HE MOVED SILENTLY TOWARD HER ON THE TOWER ROOF.

His entire life had been one steady movement toward this moment. Toward this woman. This angel.

"Alec," she said softly, closing the distance between them. Lifting her arms and encircling his neck, she murmured, "I feel as if I am perched on top of the world."

"You are," Alec whispered.

Fiona gazed at him steadily. "Is this the way a falcon feels?"

"Aye, I think it is," he murmured. "Just before she takes flight."

"Then I know why sh always will."

"And why is that?"

"For love," she said s

"I do love you, Fiona."

As they clung together, she could feel the breeze lifting them higher and higher into the evening sky—taking them aloft to a realm, a sphere, no two mortals had ever reached.

Angel
of
Skye

May McGoldrick

A TOPAZ BOOK

TOPAZ
Published by the Penguin Group
Penguin Books USA Inc., 375 Hudson Street,
New York, New York 10014, U.S.A.
Penguin Books Ltd, 27 Wrights Lane,
London W8 5TZ, England
Penguin Books Australia Ltd, Ringwood,
Victoria, Australia
Penguin Books Canada Ltd, 10 Alcorn Avenue,
Toronto, Ontario, Canada M4V 3B2
Penguin Books (N.Z.) Ltd, 182–190 Wairau Road,
Auckland 10, New Zealand

Penguin Books Ltd, Registered Offices:
Harmondsworth, Middlesex, England

First published by Topaz, an imprint of Dutton Signet,
a division of Penguin Books USA Inc.

First Printing, May, 1996
10 9 8 7 6 5 4 3 2 1

Excerpts from *The Poems of William Dunbar*, edited by James Kinsley (1979),
and *The Poems of Robert Henryson*, edited by Denton Fox (1981), are re-
printed by permission of Oxford University Press.

REGISTERED TRADEMARK—MARCA REGISTRADA

Printed in the United States of America

For Cyrus and Samuel, our own Highland rogues.

Prologue

Drummond Castle, October 1502

His ice-blue eyes locked on the castle looming in the gathering dusk.

Silent as death, he and his company of killers climbed the ridge toward the open drawbridge. Andrew would get back what was his. He would have his revenge.

Fiona bounced across the wood floor at the sound of horses thundering across the drawbridge. Standing on her tiptoes, she stretched her five-year-old body, inching her dimpled chin up onto the stone ledge surrounding the small window in her effort to peer out into the dusky light at the approaching riders. From the unglazed slit in the castle wall, the misty autumn wind swept through her fire-red hair. She could not see the riders, but she could hear their steel armor clanging as they rode into the castle's inner yard.

Her father was coming for her.

"May I please go down, Nanna?" she asked for the umpteenth time. "Please, Nanna?"

"You know what your mama said, child," the old woman responded, smiling at the irrepressible excitement of the little girl. This was a big day for her. This was a big day for them all.

Fiona skipped from the window and picked up her little stool from beside the fireplace, carrying it quickly to the high window and scampering onto it. As she pressed her face into the opening, a gust of Scottish night air filled her with a thrill of anticipation.

But her mother had given strict orders that she was to remain in her room until she was called for.

He must be very important, the little girl thought excitedly, trying to pick him out from among the horsemen in the courtyard. In the flaring torchlight she could see the varied array of tartans on the company of men dismounting below.

Though Fiona could not even recall when exactly she had last seen her father, she tried hard to remember, as her eyes scanned the sea of men below, what he looked like. She had been very little the last time. But there were things about him that she could still recollect, vaguely. His deep and easy laugh. His soft red beard. The strange, beltlike chain that she could feel under his shirt. Her mother had told Fiona that her father always wore that, but she had never said why.

"Your papa is a busy man, Fiona," her mother had said the times she'd asked for him. All her life Fiona had been hearing talk of fights with the filthy English who were trying to take Scottish lands. And all her life she'd been hearing her mother tell her how Papa had to help. How it was his job to help keep their homes and their country safe.

But now he was coming to them—making a special visit—to take her and her mother and Nanna back to his own castle. To be with him.

For the past week Fiona had been shadowing Nanna as she went about her chores. The little girl had tried extra hard to be more of a help than a hindrance. After all, she had so many questions about the upcoming visit, and Nanna was the only one who would even talk to her about it.

Fiona wished she could remember more.

For as long as the little girl could recall, no one would ever talk to her about her father. There were moments when her mother would allow Fiona a glimpse of those times when he had been near. And it was during those talks that Fiona would hear about his humor, his courage, about the kind of man he was. But then her mother would never answer her other questions about him, so he remained an enigma.

Sometimes Fiona wondered if her father still loved her. She wondered if he missed her as much as she missed him. Sometimes she even dreamed of him. When she did, he was like an angel, floating far above—away from her—but watching over her. She could see him, his red hair and beard streaming around him as if blown by a gentle breeze.

And now everyone kept telling Fiona not to disturb her mother.

The little girl knew that her mother was not her usual self. She had been very quiet for the past few days and spent many hours alone in her room. Fiona heard her crying. Nanna said that her mother was just having a hard time believing that what she had wished for, for so long, was finally coming true. But Fiona knew it had to be something else.

During their time together Nanna had told her that, for reasons beyond their control, Fiona's parents could not be married up until now, but that their love had finally triumphed.

At last, her father had told his people that Fiona was his daughter, and that he and her mother were going to be married. Fiona was not really sure what being married meant, but she knew it had to be something very special. After all, she was going to have a permanent father now. But even more importantly, she knew that it meant her mother would never have to be sad again. Nanna had told her that.

Fiona began to count the torches that were being lit in the courtyard. She knew her father would have warriors with him. Nanna had said Fiona's father had many who attended him.

"Fiona, come here so I can braid that wild hair of yours," Nanna scolded gently, smiling patiently at the excited child. The room was warm and comfortable, and the old woman felt at peace with the world.

The little girl reluctantly turned from her place at the window. Hopping off the stool, she ran across the room, flinging herself affectionately onto the woman's lap. Nanna put her arm around the child, returning her warm embrace.

Nanna had raised the girl's mother, just as she was now helping to raise Fiona. They were so different, mother and daughter, and yet so much the same. Margaret had always been the proper child, always reserved, always private. But Fiona was different. Nothing was held in. Nothing was hidden. One thing Nanna knew they had in common, though: They both had such incredible depths to their love.

Fiona squirmed in her lap, breaking into the woman's reverie. Nanna picked up the brush and began to run it through the silky softness of the little girl's hair.

"Nanna, is my hair really the same color as Papa's?" she asked, turning her bright eyes on the woman.

"Aye, child. That it is."

"And my eyes, Nanna?"

"Nay, child. You have your mama's hazel eyes. Your papa's eyes are the color of a March morning. Yours change with your mood and with the color of the sky."

"But I do look like him, don't I, Nanna?" she asked hopefully. Her mother had always said that Fiona resembled her father.

"Aye, lass. You look like him. And you have his wit. And his restlessness, and his high spirits, as well. You are his very own child, Fiona."

There had never been any question whose child Margaret had borne. He had been here at Drummond Castle beside her when Fiona had taken her first breaths in this world. Nanna had seen the tears of joy washing his handsome face. And then, later on, Nanna had seen the tears of sorrow on that face when he had to go.

As the woman braided the little girl's locks, she thought of how often she had done this same simple task for her mother as well. Margaret Drummond, eldest of three daughters of John, Lord Drummond, had grown up to be one of the most beautiful and sought-after maidens in all the realm. As a young lady of the court, Margaret had been pursued by princes and earls and lairds as well as by knights of every caliber. But she had turned her face from matches that had promised security and respectability. Instead, Margaret had accepted an impossible love. She had been swept away by a man beyond her reach. A man whose life and destiny were not his own to control. Nanna had watched her grow from childhood, and had always known her charge would never accept anything less than the union of two souls. For Margaret, impossible as it was, this love was forever.

Margaret had known the consequences of the relationship and had left the society at court when she had found herself with child. She had withdrawn to Drummond Castle, away from the prying eyes of the court gossips. She had secluded herself, even from much of her own family, content to raise her child alone, hoping all the while for his return.

And then he had followed her, to be with her during the pain of her labor, to share with her the tears and later the joy, to bask in a brief glow of happiness before the world had pulled him away—as it would again and again—but always with the departing promise that he'd come back as soon as he could.

But then one summer day he'd left, and he hadn't returned. This time had been different. His world had kept him away. Two long years had come and gone before the news of this impending visit had reached Drummond Castle. The skirmishes, the politics ... all had conspired to keep them apart until now.

Nanna knew that through these past two years, Margaret had clung to the certain knowledge that she was loved by the man who had fathered her child. Time had passed, though, and Nanna often wondered if he had changed.

But now ... now he was about to make Margaret's dreams come true. Their dreams, Nanna thought. All of their dreams.

The sound of the door's latch startled the old woman from her thoughts, and she sat bolt upright. The door opened and Margaret rushed into the room, pushing the heavy oak door closed behind her. Her eyes flickered across the room in search of her child. Finding her on Nanna's lap, Margaret's face visibly registered her relief. Fiona leaped up and ran into her mother's arms.

"Mama, is it time?" the little girl asked hesitantly, sensing something was wrong.

"Oh, my poor baby," her mother responded in anguish, hugging the child tightly to her. In an instant she turned her troubled eyes toward the older woman. "Nanna, we have no time. Take the back stairs down to the Great Hall. Find Sir Allan and have him come up here immediately. Then go out to the stables and have them ready three horses."

"What's wrong, m'lady?" the older woman asked, rushing to her mistress's side.

Margaret's bright eyes flashed toward her daughter; loose tendrils of blond hair fell around her perfect face, now filled with obvious distress. "What I have feared for the past few weeks has finally happened," she answered quickly, struggling to fight back tears. Her face was flushed with her effort to restrain a thousand emotions. "You must take Fiona away from here. But first go and do as I have said. I will send her down with Allan. And please hurry."

The older woman was torn between the desire to know more of her lady's distress and the need to comply with the urgency of her command. But one look at the fear in Margaret's eyes catapulted her into action, and she bustled quickly out the small door at the rear of the chamber.

As the door closed behind the retreating woman, Margabret's hand went to the leather purse in the pocket of her dress. Wrapping her fingers around it, she could feel the dead coldness of Andrew's broach, and, beside it, the ring, its heat burning her fingers through the leather. She had to hide them, and she had to hide them now. Her eyes swept around the room.

Oh, God, she thought. Oh, God! But where?

And then she remembered. With a sharp cry, she ran across the room to the fireplace. Counting several stones over from the opening, Margaret pulled one from the wall. Fiona just stood there in the middle of the room, confused, but knowing deep within her heart that something was wrong, terribly wrong. She could see the small dark space behind the wall and watched her mother yank a small leather purse from the pocket of her dress, jamming it into the hiding place. Quickly, Margaret shoved the stone back where it had been and whirled on her daughter.

"Fiona, my love," she said, crossing the floor quickly. "Run and get your heavy cloak and the leather purse I gave you."

"But Mama," the girl protested. "What is wrong?"

"Go, child! Hurry!" the mother said quietly, trying to control the panic in her voice. "I will explain in a moment."

Fiona ran to the pegs by the door and pulled down her winter cloak. As she turned back, she could see her mother writing furiously at the small study table. Tripping to the chest by her bed, Fiona took out the purse. By the time the little girl reached her side, she had folded her letter and tipped candle wax onto the paper, which she then sealed using her ring.

"Give me the purse, Fiona," Margaret said, reaching for the bag. She stuffed the letter in the purse and removed the ruby- and emerald-encrusted cross that was hanging from the gold chain around her neck. Drawing Fiona to her, Margaret placed the chain around her neck and discreetly tucked it inside her dress.

"Mama!" Fiona looked wildly at her mother. For as long as she could remember, her mother had worn the cross close to her heart. "You said Papa gave you this."

"Aye, my love," Margaret answered, tears now coursing freely down her cheeks. "But I'll not be needing it, and you shall."

"But Mama! I don't understand! Papa is coming!"

Margaret looked at her bewildered daughter. She was hardly more than a bairn. How would she survive this?

"Listen to me, child. We have only a moment." Margaret looked around furtively. Time was running out, but where were Nanna and Allan? She continued. "An evil man has come into our home. *Not your papa.* Do you understand me? Your papa does not even know of the evils that surround him. He is innocent of this."

Fiona tried to understand her mother's words. What did she mean? The words swirled through her head. Papa was not coming. Innocent. Of what? Why did her mother no longer need her cross? Who was this evil man?

Fiona began to cry, hiccuping and sobbing as her mother tucked the leather purse inside her clothes. Margaret then wrapped the heavy cloak around Fiona's shoulders and tied the leather thongs at her neck.

"Listen to me carefully, Fiona," Margaret continued. They were both weeping now, and she wiped her daughter's tears from her flushed face. She cupped the innocent young child's face with her shaking hands and looked intensely into the worried eyes. "I need you to be very brave. You have to go away . . . to a place where you will be safe. And you have to stay away until your papa comes to get you."

"But why isn't he here?" Fiona cried. "Where is Papa now?"

"I wish I knew, Fiona. But the evil men are already here. These men will hurt us, my love. It is too late. You must go.... They ... But listen to me, this is most important." Margaret knelt beside her child and held her tightly with one arm as she pointed to the wall where she had hidden the packet. "When your papa brings you back here, show him what is behind that stone. He will punish the evil ones who have come here tonight! I promise you, he will!"

Margaret hugged Fiona fiercely, and Fiona clung to her mother.

They both jumped at the sound of the gentle knock at the small rear door.

Holding her sobbing child against her, Margaret called for her knight to enter.

Sir Allan entered the room, his face dark with concern.

"M'lady ... should you not ... should I not be down with Lord Andrew—" he began courteously.

"No!" Margaret interrupted. "You must take Fiona far away from him ... away from here. He—"

With a resounding bang, the heavy oak door of the room burst open, and a half dozen soldiers rushed in, drawn swords in their hands. Instinctively, Allan pulled his own sword from its scabbard, stepping in front of his mistress.

Margaret gripped Fiona's hand and started backing toward the rear chamber door. As her heart slammed in her chest, she knew that it was not her own life that she feared for, but the life of her own precious child.

Holy Mother, Fiona is an innocent, she found herself praying. Please help her. Please save her.

"What is the meaning of this outrage?" the knight bellowed.

Instead of answering, four soldiers charged at him.

Gallantly, Allan parried the first blows of the on-slaught, managing to shove one of the assailants clear across the room. Slashing at the soldiers, Allan managed to plunge his brand into one of the men, where the shoulder meets the neck, but before he could pull his sword out of the dying man, two of the other soldiers found their chance; their swords pierced his chest and his back, the blades crossing somewhere between his ribs.

The valiant knight was dead before he hit the floor.

The assailants then turned on Fiona and Margaret, who watched in horror as the killers approached them.

Quickly recovering, Margaret drew Fiona behind her as she pulled a small dagger from her belt. Slowly, they continued backing toward the door.

"Stay behind me," Margaret commanded in a voice that shook with emotion. "These animals will not dare to harm—"

Suddenly Fiona felt herself being lifted high into the air. Twisting her body, she tried desperately to dive toward her mother. But a huge man, bigger than Sir Allan, held her with a viselike grip that sent shock waves of pain shooting down her arms. Turning her head, she glimpsed the ugly, scarred face and the wild, unkempt beard of the grinning madman who held her.

From the corner of her eye, she saw that another man had taken hold of her mother's arms and wrenched the knife from her hand.

Reacting to her mother's cries, Fiona felt her body stiffen with anger. Suddenly something snapped within her, and all her fear vanished. She was a whirlwind of motion, arms and legs flying in all directions at once. Wildly, Fiona kicked hard at the man's stomach, sinking her teeth into his massive paw at the same time. Her attacker snapped his hand away, and Fiona swung loose for a moment. Twisting her arm, she kicked again hard at his midsection, this time causing the man to throw her away from him.

"The devil . . ."

Fiona landed on her hands and knees, but quickly scampered to her feet, eyeing the ugly man defiantly.

"Are you going to let this wee thing best you, m'lord?" one of the soldiers sneered.

"She is a demon," the Goliath roared, taking a step toward the girl.

Fiona looked around her wildly. She could see that both doors were blocked. There was no way out. Running to the window, she picked up the stool and rushed toward the men who were holding her struggling mother. Throwing the stool at one, she bit down on the hand of the other before being grabbed by the hair from behind.

The man yanked her head back roughly and jerked her around to face him. His fist hung in the air, his eyes clouded with fury.

"I'm going to teach you how we deal with demon bairns where I come from."

Fiona's eyes shot darts of defiance into the Highlander's face.

"If you hurt me," she hissed, "my papa will *kill* you."

A look of shock flickered into the man's face as his fist opened. Then his black eyes narrowed into a hardness that froze Fiona's blood.

"Where you are going, your almighty papa will never find you," he growled menacingly.

Dragging her toward the rear door, past Margaret, who had been gagged, the leader flung the little girl at one of his men.

"Take her down," he spat. *"Now!"*

"Should we wait for you in the courtyard, Torquil?" the man clutching Fiona asked. Fiona tried to jerk her hand free, but her captor twisted her arm behind her back, taking hold of her hair with vicious force.

"No, I will catch up," the man responded gruffly. He turned with a sneer toward Margaret. "We have a very sad occurrence that needs to take place here."

A look of horror came into Margaret's eyes, and she cast a final look at her daughter as they dragged the screaming child from the room.

Lord Gray, Margaret Drummond's uncle, was the first to discover his niece's body. The shocking news traveled like a thunderbolt through the countryside.

From what could be gathered, earlier in the evening a group of strangers had kidnapped Margaret's daughter, Fiona. On the eve of such momentous expectations, after waiting two long years for the child's father's return to them, the shock of this loss had proved too much for Margaret—she had lost all sense. In despair, she had taken her own life, poisoning herself in her daughter's room. They had found the note she left, professing that life was not worth living without her child.

People searched high and low throughout the Scottish countryside. But the fruitless effort was curtailed a fortnight later when the worst gale in fifty years tore across Scotland, spreading havoc and destruction from the Outer Hebrides and the Isle of Skye to the Firth of Forth and Edinburgh itself.

Neither Fiona nor her kidnappers were ever found, and those who loved her wept, thinking her dead.

Chapter 1

The nut's shell, though it be hard and tough,
Holds the kernel, sweet and delectable.
—ROBERT HENRYSON, *"The Fables"*

Dunvegan Castle, the Isle of Skye, June 1516

He could hardly breathe.

The bodies of those around him were pressing so close that he felt he could not even lift his arms. And there were faces—faces that looked so familiar but that he could not put names to. Then, just beyond them, he could see King James looking at him with pleading eyes.

"What is it, m'lord?" he heard himself ask. His voice came from far away, as if from somewhere inside his head. He wondered if the words had even been uttered.

He tried to move toward the king, but the bodies were now pressing against him even more tightly than before. Then, like the surge of an ocean current, they pushed and carried him with excruciating slowness away from his king.

Alec continued to look at the king, following his gaze when James turned his face toward the murky shadows beyond.

Looking past him, Alec could see a door was opening. A cloud of mist streamed through the opening, swirling as it poured through the door. Suddenly he was blinded by the shimmering light of a thousand suns. Then that brilliance was eclipsed by another sight—the vision of an angel stepping through the door. Her red hair flowed about her in endless waves and framed a face of pure perfection. From where he stood, Alec could see her eyes, crystalline, radiating a spectrum of colors. Those eyes found his and drew him toward her with an unspoken promise of fulfillment. Light and warmth swept over him; his eyes were riveted on the dazzling creation.

Alec saw the king move toward the angel, beckoning to him with one hand and, with the other, reaching for the light.

But he couldn't move. Alec tried desperately to fight the current carrying him away, but to no avail. He was carried farther and farther away from the light and the vision. More and more he felt his breath being crushed from his body. Struggling for air, Alec could see the light receding. He could see his angel disappearing.

He was suffocating. He had to somehow get back to his king—to the light.

He could hardly breathe.

Gasping for air, Alec Macpherson sat bolt upright in his bed, sweat running down his chest and back.

It was the same recurring dream.

Throwing the covers aside, Alec vaulted from the bed. He looked around at the still darkened room. So cold. So large and cold and empty, he thought. The cool summer breeze flowed over his naked skin from the open slit of the window. The silence around him seemed a tangible thing, pressing on him like a millstone, crushing him.

Trying hard to rid himself of the dream, Alec walked to the window, stretching and breathing in deeply the misty salt air. Ever so slowly the sense of oppression that had gripped him began to ease. His eyes were drawn to the twin peaks of Healaval across the fog-shrouded waters of Loch Dunvegan. It didn't seem to matter how long he remained here at Dunvegan; it simply was not home. He missed the noise, the life that existed at Benmore Castle. But then again, he thought, even being home had not been enough . . . had not helped.

Looking out into the morning fog, he saw in his mind's eye the lingering images of the dream. This was the first time that he'd seen the face of the angel. Always before, she'd been nothing more than a light. But this time Alec had seen her. She was flesh and blood. But who was she?

King James IV had been dead for three years now, and Alec had fought beside him on that bloody day at Flodden Field, the day when the king had ignored all warnings and had challenged the English. The king had been cut down by an English arrow and a swarm of blood-crazed foot soldiers because Torquil MacLeod and others had held back their troops when they were most needed to save their country. That had been a bitter day for Scotland and for Alec.

How strange, Alec thought, that after so long his dreams would now be invaded by his king's ghost ... and by the strange vision of the angel. Four months ago, Alec Macpherson had arrived at Dunvegan Castle. And that was when the dreams had started. He had come here, certain that doing the Crown's work in this faraway corner of Scotland was what he needed. His life and his mind were all cluttered with events and people he just could not shake off. A false promise, a broken engagement, a faithless woman. Alec rubbed his face hard with his hands as if that act could somehow wipe away all thoughts, all traces of Kathryn.

Forcing his thoughts back to his dream, he wondered what the king could be trying to tell him. Why did he wait three years? Why did he come to him here?

As the new laird of Skye and the islands of the Outer Hebrides, Alec had hardly rested in his efforts to bring order to this wild and mysterious land that Torquil MacLeod had so barbarously ruled.

Justice had finally caught up with the murderous MacLeod, but his execution for treason had left a great void in the power structure of the northwestern Highlands. Alec Macpherson, future chief of his own Highland clan as well as a fearless warrior and well-known leader, had been given the task of correcting the ills of thirty years of brutal repression and securing the region for the new Stuart king.

As he dressed for his morning ride, Alec thought over all that he had set out to do four months ago. It seemed to him he had been working night and day, and it was still a bit daunting to consider all that remained to be accomplished. He had arrived here with his own men, expecting resistance, even bloodshed. After all, he had not been chosen by these people to be their leader. He'd been made laird by the nobles of the Regency Council and had been given the Isle of Skye to rule as his own.

So Alec had been surprised by the reception of the

men who had greeted him. The handful of soldiers still remaining at Dunvegan Castle were under the command of Neil MacLeod, a warrior crippled at Flodden, one of the few of this clan who it seemed had fought loyally for his king. He and his men had peacefully submitted to Alec's will and had sworn to aid him in his royal commission. And indeed, Neil and his men had been true to their word.

It was not long before Alec discovered that the people of Skye—the clans MacDonald and MacLeod—deserved better than they had been getting for so many years under Torquil.

They were quite different from what he had expected. Yes, there were still small roving bands of rebel outlaws left in the outlying areas of the island. But aside from them, the crofters and the fishermen of Skye were, for the most part, good people. They were solid, common folk with strong beliefs in the old ways—people who, despite their treacherous leader, had somehow maintained a heritage of hospitality and decency and, most importantly, dignity.

And Alec could see that these people were beginning to trust him, to accept his commands in the spirit that they were given—to better the lot of all who depended on him.

Alec strapped his sword to his side and pulled open the thick oak door leading from his tower room. The musty smell of the interior stairway assaulted his nostrils. This old tower was said to be nearly three hundred years old. Dimly lit by a few narrow slits in the thick stone walls, it evoked the memory of childhood stories of fairies and sprites, kelpies and sorcerers. It was no surprise to Alec that the history of Skye was a brightly woven tapestry of fact and fantasy.

But the castle had a proud and well-known history within its walls. It had withstood the assaults of Vikings and Celtic kings from the water and from the land. It had been an outpost of civilization when the Christian faith had first taken hold in this wild land of fairies and those who believed in them. And it had been a center of rebellion against each of the four Stuart kings that had occupied the Scottish throne.

But that final part of Dunvegan's history was over, Alec thought.

Descending the two flights of stone stairway, Alec consciously attempted to shake off the remnants of his troubling dream. This morning hunt was becoming a habit, but at least he knew it was one way to clear his head. Entering the dark Great Hall, he peered at the men who were sleeping on benches around the last glowing embers of the fire in the center of the room. It was all quiet, and the hounds hardly stirred as he strode across the floor.

"Going hunting, m'lord?"

"Robert!" Alec started. "How many times have I told you not to sneak up on me?"

"Just practicing the ways of the warrior, m'lord," the squire responded in hushed tones. "Someday, m'lord, maybe someday when you find me ready to train with the warriors, I could prove to you that I've learned well all you've taught me. Remember? You told me that a warrior must be prepared at all times. You told me that stealth—"

"And I have also told you not to practice on me the things that I teach you."

Alec had taken Robert to be his personal squire a year ago. The boy had proved himself eager and hardworking, and in the past year he had shot up like a beanstalk. Seeing how he had grown, Alec smiled to think how often he had been drawn back from the hard-edged world of Scottish politics by the confused and sometimes comical perceptions of the adolescent boy. Though he was often a thorn in Alec's side, Robert was devoted to the warlord—and not in the least frightened by his moods.

"Aye, m'lord." The young man nodded. "But you have also told me to use my judgment and to make decisions. Especially when it comes to the welfare of people that I care about."

"That is true, Robert."

"And so, m'lord, some of what you have told me I have to practice on you, because if I do not . . . then you might not be around to tell me more. And if you are not around—"

"Enough, Robert!" Alec growled, leading the young

man through the Great Hall toward a small door on the far side. "It is too early for me to keep up with you. Go back to sleep."

"But m'lord. I have your breakfast ready," Robert responded with concern. "You have to eat something before you go. You don't eat enough. Even Cook says so. And all this early morning hunting. Your brother Sir Ambrose says you are just looking—"

"I am fine, Robert," Alec said, stopping on the iron mesh that covered the open well that provided air to the castle's subterranean vault. "There is no need for any of you to worry about me."

Alec glanced into the darkness of the well, thinking of the horrors that had occurred in that dungeon not so long ago. He caught a movement out of the corner of his eye. As he peered down into the darkness, he thought he saw a shadow move in the depths. A rat, he thought with disgust.

"But m'lord," the lad continued. "Sir Ambrose thinks that with no ladies of quality to take your mind off your work here, you just—"

"Robert!" Alec turned his glare on the lanky youth standing beside him. Ambrose clearly needed something else to occupy his mind. But how could Alec even begin to explain what a refreshing change it was to be without those grasping women of the court? To be without Kathryn, his treacherous onetime fiancée. Alec was willing to admit—to himself, anyway—that there was something missing in his life, but it was not the companionship of those he had deliberately turned his back on.

No, he could not explain it to Robert, but Alec would need to make that very clear to his brother before Ambrose arranged for any surprise arrivals at Dunvegan's doorstep.

"But all I was saying, m'lord—"

"Will you shut up?" Alec growled menacingly.

"I will, m'lord." The young man flushed, suddenly remembering the reason for his master's sensitivity on this topic. "By the way, m'lord, I told Sir Ambrose that I would wake him up so that he could ride with you this morning. He is really quite worried about you. We are all worried about you. Why, I was just talking with Cook last night, and he says that—"

"Robert," Alec rumbled menacingly. "I am warning you. Ambrose is going home soon. If you say even one more word, I will send you ... and Cook ... away with him."

"Not another word, m'lord. I will not say another word. I promise. And I will stop Cook from talking, too. You will not hear anything. And if you do not want breakfast, it is up to you ... m'lord." Robert stopped short, knowing from the laird's threatening glare that he was doing it again. The last thing he wanted was to be sent back to Benmore Castle. The squire squirmed uncomfortably, thinking of Lord Alexander and how, in the past, he had so very often tried the patience of the old laird. And Robert liked Lady Elizabeth, his master's mother, but he wanted to be a warrior someday, not a lady's maid, for God's sake. He stood silently, his eyes riveted to the floor.

Alec shook his head and turned toward the door. This boy could certainly talk. In fact, his chatter had awakened everyone in the hall. Oh, the lad would pay for that, Alec thought with a smile.

"I will not starve, Robert. You don't need to worry," Alec called back over his shoulder. "I will eat something when I get back."

The squire legged it quickly to the door and opened it for Alec as he reached it. Before going through, the warlord paused.

"Oh, one more thing, Robert," the laird said, scowling fiercely. "Neil tells me you've been shirking your household duties and skulking around the training fields."

Robert paled under his master's withering glare. "Nay, m'lord. I've ... I've kept up with my duties ... I ... It isn't true! I mean, I have been going to the fields, but I'm ... I'm ..."

"Listen, Robert," Alec said, taking the lanky lad roughly by the arm. "Starting today, I want you to train full-time with the warriors. Tell Cook to pass on the household duties to one of the younger lads."

Robert stood, speechless, trying to fathom what he'd just heard and gawking through the open door after his departing master.

Alec smiled to himself as he strode out into the murky predawn light. He'd been looking for the right moment to reward Robert for his diligence and effort. Despite his adolescent ways and his gregarious nature, he was maturing into a fine young man. This change in his status would only reinforce his development in the ways of the warrior. Resourceful. Cool. Reserved. Quiet.

As Robert began to yelp in delight, Alec laughed openly at the gathering sound of curses the awakening warriors in the hall were uttering at the lad capering happily in the doorway.

A few moments later, the laird nodded to the gate-keeper and ducked his head as he steered his black charger through the ten-foot-thick curtain wall of Dunvegan Castle. Emerging from the gloom of the passage into the only slightly brighter predawn light, the warrior wheeled his horse to the right and galloped along the saltwater inlet dominated by the fortress walls.

On his left wrist, Alec held his prize falcon, the snow-white peregrine, Swift. Hunting with the rare Welsh albino bird had become more than the warlord's chief exercise and escape. It had become a morning ritual.

Pounding over the rolling moorland, Alec headed toward a thickly forested valley a mile inland. Surrounded by wild hills and jagged rock ridges, the land was rich with red deer and with the fat pheasant that Swift was so good at plucking from the air.

Descending into a small dip in the terrain, Alec found himself enshrouded in a pocket of morning mist. His vision was cut to a very short distance, but he knew that the path would rise in just a few short yards.

This was one of the things he liked best about Skye. Here he had the freedom to ride hard on his own land amid the unearthly rock formations and the heather-covered hills. Here he was free to enjoy the solitude of the morning air, free from the stifling closeness of the court, from its parasites, and from its women.

Alec entered the wood as the land began to rise, and with it the thick vaporous cloud gave way to patches of the mist. He looked around him in awe. Still, after so many days of riding the same path, he was amazed how the beauty and mystery of these woods touched him. The oak trees, hundreds of years old, entwined their branches into a canopy above him. He looked up as the first rays of the sun strained to gain access.

Suddenly Alec saw a dark shape form on the path before him. Jerking the steed's head to the right, Alec saw a white arm flash up from the fold of a cloak. Swift shrieked, his fluttering wings obstructing Alec's vision momentarily. Then, as they flew past the diving shape, Alec yanked the horse's reins tight, struggling to hold the plunging, rearing beast in check. He turned his head to the figure lying beside the path.

"You madman!" came the enraged voice of a woman.

The shock of hearing a woman's voice stunned the warrior. The epithet she hurled at him was lost to the realization that he had nearly ridden down a defenseless peasant woman.

"It is one thing to break your own neck. But mine is another matter," the voice scolded, the pitch rising with her anger. "You nearly trampled me!"

"Hold, there! I will help you," Alec responded. "Whoa, Ebon!"

The steed continued to strain against Alec's efforts to calm him, and Alec could not see the woman clearly, but he glimpsed brilliant red hair spilling out of the dark hood as she scrambled to gather up the contents strewn around a large brown satchel on the ground.

"Are you hurt, wom—" Alec tried to shout above the din of the shrieking bird. But the charger wheeled again, and when the warrior looked back down the path, the cloaked figure had disappeared. There was no movement of branches nearby. No shadows. No trace. One moment she had been standing there—the next she was gone.

Fiona stood a few paces off the path, peering through the mist at the power struggle going on between horse, rider, and the strange white hawk. Three beasts, she thought angrily, rubbing a bruised shoulder. Three wild beasts. She quickly straightened the cloak around her, shoving her hair back under the veil she was wearing beneath the hood of the cloak. Her heart was slamming against her rib cage. She tried to take deep breaths to slow her pulse . . . and to cool her anger.

Finally, the giant warrior subdued the snorting black stallion, and the hawk's cries ended. She watched as the rider looked questioningly about him. Fiona knew that she could not be seen and that she could escape easily through the thickly wooded grove behind her. She knew this area like the back of her hand.

The huge, golden-haired warrior trotted his horse down the path to where he had passed her. Looking around him in every direction, he stopped the horse and cocked an ear, listening for a sound. Rising from the saddle, he stood in his stirrups for a long moment without any movement. It seemed that horse and hawk were taking their signals from their master as they waited patiently, motionless.

Finally, pulling out his sword, he speared the string of wooden prayer beads that lay on the turf. Sheathing his sword, the rider looked at them curiously and then clenched them in his fist.

From where she stood, Fiona could not quite make out the expression on his face. The giant wheeled his horse in her direction. Now horse and rider faced her. She slid as quietly as she could behind the wide trunk of a gnarled oak. Oh, my Lord, did he see me? Her mind began to run wild. Can he hear me? She held her breath, wishing she could stop the pounding of her heart. Then she nearly laughed aloud at the silliness of the thought, considering the distance between them.

"Are you hurt?" the rider called out, his voice echoing in the wood. "You do not need to fear me."

He paused, listening for a response, but getting none. "If you are hurt, but can get to Dunvegan Castle, go there. They will care for you."

He paused again, listening. Fiona could hear the hooves of the impatient horse stamping at the edge of the path. There was annoyance in the warrior's tone when he called again. "Answer me! These woods are dangerous if you are hurt. There are all kinds of wild beasts out here."

There certainly are, Fiona thought, chuckling softly to herself. My thoughts exactly.

"Now, listen," he shouted, anger now apparent in his voice. "I am trying to help you. I don't know why a woman would be out here roaming the woods alone at this hour, but speak, for God's sake."

Once again, Fiona peered cautiously from behind the

tree and watched him as he waited for a response. She smiled at his evident anger and frustration. Good, she thought. He had some nerve riding like a madman on trails honest peasants use to earn a livelihood.

The warlord just remained where he was for a long moment, clearly trying to make up his mind.

"If you will not answer, then ... to hell with you!" he roared, and wheeling the horse nimbly, he thundered off down the path.

Fiona let out her breath as he disappeared into the mist. Then she stamped her foot hard in anger. "Well, Lord Macpherson, you certainly learned nothing from that!"

She moved from her hiding place in the trees and onto the deer trail she had used each morning for the past few years. Since the new laird had arrived, Fiona had spent many days watching him gallop through the countryside, the white bird or some other falcon on his arm. Always riding like a madman, always pounding his horse full speed, as if running away from, or perhaps chasing after someone. Whatever it was, though, today he was early and had caught her off guard.

But he wasn't entirely to blame, Fiona conceded. She was late returning from the cluster of huts deep in the forest where, four years ago, her old friend Walter and his company had taken refuge from the cruelties of Torquil MacLeod. And Father Jack, the old hermit, had been there today as well, and time always passed quickly when he began telling his tall tales.

The Priory on the secluded Isle of Skye had been a refuge for lepers for as long as anyone remembered. The church lands used to feed them and provide them with shelter. That had all changed four years ago, when Torquil decided that Skye would no longer be populated by disease. So for four years, Fiona had been traveling this route between the Priory and the people who hid like hunted animals, trapped on the island they now called home. Trapped by the unreasoning hate of a nobleman who thrived on the misfortunes of others. Trapped by a powerful leader whose very word had unleashed a torrent of violence on a sickly people who could neither escape nor defend themselves.

At the thought of the injustice, Fiona's hand went in-

stinctively to the wooden clapper at her belt. It was use-
ful having the clapper now. Most folk gave wide berth
when they heard the leper's wooden warning signal. But
wearing it even four months ago would have made her
trips far more risky. That is, wearing it before Lord Macpherson came.

So, whenever she could get away unnoticed, she continued to go down this path, carrying food, medicines,
and whatever else Walter and his people needed. Father
Jack had taken the lepers into his own flock when they
had moved into the forest near his stone hut. But Father
Jack was getting old, and Fiona wanted to help him. She
needed to help him.

For, despite the dangers, Fiona was not going to abandon Walter, the man who found her so many years ago
. . . washed ashore, nearly dead. The one who took her
to the Priory, to the place that had been her home
ever since.

Suddenly Fiona's foot caught on a raised root branch,
and she nearly tumbled headlong to the ground. Though
she caught herself at the last moment, a shock coursed
through Fiona when, to her right, a rustle in the under-
growth exploded as a fat pheasant took flight. The noise
and surprise of the bird's emergence rattled her. Fiona
froze in her tracks as a shiver radiated through her body.
She looked about her nervously, and for a moment the
very shadows of the dawn woods took on a threatening
look. Straightening the hood that had fallen from her
head, Fiona pulled the cloak tightly about her, as if the
thick cloth could control the chill that was coursing
through her.

"These are your woods, Fiona," she said aloud, breaking into the silence that had fallen around her. "You
have traveled this path more times than you can count.
Get a hold of yourself. Get a hold of yourself!"

As if her words were not enough, she found herself
reaching down to pick up a stout branch lying beside
the path. As she did, she felt the rattle of crockery in
the satchel she carried. Crouching in the path, she
opened the bag and looked sadly at what had been three
empty jugs. Only one jug still intact lay amid the wreckage of two broken ones.

"Thank you, Lord Macpherson!" she said, fingering

the jagged pieces. "Now you have seen to it that I have some explaining to do."

Slinging the satchel back onto her shoulder, Fiona grasped the sturdy piece of wood in her other hand and continued on her way, her momentary lapse of confidence forgotten.

She began to rehearse what she would say to her mistress. "Aye, m'lady prioress," she said, smiling at the thought of such an unlikely confession. "Two more broken jugs. But it was not my doing this time. It was a chance meeting with that ill-tempered Lord Macpherson. Oh, no, m'lady, you know I would not dream of disobeying you and going to the lepers' camp alone ... again."

Fiona came to a stop at a fork in the path. "Let me see," she whispered to herself. "Safe way home or short way home?"

"Definitely, the safe way home! Enough excitement for one day." She turned onto the more traveled path and felt her spirits rising as she continued the imaginary discussion she had just begun.

"Let me see! Where were we? Aye, m'lady! Lord Macpherson ... Lord Macpherson? Why, he just galloped right through the priory laundry while I was hanging the wash. What, m'lady? It is true that I have not done the wash for some years now. I know, m'lady! I have other responsibilities. But you see, it was such a beautiful day. And I was trying to help the other sisters. Especially Sister Beatrice. She has a summer cold she cannot be rid of.

"Aye, you should have seen him. The laird is quite an imposing figure riding his horse the way he does. But that innocent bird tied to his wrist. The poor creature. The jugs, m'lady? Oh, no, they could not have been filled with herbal teas for the leper folk. They were filled with ... water ... aye, jasmine water. What, m'lady? We do not use jasmine water to scent the laundry?

"Hmmm!" Fiona slowed her pace, now thinking about that one. "No jasmine." But then her eyes sparkled and she picked up her pace again.

"I am sure you are correct, m'lady. Clearly, I must have been so enraptured with the spiritual aspect of my task—you are forever telling me that God resides in the most mundane of our labors—that, well, the scent of nature's glories must have been upon those linens. Aye, m'lady, I could have sworn I smelled jasmine. What, m'lady prioress, Lord Macpherson in the laundry? Aye, m'lady, I was the only one to see him, but I assure you his horse did not soil so much as a single handkerchief. Just the jugs, m'lady. Aye, smashed, m'lady."

Fiona chuckled at the thought of such a conversation . . . on such an improbable topic. Lord Macpherson barreling through the laundry while she was hanging the wash. But then Fiona's expression clouded for a moment. She had to talk seriously to the prioress about assigning Sister Beatrice's tasks to others for the time being, until she got better. The older nun would never utter even a word of complaint, and would certainly never shirk her responsibilities. Fiona knew that the prioress would have to intervene and order her to rest.

The prioress had always pushed Fiona to take on more responsibilities in the administration of the Priory. And she had always supported the young woman in the decisions she made. Always, Fiona thought. It was not that the tasks that some of the other nuns performed were beneath her. No, it was just that the prioress felt it more appropriate to give her jobs that, as the older woman put it, better suited Fiona's talents. But Fiona had a lingering suspicion that the prioress saw her as good with numbers and terrible with everything else. Hmmph! she thought.

Special gift from God, that is what the prioress had often said of her, a smile on her wrinkled face. And it was true: Sometimes Fiona had taken to her tasks like a fish to water. What had taken the prioress hours to do, particularly with numbers and the books, Fiona could accomplish in a fraction of the time. More recently, though Fiona's restlessness and mildly insubordinate acts had caused the prioress to take to calling Fiona "an endurance test from God." Oh, well, the young woman sighed.

Entering a clearing, Fiona blinked at the brilliant morning sunlight that had quickly burned through the predawn mists. The sun was dazzling as it reflected off the small pond in the center of the small meadow. She was still a half hour's walk away from Priory lands. As

Fiona picked up her pace, she wondered what her old friend David would say about her adventure this morning. Naturally, she would tell him the truth. All of it. He was the only one she would dare speak the truth to. He was the only one who never panicked and scolded her for the smallest of risks.

Certainly there were times when they had their disagreements, but they inevitably worked them through. This was the way it had always been between them. David never tried to rule her or intimidate her. He told her about the real world, about places outside of Skye. About the beauty of the Scottish mainland. He'd been there. He taught her the survival tricks, as he called them. And he taught her how to apply what she knew to the needs of real people. These lessons were such a refreshing change from all the French and English and Latin lessons the prioress had her sit through.

And the lesson he had stressed most—from the time she first arrived—had been to stay far away from Torquil MacLeod.

David, the Priory's jack-of-all-trades, was also the prioress' half-brother. He was a younger son, illegitimate, but nonetheless an uncle to Torquil, so he knew him well. His stories of the laird's brutality rang true to the imagination of a little girl whose mind had securely locked away all memory of what rough men could do. But from the time Fiona had been a young child, David had taken her under his wing, and his gentleness had won her trust. He'd made her feel safe while always pushing her to test herself. He had always encouraged her independence. He'd once considered himself to be like a father to the orphan lass, but he'd ended being her friend. A dear friend.

"It is fine to make mistakes, so long as you learn from them." That was what her friend had instilled in her. Fiona was not sure life in the Priory would have been quite so interesting without him.

And then a little more than a year ago Malcolm had been returned to them. At the thought of the young boy, Fiona picked up her pace. He would be waiting for her.

Passing a jagged outcropping of rock that stood beside the pond, Fiona shifted the satchel to her other shoulder and dropped the stick to the ground.

Looking past the rolling hills toward the wild peaks of the Cuillins far to the south, Fiona was suddenly aware of a figure standing in the shadow of a great oak tree only a stone's throw ahead. Stopping dead in her tracks, the young woman pulled her hood farther forward to hide her face and reached inside her cloak for her wooden clapper.

The figure stepped out of the shadows, and Fiona shuddered involuntarily.

The man's filthy face was crisscrossed with scars, and the young woman could see the bright red cross that had been branded on his right cheek. From the mark, she knew instantly that he had been found guilty of stealing from a church. That brand was enough to make him unwelcome in every village and town in Christendom. But it was the look in his black eyes that frightened her the most. It was the look of a hungry animal.

Fiona swung her clapper, and the noise made the man stop momentarily on the path. Then she heard what must have been a laugh, but it was a sound so resonant with evil that it was hard to identify as such. Fiona felt a clammy chill spread upward from the small of her back.

"That don't matter none to us," he said, spitting out his words with a bitterness that Fiona had never experienced before.

He took a step toward her, and she swung the clapper more desperately, hoping that the sound would ward him off.

"We've watched you before," he continued, taking another step toward her. Fiona could smell his foul odor, and she turned her head in revulsion. "You ain't no leper. You're that pretty face in that churchyard full of old women. We've been watching you."

Fiona felt the hair rise on the nape of her neck. Taking a step back, she turned to run for the woods, but as she did, two others stepped from either side of the rock outcropping she had just passed. Their arms were spread wide, and Fiona knew what it felt like to be a hunted animal at bay. She turned her eyes from one predator to the next. Their eyes glistened in the morning sun. They all looked ... hungry. But she sensed it was not food they were after.

"Where are you going ... angel? Ain't that what they

call you ... 'angel'?" The heavier of the other two brutes spat the words out, and Fiona could see the fleck of drool at the corner of the man's mouth. She felt her stomach tighten. "We just want to see what kind of an angel you are."

Fiona again glanced quickly around her. She was trapped on all sides by these outlaws. They were circling her, and she could tell that their evil excitement was building. Fiona saw Crossbrand, obviously the leader, wave to the others to close in.

"You are brave men coming this close," she wheezed with a mocking tone. Fiona gave her clapper one last shake, and then let it fall to her side. She tried desperately to keep any sign of fear from creeping into her voice. "But you ain't going to be happy with what you get."

The three men slowed, exchanging glances, but when she began to cough, they all came up to a full stop.

Fiona's whole body heaved with the racking coughing fit that shuddered through her. As if her insides would turn out in a moment, the young woman convulsed with the effects of the fit.

"I ain't who you think me to be," she said in a sickly voice, gasping for air. "I have the disease bad. I am telling you, the other lepers have even kicked me out of the village, 'cause they say I got something different. They know I'm dying. They're afraid it's catching."

As Fiona doubled over in another coughing fit, she saw the two who had emerged from behind the rock back up a step. The leader straightened up, peering at her suspiciously.

"You won't be fooling us that way," Crossbrand finally said with a sneer, though his tone was less certain than before.

"It is true," she insisted, her voice raw. Her throat was now really hurting from the forced coughing. "I am going to the Priory for medicines for my sores. They are oozing a black pus. You can see for yourself. And this morning my coughing was black with blood."

She pointed to the patches of darkened mud that spotted her skirt from her earlier fall, and then doubled over.

As she began to cough again, one of the two followers spoke up.

"She's got the plague," he muttered, moving toward Crossbrand's other follower. "I seen it last summer in Edinburgh. It's the damned plague."

"She ain't got no plague, you fools!" Crossbrand shouted. "She's the lass they call the angel from the convent. The one some say is a fairy. By the devil, I tell you she's the same one we been seeing these past two days."

Fiona emitted a weak laugh that gave way to another hacking spell. She managed to spit up a sizable amount of phlegm ... in the leader's direction. Now Crossbrand himself backed away.

"I wish I was, but I ain't!" Fiona gasped, wiping the spit from her chin with the back of her hand and stepping toward the leader, who was now between her and the woods. "I know who you mean, though. The one who comes to the leper village. But they say the prioress won't let her come no more, on account of the ... begging your pardon ... outlaws and all."

Crossbrand pointed his drawn sword in reaction to her movement. Taking a step to the side, he waved at his companions to move in. Their response was an immediate retreat.

"I ain't going to touch no damn plaguey leper," one of them yelled in disgust, as the other nodded.

"Don't go away," Fiona pleaded, continuing to move toward Crossbrand, causing him to move farther around her in the direction of the others. "If you ain't afraid, I'll bring food back when I come. I got nobody for a friend, you know, and I'm sure they'll give me enough to bring. I'm still plenty strong enough for—"

She stopped midsentence as once again a coughing fit erupted from her hooded frame. Peeking at the open field as she gasped for breath, Fiona considered her chances. If she turned and ran now, she might make the woods, but she shuddered to think what would happen if she didn't.

"And if you promise to keep me with you, I won't touch it," she continued, looking at the three. "I swear. I'll bring bread ... and mutton ... I'll bring—"

"You hear?" one of the followers said. "She'll bring bread."

"Bread!" the other shrieked. "Just let her go. I don't want nothing to do with her."

"And let her bring the law down on us!" Crossbrand spat coldly at the two. "I say, leper or angel, we put her out of her misery!"

"But Gavin," the other said heavily, pulling Crossbrand around to face him. "She's too stupid to know it, but she's as good as dead already, and getting close—"

"I say we kill her now," the leader shouted.

Fiona did not wait for the response. Turning, she pulled her skirt and cloak up and fled for the woods. It was only a moment before she heard the shouts from behind her. Knowing her life depended on her speed, Fiona flew across the uneven ground of the meadow. She cursed as she nearly tumbled to the ground, tripping on the edge of her long cloak. The sound of her pursuers growing nearer was nearly drowned out by the pounding of her own heart.

After her stumble, the men were nearly upon her. The sound of their footsteps in the grass right behind her shook what confidence remained. Panic crept into her bones, and she felt her strength suddenly draining from her. She could almost feel the heat of their breaths on her back. Realizing that she was still carrying the satchel, Fiona shrugged the bag from her shoulder.

As the bag fell from her arm, Fiona hit the ground with a thud that knocked the wind right out of her. Her foot had found a rabbit hole, and her body pitched forward to the earth. In a split second, she knew she was finished. In a moment these animals would be upon her.

Then all Fiona could see were the shining black hooves that pounded to a pawing, prancing halt beside her head.

Chapter 2

Death takes the champion in the fight,
The captain in the tower at night,
The lady in the bower of beauty,
Timor mortis conturbat me.
—WILLIAM DUNBAR,
  "Timor Mortis [Fear of Death]"

The cough had the ring of death to it.

Alec reined in Ebon at the sound that echoed from just beyond the trees. Trailing the woman had not been tremendously difficult, and now he knew he was right behind her.

At the thought of this being the same woman, Alec's desire to help her grew even more when he heard her wretched coughing. Although he was angry at first, there had been no hunting after the mishap on the path. Then, as he followed her, a strange urgency had overtaken him, had driven him forward.

He had to find her. The prayer beads in his hand did little to relieve the unsettling effect of the mysterious encounter. He needed to know that she was not hurt.

Alec could not blame her for running off. These short months at Skye had made him better understand the reasons for the way these people behaved. Under the rule of Torquil MacLeod the peasants' survival had depended on their ability to become invisible. The rough hand of MacLeod and his men weighed heavily on those who dared—or were unlucky enough—to cross his path.

Nudging Ebon forward through the thinning wood, Alec followed the sound of the ailing woman. The falcon rested easily on his wrist, and Alec ducked under the low overhang of branches and vines.

The gloom of the wood soon gave way to the brightening of a clearing just ahead. As horse and rider stepped out into the sunshine, Alec reined Ebon to a halt and his eyes took in the scene before him.

She was not alone. Again she coughed, doubling up with obvious pain from the fit. Before her, three men stood watching—one with a sword drawn menacingly. Alec's jaw clenched at the sight. They were not there to help her. For years this had been a common occurrence here. Another victim.

At first, Alec could not hear the exchanges between the woman and her assailants, but suddenly the one with the drawn sword could be heard clearly. Those words sent her running across the field and ignited Alec into action.

Fiona never thought of angels as having hooves, but she was surely glad that this one did. Turning her head slightly, she could see the three shocked faces of the would-be attackers staring at her rescuer. The horse's hooves stamped and pawed at the ground beside her. She did not need to look up to know who the rider was, but a glance told her that Lord Macpherson's sword was still in its sheath.

Though obviously forgotten, Fiona leaped to her feet and stepped back toward the horse's midnight-hued flank.

The giant astride the charger glared at the three outlaws. With an economy of motion, he whipped the hood from the white falcon's head and launched her into the sky. The flurry of the bird taking flight was enough to startle two of the attackers, enough to take the breath away from Fiona. The two jumped back a pace. Crossbrand stood his ground, sword in hand . . . but only for a moment.

Lord Macpherson is magnificent, Fiona thought. His eyes flashed in anger at the adversary before him, and his look was piercing. When the warrior's hand went to the hilt of the weapon at his side, Fiona watched the outlaw leader drop his own sword and spring backward toward his cowering cronies.

The silence in the meadow was awe-inspiring. The towering figure continued to stare as the falcon circled ever upward. Fiona's eyes were drawn to the bird spiraling in free flight. In her mind the peregrine's graceful soaring etched the word *freedom* on the blue canopy of sky above. When Crossbrand finally spoke, his tone was deferential. They know who he is, Fiona thought, and they know they are no match for him.

"M'lord," the outlaw began humbly. "She's got the plague. She's a leper, m'lord. We were just—"

"That is no crime," the warlord interrupted in a tone that washed all color from the men's faces. Only the leader's brand retained its bright red hue. "Sickness is no longer a crime on the Isle of Skye."

Alec had learned soon after his arrival about the appalling MacLeod policy of paying bounties for the lives of lepers. Alec had spread the news far and wide that such brutality would no longer be tolerated.

"M'lord," Crossbrand pleaded in faltering terms, his eyes searching the ground as if he might find the right words there. "M'lord, we ... please, m'lord ... she ... well ... the plague, she—"

"Enough." Alec cut him off, his voice conveying the steely edge of his anger. "I have made it very clear what the punishment would be for those hunting the innocent."

"But, m'lord, we didn't know," the outlaw cried, his lying words seconded by the mumbling noises of the two standing behind him. Fiona wished his false tongue would swell in his throat and choke him, God forgive him. "We were away ... in the service of the King James, m'lord ... at Flodden ... for three years, m'lord. ... But it's her, m'lord ... she spreads the Death, m'lord. We being healthy, we thought ... m'lord ... maybe as service—"

"I have heard enough," Alec said. These lowlifes would say anything to save their miserable hides. "There is no longer any room on Skye for the likes of you three."

The three took another step back.

"But m'lord," Crossbrand begged, "we've done service for the king. We were just doing what was—"

"You should go down on your knees and thank God that I do not give you exactly the punishment you deserve," Alec growled.

"But m'lord—"

"Leave this island!" the warrior commanded, his voice low and steely. "I tell you this: If, after sundown tonight, you are seen on Skye, your punishment will be death. Go."

"But m'lord—" the outlaw whined.

"Now!" Alec nudged his charger forward a pace.

The three turned and ran across the field, but not before Fiona saw the look of hatred that Crossbrand shot in her direction. She uttered a silent prayer that their paths would never cross again.

Fiona cast a glance at Lord Macpherson and then at the woods behind her. She was grateful, but hesitant.

Years of the prioress's warning words crashed down upon her. She was to stay away from nobles, warriors, lairds. She was to hide away from Torquil MacLeod and all of his men. But this was different—this was Lord Macpherson, the man she had watched for months. The man who had stormed past her in the mist of many dawns. The man who was bringing prosperity at last to the people of Skye.

The one who had crept into her dreams for more nights than she cared to admit.

She had to leave.

Fiona knew that she was crossing forbidden boundaries in tarrying with this man. It was one thing to dream, but this was far too real. And she could not risk any further involvement with the laird looming above her. She had to get back to the Priory. There was enough explaining to do as it was. Fiona took a step back with the idea of running for the wood.

"Stand where you are," the warlord ordered, watching the three disappear into the trees. He had found her at last. He wasn't about to let her evaporate into thin air again.

Fiona stopped short at his words. She pulled her hood farther forward over her face as the warrior climbed down from his steed. The young woman realized that the laird had never even glanced toward her.

This was the closest Fiona had ever come to Lord Macpherson. As he strode confidently over to the sword lying in the grass, she knew that she had never seen a man quite like this one. Something stirred within her as she watched his every move. He stood for a moment, studying the blade as if trying to identify its origin. He was tall and powerful. His blond hair was tied at the nape of his neck, though golden strands that had escaped their bonds framed his ruggedly handsome features. She had not been able to pick up the color of his eyes or look into them, but somehow she knew that they, too, would be beautiful. He turned toward her, and she lowered her face, blushing at her own forward thoughts. Her heart pounded and something melted within her.

Run, she told herself. Run while you can.

Alec eyed the cloaked figure standing like a statue before him. The hood covered any possibility of seeing her face, and her hands were hidden in the folds of her garment. The clapper hanging from her rope belt signaled her illness, and the cough had been wrenching to hear—but he had seen her run. She had the speed of a doe, and she had not coughed once since he'd entered the clearing. And then there was her stance, her straight-backed, fearless stance. There is more here than meets the eye, he thought.

"There is no need for you to run away," he began, noting her discomfort as she edged away from him. "If you had let me help you before, this would never have—"

"There was no need for your help, m'lord," she interrupted in a husky whisper.

If there was any doubt in his mind that this was the same woman, it washed away. It was the voice ... the same voice.

"You're wrong about needing my help. But come, I'll take you to your destination," he replied, looking up and waving his fist in a circle at the falcon that was gliding on the air currents far overhead.

"I stand corrected, m'lord," she conceded. "There is no further need of your assistance. I travel this way often."

"And I suppose you run into these types often?" he snapped, gesturing toward the woods where the three outlaws had disappeared. Could this woman be so dense?

Fiona could not answer him immediately. His directness, his nearness was disarming, and her inability to respond to him was disconcerting for the young woman. She simply shrugged her shoulders in silence.

Alec looked away from the woman and held his hand aloft. When he whistled shrilly, Fiona looked up and watched the powerful bird change direction immediately and dive with incredible speed. Just above them, the falcon pulled up suddenly, settling gracefully on the man's leather-covered wrist. With a twinge of sadness, she watched the snowy peregrine surrender her freedom. But when the bird alighted, Fiona realized that the warrior's eyes were not on the hawk. They were on her face. Flustered, she looked down immediately.

"Those three louts could be waiting for you just inside these woods," Alec said, trying to smooth the irritation out of his voice. He did not want to dwell on the situation that had just occurred. But in truth, he was angry with himself for just letting them go. "It is not safe for you—"

"*You* let them go," she interrupted, adding belatedly, "m'lord."

The warrior raised an eyebrow, considering the small cloaked figure standing so assertively in the shadow of the huge horse. What was she, his conscience? She wore a crofter's garment, but she hadn't the tongue of a peasant. She certainly shows no fear of me, Alec thought with curiosity. Indeed, he had caught a glimpse of the lower portion of her face within the hood, and what he had seen had surprised him. She had the most sensuous mouth and the smoothest skin of any leper he had ever run across.

"Aye," he said with a note of weariness, feeding Swift a tidbit of meat from the pouch at his waist. "I did let them go. But then again, if I killed every outlaw on this island, there would be no one left."

Anger flashed through Fiona at his words. He had been here long enough to know that the people of Skye were not outlaws. She successfully checked her temper but could not hold back from responding somehow.

"Why limit yourself just to Skye, m'lord? Why not depopulate the entire Highlands?"

"Your idea has merit, lass," he responded. "But don't you think the clan chiefs would object?"

"How could they object, m'lord?" she said mildly. "They would be the first to go."

"Are you suggesting that every laird in the Highlands is an outlaw?"

"More likely that than every peasant on Skye."

"That's difficult to believe," Alec responded, enjoying her challenging wit. "Especially considering I have yet to come across a law-abiding peasant since arriving."

"Clearly, you are meeting the wrong sort of people . . . m'lord."

"Am I meeting the right sort now?" he asked with a smile.

"That is for you to decide," she answered seriously. "But I will tell you one thing, I'm no outlaw."

"If that's so, then why did you run from me this morning? Who are you, lass?"

"You can see what I am, an innocent islander . . . unlike those you let go."

"Perhaps. But it's thanks to *me* that you—as a leper—are not an outlaw as well," Alec said defensively, stung by her accusation.

Fiona's temper flared at his words.

"An outlaw commits harmful acts," she responded. "And with or without your interference . . . m'lord . . . I have never been an outlaw!"

Alec took in, with some amusement, the change in the woman standing before him. Her posture was no longer that of the sickly creature who had faced the three brutes. Her voice was clear and strong, her attitude challenging. If she tosses her head one more time, he thought, that hood might fall right to her shoulders. He restrained an urge to step up and push back the hood. He wanted to see the expression he imagined on her face. And what kind of face is it? he wondered. She was a bit of a puzzle that needed solving.

"Even if I accept that you're no outlaw, you still have much to thank me for," he answered, absently stroking the downy feathers of the bird on his arm.

Fiona watched his long, strong fingers on the odd, white plumage of the falcon. She noted the man's gentleness.

"Aye, m'lord," she said after a pause, trying her best to inject her voice with irony. "I have *so* much to be thankful for. Why, for the second time today, you have nearly *killed* me with your kindness."

"What?" This was too much. "Have you already forgotten? In addition to your felonious background, I see you also suffer from lapses of memory. I did not try to harm you. I saved you."

"You call crushing my skull beneath the hooves of your horse 'saving'?"

"Hooves can be far less painful than a sword in the back."

"For you, perhaps," she muttered.

"Don't make me sorry I saved your neck."

"Now it's my neck you've saved."

Alec glared for a moment at the hooded figure.

"Ebon was not even *close,*" he continued. "However, if your head *had* been crushed, you would not be here standing and arguing."

"Oh, so it bothers you to have a person accuse you—"

"Aye, when I'm being unjustly accused of crushing someone's skull."

"It's all the same. You *tried.*"

Alec stared for a moment at the fiery creature before him. He could not see her eyes, but he could feel the sparks of wit flying out at him from the dark recesses of the cloak. He shook his head, and amusement crept into his features.

"Your gratitude overwhelms me ... not to mention your manners." He smiled, placing the hood over Swift's eyes.

"I am sorry, m'lord," Fiona responded immediately, "if I do not measure up to what you are accustomed to—mainland peasant manners!"

"Oh, don't be sorry," Alec quipped nonchalantly. "You measure up."

Fiona stared up at the bird. Lord Macpherson might represent absolute worldly authority on this island, but even so, she was unwilling to allow him the last word. Nonetheless, she could not go on with this.

She needed to get back to the Priory. Fiona looked around for her bag and saw it lying beneath the front hoof of the great black beast.

Alec watched as she moved to Ebon and shoved with two hands at the shoulder of the massive charger. The horse's ears flicked back, and the animal lifted his hoof as the woman snatched her satchel from the ground. She looked inside and stamped her foot before whirling on him. Clearly she was ready to say something to him, and Alec waited with interest. But instead of words, the woman dumped the shattered contents of her bag at his feet. Then, without further ceremony, she turned away from him, throwing the bag over her shoulder.

"Good day, m'lord," she said dismissively, striding toward the woods on the far side of the meadow.

Fiona couldn't help but smile as she moved through the grass. Of all the qualities David had mentioned in his description of the new laird to the prioress—and to Fiona—he had not brought up his incredible arrogance. The man was nearly impossible, but she, in this encounter at least, had more than matched him. The prioress, though, would surely be shocked if she knew Fiona had even met the laird—never mind the tone she had used with him. Fiona knew that, even though she had never met him, the prioress thought Lord Macpherson a gem. Day in and day out for the past few months, Fiona and the prioress had heard David go on and on about the virtues of this man.

"It is a good thing David never mentioned humility," she murmured to herself. "Humility is still a virtue, I believe."

"Then why don't you practice it?" Fiona jumped at the sound of the voice over her shoulder. Stopping and turning abruptly, she found herself looking directly at the massive chest of the giant, who nimbly halted just short of barreling her over. The falcon was still on one wrist, the black charger trailing along in the grass.

Her next words caught in her throat. She had not expected to find him following her. Now his close manly presence stunned her into silence. She felt her heart begin to race at the excitement his nearness evoked in her, and this continuing response confused her momentarily. After all, she had encountered many men in her years at the Priory—she had never been cloistered. The Priory had always been shelter to travelers and those in need of protection from the fierce MacLeod clan chief. And she had for years brought what comfort she could to the men, women, and children of the leper community hidden away in the forests of Skye. But with all of that, never had a man's closeness caused such a reaction in her. In truth, though, she had also never been so close to a warrior, to a laird.

Fiona shook her head to clear it of these unwarranted notions and backed away uncertainly.

"Why are you following me, m'lord?" she asked huskily, looking at the ground between them.

Alec watched her for a long moment before answering.

"Two reasons," he responded finally, trying to draw her eyes upward to him. "First, I told you that I would accompany you to your destination ... unless you would care to accompany me to Dunvegan. And second, I wanted to return these."

Fiona hesitated, then looked up quickly. Lord Macpherson was holding the rosary beads in his outstretched hand. She reached up and took them from him, but not before he snatched her hand, turning it and holding it palm up for the briefest of moments.

For a fleeting moment Alec got a glimpse of a beautiful face and uncertain eyes that glanced up at him. Then, as her head lowered, he considered the perfect white hand that had taken the beads from him. They were not the callused working hands they should have been. He smiled. Whoever she was, she was no peasant. Almost in spite of himself, Alec found himself wanting to know more.

His eyes are blue, she realized. They were the same deep azure color as the sky above the Cuillins' peaks. And for Fiona they were as full of mystery—and as alluring—as the Cuillins themselves.

"Umm ... well ... thank you, m'lord," Fiona said haltingly. Her heart was pounding furiously in her chest. This was becoming quite difficult. She needed to get away. She was losing control of the moment; she was losing control of herself, of her very thoughts.

She also had to get back before the prioress really began to worry. "I ... I honestly do not need your help. Please believe that."

"Regardless of what you say, your options have not changed," Alec said sternly. "Which is it? Dunvegan or ... wherever it is you're going?"

Fiona paused, weighing her options.

"If you must know, I am going to the Priory ... for medicine," she said, standing in front of the towering figure. "But are you not at all afraid of my sickness? One of those men back there said I have the plague. The other lepers said the same thing. Does that not concern you?"

"Nay!"

"Why not?" Fiona asked, taking in a deep wheezing breath and preparing to unleash one of her well-practiced coughing fits.

"Stop that counterfeit cough right now," he ordered. "Don't you know you could hurt yourself coughing like that?"

"I cannot help—"

Alec reached with his free hand and grabbed her by the shoulder. His action shocked her, forcing her to look up into his eyes. Into those dangerous blue eyes.

It was the first time Alec looked directly into her hazel eyes. They were the color of the ocean on a summer day. Alec saw within them the same power of the depths that had frightened him for so long ... until he had learned to master his fear. But these eyes also drew him on, enticing and yet challenging him.

"You may be able to gull ignorant dolts like those three fools," the warlord said quietly, "but I have seen enough of the plague to know you don't have it. And as for your ... other acting, you are neither peasant nor leper."

Fiona found herself admiring his handsome features. The long lashes and the stern set of his jaw. And then, as if suddenly remembering who she was, who he was, Fiona became aware of his hand on her shoulder. His hold was anything but gentle.

"I don't have to tell you who I am," Fiona whispered determinedly.

"No, you don't. But your options—"

"They're not my choices. They are yours. Why don't you just let me be? Why don't you go?"

"I'm through arguing with you, woman." His voice was now authoritative, commanding. "I'm tired of giving you choices. We're going to—"

"Fine," she said, interrupting quietly. "The Priory. But we must go now."

From the hard edge in his tone, she knew he meant every word.

The warrior released his grip on her shoulder, and as she turned toward the wide path leading through the woods, Alec wondered what had come over him to take hold of her in that way. She definitely had gotten under his skin. That was it. Why, she'd come very close to riling his temper.

For some time they walked together in silence, each deeply involved in thoughts and the mystery of the other. But the sounds of the spring woods broke into their individual musing, lightening their thoughts the farther they went.

Quite soon the forest gave way to open fields. A shepherd drove a flock of sheep past the two travelers. No doubt on his way to the pond in the meadow. The warrior thought the lad was about to speak to the hooded figure, but on recognizing Alec, the shepherd started uneasily and said nothing, moving cautiously to the other side of his flock.

They were now on Priory lands, Alec realized.

From what he had learned, these lands and all those areas administered by the Church had always been spared the customary violence and looting supposedly controlled by, but actually conducted by, Torquil MacLeod and his men. Rumor had it that Torquil was actually afraid of the prioress' wrath and had kept his men away. From the looks of the carefully plotted fields and the hedged pasture land, Alec thought that the area showed a prosperity that only years of peaceful industry could produce.

On various occasions since his arrival Alec had had occasion to meet the prioress' brother David at Dunvegan, and he liked the man. It was from him that Alec had learned of the nun's iron rule and the respect that she was able to instill in all. It was perhaps because of this that she had, for many years, continued to be a beacon of hope for the people of Skye ... and Alec meant to keep it that way.

"Have you ever chanced to meet the prioress?" he asked, breaking the silence and casting a look at the woman beside him.

Fiona fought back a wry smile. "Aye, Lord Macpherson, once or twice."

"You seem to know who I am, but I still do not really know who you ... are," he said, stumbling over the last word as the woman's hood fell back, revealing for the first time the full extent of her beauty. Beneath the hood she wore a linen veil that only partially concealed the stunning waves of red hair framing a face of perfect proportion and complexion. The hazel eyes, the straight nose, the full lips, and the sculpted chin ... enough to distract any man, but there was something else about her. He was certain that today was the first time they'd met, but he felt he knew her. His mind told him so. But where? How?

"No, m'lord?" Fiona responded. "How curious! You seem to know well enough who I am not!"

She looked straight ahead at the path when the warrior turned his gaze on her.

"I thought this morning you were a fairy," Alec said. "Crossing my path and then disappearing in a wisp of misty air."

Fiona shot a quick look at the warlord. "I can see the old wives' tales of our island have made an impression on you."

"Aye, but you are clearly very real," Alec continued, admiring the color that was lingering on her cheek. He studied the perfect beauty of her face. His eyes lingered on the heavy drape of her cloak, obviously worn to hide a slender body. "Now I am beginning to think you are more like my falcon Swift."

"Are you, m'lord?"

"Aye. Each of you wears a hood, but I should tell you that hood does little to hide what is beneath. In fact, I believe it only served to get in your way when you tried to fly across that meadow back there. Swift, as you saw, flies quite well without her hood."

"Swift flies when you allow her to," Fiona said pointedly. "Her freedom is a matter of your whim, m'lord."

"Her desires and mine are not so far apart," he answered. "Why do you think she returns to my wrist?"

"I can't imagine." She smiled. In spite of her feelings about captive birds, in spite of her feelings about everything, Fiona was beginning to feel quite comfortable as they got nearer to the Priory. But looking up at his strong profile, Fiona felt a pulse-quickening thrill race through her. She turned her eyes to the path ahead, forcing herself to ignore the unexpected emotions that were drawing her attention from his words. But she could not ignore this sudden glow of happiness that was stealing through her.

"Because she knows that the hood is only worn temporarily ... and she trusts me." Alec threw a quick glance at the lass. "Not to mention the simple fact that she ... well, clearly enjoys my company."

"Is that so?" Fiona laughed. It was the first time he had heard her laugh, and Alec liked the sound of it. "Well, I am sorry to disappoint you, m'lord, but your falcon and I are not so much alike."

"You don't enjoy my company? My charming wit? My courtesy? My manly good looks?"

"Nay, m'lord," she answered, pausing for effect and suppressing a laugh before continuing. Lord Macpherson is certainly well aware of his own charms, Fiona thought. "Actually, what I meant is that, unlike your falcon, my hood is permanent."

"Nothing is permanent," he said, but suddenly he grew serious, his thoughts recalling the events in his own recent past. On things he had once truly believed to be permanent.

"The vows of the convent are not just permanent, m'lord. They are eternal."

Shaken from his own thoughts by her statement, Alec whirled to look at her. He was not even sure he'd heard her correctly. A nun! Instantly he retraced in his mind the events and the conversation of the morning. Turning his attention to the path ahead, he could not help dwelling for a moment on his own attraction to this nun, and it made him feel strangely uncomfortable. And what exactly had he said to her? A nun!

Fiona peered up at the man walking beside her and smiled. This warlord, sent to control the wilds of Scotland's Outer Hebrides, suddenly looked like a schoolboy. First shock, then a flush of embarrassment registered on his face, then his features tightened into a scowl of displeasure. When he directed this glare back to her, Fiona looked away. What a wonderfully unexpected response, she thought. She should have tried this sooner.

When Alec did speak, though, his voice was anything but angry.

"So you *live* at the Priory?" he asked in as cordial a tone as he could muster.

"Aye, m'lord."

"Then why do you dress this way?"

"To tend the sick."

"Have you been at the Priory long?"

"Aye, m'lord. As long as I can remember."

"And you are not sick in any way?"

"No, m'lord," Fiona responded sweetly, turning her bright eyes on him. She gave him a brilliant smile. "But thank you for asking."

Alec's heart pounded in response. Her eyes and her smile could bewitch a man. Those lips of hers.... He needed to get hold of his thoughts.

"Tell me," Alec asked after a moment, "do they still teach religion at the Priory?"

"Naturally."

"And they teach the value of virtue?"

"Aye, indeed they do, m'lord."

"Are meekness, truthfulness, and obedience still considered virtues?"

"Absolutely, m'lord."

"Then are you not ... are not all the nuns of your Priory expected to practice them?"

Smiling to herself, Fiona thought back over the morning's events. Of her forwardness, of the tales she'd told, of her bland refusal to obey his simplest commands.

"Nay, m'lord. That is a different order."

Coming over a rise, the two saw the walls of the Priory rise up in the distance. A huddle of huts formed a neat village at its gates, and the smoke of the morning fires hung comfortably in the air above. A brown and white dog ran out from a pen beside the closest cottage, and his friendly barks blended with the rhythmic hammering of the smith already hard at work in the forge. The smell of roasting mutton reached Alec, and the stirring in his belly reminded him that he hadn't anything to eat today.

The folk of the village directed surprised looks at the two as they walked along the lane that led to the gates of the Priory, and Alec did not wonder at their interest or their surprise. He had been encountering the same looks in other villages for the past four months.

The gates that led through the high wall surrounding the buildings and the church comprising the Priory were open, and when the two entered, an ancient blue-robed porter carrying a long and stout staff hobbled over, nodding his yellowed mane at the warlord and directing a warm and toothless smile at Fiona. She touched his hand affectionately as they passed.

"As I told ye, lassie, no rain," he chuckled. "Nary a drop."

"Aye, James." She smiled. "A fine morning."

Alec looked around at the orderly plan of the Priory grounds, at the church directly ahead, and at the stables and guest quarters to the left, with a small orchard rising behind. To the right, the chapter house, with its business offices and school, and what he assumed to be the nuns' quarters beyond. Alec could see the smoke rising from what must be a kitchen building behind the living quarters, and he guessed there was probably a well-tended garden behind that. Between the nuns' quarters and the church, paths of white crushed shells crisscrossed a small quadrangle of greensward, cultivated herbs, and flowers. Neat, efficient, and pleasant, Alec thought approvingly.

His eyes had no sooner taken in the buildings and grounds than a young boy came racing and whooping across from the stables. The warrior watched the lad come full tilt, never slowing a whit and throwing himself into the embrace of the young nun. She stumbled a step back to keep from falling down but quickly regained her footing, hugging the child tightly to her.

"Sorry, Malcolm. I know you've been wait—"

"The prioress is angry. She is *so* mad at you," the boy blurted out. "She went right to the chapter house after Mass this morning. She would not even talk to the chaplain. She—"

"Hush," Fiona soothed, crouching before the boy as she glanced nervously in the direction of the chapter house. "I'll take care of it."

"She kept waving her hands as she walked, talking all the time about 'patience' and 'asses.' David called me to the stables."

The lad nodded toward the heavyset, middle-aged man whom Alec could see running toward them, shouting directions over his shoulder at the hostlers in the stable yard.

A fearful look crept across the boy's face as he snuggled in against Fiona, wrapping his arms around her neck.

"Will she make you slop out the pigsties for a month?" Malcolm whispered anxiously. "She'll not use the birch rod on you, will she?"

"Nay, Malcolm," she answered with a sigh. "Though either of those punishments may be preferable to what she has in mind for me."

Fiona looked at the little boy. He was now warily eyeing the stranger standing nearby with the falcon and charger.

"Lord Alec!" David boomed, running up breathlessly. "You honor us, m'lord. If we had known you were coming ... Are you alone, m'lord?"

"Good day, David," Alec returned pleasantly. "I was out hunting, and just thought I might take you up on your offer to show me the Priory."

Alec and Fiona exchanged a quick look.

"I would be delighted, m'lord, but—" the older man turned to Fiona. "You, lass, had better run. You have a hornet's nest waiting for you." He nodded in the direction of the chapter house and arched his bushy gray eyebrows.

Fiona took a deep breath as she stood up and started for the building.

"Fiona ..." Malcolm said, following her.

She turned and took the little boy's face between her hands. "You stay with David." She straightened up and glanced at Alec.

"Good day, m'lord," she whispered, turning on her heel and striding across the yard.

Alec watched her go, her chin high and her back straight. But it occurred to him that she looked like a soldier going with full awareness into an ill-fated battle.

"Is the prioress so heavy-handed with the nuns?" Alec asked sympathetically.

"Not at all, m'lord," David responded, surprised. "In fact, The prioress is quite gentle when it comes to her own flock."

"Then why is this good nun ... this Fiona ... an exception?"

David looked at the laird quizzically.

"Because, m'lord, this good nun is no nun."

Chapter 3

Of all fairhood she bore the flower ...
—ROBERT HENRYSON, *"The Bludy Serk"*

"Patience is the virtue of asses."

Fiona squirmed where she stood in the center of the room. The prioress had not even paused for a breath since the young woman entered. Mara Penrith MacLeod, prioress of the Convent of Newabbey, was not about to let her charge off lightly.

The prioress had been the undisputed superior on these lands for nearly thirty years. From the time she had proved herself able at the age of twenty-two, no one had ever thought to challenge her authority. She had always been fair but strict in her administration. Over the years, she had earned the respect of those around her, but had demanded obedience as her due. Through times of turbulence and times of peace, she had drawn a straight line, and all had followed where she led. Life in the Priory had been orderly, serene. Until Fiona arrived.

She was at least a head shorter than Fiona, but she had the force of personality that made others feel she towered over them, especially when she was displeased. And right now the older woman was more than displeased. She was angry. Quite angry.

"I know, m'lady prioress, but—"

"So you admit you think me an ass?"

The prioress glared at Fiona from where she stood by the little window of her business room in the chapter house. Her fierce look was inconsistent with the gentle garments she wore. The dark blue robes and the white

veil, symbols of her kindly vocation, did nothing to
lessen the impact of the tongue-lashing she was giving.

"No, m'lady, but—"

"As well you should think me an ass, for all the defer-
ence you pay me."

"But, m'lady prioress, I—"

"And I might as well be a mute and brainless beast,
for all the attention you pay to what I tell you." The
prioress began pacing the room again as she spoke, her
limp more pronounced. Her knee was aching more this
morning than it had in weeks. "Fiona, you never hear
me at all, do you?"

"I do, m'lady," Fiona answered, looking with concern
at the older woman's discomfort. "If you would only let
me—"

"Explain?" the prioress exploded. "How many times
have I listened—patiently—to explanations for your rebellious disobedience? Fiona, why do you insist on defy-
ing me?"

"M'lady prioress, please, I have never—"

"Young woman, do not even *think* of denying that
you have continually disobeyed my instructions at every
turn ... for the last *fourteen years!* If I had pulled one
of my gray hairs out every time you defied my orders, I
would still be an ass—but a bald-headed one by now!"
Her gray eyes rolled skyward. "Holy Mother, what do I
need to do to get through to this wayward child?"

When the prioress paused, Fiona knew this was her
chance to speak. She also knew from past experience that
if she did not jump in now, she would be standing there
for the next hour. Nonetheless, Fiona picked up the
three-legged chair by the window and placed it by the
fire for the older woman. Because of her ailing joints, the
superior allowed herself a wood fire year round. Aye, a
luxury ... but it was the only luxury she indulged herself,
now that her falcons were gone. The prioress sat gingerly, wincing as she flexed her knee before her.

"M'lady, I have changed," the young woman said,
moving back to the center of the room. She was somewhat surprised that the prioress was allowing her to continue. "You *know* I have. Aye, I admit that every now
and again I might have done childish—"

"Every now and then? Childish?" the prioress interrupted, looking at Fiona in exaggerated shock for an instant before focusing her glare once again. "Why don't we get a bit more specific for a moment?"

Fiona dropped her head in resignation before speaking again. Defeat, that was what the prioress was after. Nothing less.

"Aye, m'lady," she surrendered humbly.

"I am waiting," the older woman said, sitting erect in the chair. Her hand rubbed at her swollen knee.

Fiona pulled together her courage to start again. "Aye. I did chil—dangerous things. But, m'lady, I was only a bairn."

"Malcolm is a bairn. And you ... you never were. You were thirteen years old when you set all of my falcons free. And sixteen when you first swam across the loch. And I repeat ... *first* swam across the loch. Should I continue? Hardly a *bairn*, Fiona."

The young woman flushed. The prioress never forgot anything. Ever! Unconsciously, Fiona went to the fireplace and picked up the thick cloths that were hanging on the warming rack. Folding them carefully, she knelt before the prioress.

"Please, m'lady, I cannot undo the foolish things I've done," Fiona said, placing the warm cloths over the knee of the older woman. The swelling is getting worse, she thought. "But this is different. When I go into the forest, I do not disobey you for childish or selfish reasons. Walter counts on me. Please understand! You know that for years I have—"

"Been risking your life going there alone. You've paid back that man's good deed tenfold, child. When are you going to understand?" The prioress paused as another emotion besides anger wedged its way into her consciousness. "Fiona, nothing you have ever done has been selfish. Foolhardy, aye. Selfish, never. I fear for you because you put the well-being of all God's creatures—man and beast—ahead of your own. You don't think of yourself, nor of your safety."

Fiona looked up at the woman who had raised her and loved her—and put up with the hell that she had sometimes brought to her door. Fiona knew, without question, that the prioress's anger always stemmed from the worries that Fiona herself wrought in her. Well, except, perhaps, for the episode with her falcons, Fiona thought, hiding a smile.

The older woman's now gentle voice brought her back to the present.

"Fiona, child. You know I love you like a daughter. Every time I think—or find out—about you being out there alone, something shrivels up within me. I worry about you. Do you understand? You know that there was a very good reason for the lepers to hide themselves from Torquil's brutality."

"Aye, m'lady. But he's gone now, and—"

"Aye, Fiona. But those ignorant swine who served him are not!" The older woman's temper flared once again. "Because of the new laird, Lord Macpherson, the lepers have been given a chance to live out their miserable lives in peace. And besides, they have Father Jack. That old hermit can see to their needs. But a young lass roaming the woods alone—"

"But m'lady, that is a nun's work. Helping the sick and needy ... I mean."

"Fiona, how many times do I need to tell you, *you are not a nun!*" The older woman took a deep breath, trying to regain control of her raging temper. When she spoke again, her voice was clipped. "I do not know where I have gone wrong in your education, but Fiona, I am saying it again: You are *not* a nun, young woman."

"M'lady prioress, I know I'm not. But that does not alter my wish of becoming one ... someday."

"Fiona," the prioress responded, considering her words and pausing for a moment to marvel at her own patience. "Fiona, that cannot happen. It will not happen. Not in this lifetime. Now, I want you to forget about it."

"But why?" The young woman looked helplessly at the prioress, her hands spread imploringly.

The nun looked feelingly at the beautiful and disappointed child leaning in front of her. She had never told her that becoming a nun was an option for her. Never. But neither had she told Fiona that life still had so much in store for her. That her destiny lay in other places, in other hands. There was so much that she wanted to reveal but could not ... yet. The prioress wanted to have all the answers before she would reveal the truth. She knew the time would come, though, and soon. After all, the messenger to Lord Huntly had returned, having successfully delivered her letter. Now all she had to do was to keep Fiona safe and close. But that was the biggest challenge of all. It always had been.

The prioress reached over and took Fiona's hand in her own. When she spoke, her words were gentle. "I have told you many times that you should not call yourself a nun or feel as though you should act like one. You have lived and worked and learned in this Priory. We have shared a wondrous part of your life. What the future brings, we can never be sure of. But a religious life is not your calling, that I *am* sure of. So we will not speak of it again, Fiona, and that's my last word on the subject. Do you understand?"

"Aye, m'lady. But you must understand that I cannot turn my back on those who need me."

The older woman's temper flared again in the wink of an eye.

"Fiona," she erupted, "you are intelligent enough to know that roaming the woods ... alone ... is absolutely—"

"But m'lady, I know this place, and nothing has ever happened to me that I could not—" Fiona broke in, cringing as she spoke the words, at the thought of what the prioress's response would be if she knew about this morning's incident.

"A young lass is still prey for the dirty, heathenish pigs who call themselves men around here these days. Why, when I was a young girl, men respected a woman—"

Fiona had heard this speech before, as well.

"M'lady prioress," Fiona soothed. "You have been like a mother to me. And I do respect you—"

"And obey me, too, I suppose you'll be saying next," the older woman grouched. "Fiona, why can you not understand that you are my responsibility? The things that you do and say, the way you look, they all are a reflection of me." Then, really eyeing Fiona for the first time, the prioress stopped short and looked at the young woman crouching before her.

Suddenly Fiona was uncomfortably conscious of her disheveled appearance. She had hung her cloak on the peg before entering the prioress' office. Now, following the gaze of the older woman, Fiona's eyes were drawn to the shoulder of her dress, torn from one of her falls. She could see the fire again building in the prioress' eyes.

"What happened to you, Fiona?" she shot at her, forgetting her previous train of thought.

"I fell, m'lady."

"On your shoulder?" the prioress began fiercely. "How did you fall, Fiona? *Where* did you fall? You *tell* me what happened."

The knock on the door interrupted the prioress' string of questions. Something happened this morning, she thought hotly, and I am going to find out what. And who could this be? Everyone knows I am not to be disturbed when I am ... counseling Fiona. She shot an angry glance at the young woman retreating to the door.

Fiona whispered a quick prayer of thanks to her guardian angel for her deliverance. She pulled the heavy door open. But seeing the giant figure that filled the entryway, Fiona realized that she might have sent her prayer off too soon.

Alec watched her expression change from relief to disbelief. She had clearly not expected him to be standing there.

And he had not expected her to be so stunning.

Suddenly the full impact of the young woman's beauty struck deeply into the warlord's consciousness. Alec's body tensed with a response he had not anticipated.

His eyes took in the figure standing before him. The veil, like a halo, framed the loose strands of red hair and the flawless ivory skin of Fiona's face. Her deep hazel eyes glowed, showing her change in mood, and Alec watched as she returned his appraising look with her own. As his glance fell on her full red lips, a blush crept from the satin skin of her throat into the milky softness of her cheek.

Alec found himself responding to the young woman with unexpected intensity. He fought to control the clenched muscles of his body as his heart pounded furiously in his chest.

"Who is it, Fiona?" the prioress snapped from her chair by the fire.

Fiona started, surprised by her own bold reaction to the nobleman. She stepped back quickly, taking herself out of the prioress' line of vision as the laird crossed the threshold.

The diminutive nun who had spoken with such vigor sat at the fire, and Alec directed his attention to her. She was a tiny thing, and the intelligent eyes nestled in a stern face were scrutinizing him carefully. It took only a moment for her glance to fall on the Macpherson broach that held his tartan in place. Alec watched her frown disappear as she recognized the family crest depicted on the iron clasp.

Fiona was the first to speak.

"You have an unexpected guest, m'lady prioress," she said in a low voice. "I believe this is Lord Macpherson, whom David has spoken so much of."

"Of course," the prioress responded, excitedly springing from the chair and reaching her hand out to the man towering before her. "Lord Macpherson, welcome. It is indeed a pleasure to meet you at last."

Alec bowed at the waist and took the tiny hand of the nun. After kissing the ring of the Order that she wore on her left hand, he allowed himself to be led into the room.

"Thank you, m'lady prioress," he said with a smile. "The pleasure is mine. I have been remiss in not coming to see you sooner."

"David has told me how busy you've been since your arrival," she answered, smiling back at him.

"Still, that is no excuse," Alec responded apologetically. "And please forgive my dropping in without sending word ahead."

"You never need to worry about that, Lord Alec," she said. "Think of us here as old family friends."

"Aye," Alec said. "My father always speaks of you with the highest regard. He told me before I left Benmore Castle that I should convey his best wishes."

"He is a fine man, your father."

"He says that he first met you many years ago ... when you were children."

"That's true. The Highland gatherings years ago were wonderful times for children. And after that, Alexander

always visited when he came to Skye, but I have not
seen him for years. Is he doing well?"

"Very well, Prioress. He does not travel much anymore, though he and my mother are rather impatient to
be grandparents."

"Alexander Macpherson a grandfather. That presents
a very pleasant image in my mind." Her smile faded a
bit as she shifted uncomfortably where she stood. "So,
Lord Alec, any plans that way?"

"Nay, Prioress," Alec responded, smiling at her unabashed question. "I believe you would have a better
chance, though, asking that of my brothers Ambrose
and John."

Fiona stood seemingly forgotten in the background,
and though she had covered her torn shoulder with a
shawl lying across the prioress' worktable, she wondered
how she might slip out of the room without attracting
any attention. But at the same time, she found herself
unaccountably drawn to these bits of information she
was gathering about Lord Macpherson.

Alec noticed that, in spite of the prioress' speed in
rising from the chair, the older woman was favoring one
leg as she stood. Leading her back to the fire, he sat her
in the chair, picking up the dropped towels. They were
still warm.

Fiona rushed to his side, trying to take the towels
without ever raising her eyes to his, but Alec held on
tight. She looked up, scowling into his smiling eyes, and
tugged hard as Alec loosened his grip. Fiona nearly fell
over backward. He smiled.

"You can see I am getting old, Lord Alec," the prioress said, pretending not to have seen the exchange, and
stretching her leg toward the fire.

Fiona was thankful that the prioress had not noticed
the foolishness displayed by the handsome laird. She replaced the towels over the nun's knee, and Alec stood
beside the open hearth watching her.

"It cannot be your age, Prioress," he responded
kindly, forcing his attention back to the older woman.
"It is most assuredly the dampness of this island
weather."

The prioress looked at him gratefully, taken with his
courtesy and consideration.

Wordlessly, Fiona brought over a chair—one which she knew was in desperate need of repair—for the laird beside the prioress. Perhaps, she thought wryly, his weight will be too much for this. The image of him sitting among the splintered wreckage would be precious.

"Will you sit, Lord Alec?" the older woman asked. "We have much to talk about."

Alec looked over at Fiona, who was standing quietly behind the prioress. Striding across the floor, he effortlessly snatched up the larger chair by the worktable and added it to the group.

"Will the young lady join us?"

Fiona spoke at once. "Nay, m'lord. I . . . I . . . have—"

"Nonsense!" the prioress erupted. "Of course you'll join us."

Fiona could not conceal her shock at the superior's words. In the past the prioress had practically hidden her away whenever any well-to-do gentleman had visited the Priory. The prioress had been particularly careful whenever Torquil MacLeod or any of his men had come around.

"Lord Alec," the older woman said, a mischievous twinkle in her eye. "I've failed to introduce you to Fiona . . . our beloved rebel."

Fiona blushed scarlet and bowed her head toward the warlord. Her hands were clasped tightly, and she hardly dared to look up at him.

"A rebel, Prioress?" Alec asked, raising an eyebrow at the young woman.

"Only at times, Lord Alec," the prioress answered. "The truth is, Fiona is an angel who was dropped at our doorstep years ago. But then, the Lord has strange ways of . . . testing his servants."

"He certainly does, Prioress." With casual grace Alec moved to stand beside her, one hand on the smaller chair. When he pulled it back, holding it for her with a slight bow, Fiona looked down at the chair and again at him.

She paused. Then the prioress' expectant look flustered the young woman momentarily. Feeling awkward and self-conscious, Fiona seated herself cautiously on the edge of the chair that the warlord held for her.

Alec hid a smile and took his seat beside her.

The prioress and the laird talked, and as they did, Fiona considered how quickly this handsome nobleman was charming his way into the older woman's good graces. And she found herself listening attentively to the intelligent conversation, his pleasant voice ringing with easy laughter as he and the prioress exchanged both news and barbs of wit.

Their discussion ranged from the politics of court to the state of the year's crops. With every shift in topic Fiona listened anxiously for any possibility of the conversation turning to the morning's mishap, all the while afraid to move for fear the chair would collapse beneath her.

Then, once, when the prioress mentioned her concern about the bands of outlaws roaming the island, Alec gave Fiona a mischievous look before explaining his plans regarding their control and turning the conversation. He had the opportunity, she thought, but he didn't bring it up. It was then Fiona knew her secret would be safe with him.

As the two talked, Alec often directed his comments at Fiona. But the young woman avoided entering into the chat with the same determination that she avoided returning his lingering looks.

When the discussion turned to the running of the Priory, Fiona knew that her silence was coming to an end. It was the prioress who forced her into the conversation.

"Fiona, tell Lord Alec about your system," the superior ordered.

Their chairs were so close.

"M'lady," Fiona stammered. "There is really so little to tell."

"So little," the prioress scoffed before turning proudly to Alec. "She has only improved the Priory's financial standing from break-even stature to a profit-making one. And those profits are feeding more mouths every day...."

The prioress rose and went to the table, shuffling through papers as she continued to speak. With the older woman's attention momentarily diverted, Alec shifted his weight and placed his knee against Fiona's skirts. Though he was very nonchalant about it, Fiona was sure he was well aware of the pressure of his leg on hers. She felt her cheeks color—he was doing this on purpose. She moved her leg slightly to the side. His knee followed. She tried to push back with her knees, but still he didn't take his leg away. Casually positioning one foot behind the other, this time she kicked him.

Alec calmly moved his knee away and smiled as he once again captured her eyes. Another flush of color crept into Fiona's face.

". . . And I tell you her ideas are truly inspired," the old nun concluded. "The farms' yields improve with every harvest."

"I could see coming here this morning," Alec agreed heartily, "that these are the most productive lands in Skye. I never expected to run into such treasure."

"Lord Alec, you haven't seen anything yet," the older woman asserted. "But I would like you to see the farms, the storehouses, the orchards. This young woman is responsible for the most significant changes. Fiona, take the new laird for a tour of the grounds. Show him some of the changes."

Alec looked at the young woman in a new light. At first he had come in here determined to rescue her from the prioress' wrath and, if he could, to get back at her somehow for letting him think she was a nun. But now, hearing of her intelligence and administrative abilities, Alec's interest in the blushing beauty unconsciously took on a new dimension.

"M'lady, why don't *you* take Lord Macpherson around?" the young woman pleaded. A kind of panic was overtaking her at the thought of being left alone right now with Lord Macpherson. His playfulness notwithstanding, something was happening to her. Something she dared not think about. "Certainly you—"

"I cannot, Fiona," the prioress retorted. "But perhaps Lord Alec will join us for a noon meal."

"I would be delighted, Prioress."

Alec stood, and as Fiona rose resignedly, the sound of cracking wood was heard, and the chair crumpled to the floor.

The three looked down at the splintered mass, and then the prioress and Alec glanced at Fiona.

"I had no breakfast, either," she said innocently.

They all laughed in unison, and Alec scooped up the pieces as they started for the door.

As they took their leave, the prioress gestured to the leather wrist band that the warrior wore.

"I understand that you are an avid hunter, Lord Alec."

"Aye, Prioress. Though I value the birds and the sport of it more than the hunting. In fact, your brother is right now holding a fine peregrine outside."

"I, too, am a fancier of hawking."

"Are you, Prioress?" Alec responded with delight.

"Aye." She sighed. "Well, I was. But if you would like to put your falcon somewhere, I have some *empty* cages."

"I will do that. Thank you."

"But, Lord Alec?" she said as the two started out through the door.

"Aye, Prioress?"

"If you truly value your bird, do not let Fiona out of your sight."

Chapter 4

The courtly knight did a great oath swear,
He would serve Satan for seven year ...
—WILLIAM DUNBAR,
  "Renounce thy God and Come to Me"

"I never saw her again!" Alec said, retelling the story of his encounter with the strange woman.

Alec and his younger brother Ambrose were the only ones left at the head table in Dunvegan Castle's Great Hall. The weather had gradually deteriorated as the day had progressed, and now the wind-whipped rain slapped past the open slits of the windows at the far end. An arm-wrestling match at one of the lower tables caught Alec's eye as Robert was holding his own with one of the Macpherson warriors. The lad was getting stronger by the day.

"What do you mean?" Ambrose asked incredulously.

"It was the damnedest thing," Alec answered. "She never came back!"

"She said nothing?" Ambrose asked, unable to imagine the scene. "This woman just turned her back on you and left?"

"That is exactly what she did."

In the hallway outside the prioress' office, Alec and Fiona had been met by a nervous, waiflike boy who was waiting anxiously for the young woman. Fiona had drawn the boy aside and spoken in hushed tones with him as Alec stood by. Then she had retrieved her cloak from the peg by the wall and had headed down the corridor with the lad in tow.

Alec had followed, and he might have been amused by the proceedings had it not been for Fiona's obvious

agitation. Whatever the lad had said, it had upset her.
Outside, David had quickly joined them, but without a
word, Fiona and the boy had disappeared.

"And you let her? Did you tell the prioress what
happened?"

"No."

"But why not? Who does this woman think she is?"

"A nun."

"A *nun!*" Ambrose looked in shock at his brother.
"By God, Alec. You did not tell me that before. You,
Alec Macpherson, smitten by a nun! Big brother, you
are in a lot worse shape than I thought."

"Smitten," Alec scoffed gruffly. He realized that, in
telling Ambrose of the morning's events, he must have
made more than a few references to Fiona's looks. "I
never said I was even attracted to the woman."

"A nun! Perfect! You will be joining the monastery
next."

"Ambrose . . ." Alec threatened.

"Why not?" Ambrose continued. "You are living the
life of a monk now. When was the last time you had
a woman?"

"I am warning you, little brother."

"Admit it," the young warrior pressed, rocking back
on the chair. "You hardly drink anything anymore, it is
impossible to get you into a brawl, and you've already
sworn off women. My God, not even the monks are *that*
good! You two will make the perfect pair. You can hold
hands at Mass. Do they allow that, Your Holiness?"

With a quick sweep of his boot, Alec sent his brother
crashing to the floor. At a table at the far end of the
hall, several Macpherson warriors looked up in surprise
at the commotion at the head table. Seeing that it was
Ambrose who had been upended, they shared a laugh
among themselves and went back to their conversation.

Ambrose lay stock-still on his back, staring at the
blackened ceiling.

"I am hurt," he said, feigning injury. "But not too far
gone. I can still take care of the announcements for
you."

"Get up, you worm."

"Colin and Celia would want to be here," he continued, still lying motionless. "Your new goddaughter will

enjoy the ceremony. And there are all the folks at home."

"Get up, Ambrose," Alec said disgustedly, offering him a hand up. "You've put on enough of a show."

"A nun." The younger brother laughed, accepting Alec's help and seating himself again on the chair.

"If you care to hear the rest of it, then hold your tongue."

"You mean there is more?"

"I started to tell you about what she's done there."

"You said she left."

"David took me around and explained the new ways. And at the noon meal, the prioress told me more. This Fiona has made some amazing changes."

"Oh, it's 'Fiona,' is it?"

"Will you give it up, Ambrose? This is serious."

"Very well, big brother. What has she done?"

"Three years ago, the prioress was training her to administer the church lands. Apparently, it was then that Fiona came up with a very different idea of how to manage things. She suggested that the prioress divide the land and lease it to families long-term in return for half of what they produce initially."

"Divide the lands?" Ambrose repeated, his interest piqued.

"Aye. The prioress thought she was crazy at first, but this Fiona is very persuasive. She suggested trying it with two families to start. Well, after the first year, the prioress was convinced. The two leasing families outproduced the others by quite a bit. Now the church lands are almost completely leased out, and the Priory serves as a center for exchanges and bartering while still overseeing the farms' planning. With the increased yields they have been able to build a new stable, expand the orchards, and give more help to the island folk. Ambrose, they're doing the things a Priory is intended to do."

"She made the peasants into landowners? Where did she get that idea?"

"I'd like to know that myself," Alec responded. "As far as I know, she has never even been off the island."

"Do you know who she is? Her family? Her name?"

"Nay, she was a foundling. One thing I do know, though, is that she's damn good at disappearing."

"Well, here's one more thing about Skye." Ambrose laughed. "Even the nuns are a mystery."

"Actually, Ambrose, she is not a nun . . . yet."

Ambrose stared at his brother, leaning his elbow on the rough oak boards of the trestle table. "First you tell me she's a nun. Now you say she isn't. Which is it?"

"You asked me who she *thinks* she is. She thinks of herself as a nun. But apparently she is not."

Ambrose continued to look quizzically at Alec.

"I see. She's a bit daft . . . is that it?"

"No! She . . . just has not yet taken her vows," Alec explained.

Ambrose sat for a moment, nodding as if a great truth had just been conveyed to him.

"Then I say you should wait, Alec," he needled with a straight face. "I mean . . . as far as pursuing her goes."

Alec drained his cup of ale and set it on the table, ignoring his brother's last dig.

"But Fiona was not the only surprise I found at the Priory this morning," the warlord said. "There is a lad—"

"She has a child," Ambrose broke in. "A nun with a child. Well, that explains the attraction."

"Ambrose, it's time—"

Alec halted midsentence as a cloaked figure strode to the table on the dais.

With his one good arm, Neil MacLeod whipped his sodden cloak from his shoulders. Throwing it to a serv-ingman, the tall man moved around the table to a bench beside Alec. As he seated himself, he lifted the dead weight of his right arm and dropped it on the table.

The thud of the useless limb sent a pang of sympathy through Alec. Glancing from MacLeod's crippled arm to the scar that marked Ambrose's forehead, Alec thought of the king's battle at Flodden. And of the sacrifices that had been made.

Neil MacLeod noted with grim satisfaction the look of sympathy that flickered on the warlord's face. *Aye,* he thought. *Think hard on the wrongs of this world, hero. You've nothing but rewards to show for a day when we were all nearly wiped out. Here you are, laird of Macleod land . . . land that never belonged to you. For your brav-ery? For your sacrifice? Ha! You just stood with the rest*

of the sheep. While I . . . while I was misled by Andrew.
I should be chief of this clan . . . as he promised. And
Torquil can burn in hell for ruining it all. And you can
burn with him, hero. I fought at Flodden. But tell me,
warlord, what have the MacLeods to show for it? What
have I to show for it?

"The devil's abroad tonight!" Neil declared grimly,
reaching for the tankard of ale before him.

"Aye," Ambrose answered. "But surely you must be
used to it out here."

"We are," MacLeod responded, downing the ale and
gesturing for another. "The foul fiend is never far from
us on Skye."

"This island is also the abode of angels, from what I
hear," Alec countered.

"Perhaps," he conceded grudgingly. "But I do not see
them helping us much with the weather."

"They say 'Every man's heaven is simply the thing he
most deserves,' " Ambrose stated shortly, ignoring the
nasty look MacLeod was directing toward him. Then he
added vaguely, "Or was that 'desires'?"

"Maybe, but what I desire now has nothing to do with
heaven," Neil said, turning his attention to the trencher
of food that was being placed before him.

"They also say that the devil always has the last
word," Ambrose muttered to Alec under his breath.

Alec was beginning to feel the constant pressure of
serving as mediator between these two. Though the warlord was not completely enamored of the MacLeod
leader, he was determined not to let his feelings show as
blatantly as Ambrose was willing to. And he had more
important tasks to accomplish than continually worrying
about two clashing personalities. Considering those
larger tasks, Alec's thoughts returned to Malcolm.

"I visited the Priory today," Alec said, directing his
words at MacLeod.

Neil turned to him, a look of genuine surprise on his
face.

"No one from Dunvegan has found much welcome
over there. Not for years." The man pushed his empty
plate away from him and busied himself with cleaning
his knife. Even three years after his injury, it was obvious to all who watched that he still had difficulty dealing

with even simple tasks. "That woman, the prioress, would bring down fire and brimstone if Lord Torquil even stepped close to the place."

"After seeing the condition of the rest of the island," Ambrose said, gazing into his cup, "I can understand her feelings."

Under hooded eyes, Neil shot a silent dart at the younger Macpherson warrior.

"I met Malcolm," Alec went on quietly, looking hard at the man. Before today, the new laird had heard nothing about the existence of a MacLeod heir. Nothing about Torquil's son Malcolm.

The man shrugged indifferently.

"Who is Malcolm?" Ambrose asked.

"One of Torquil's bastard brats," Neil spat, draining another tankard of ale.

"From what I understand," Alec interjected, "he is the only direct heir your laird left behind."

"He is still a bastard," the MacLeod argued noncommittally. "And a convent-trained milquetoast, at that."

"Judging a seven-year-old a bit harshly, aren't you?"

"I am not judging anyone," Neil responded after a thoughtful moment. "But what good is a seven-year-old laird in a wild place like these outlands? He could never survive power like yours."

"There are others with more faith in my character. I've told you I'm not here to destroy MacLeod lands. Neither am I here to destroy their heirs."

Neil MacLeod eyed the warlord, obviously considering his next words carefully. Finally, he chose to say nothing and turned back to his ale.

"Malcolm is coming back to Dunvegan."

"To stay?" Neil asked, a note of surprise in his voice.

"To visit, at first. Once he feels comfortable, he'll stay."

"The prioress will never let him go," Neil answered, recalling the old woman's barely controlled fury when she came personally to fetch the child back the last time.

"It was the prioress' idea," Alec said, adding with an air of finality, "The lad *will* be coming."

"It was that bastard Macpherson who rode Walter down."

"I tell you, Father Jack, it couldn't be," Fiona said with equal force.

When she and Walter's grandson Adrian had gotten to the hermit's hut this morning, Walter was in great pain. As they walked, Adrian explained what had occurred. After Fiona's departure just before dawn, Walter, Father Jack, and Adrian had started toward the priest's hut. They had been taking one of the less traveled roads when, out of the mists, a rider had appeared. Adrian told her that the rider had slowed upon seeing them, but then had spurred his horse into a gallop. They had all watched in horror, paralyzed as the charger descended upon them. Then, at the last moment, Walter had stepped out toward the attacker, and the black charger's hooves had trampled the old leper, breaking the brittle bones of his right leg.

Fiona and Father Jack had worked throughout the day, carefully setting the leg as best they could and trying to ease the old man's suffering. By nightfall, the medicines she had brought from the Priory began to take effect. Her old friend was now resting—fitfully, but at least resting.

Fiona moved quickly to the window and hung her cloak across the opening. The stretched-skin shutters over the two small windows were doing little to keep out the wind-driven rain pounding against the walls of the hut. The last thing Walter needed now was to get a chill.

"I tell you it was the Macpherson plaid," the hermit asserted. "Before I found my place here by the wood, I traveled the length and breadth of Scotland, and I know their tartan as well as I know the back of my hand."

"He would have stopped," Fiona countered fiercely. "I know he would."

"Then you tell me how many others race across this island—Macpherson plaid flying—with a hawk on their arm."

She could not believe it. She did not want to believe it. The man she met this morning would not purposely trample a harmless old leper. Even if it was an accident, Lord Alec would have stopped.

It had to be a mistake. But she had to convince Father Jack of this. He was an important spiritual force on the island, albeit a reclusive one. But when he chose to speak, the people of Skye listened. The short, brawny man disdained the company of those in power, but his words and his advice moved across the island like an ocean swell—an undercurrent that reached and affected all.

Fiona shuddered to think what damage news like this would do to the warlord. Everything he had done would be for naught. People would either become openly hostile or would go back to being invisible. Things would get worse. Things would go back to the way they were.

"I know it sounds like him, but even a laird cannot be in two places at one time."

The old priest stared at Fiona. He knew her, and he knew that she had no reason to lie for the new laird. Walter was as much family to Fiona as anyone else she had. She owed no loyalty to the Macpherson warlord.

"What do you mean?" he asked gruffly.

"Lord Alec was with me this morning."

"With you?" the priest asked, his gray eyes flickering in surprise. "You *know* the man, Fiona?"

"Aye, since this morning. He went with me to the Priory."

"How did you meet? When was this?" The old man was perplexed. She had been with him at the leper's village and hadn't mentioned any of this. "Come, Fiona. What is this all about?"

She knew she could not tell him what had occurred in the misty morning hours. Despite the priest's approval of Fiona's mission with the lepers, she knew he would try to stop her from coming to the wood if he knew of the men who had attacked her.

"I met him near the Priory lands when I was going back this morning."

"When, Fiona?" he pressed. "He could have ridden down Walter and still caught up to you before you reached the church lands. Do you realize if Walter survives, he could be a cripple? A crippled leper!"

"But he didn't do it!" she exclaimed. "Why are you so determined that he is guilty? You do not even know the man! There are many Macphersons on Skye now. What makes you so sure it was him?"

"It was him. I saw him with my own two eyes."

"When have you seen him before, Father?" Fiona argued. "Do you know of his size, or his build, or the color of his hair? You have never met the man, Father. Why are you so determined that was him?"

"It was the same man who rides across the land like some crazed fool every morning," the priest growled stubbornly.

"Father, with all respect, you cannot even see your way home without Adrian. What makes you so sure?"

"Because, with my own eyes—dim as they may be— I saw him ride down my friend."

"Nay, you didn't, Father," a small voice was heard to say.

Adrian stood beside the straw bed where his grandfather lay. His big eyes looked steadily at the two.

"I saw Lord Macpherson with Fiona at the Priory, and I was beside Grandpa when he was trampled." He looked directly at the priest. "It was not Lord Macpherson, Father Jack. If you were to see him up close, you would agree. The laird's hair is like gold. The rider's hair was like dirt. The boots the laird wears are lighter-colored than the man we saw. They're much finer. I saw him, Father. The man who rode down my grandfather was carrying a brown-colored hawk. At the Priory, the warlord had the white peregrine."

The old priest gaped at the lad, looking as if the wind had been knocked from his body. After a long moment he sagged onto the block of wood that served as a chair. Fiona placed her hand on his stooped but still broad shoulders.

"Father, Lord Alec is nothing like the last laird."

"Only Satan himself could match Torquil MacLeod, lass," the priest said, looking up at Fiona.

"This one cares about us. About the people of Skye." She remembered his fearless concern for her. "He is a good man, Father Jack. You know he was the one who stopped the hunting of innocents."

"I know, lass. But public power and private weakness often abide in the same man," the hermit said with a deep sigh. "Then who did this terrible thing?"

"We will find out, Father," Fiona responded, turning to her injured friend, who was groaning with pain. She put her hand on his forehead. It was burning with fever. "Right now we need to tend to Walter."

Chapter 5

Alone as I walked up and down,
In an abbey fair to see,
Thinking what consolation
Was best in this adversity.
—ROBERT HENRYSON, *"The Abbey Walk"*

Oh, God. He's gone.

Fiona wrung her hands and whipped the veil from her head as she paced her small workroom adjoining the prioress'.

She had heard stories of the dungeon at Dunvegan Castle. Of how enemies of the MacLeods could languish there for years. Of how death would come violently and painfully to those who even thought to oppose the power of the laird.

And now Malcolm. How could the prioress let him go?

Fiona had returned to the Priory when, after four restless days and nights, Walter had at last regained consciousness. Though he was far from being out of danger, he now showed signs of improvement, and Father Jack had ordered her to go and get some rest.

Then, on returning, she had learned from David that Lord Alec had taken Malcolm to Dunvegan for the day.

Standing beside the small window, Fiona shook with anger and fear, recalling the nightmares that had haunted the child's sleep for so long after his last visit to the MacLeod stronghold. She remembered the little boy's sobs. She remembered the promise that she had given never to allow anyone to take him back there.

She angrily pounded her fist into her open palm. How could they let him go? Why could they not at least have

asked him? Malcolm was not a five-year-old child anymore. He was a young lad with brains, with intelligence.
He would have told them no. Why did the prioress not
wait for her return? Fiona slumped into the chair at her
worktable and buried her face in her hands.

Malcolm's mother had died delivering him. She had
been no more than a child herself, and when she made
her way to the Priory, a victim of Torquil's lust, the
prioress had taken her in.

Fiona had only been twelve the night Malcolm was
born. In the months before, she had befriended the shy,
frightened girl who was not much older than Fiona was
herself. And during those months she had shared with
Fiona all the sorrows of her young life.

The prioress had allowed Fiona to stay beside the pale
girl during labor, sponging her face as the contractions
increased both in duration and intensity. Once, after her
friend's wrenching cries had proved too much for Fiona,
she'd burst into tears. It was then that she had looked
at the prioress, her eyes pleading to go, but the prioress
had said gently that this was how she would learn to
tend those who needed help.

Sitting alone in the darkening workroom, Fiona felt
the tears begin to slide down her face. She closed her
eyes and remembered the helplessness that she'd felt.
Remembered the overwhelming sense of loneliness in
her friend's large, anguished eyes—in the death grip with
which she held Fiona's hand.

Looking into the sad brown eyes, Fiona's resolve had
strengthened. She could not turn her back on the girl.

She no longer wanted to go. She was needed.

The hours of labor had dragged on interminably.
Through the night-long ordeal the young woman had
become weaker and weaker. Her panting breaths
seemed unable to take in enough air to sustain her.
Fiona had held her hand, trying to support her with her
own strength, willing her to go on.

Finally, the young mother had cried out once more in
pain, and then the sound of an infant's cry had rung out
in the torchlit room. When the nuns had finished their
ministrations and the bairn had been laid in the fading
mother's arms, the girl had smiled and looked into Fio-

na's face. Reaching out for her, the mother had placed
Fiona's hand on the infant's head.

Then she had closed her eyes, never to open them
again.

Malcolm had been Fiona's responsibility ever since.
She'd bathed and fed him. She'd watched him crawl and
had helped him walk. And they had grown together.

Until Torquil took him. In the late winter two years
ago, the MacLeod chief had decided to bring his heir to
Dunvegan. He was gathering the Highland clan leaders
at Skye after the king's death at Flodden, and he'd
wanted to show off his son. Despite all the women that
Torquil had lain with in his violent and lecherous life,
Malcolm had been the only child of his to be born alive.

But the bairn had been a disappointment. Young Malcolm, faced with the boisterous brutality of the father
he'd never seen before, had been silent, teary-eyed, and
homesick for the Priory. The five-year-old was not the
tough and unruly youngster Torquil had wanted to display, so Malcolm had been kept hidden away in the dark
chambers of the damp and grim castle keep.

Malcolm had been away for six months, and that had
been the longest half year of Fiona's life. The prioress
had strictly forbidden her from ever trying to visit Malcolm, and something within had told her that this was
one time she had to obey, for fear of her life.

Then the news had reached them of Torquil's imprison-
ment at Stirling Castle, and the prioress had gone herself to Dunvegan to take Malcolm back. The neglected,
wild-eyed boy who had been returned to them had required much love and patience—and Fiona had supplied both.

Fiona leaped to her feet, pacing the room again. She
could not believe the prioress would allow the same
thing to happen. Not again.

True, Lord Macpherson was not Torquil MacLeod,
but Malcolm was not what these men expected him to
be. He was not a brute.

Malcolm was kind and considerate. He was patient
and intelligent. His blood might be noble, but so was his
soul. He could never be a chieftain among the savage
warriors of the Highland clans. And Fiona feared for
him, feared for his survival in a place like Dunvegan—

even if he were beside a man like Lord Alec Macpherson.

Why had he taken Malcolm?

"You enjoy beating me, admit it."

"You are pretty slow, for being so big."

"I am not slow," Alec protested. "You cheat."

"I do not." Malcolm giggled. "It was a straight race from the refectory. You just eat too much."

"You don't eat enough," Alec answered sternly.

"You sound like Fiona," the boy responded seriously. "She eats like a bird, yet she still complains that I don't eat enough."

"She's right," the warrior said as they entered the chapter house.

"I'll beat you to Fiona's workroom," the boy blurted out, springing ahead of Alec.

"You are cheating again, you elfin thing," he called after Malcolm, chasing him through the darkened entryway. "You know the way."

Following the lad through the maze of corridors, Alec hung back enough to let Malcolm lead him all the way to Fiona's workroom. But when the boy reached a door at the end of one hallway, Alec crashed thunderously into the heavy oak portal right behind him. Without knocking, Malcolm lifted the latch and shoved his way into the candlelit room.

Alec stepped into the room right behind the laughing boy, but then the world stood still.

She must have been asleep at the table because her look was one of a person in total disarray. Her dreamclouded eyes cleared with comprehension and then joy as Malcolm threw himself onto her lap.

Alec stood mesmerized by the sight of the two before him. But then it was her beauty that made his pulse rise.

She was perfection.

Her red hair hung in a tangle of ringlets about her face and flamed in the light of the candle sputtering on the table. Her perfectly sculpted features—her nose, her mouth—were too real to be the work of any artist. The warlord's breath caught in his chest as she raised her eyes to him. She was even more beautiful than he remembered.

But then Alec's eyes narrowed as a flicker of recognition passed through his brain. Something in the way she looked, in the way her eyes brilliantly reflected the glow of a thousand lights. A sense of warmth swept over him as a question formed somewhere within him. His dream. She had the face of the angel who haunted him. The one that he could never reach. The one beyond the king ... brilliant, beautiful, and unattainable.

When Fiona looked up at Lord Macpherson, something ignited within her. His blue eyes seemed to penetrate her flesh, searing her soul with an intensity she had never before experienced. Uncontrollably, her eyes swept over the magnificent man filling the doorway. His blond hair hung in loose waves across his shoulders. Her eyes lingered on the strands that dangled over his finely chiseled features, around the strong line of his jaw.

Fiona's eyes took in every bit of him. His perfectly white shirt, pulling across broad shoulders, highlighted the sun-kissed skin of his neck and exposed forearms. The Macpherson tartan that was draped over one shoulder and cinched at his narrow waist with a belt drew her eyes downward. Her gaze followed the curve of his kilted hips to the exposed tan of his legs to the knee-high boots and all the way back up again. They halted at his face, arrested now by his smiling azure eyes.

She blushed uncontrollably and hid her face in Malcolm's mass of curls, now resting on her shoulder.

"Fiona, I am glad you are back. You've been away so long. I missed you," the young boy said, his voice muffled as he hugged her fiercely.

"It hasn't been so long, Malcolm."

"It's been four long days," he exclaimed. "I've been counting."

Fiona laughed, ruffling his hair. "So I can see. And I've missed you, too!"

"Is Walter feeling better?"

Fiona nodded and opened her mouth to answer, but Malcolm's enthusiasm got the best of him.

"Oh Fiona, we had the best day!"

She could still feel the heat of Lord Alec's gaze. She dared not look up. She had been caught doing something she had never dreamed of doing before.

"Alec made me king for the day," the youngster

blurted with excitement. "I could command whatever I wished."

"*Lord* Alec, Malcolm," Fiona corrected gently. "So tell me, what was it that you wished?"

Malcolm squirmed out of Fiona's lap and scampered to the laird in the doorway, taking hold of the giant's hand. "My first wish was for you to be there ... with us at Dunvegan. That was Alec's wish, too. He told me so. But my second wish ... You tell her, Alec. Ple-e-ase!"

Fiona raised her eyes to the courtly nobleman. Flattery, she thought. Lord Alec has taught Malcolm flattery. The laird stood where he was, smiling. And then she looked at the excited and expectant Malcolm.

"Would you like to come in, m'lord?" she whispered, standing up. Even to her own ear, her voice had a strange quality.

Alec entered the workroom, his hand on Malcolm's shoulder as they crossed the room. Glancing about, the warlord noted the orderliness of the workplace. An open cabinet with a crisscross of pigeonholes holding hundreds of scrolls lined one wall, rising to the unpainted wood ceiling. Two tables and two chairs were the only other furnishings. There was no sign of any adornment present in the room, and Alec was mildly surprised at the efficiency evident in the chamber. This could be my room, he thought appreciatively.

"Would you care to sit, m'lord?" she asked, indicating the chair by the table across the room.

"Is the chair safe?"

She smiled and nodded.

"I thank you," Alec said. "This little kelpie has worn me out today."

Malcolm skipped ahead of the laird and grabbed the chair, dragging it closer to Fiona's chair. Alec stopped short, amused by the little boy's antics.

The warrior waited beside his chair for Fiona to sit, and the young woman was once more taken by his chivalrous behavior. She felt her color rising into her face again, and wished she had somewhere to hide from such attentions. He was treating her with unwarranted courtesy.

Malcolm nearly pushed Fiona into her chair, climbing

back into her lap as Alec sat across from them. Fiona was glad to have Malcolm between them.

"So what was it you wanted Lord Alec to tell me?" she queried the boy.

"We did so much, Fiona," the boy blurted out, twisting his body to look at her. His eyes were shining. "Alec let me ride Ebon! And I had a lesson in swordfighting! And I met so many people! And the castle ... Fiona, Dunvegan is so different now! It isn't nearly so scary. There are tapestries and all sorts of things on the walls. And there's furniture now. And there's ... what else? Aye, there are lots of Alec's men around all the time. They aren't mean at all, and they even joke with each other. And there's Robert, Alec's squire. He talks way too much, but he's going to be a warrior!"

Fiona couldn't help but smile at the young boy's excitement. She looked over at the laird, and their eyes met for an instant. Suddenly she had an urge to thank him for this. For what he had done for Malcolm. This was certainly far different from what she'd envisioned Dunvegan to be.

"And Ambrose, Alec's brother ... he has a great scar that he won at Flodden fighting for the king! I want a scar like that. And I ... and I ..." Malcolm stopped midsentence. He turned and looked expectantly at the laird seated comfortably across the room.

"Malcolm, what was it that you wanted *Lord* Alec to tell me?" Fiona asked, looking pointedly at him.

"I want ... Alec asked me ..." The lad responded, casting a last hopeful look at the laird.

"What do you have against falcons?" Alec asked casually.

"What?"

Alec smiled at the bright-faced boy and turned his eyes back to Fiona. "He wants a hawk."

"A hawk? And have another free animal caged? For God's sake, why?"

"Why not?" Alec responded quickly.

"I need a mistress, Fiona," the boy explained seriously, interrupting the two.

"You need *what*?" Fiona looked from Malcolm's somber expression to the warlord's barely restrained laughter.

"He needs a mistress," Alec repeated. "You heard him."

"Wait a moment—" she began.

"I do, Fiona!" Malcolm interjected, taking her by the chin. "Ambrose said so."

"Oh, he did, did he?"

"Aye," Malcolm continued. "Ambrose said Alec has a mistress, and that I should have one, too!"

Fiona felt an unexpected pang of disappointment, then she considered for a moment. "Malcolm, first of all, you are too young to be discussing such things. And second, I think I would prefer not to hear about Lord Macpherson's private affairs."

"She's not a private affair," the lad grumbled. "Tell her, Alec."

Fiona looked questioningly at the amused laird.

"You really need to meet Ambrose," he answered, nodding. "Before I set him adrift in a rudderless boat, that is."

"If he is anything like his brother," she responded, "then perhaps I will wait."

"So I can keep a hawk?" Malcolm interrupted. "I'll bet the prioress would agree."

"I am lost," Fiona said, ignoring the boy's comments. "Hawks? mistresses? scars? swords? What other things of value have you taught Malcolm?"

"I think I should clarify this before we move further afield."

"That would be nice," she said, raising an eyebrow at the laird and hugging Malcolm to her protectively.

"My brother made a rather off-color comparison of Swift, my falcon, to ... well, ... to a woman." Alec searched for just the right words. "His comments went something like ... to the falconer, a dog is a servant, a horse is transportation, but a hawk is his mistress."

"How is that so, m'lord? Though I'm afraid to ask." Fiona had always believed these animals to be God's creatures. Beneath man in the natural schema, perhaps, but objects of man's will ... never!

"Others besides Ambrose have said that the relationship between a falconer and his bird is very much like the relationship between a man and a woman. When a falconer trains, or rather teaches a bird to trust him, he can only coax her. If he is successful, he is rewarded with the companionship of a creature that could disappear forever in the wink of an eye."

"A rather tenuous view of the relationship between men and women, m'lord."

"We can only learn from what experience deals us," he answered seriously.

" 'Only,' m'lord?" she asked, a note of friendly challenge in her voice. "I don't know that women are as inconstant ... or so much in need of man's training ... as you or your brother suggest."

"Nay?"

"Consider, m'lord, the relationship between falconer and falcon ... between man and woman. Suppose, as you say, the man teaches, coaxes, forms her in a way he discerns as desirable. But what of the woman?"

"The woman? Tell me."

"Let us accept, for the moment, that what you say is true. The woman is learning about life. In so doing she is ... well ... growing a set of wings. For perhaps the first time, she is now able to see more of what the world offers. For the first time she is *able* to soar. And as she rises higher, she can also see a changing horizon. As you say, she *could* use these wings to fly away. But she does not."

"What stops her?"

Fiona paused for a moment as Malcolm squirmed in her lap. The laird sat still, watching her intently. She took a deep breath.

"Her man. She sees the horizon, but she also sees her man. The woman wants him, but her needs have changed. She now seeks more than *simply* what her man can teach. She wants trust, companionship. The same basic qualities we want in our friendships. And she knows these things are shared, not taught. She stays, m'lord, sometimes in the hope of these things. But when this sharing does not happen—when she knows it will not happen—the falcon flies."

Alec rose from his chair and crossed to the window. The moon was just rising above the roof of the church. He turned and leaned against the sill.

"Do you think men are unable to learn?"

"Nay, m'lord," Fiona responded quickly. "But most

see no need to change. And is it not true that men learn only what their passions allow?"

"Tell me, Fiona," the warlord said, his eyes capturing hers, his tone lightening suddenly. "What do you know of men's passions?"

Fiona blushed, averting her eyes.

"I only ask the question, m'lord," she answered, her eyes sparkling with mischief. "I believe someone once said, 'We can only learn from what experience deals us.' "

"So can I have a hawk, then?" Malcolm asked, punctuating his question with a yawn. Grown-ups talked too much.

"We can talk about it in the morning, Malcolm," she said gently, very aware of the standing laird. "You're falling asleep right here."

"I've heard that before. But I'll remind you again tomorrow, Fiona. I won't forget," the boy grumbled, edging off her lap. Brightening, he turned to her. "Carry me up?"

"Get along, you imp." Fiona laughed. "If you're big enough for a hawk, then you're big enough to go up on your own two feet. But I will walk with you."

Malcolm whirled toward Alec. "Will you walk with us?"

The laird nodded, his eyes drawn to the beauty seated at the table. The candlelight behind her caused the red in her hair to flame brilliantly around her face. She was truly radiant, but there was more than just her beauty drawing him on.

"Good night, m'lord. Thank you for showing Malcolm—"

"Wait!" Alec stopped her, reaching out and touching her elbow as she was about to turn away. Malcolm had just disappeared into the nuns' quarters, and Fiona was about to follow him in.

Alec did not know what had come over him. But he knew he could not let her go, not yet. Since he had seen her last, Alec had not been able to stop thinking about her. There was something about Fiona that haunted him. He was not sure what it was. She was like a waking dream, following him.

"The porter will let you out, m'lord," she said. "Unless there was something else?"

"There is."

Alec's pause after his last word was enough to send both a thrill and an accompanying flush through Fiona's body. His look was direct, and its effect coursed through her in a way unfamiliar to her.

"You still have not shown me around, Fiona."

At the sound of her name on his lips, Fiona felt her color rising again. How could this be so? she thought, glad for the cover of night.

"It is dark, m'lord. We . . . we would not even be able to see the flowers in the garden."

"The flowers are not the only thing that interests me."

"Nay?"

He shook his head.

What was happening to her? She knew she should go, but she wanted to stay. The idea of walking in the darkness of the night, under the blanket of stars, beside this man, sent a shiver down her spine. But it was not proper. It would never be proper . . . for her. And yet . . .

"Perhaps another time?" she heard herself say.

"Nay, lass, there is no moment like the present," he answered, speaking from his heart. He was attracted to her, and he already knew the reason for it. Yes, she was beautiful—stunningly so. His body was telling him that right now. But more importantly, this woman had spirit and wit. Moreover, despite her willingness to don a disguise in her effort to help those in need, she was devoid of the insidious falseness that defined the courtly ladies he had been dealing with all his life. "You are very difficult to corner."

"I am?"

"Aye, you are. I have been here every day since we last met, looking for you. But you're never around."

Fiona's eyes were drawn to his. She had heard about him coming here and spending time with Malcolm. But it simply could not be that he'd come here for her. Something stirred within her at his candid admission . . . a seed of hope . . . but it was a hope for something she dared not admit to, even to herself. But had she heard him right? What had he said?

"I . . . I did not . . ."

"How about it, Fiona?" Alec pressed. "We will not go far. Perhaps we could just sit and talk. It is a beautiful night, and it would be a shame to waste it."

She looked at him again. She was out of her element. All the training that she had gone through in her life had not even come close to preparing her for this incredibly handsome and persistent laird.

"Is there something specific you want to talk to me about?" she blurted. She knew it was a last defense, but she was trying to control a sudden panic. She had to focus on the reason behind all this. She could not in her wildest dreams imagine why Lord Macpherson would want to sit in the moonlight with her.

"Aye, there is." Alec peered through the darkness at the young woman. He needed to calm her fears, allay the causes of her skittishness. Like the new falcon that bates in panic in her first contact with the falconer, rising from her perch with a wild beating of her wings, Fiona looked ready to vault the stone steps of the dormitory. And yet, something told Alec that she would not. "I want to talk to you about the poisonous gases that lie just beneath the ground in the Spanish New World. And I really need to learn your feelings about the Tudor king's new warships. And I was wondering if you had heard about Erasmus's response to Martin Luther. Or about Suleyman the Magnificent's harem of a thousand wives. . . . A man needs to learn."

She laughed. "You've just crossed far beyond my realm of knowledge, m'lord."

"Very well," he said, taking her by the hand. "Then we can explore territory new to both of us."

The touch of his fingers sent a shock through Fiona. As he led her toward the garden paths, the sensation traveled like a river of heat. Up her arm and into her chest. It swept through her and spread. Something within her wanted to resist the pull of his hand.

But something even stronger drew her on, and ahead the moonlight spilled glowing, white, and liquid into the ordered greenery of the open gardens.

"Tell me, is this place very old? No one at Dunvegan seems to want to tell me anything of the Priory's history. How did it come to be founded here? What happened to Newabbey?" Alec knew he had to draw her out. He

wanted her to feel comfortable, to be as at ease with
him here as she had been in her workroom. "For that
matter, what happened to the old abbey?"

And then, gently, Fiona slipped her hand from his
grasp and started to talk. They walked past the darkened
buildings, past the rear of the church, and as they did,
she spoke of it as the place she called home. She told
him of the Priory's sometimes colorful history, of the
nearby abbey that had been raided, burned, and aban-
doned in the times of the Norse invaders hundreds of
years before. She spoke of the succession of women who
had guided the construction of the various buildings.
Women who had seen the need for changes and had
made them. She told Alec of the work of the present
prioress, of the improvements that were even now
happening.

Alec listened, amazed by the depth of her concerns
and the vast degree of her knowledge. He knew from
his discussions with the prioress and with David that
Fiona was neglecting to take credit for her own efforts.
He looked at her in the glow of the rising summer moon.
She was so young, so beautiful, so resourceful, so inven-
tive. And tonight he had discovered something else
about Fiona. She was so candid about her emotions and
beliefs. She expressed them with no fear or reservation
and displayed them with a great degree of animation.
Nothing was hidden within her, and no opinion was
held back.

They had been skirting the gardens. Fiona hesitated
at the edge of the shadowy grounds which lay ahead. She
fell silent, but watched as Alec started to move along the
crushed shells of the pathways. She followed.

As they walked, Fiona became aware of a gentle humming emanating from the golden-haired warrior. She
smiled at the ease in which he fell into the tune; she
took comfort in the sound of his voice. The rich night
scents were rising from the garden beds and mixing with
the odor of crushed thyme produced with each step they
took across the greensward between the paths.

Their senses came alive as each found a kind of restless joy in the place and in the magic that was stirring
within them. Hardly wanting to end the night, Alec
looked about him for a way of prolonging it. Spotting a

stone bench, he guided Fiona toward it, stopping at the last moment and cutting off her path.

"I could use a short rest," he said, seating himself and not leaving Fiona much choice in the matter. "How about you?"

"So Malcolm did wear you out," Fiona said with a laugh as she watched him stretch his long legs out before him. She sat at the end of the bench, a discreet distance between them.

"Aye, he is quite a lad."

"May I ask you something, Lord Macpherson?"

"Anything." Alec turned, looking at her profile. She had gathered her hair and tied it at the nape of her slender neck. She was looking straight ahead, avoiding any eye contact. He took in the beautiful features: the fiery hair, the straight back, the modest dark dress, the rise and fall of her bosom with each gentle breath.

"Why ... I was wondering ..." she stammered. She could feel the heat of his gaze on her. "Why your attentions to Malcolm? I mean ..."

"The visits here, the trip to Dunvegan, the riding, the hawking?" Alec asked.

"Aye." She nodded. "He even calls you by your given name."

"You might, as well."

"That is not what I am getting at," she insisted, the flush rising to her face once again.

"I know," he answered. "Well, I like Malcolm."

"Malcolm is a wonderful lad," she pressed. "But surely that is not the only reason. After all, his father was your enemy."

She turned and looked directly at him, awaiting his response.

"My understanding is that his father was not all that popular here, either," Alec responded quietly, meeting her gaze and indicating the Priory with a sweep of his hand. "If you don't hold it against the lad, why do you think I would?"

"Because blood feuds seem to drive the actions of many in your class."

The warlord paused for a moment before answering, arrested once again by her frankness and her honesty. And her beauty.

Gazing into her face, at her finely sculpted features so delicately lit in the glow of the moon, Alec fought hard at the sudden urge to throw caution to the wind, to pull her fiery locks free of their bonds, and to lace his fingers into the silky tresses as he drew her to him. Caught up in the moment's fantasy, the young warrior was left torn between his desire to communicate with this young woman of wit and intelligence ... and his growing need to feel her slender body against his, to mold her soft, full lips to his own.

"M'lord?"

"Aye ... blood feuds. But do you mean the baker in the village does not occasionally argue with the blacksmith?"

"Of course they do," she conceded with a smile. "Though I have only once or twice seen the baker raise an army to settle the dispute."

"You see? I am already behind in this area."

"I have a hard time believing that, m'lord," she teased, raising an eyebrow at the long sword tied at his belt.

"It is true," Alec protested. "Although I have personally slaughtered thousands upon thousands—this week—I am certain that I have only gathered an army *once*."

"Well, m'lord, you had better hurry. Think of how your reputation will suffer among the other clan chiefs when they find out our baker is ahead of you in raising armies."

My reputation will suffer tenfold, Alec thought, if anyone—including Ambrose—ever discovers that I sat next to such a beauty as this and let her escape without so much as yielding a kiss.

"You have nothing to say about it?"

"About what, Fiona?"

"Your poor reputation."

"Until a moment ago, I had no idea that my reputation was even in jeopardy. Now it sounds as if my honor has been called into question. Has it?"

"It certainly has in my mind."

"Fiona, I am truly shocked to think you would feel this way about me," he complained smilingly. "What have I done to deserve such low opinion?"

Shifting his position on the bench, Alec moved toward her slightly, taking hold of Fiona's hand.

She looked at him with mischief and let him hold her hand in his. "You can be assured that I have no opinion of you whatsoever—high or low. It is merely your reputation that I am concerned about—a reputation, m'lord, which has preceded you."

"Wait!" he cried, feigning a deep wound to the chest. "Now you have no opinion whatsoever?"

"None, m'lord," she responded innocently. "But seriously, going back to where we started, you have not answered my question."

"Your question?" He ran his thumb over the silky skin on the back of her hand.

"Regarding your interest in Malcolm, m'lord." Fiona shivered at his caress, but still did not withdraw her hand.

"I like Malcolm," Alec replied earnestly. "But you are correct. That is not the only reason."

She gently withdrew her hand from his grip.

Alec looked at the young woman whose direct gaze spoke volumes about her affection and concern for her young charge.

"I do not want Dunvegan forever."

"But you are the laird," she exclaimed, stunned by his comment. "The Stuarts gave these lands to you."

"Only because they needed to secure Skye and the Outer Islands. But they belong to the MacLeods and to the other clans that have lived here from the beginning."

"So . . . how does Malcolm play into this?"

"Malcolm is the rightful heir. He is the future laird."

"Malcolm is a child," Fiona said. "You do not know what happened before."

"Then why not tell me," Alec suggested.

Fiona started, uncomfortably at first; but then, as more of the events of the past flashed in her mind, the more she realized how important it was for this laird to know about Malcolm and his experience with Dunvegan Castle.

Fiona talked, and as Alec listened, his own revulsion at those first glimpses of Torquil's dungeon sprang to mind. Upon their arrival, they'd found a tangle of skeletons in the manhole that had been carved deep in the rock beneath the castle's dungeon. To think that a mere child had been exposed to that made him even more determined to help Malcolm in every way possible.

"So . . . what if Malcolm is not the kind of leader that is needed?" Fiona concluded. "He has seen brutality, but he has been raised by people who preach gentleness and peace. He's been raised in a convent. He is smart, do not mistake my words; but he is not a fighter."

"Leaders are what Scotland needs for the future, not fighters. And leaders must have much more than a strong arm and a quick sword." Alec looked at the woman before him. "But don't shortchange Malcolm. He has spirit, even if Torquil couldn't see it."

"Aye, I know he has spirit . . . but—"

"As his teacher does," he interrupted, placing his hand momentarily over hers.

Flustered, Fiona lost her train of thought. Even after he removed his great hand, she could feel the imprint scorching her skin. The man had a way of distracting her. Of sweeping her up on some unseen current. Like a rolling ocean wave. Like the wind.

"I . . . I just don't want to see him hurt. Disappointed," she continued after a pause. "He obviously likes you and wants to spend time with you. I think that is wonderful. He has never had someone like you to look up to. But do not give him promises that cannot be."

"Cannot be?"

"Aye. I know how easily promises are made and how easily they are broken. I do not want Malcolm to become a fool, dining on hope."

The warlord's tone changed abruptly. "You are talking of my word, Fiona. A promise is a promise, and *my* promise will not be broken or tampered with."

Fiona heard the irritation in the warrior's voice. She had not meant to be offensive. She had not meant to be disrespectful. But she was the only voice that Malcolm had right now. Rather than have Malcolm hurt later, she was more than willing to take the heat from Lord Macpherson now. "But what of your own heir? Are you not making decisions now that might be changed later? Will your future heir be so generous? Are you not giving away things today that you might regret not having tomorrow?"

Alec felt the tension charge his body. Memories of broken promises still ruled his life. He looked up at the sky above. The stars scowled down upon them.

When he finally spoke, Fiona saw a face that had hardened, and there was no hint of softness in his voice. "These lands will be Malcolm's. That is my final word."

Fiona watched as the laird stood, ready to take his leave. She had wrought a change in him with just a few careless words. She had questioned his honor. And perhaps unjustly so. As they walked back beneath a cold moon toward the nuns' quarters, she felt a gnawing regret over what she had said . . . and about the short-lived friendship that seemed to have wilted as quickly as it blossomed.

It is true, there is much I have to learn about people. So much I do not know, she thought. A knot was forming in Fiona's throat, and she dared not look up from the path.

So much I will never know about Alec Macpherson.

Chapter 6

He that is without pain or strife
And lives a lusty, pleasing life,
But then with marriage he does mell
And binds himself to a wicked wife . . .
—WILLIAM DUNBAR,
  "He Brings the Sorrow to Himself"

She wanted Alec Macpherson.

Everyone at court knew Kathryn Gray had set her cap for the heir to the Macpherson lands.

He was everything she wanted. He was of noble blood. He was handsome. He was charming. He was rich. He had been the favorite hunting companion of King James, and he was now celebrated for his role in saving the life of the new infant king. He had all the finest qualities of the courtly gentleman . . . and more. He had her father's approval.

And, after all, how could he refuse?

She was of the noblest blood in Scotland. She was beautiful. She had grown up in the courts at Paris and Avignon. She was also rich . . . but not rich enough. She had power . . . but not enough. Never enough. Not as much as Alec Macpherson could give her.

And she was the mistress of seduction.

The court buzzed with activity when the news of their intended betrothal was made known. They were seen everywhere together, and all the ladies at court pined at the loss of such a dashing and eligible bachelor. But all the gentlemen at court smiled into their cups and exchanged knowing looks. The lady would soon tire of this one. After all, she had tired of all the others.

And she soon did.

But there was too much to gain through marriage to this man for her to let him go. She was the model of propriety in his company. But she was infidelity personified when his back was turned. Whenever his back was turned.

But Alec Macpherson was not long fooled.

"She is a faithless whore," Alec muttered, pounding his fist on the table. "And if she is anywhere near Benmore when you go home, Ambrose, throw her and her whole filthy lot out in the moat."

A messenger had just come to Dunvegan with word of Kathryn Gray's visit to Benmore Castle. She had stayed a few days before continuing her journey through the Highlands. From all that could be gathered, she was heading for Kildalton Castle and the Western Isles.

"Well, it is clear she has not yet given up on you, big brother," Ambrose offered tactfully. He knew this to be a dangerous subject for discussion. "Do you think she will come to Skye?"

"If she does, I will drown her with my own hands." He'd thought he loved her. He had tried to be what she wanted. But now the only feeling left was disgust.

It was truly over between them. Her own conduct had nailed that coffin shut. But even before Alec had found out the truth about her, she had made clear to him that the sparkling courts of Europe were the places she wanted to be. She had called the life at Skye barbaric, devoid of culture. She had said she never had any intention of living in a place so far beneath her. Journey through the Highlands? Whom was she trying to fool?

After he'd discovered her with her latest conquest at Drummond Castle, Alec had wanted nothing more to do with Kathryn. So Lord Gray had tried to intervene on his daughter's behalf. The betrothal agreement was nearly finalized, and he made sure they knew that the damage in breaking off the relationship at such a late date would be costly and extensive for everyone concerned—especially for Alec. Or so he thought.

But then the Macphersons—backed by the Campbells and Lord Huntly—had stood together, and the contract had crumbled to dust.

"Our parents obviously did not abide her company

for long," Ambrose suggested. "I am surprised that she would be so bold as to stop there at all."

"Bold?" Alec asked, facing his brother across the table. "She will do anything that she thinks will profit her. I learned a great deal about her once my eyes were opened, and I know she has absolutely no conception of right or wrong."

What was it that Fiona had said the night before? About learning from each other? About trust? That beautiful young woman was living in the shelter of a convent. How could she know about life in the real world? Indeed, he had been that naive once. He wished he could even now draw on her idealism. But it seemed to Alec that he was living in another world. Perhaps it was a world that Fiona could not even exist in—a world that included such creatures as Kathryn Gray. Fiona dwelled far above them, he thought, like an angel.

And yet, etched so clearly in his memory, the recollection of that final confrontation still smoldered within him. After Kathryn's lover had scrambled out the high window to save his own hide, she had stood there—confronting him—as if nothing were amiss. She told him of her physical desires and how they had nothing to do with their marriage. With their union she would have his name, but she would accept no "chains." She would be independent, and she would soar free as she pleased.

"I recommend you do the same," Kathryn said, her voice and her eyes as cold as ice.

Their coming marriage would be an excellent move—politically—for both families, and she suggested that Alec accept it as such.

"What do you think she is hoping to gain by this little excursion of hers?" Ambrose asked, breaking in on Alec's thoughts.

"Sympathy, perhaps. The hope of gaining allies among the parents and others who know me in the Highlands. She's very good at playing the pathetic, misunderstood martyr when she wants to."

"That would explain her next move to Kildalton," Ambrose suggested.

"She'll be in for a cool reception there, though. With Colin and Celia at Stirling, Lord Hugh Campbell and Agnes will not give her the time of the day." There was some satisfaction in the thought of Kathryn's being treated as she deserved. "But one thing is for sure, the slut is not accustomed to being dumped."

That day Alec had walked out, disgusted and shaken by the hollowness of the life she envisioned. A life of deception. But his inner strength had soon burst to the surface. He never looked upon her again.

"I'll tell you one thing. Because of her own web of false friends," Ambrose added, "the outcome of her bad luck made for a noisy affair at court."

"Court!" Alec spat with contempt. A place he had no desire ever to return to. "I was blind not seeing her cronies as the worthless parasites they are."

"We all make mistakes, Alec," Ambrose responded. "But look at the bright side. In the end you made some worthless parasites' lives *very* miserable."

"I just hope that was the end." Alec paused, standing and looking over the pile of work that awaited him. "I would be happy if I never had to step foot in that court again."

"Come, Alec, it is not really the court that is to blame," Ambrose suggested. "At least there is something to do there . . . besides work!"

"Work?" the warlord exploded with a laugh, looking over at the younger man sitting comfortably in the chair. "What do you know about work? You have not yet done a good day's work in your entire life, you lazy beast. One scar in one battle and you figure your future is secure. When I heard you telling Malcolm how you—"

"If you are going to slander me," Ambrose cut in, his face the very picture of the tragically wounded, "I am not going to tell you what I have accomplished this morning."

"You mean other than sleeping the morning away and lazing around?" He nearly laughed at the shocked look on the younger warrior's face. After a pause, Alec sighed with comic gravity. "Very well, at least I know this should not take very long."

"I think I may have learned of a way to get the Mac-Donald clan to work with us."

Alec sat up again, his attention riveted on his brother's now smiling face. Alec had seen that the time was right for Scotland to develop a new industry in the west.

News of the riches of the New World had swept through a Europe that was bursting at the seams. But Alec knew that to explore and to develop these new lands, great new ships would be needed.

After arriving here, the new laird realized Skye offered opportunity for such a venture. The island had timber and pitch for hulls and masts, and stone for ballast. It was well situated on the west coast of Scotland, with a number of ideal inlets and coves to choose from for a shipyard. That was when he had asked Ambrose to join him. The younger Macpherson's knowledge of ships and shipbuilding was well respected across the land. Ambrose brought the expertise that Alec was in search of.

The only thing Alec lacked was labor. The MacLeod clan had a tradition of fishing as well as farming, but there were simply not enough available workers.

Half of Skye, however, was populated with MacDonalds, an old and proud clan that had been subjugated by Torquil and his immediate predecessor. There were many available men, but when Alec had approached their ancient clan chief at Dunscaith Castle on the southern tip of Skye, MacDonald had liked the idea, telling him, though, that his clan would never work with either the MacLeods or their new mainland overlord. The people had lived too many years in fear of them just to come out and get involved in this venture. And even though the chief himself saw good in the new laird's plans, he knew he would be ineffective in convincing his people. After all, he was no longer seen by the clan as either counselor or leader. So Alec's efforts had been stymied, for the time being.

"How do we get the MacDonalds to work with us?" Alec asked, quite interested in Ambrose's discovery.

"While I was *lazing* around this morning, riding up the coast and *working* with the fishermen, one of them mentioned a possibility we were unaware of."

"Aye? What, Ambrose?" Alec fired at his brother, who was definitely taking his time.

Ambrose became serious, leaning on his elbows and looking directly at Alec. "There is an old priest on the island. His name is John. Father Jack, they all call him.

He is a hermit of sorts, but he lives not far from here. Inland, by the edge of the great forest."

"Aye," Alec responded, musing. "I believe I may have seen him on my way to hunt. The fields by the wood are wonderful for hawking. I have never been able to stop and speak to him."

"The fishermen tell me he is the way to reach the people of both clans. He is a good man, they say. A man who is not impressed by either violence or wealth. They say he treats all God's creatures the same. The clan folk listen to him ... more than they do to their own chieftains."

"Can he convince the islanders to work together?"

"It seems if anyone can, he's the one to do it."

"You just made my day quite productive, Ambrose."

"What? Why do you say that?"

"Because I was just about to ride over to see this Father Jack."

"You already knew about him?" Ambrose asked, surprised by his brother's revelation.

"Aye. Of course. A good laird knows everything."

"This is Ambrose you are talking to, Alec."

"Very well," Alec admitted. "He sent a message that he would like to talk with me on an urgent matter."

"Why is the priest not coming here?" Ambrose asked. "Alec, part of being laird is having people come to *you!*"

"Ambrose, this is one laird who will go where he is needed." Alec stood and called for Robert.

"I'll go with you."

"Then you'd better get off your buttocks, my hard-working little brother. I'm leaving now."

"Why is he not coming today?" Malcolm asked Fiona. Alec's squire had just left the warlord's message with David, who brought word into the lesson room.

Fiona had kept Malcolm close to her all morning. She had hoped to see Lord Alec and explain her words of the night before. As tired as she had been last night, Fiona had lain in bed going over their discussion again and again. She had thought back over the words said and had tried to remember why and when he had taken her words wrongly. It was important to her to try to undo what had been said.

After all, she didn't want Lord Macpherson to think her a wisecracking ingrate. Even if she had acted like one.

"Fiona, why?" the boy's voice cut into the young woman's thoughts.

"He is a busy man, Malcolm."

As the words left her mouth, Fiona felt a chill spread rapidly through her body. She did not remember much about her past, about her life before the Priory. But she already knew that was partly by choice. Thinking back had always been painful. Her memories were filled with the vague cries of a woman, with wind so strong that it seemed to bite into you, so intense that it forced your eyes closed. Then water. Cold, cold water. And being alone. That was all she remembered. That was all she allowed herself to remember.

"Do you think he will come tomorrow?" Malcolm pressed. "He promised me that if you agree to it, he will take me hawking. My own hawk, Fiona! Can you imagine? With the hawk on my arm and all, do you think I will look like him?"

Do I look like him? Do I look like him? Somehow these words sounded familiar to Fiona. She grew pale.

"Fiona, are you well?" Malcolm's hand rested on her arm. His anxious brown eyes looked with concern into her pale, tired face.

"Aye, lad," she answered, mustering a weak smile. "Shaking off the past is a tiring task."

Fiona shifted the heavy satchel to her other shoulder and looked wearily at the threatening gray sky. She was getting close, for she had been skirting the edge of the wood for nearly a quarter of an hour, and she thought it would be good to have a roof over her head before the rain began in earnest. Though it was only midafternoon, the sky had taken on a dusky look. Only an occasional bird flitted from the treetops to the meadow that stretched out to her left. In a few moments the hermit's cottage came into sight, and Fiona directed her steps to it as the first drops of the summer shower fell.

Hurrying around the corner of the building as she peered into the small window on the side, the young woman ran headlong into a tall, cloaked figure leading a charger.

"Oh!" she exclaimed, stumbling to the side as a hand reached out to stop her from falling.

"Steady, there," the man responded, a hint of warning in his voice.

Fiona looked up into blue eyes that were surveying her closely. She pulled her arm away and stepped back.

"Excuse me, m'lord." She looked up into the man's hard face. Sand-colored hair was plastered to his head. Suddenly her eyes fixed on his features. There was something familiar about him, but his unshaven face did not quite match the image that was floating somewhere in the recesses of her memory. She could not quite remember. As much as she wanted to, she simply could not.

"Do I know you?" Neil MacLeod asked shortly, looking carefully at the woman before him. A frown clouded the man's eyes.

Fiona took another step back. Whoever he was, there was something about this man that sent a chill through her body. The rain was coming harder now.

"N-no," she stammered. He was a MacLeod man; she knew from the tartan he wore. A warrior. But that was no help. She had spent her entire life avoiding his kind. Still, there was something in that face. She felt her tongue swell in her mouth. Fear seeped into her bones and spread through her body until it dominated her senses. Fiona stepped back. She wanted nothing to do with him.

"You are from around here, are you not?" he pressed. "Who are you? Speak up, lass."

Fiona stood, momentarily frozen by a snatch of memory. She glanced down at the man's hand, hanging limply at his side. Somewhere in her head she could hear a woman's cry—the same cry that continued to haunt her dreams. Her glance darted again to his face, gleaming in the falling rain. His look was piercing, as if he, too, were trying to remember something.

"Well?" Alec's voice growled as he suddenly appeared beside Fiona. His face a mask of steel, he turned toward the MacLeod warrior. "Well? I thought you were in a hurry to get back."

Neil MacLeod shifted his glance under the other's withering stare.

"Aye, that I am."

Alec glanced over at the young woman beside him. She certainly did not look well to him. He had caught a glimpse of her as she passed the cottage window. Looking at her now, standing beside him in the falling rain, he thought she looked pale and tired . . . and frightened. He grasped her arm, and as he did he felt her pull his hand tightly to her side.

With the pressure of Fiona's arm, a sense of possessiveness swept through Alec. For the first time, he had a sense that she was communicating a need to him—and he instinctively responded. Pulling her toward him, the warlord leaned forward, partially shielding Fiona from Neil MacLeod with his body.

When Alec's eyes snapped back to the warrior, MacLeod was gazing curiously at the laird's protective grip on the young woman's arm. Hastily averting his eyes, he reached back for the bridle of his charger.

"I was just taking my leave," he said, nodding to Fiona with a last look as he led his gray horse past the two.

Fiona turned and watched him mount up and ride slowly away in the pouring rain. As MacLeod disappeared into murky distance, relief washed over Fiona. Now she could feel the laird's closeness beside her, the muscular grip of his hand. And for the first time all day, she felt buoyant, almost exuberant.

With a sigh she turned back to Alec, but her look was greeted with an angry glare.

"Could you tell me what in God's name you are doing here?" Alec turned and faced her fully as he asked the question. He was furious with her. But even through the haze of his temper, he was stunned once again by the effect she had on him. He stood, momentarily transfixed by the drops of rain beating against her ivory skin. Her dark cloak fell far short of hiding the brilliant locks of hair that were now dripping with water. In spite of her weary look, her large hazel eyes were sparkling with happiness, and his question did nothing to alter her look.

She simply smiled back at him. He was here. That was

all she could think of. Once again he had been here . . . for her.

"I saved your hide not saying anything to the prioress the other day, and here you are again, out alone, vulnerable to anyone or anything. Have you no sense at all?"

"Some, m'lord," she said vaguely, looking into the deep blue of his eyes.

"Do you know what being defenseless means?"

Fiona nodded.

"Why do you not have someone accompany you? Never mind the two-legged animals wandering around this island. What about the four-legged ones? What would you do if you stumbled on a boar or a wolf? There are still wolves on this island, you know."

"So I have heard, m'lord."

"Heard? You are not hearing one word. You are not frightened in the least, are you?"

Fiona shook her head slowly from side to side.

Alec's eyes surveyed her from top to bottom. She had discarded the ragged cloak and wooden clapper that had helped disguise her the other day. From her shoulder, beneath her dark cloak, the same bag she had carried before hung heavily at her side.

He wanted to strangle her for being so careless. But at the same time he wanted to hold her tightly to him, to kiss her.

"What have you in that satchel?" he continued gruffly, trying to hide the powerful impulses that were rushing through him. "Nothing you could use to save that pretty little neck of yours, I would wager."

"My satchel?"

"Fiona . . ."

Alec was very close to her, and he could see the beads of rain on the bridge of her nose, on her cheekbone, her lips. Without thinking, he reached out and brushed the droplets from her cheek. The side of her face rested against his gentle touch.

His hand paused at the shock of contact with her skin, and their eyes locked for the longest while. They stood, secure in the eternity of a moment. Fiona felt her breath catch in her chest. She was frozen, immobile, panic-stricken with the thought that the slightest movement would break the spell.

Alec's gaze fell to her lips and lingered there. He found himself wanting to lift that mouth to his. He wanted to taste the sweetness of the summer rain that wet those ruby lips. He wanted to kiss her. Abruptly, he shook his head to clear it and moved his fingers from her face. Dropping his hand to her shoulder, he took hold of the light wool of her cloak. He took a deep breath before speaking, and when he did, his tone was softer.

"You are soaking wet, and you are as pale as a ghost. Why, you have probably caught a chill already. Do you have nothing to say?"

Fiona stood looking up at him with the same dreamy expression and shook her head.

"Nothing, m'lord."

"Fiona, you look like hell," he lied.

Her smile widened, and her eyes cleared. "Thank you, m'lord. I am very glad to see you, too."

Turning softly toward the cottage, Fiona glanced back once more before leaving the laird gazing after her in the rain.

Chapter 7

Her sweet bearing and fresh beauty
Have wounded without sword or lance ...
—William Dunbar, *"Beauty and the Prisoner"*

"I know her!"

Ambrose held Alec's arm and whispered as the warlord ducked into the low doorway. The younger brother never took his eyes off Fiona as she hovered over the injured leper lying on the straw mattress in the corner.

The priest had introduced her to Ambrose briefly and unceremoniously, and Fiona had barely paused to nod at the warrior before going to the side of her ailing friend. She had been too concerned about Walter's condition to even remove her rain-drenched cloak.

"That seems to be everyone's first impression," Alec said, responding to his brother's comment. "But you knowing her would be wishful thinking on your part, I'd say."

"Please do not tell me this is *your* nun," he muttered under his breath.

"As I told you before, Ambrose, she is not a nun," Alec growled with satisfaction, walking past him to the rough table where Father Jack sat talking with Fiona across the small space of the cottage's single room. Alec sat on the wooden block and watched her as she straightened to remove her wet cloak and hang it from the peg on the wall. The modest cut of her dark blue dress did little to hide the sensuous curves of her body, and the effect of her physical presence was hardly lost on Alec. She was wearing no veil, and the single braid hung down her back to her waist. With the back of her hand, Fiona pushed the loose, wet ringlets from her face, but they sprang back rebelliously. Alec had a sudden desire to smooth them back himself. But then she turned slightly, crouching over the open satchel by the smoldering turf fire and emptying the bag of its contents. Quickly, she poured a jug of liquid into the cooking pot that hung over the fire.

"He has been sleeping nearly the entire day, Fiona," Father Jack said. Turning to Alec, he noted before continuing how the young warlord's attentions were fixed on the movements of the young woman.

Fiona had been right—though the priest had not had the clearest of views, he knew that this young warrior was not the rider who had trampled Walter. The short time they had spent together had already given Father Jack a very favorable impression of these Macpherson lads. Although the MacLeod man who had brought them had balked at entering the hermit's cottage upon hearing of the presence of an injured leper, Alec Macpherson and his brother had entered without the slightest hesitation. Father Jack did not know many noblemen who were enlightened enough to harbor no fear of a leper who was far beyond the point of contagion.

"Angel," Walter whispered weakly. "Are you here, my angel?"

"Aye, Walter," she answered brightly, caressing his distorted, masklike face. "Can I get you anything?"

"Water, lass."

Fiona moved quickly to the table, where a rude wooden jug sat by Alec's elbow. The blond warrior picked it up and poured its contents into the cup she held. Their eyes met for only a moment before she blushed and looked down.

The warlord's attention was drawn to the simple wooden cross hanging from a leather thong around her neck. As she straightened up with the full cup, the cross fell lightly back against the soft wool that covered her breast, and Alec thought he had never seen a religious symbol so perfectly enshrined. He took a deep breath and tried to clear such a sacrilegious thought from his mind. Something about her was driving his thoughts, though, and his senses were aflame in pursuit.

"You were starting to tell us how this man . . . Walter

... was hurt," Ambrose said quietly from the doorway. He had been watching the young woman as well, and he was impressed by her gentle ministration of the wounded man. But he had also been watching his brother. Alec appeared bewitched. Not that Ambrose could blame him. The woman had beauty, that was undeniable. But she also exuded goodness. The younger Macpherson thought that this was certainly a departure from the kind of women he had seen Alec with in the past. He liked the change.

"He was ridden down like a dog," the priest growled. He had sent a message to the laird earlier today requesting a hearing. If this man was all that everyone believed him to be, then it was time for him to know that someone was trying to discredit him.

"Tell me who did this," Alec demanded angrily. "I will not stand for this kind of barbarity."

"Then you had best look to your people," Father Jack said, looking steadily at the laird. "The man who rode him down was wearing—"

"Was disguised," Fiona broke in with a hard look at the hermit. "Whoever it was, he was wearing the Macpherson tartan, was riding a black charger, and had a falcon on his arm."

"What?" Alec glanced from one face to the other. His look hardened, though, in spite of their nonaccusing expressions. "You asked me to come here, Father. How do you know it wasn't I who rode him down?"

"Because of Fiona," Father Jack answered matter-of-factly, glancing in the direction of the young woman. "She was certain from the first, and Walter's grandson, Adrian, who saw the whole thing, also saw you with her at the Priory. We know it was someone else, but we don't know who."

"Could Walter's grandson identify the man?" Ambrose asked. He could see Alec's anger-clouded face and knew his brother would need a moment to check his temper.

"I don't know, Sir Ambrose," the hermit responded. "Perhaps he could. I was there as well, and though the lad's eyes are better than mine, the whole thing happened very quickly."

"Might it have been an accident?" Ambrose suggested, doubting it even as the words left his mouth.

The priest snorted, and Alec banged his hand on the table.

"How many of our men do you know, Ambrose, that go riding through the countryside at that hour with a hawk? None!"

"'Tis true. It was no accident," a weak voice replied from the straw.

Alec stood and went to the injured man. Fiona was kneeling on the straw, holding Walter's hand, and the warlord crouched beside her.

"Whoever did this," Alec said quietly, "will face the king's justice."

The old leper looked at the young laird, and a tear sprang from the corner of his bloodshot eye, leaving a fiery trail across the red leather of his destroyed skin.

"The king's justice has never before done much for the likes of me," the man said, his voice breaking. "You, m'lord, are the first of your class who has even looked upon me as a human being in the last twenty-five years."

Alec placed his hand on the man's arm.

"There is no excuse for the ignorance of man, Walter, highborn or low. And I will not make any attempt to find one." Alec looked steadily into the injured man's eyes. "But right now, I would like you to tell me anything you can about the rider. Why did you say it was no accident?"

"He was waiting for us, m'lord," Walter responded, his breathing becoming more labored. "We had just come from the woods. I saw him. Hiding in the brush. He was just standing there. And then he spotted us. When he did, he came at us."

"Why would someone want to harm you?" Ambrose asked.

"I was not the one he was after," the leper replied, turning his eyes toward the young warrior.

"Not you?" Fiona asked, surprised by her friend's words.

"Nay, lass. He was after Father Jack."

"I?" the priest exploded in disbelief. "You didn't stumble into the path of the charger, did you? You stepped in front of the blackguard for me!"

"He never took his eyes off the priest," Walter said, looking back at Alec.

"Could you identify the man?" Alec asked.

"I do not think so," he said. "But even if I could, what would my word be against the word of a—"

"It would be good enough for me," the warlord declared.

"You are a good man, m'lord," the leper said, shifting uncomfortably where he lay and wincing as he did. "Clearly, everything the crofters are saying about you is true."

"This broth is ready for you," Fiona said, dipping the wooden cup into the simmering pot. "You need to drink all of this, Walter. Then you need to rest."

She reached over and gently propped Walter into a half sitting position. Without pausing, she spread the dressings beside her to change his wounds. Alec watched in admiration at her quiet efficiency. He couldn't tear his eyes from her. And his attention did not go unnoticed by anyone in the room.

"Now you see why she is called the Angel of Skye," the leper said, looking at Alec.

"*Is* she?" Alec asked, raising an eyebrow.

"Hush, Walter," Fiona scolded gently.

"Aye," he continued. "This is the land of angels and fairies, you know."

The warlord smiled. "I'm becoming more convinced of it every day."

"Tell me, m'lord, have you heard tell of our 'Fairy Flag'?" Walter whispered.

"*Fairy* flag?" Alec repeated, pausing to think. "Aye, now that you mention it, I do recall hearing as a child some story—what was it—aye, about a saint's robe or something, that the MacLeods used for a banner. But it was lost, was it not?"

"The folk here believe that it is no saint's robe, Lord Alec," Father Jack corrected as the warlord stood and returned to his place at the table. "There are a few stories about it, but most believe that the banner was given to an ancient MacLeod chief by his wife . . . a fairy."

"A fairy, Father?" Ambrose repeated.

"Aye, lad," the hermit continued. "The story goes that a long time ago, a fairy maid fell in love with the leader of the MacLeod clan. The King of the Fairies would not allow the fairy to live out her life in the world of men, but she could marry the chief only on the condition that she return to Fairyland after twenty years. They agreed and were married.

"The years passed too quickly, but when the sad time came for her to leave, the MacLeod chief took her, as they had promised, to the Fairy Bridge. They wept many tears, and embraced with a love undimmed by their years of marriage. As she took her leave, folk say the fairy gave her husband a box and disappeared forever. In the box was a silk banner, Am Bratach Sith . . . the Fairy Flag.

"From that time, when the people of Skye were in distress, the Fairy Flag has come to their aid."

"How did it come to disappear?" Alec asked, enthralled by the story.

"Folk believe that the last laird was not deserving of the magic." Father Jack looked closely at the young warlord. "The banner disappeared nearly twenty years ago, and no one knows where it went."

"No one?" Ambrose asked curiously.

"Well, let's put it this way," the priest responded. "The belief is that the flag will only reappear when a worthy MacLeod heir wears the chieftain's broach. But that's not why I started telling you this story."

The hermit looked over at Fiona. She scowled at the old priest, shaking her head threateningly. She knew what was coming.

Alec turned and looked with amusement at the silent exchange of looks. This was sure to be good.

"As he said, that's not where the story ends," Walter put in. "Tell them, Father."

"Nay, Father Jack," Fiona broke in. "And you hush, Walter."

"Ah, lass, we cannot change history," the priest scolded wryly.

"This is not history," she retorted, standing with her hands on her hips beside the straw bedding. "This is the result of you and Walter drinking too much ale together. All these foolish stories—really."

Father Jack smiled and turned to Alec.

"Walter found this mild-mannered lass half drowned

by the Fairy Bridge one stormy night. Some folk around here think she's an angel." He looked slyly at her. "But there are others who just say she's a fairy maid."

"This is ridiculous," Fiona admonished, her face flaming red. "And from a man of God, no less! It is ... indecent. That is just what it is. Indecent!"

"'Tis true," Walter put in. "I found her on the wildest night I have ever known. Angel she might be, but the lass is our own fairy."

"You see," the priest started again, but this time matter-of-factly, "from the time she was a wee thing, Fiona has roamed these woods as if she knew them better than the back of her own hand. As if she'd been here before. She had no fear. She was invulnerable. And the lass was everywhere that help was needed. There are stories, lads. Once, not much more than a child herself, she carried a bairn from a hut ablaze with fire while everyone outside quailed with fear of stepping into the roaring inferno. No one even saw her go in. They say she appeared from nowhere. And there is another one of her swimming the loch in the midst of a storm to save a fisherman tangled in his own nets. And then there is the one about the cattle that—"

"Please stop, Father," the young woman pleaded from where she stood.

Alec's gaze had been riveted on her the whole time the priest had been speaking. He had seen the emotions darkening her fair features. It was obvious that Fiona was not comfortable with talk of her own exploits. But she denied none of it. She had tried to busy herself tending to Walter. But in the end she had not been able to take it any longer.

Alec thought back on his first encounter with her. Indeed, she had been like a fairy, appearing from nowhere in the path before him. There was so much about this woman that he wanted to know. So much more.

"But you must promise to keep our secret, lads," Father Jack said, looking at the two warriors confidentially. "For no one—not those in the castle, anyway—knows for sure that our Fiona, who lives at the Priory, is the fairy—or rather, the angel—who watches over the island folk. So I need to ask you to keep our secret."

"You have our word on it," Alec declared solemnly.

Then, with a serious expression, he turned to the young woman. "So where is your flag, Fiona?"

She threw her arms up in resignation and turned her back on the laughing group of men.

But she did not ignore them long, for soon the talk turned to serious issues of economic survival involving her island folk. Alec presented his plans for shipbuilding on the island and explained his need for workers. They spoke of the difficulties of raising cattle in a land that required hard work for self-sufficiency. They spoke of bartering and the past inability of the MacLeods and the MacDonalds to communicate effectively. Of how the two ancient enemies simply could not negotiate with one another. Of how neither clan had anything to offer that the mainlanders did not already have.

Alec argued that with a need for wood, and with the Macphersons and their allies, the Campbells, the Isle of Skye would be in a position to profit and grow stronger and healthier. Alec told them that royal trading charters would ensure the working people food and goods to meet their needs.

Fiona raised concerns regarding the incentives for people to put aside age-old feuds and to work alongside traditional enemies. But Father Jack responded that it is an empty stomach that causes a MacDonald to steal a MacLeod cow, and vice versa. With food in their bellies and honest work to occupy their hands and their minds, perhaps such foolish feuding would gradually disappear.

Father Jack saw the good the new laird's plan could bring the people of Skye, and agreed to spread the word among the MacDonald and MacLeod clan folk.

As the discussion came to an end, Ambrose noted that the rain had let up ... for the time being.

"Lass," Father Jack said, turning to Fiona. "This would be a good time for you to go back to the Priory."

"I thought I would stay tonight, Father," she replied, "and give you a chance to rest."

"You need the rest more than I do. And besides, look at your patient. He is much improved."

Walter looked up from his place. "I am feeling much

better, lass. And perhaps, if the laird is traveling toward the Priory—"

"That will not be necessary, Walter," she said, focusing on the injured man. "But are you in much pain now?"

"My leg is throbbing, lass, but it is nothing I cannot put up with. But you look quite weary, Fiona. And if our angel gets ill, who will watch over us?"

"Very well, Walter," she conceded, turning to the others. "But I want you to send someone after me, Father, if Walter needs me."

"Aye, Fiona. That I will do."

The young woman took her cloak from the peg and wrapped it around her.

Alec and Ambrose stood to take their leave, as well.

"I would like to talk with Walter's grandson about what he saw, Father." Alec wanted to discover the identity of the assailant as soon as possible.

"Adrian is with the fishermen for a day or two," the old priest said. "But when he returns, I will send him to you. In a few days, I will pursue your other matter, but that will not be a speedy process."

"I understand," Alec said as he followed Ambrose out the door.

Standing by their horses beneath the trees, Ambrose hesitated before mounting.

"I know you must be in a great hurry to get back to Dunvegan and get some answers about the attack, Alec."

"I am," the young warlord replied seriously. "But I know none of our men would attack this priest. What reason would they have for such treachery?"

"None," Ambrose responded. "But on the other hand, there are so many MacLeods and MacDonalds in and out of Dunvegan Castle . . ."

"As soon as we get back, I think I'll talk to Neil about the attack. It's time we took a slightly closer look at our friends."

"Aye," Ambrose agreed. "Well, then, perhaps it would be better if *I* escorted your . . . uh . . . nun back to her convent."

"She's not a nun, Ambrose."

"Ah, yes. That slipped my mind, big brother. Well, then, you have no objections to my taking . . . Fiona . . . back to the Priory?"

Alec knew it would be better if Ambrose took her back, but he just couldn't bring himself to give up an opportunity for time alone with her.

"Every objection in the world, Ambrose, because I know when it comes to women, you are a base and scurvy dog."

"Now, Alec," he replied, looking hurt. "Must you exaggerate so? You know I am not 'scurvy.'"

"I know just what you are, little brother. And that is why *I* am going to take Fiona back to the Priory. She would stand a better chance with a pack of wolves than she would with you."

Ambrose grinned. He liked the possessiveness that Alec was exhibiting toward this woman. And a woman like Fiona would be the best thing that could happen to Alec right now. She has a freshness . . . an honest openness, he thought. She has the ability to bring back the old Alec.

But again there was something that was nagging at him. Fiona was a woman with a life of religious devotion ahead of her. As Ambrose gazed at his brother, he was certain Alec would respect that. But then what was their relationship to be? Friendship? That was the extent Ambrose could hope for. The last thing Ambrose wanted to see was Alec hurt again. But then, there was Fiona to consider as well.

"You have it wrong this time, Alec. After all, she is the fairy—we both heard it. Neither you nor I would let any harm come to this gentle creature."

"I know, Ambrose. And I do trust you. But I will take her back."

"Very well." Ambrose sighed, mounting his horse. "I'll ride—by myself—back to Dunvegan. With any luck, *I* won't be attacked by wolves. Would you like me to leave a candle in the window for you?"

"That won't be necessary." Alec smiled. "I should be able to find my way home. But thank you, anyway."

The younger Macpherson started to pull on the reins of his charger when Alec stopped him.

"Ambrose . . ."

"Aye, Alec?" he responded, noting the serious expression on his brother's face.

"Do not say anything to Neil MacLeod about Walter's accident until I get there. I don't want you getting into a brawl with him over this until I get back."

"Very well," he said, wheeling his horse and grinning down at the laird. "But what will he and I talk about, then, over supper?"

And with a wave of his hand, Ambrose cantered off across the meadow.

When Fiona left the cottage a few moments later with Father Jack on her heels, Alec was standing alone beside his horse.

"You see, Fiona?" the old priest said. "I knew you would not be walking back to the Priory alone."

As Fiona paused to look at the handsome warlord, the evening sun broke through the clouds. Beams of light streamed through breaks in the leaves behind Alec, and the charger standing behind him shook his head impatiently.

"I thought I would go by way of the Priory," the warrior said casually. "I'll take you back."

"That really will not be necessary," she objected mildly, standing firmly before the door.

"It will be dark soon, and I'll feel better if I know you are safely home."

"As I said before, I travel this way often. I will be—"

"Safe?" Alec interrupted. "Do you really believe the dangers in these woods cannot harm you?"

"Of course not. It's just ..."

"I believe we have been here before, Fiona," Alec reminded her, raising his voice slightly. He knew his glare was worth a thousand words. And it seemed to become more effective as he aged ... his men told him so. And now Alec directed it meaningfully at her. "You would do well not to forget that some of us have indeed had encounters with these dangers. Many of us, I might add." If she was going to be so thick as to reject his offer to see her to safety, then he was more than prepared to tell the world of the encounter he had witnessed the first time they met.

Father Jack looked from one combatant to the other. This had all the makings of a good row.

"I suppose this is just the right moment to say good evening to you two," he rumbled. He could monitor these events well enough from the window of the cottage. Starting back toward the hut, he paused to look at Alec. "Angels are notoriously argumentative creatures, my son. And don't forget, this one *is* part fairy!"

Without another word, the priest turned his back and plodded off toward the hut.

Fiona and Alec stood looking at one another. She had been watching him in the cottage all afternoon. There was a tingling sensation that was running up her spine as it had all afternoon . . . every time he chanced to look at her. Fiona had been surprised, a bit embarrassed even, at how a simple turn of his head could make her heart pound faster in her chest. And now, truthfully, nothing would please her more than to spend an hour walking alone with him.

"Fiona, I do not care to argue with you about this any longer. Some folk may think you're invulnerable. You may think you're invulnerable. But you're not. And your safety is my responsibility. I just heard in there that a madman is riding around this island trampling defenseless folk. If you think I'm going to let you—"

"Very well, m'lord," she said simply.

"Very well what?"

"I will go with you to the Priory."

"You will?" Alec paused, the string of additional arguments he'd been formulating withering away. "Why?"

"Why?" She laughed. "I thought you wanted me to."

"I do."

"Well, you certainly have an odd way of showing it." She smiled at him from beneath her lashes.

"I do not. It's you."

"Well, m'lord, we do not seem to be getting anywhere just standing here." She walked toward him until she came within a step. "I do have to get back. So, if you do not mind, we could continue this argument while we walk. How does that sound?"

Alec nodded in amusement, and Fiona adjusted the satchel on her shoulder. Quickly, she tied the cord of her cloak in a bow at her neck and pulled the hood over her head, looking up at him expectantly. "I am ready. But I have to warn you that I am a fast walker. So if at any time you feel you cannot keep pace, just let me know and—"

"Keep pace? Fiona, your step I can keep pace with. Your tongue, however ..."

She smiled at him. But somehow she knew she had to keep talking. Somehow she knew that as long as she could sustain the dialogue, then she could keep hidden other feelings that were running through her, bubbling beneath the surface, searching for a quiet moment to burst through. Perhaps walking with this handsome laird was not the best of ideas. Perhaps walking alone was the best course, after all.

"If my talking is a problem, m'lord, I'm sure I can think of a simple remedy."

"So can I," Alec responded slowly, letting his gaze fall to her lips. He knew his meaning was unmistakable from the flush of color that highlighted her beautiful skin. "But we had better go."

And then, before she could voice a complaint, the warrior stepped toward the young woman and lifted her easily onto the black charger. With a quick look at her surprised face, Alec swung up behind her.

"What do you think you are doing?"

"We are going to the Priory."

"Aye, and we are walking," she said, struggling to slide off the side of the horse.

Alec wrapped one arm firmly around her waist and drew her onto his lap and snugly against his chest.

"Ebon is walking. We are riding."

Fiona struggled only a moment more, realizing the futility of the effort. His brawny arm was a band of steel around her, so she had to satisfy herself with straightening the skirt of her dress and pulling her cloak tightly closed, which allowed her the opportunity to put her elbow squarely in his ribs a number of times in the process.

With a grunt, Alec tightened his grip on her and spurred Ebon into motion.

"I wonder what Father Jack is thinking right now, Lord 'Steal the Maiden.' "

"I do not see him running out to save you ... Maiden."

"Of course not, the poor dear. He is probably beside himself with distress right now."

"He is probably beside himself with laughter, telling your friend Walter how you cleverly maneuvered me into giving you a ride."

"I did no such thing."

"Clearly, you did. After all, right now I would be heading toward supper at Dunvegan Castle if you had not engaged me in an argument."

"Engaged *you* in an argument?" She shook her head with a wry smile and loosened the ties around her neck. The way she was seated on his lap, her cloak pulled, making the cord tighten at her throat. "What a boring life you must lead, m'lord, if you consider our little discussion an argument."

"Boring? My life is not boring. I ... Stop wiggling and get your elbow out of my ribs."

"If you would stop trying to squeeze the breath out of me, I might be able to get comfortable."

"Then promise you won't vault off this horse and break your neck."

"Why?"

"Why?" Alec repeated. "Because I'd like to keep that pleasure for myself."

Fiona pushed back the hood as she turned and smiled up into his tanned face. His blue eyes were kind, and for the first time, she could see the wrinkles crease the corners as his expression gradually relaxed into a smile. The breath caught in her throat as she felt his breath caress her cheek. His grip eased around her waist, and she made no attempt to move away from him.

"In that case, I promise."

"Good," he said as Ebon started down a short hill. Alec felt Fiona nestle her shoulder and arm against his chest. Even through the cloak he could feel her begin to relax, in spite of the occasional jouncing of her body against his. His own response, however, was exactly the opposite, and he fought to control the stirring in his loins. This is going to be an interesting ride, he thought.

The path south toward the Priory took them through golden meadows and wooded glens. Everywhere, the droplets of the day's rains sparkled like diamonds in the golden evening light. In the distance to their right, the sun was resting atop one of two flat-topped, heather-covered peaks that rose above the rolling hills by the coast. Fiona was gazing out toward them, and Alec heard her sigh.

"A bonny sight," he said, looking down at her.

"Aye," she replied. "They call that place Healaval. Those are MacLeod's Tables."

"The MacLeod chiefs have long been famous for their appetites." Alec smiled. "But I don't think even a Mac-Leod needs a table that large."

"Hmm ... I would say it depends on what is being served," Fiona suggested innocently.

Alec laughed, and felt his breath shorten as Fiona shifted her weight on his thighs.

"That's true," he agreed. "The Macphersons, on the other hand, have always held that the quality of what is being served is more important than the quantity."

"Well, I guess it simply depends on the individual's preference, then."

"Do you want to know what my preference is?" he asked in a low voice that sent a shiver down Fiona's spine.

"Your preference regarding what, m'lord?" she asked quickly, trying to ignore the warmth of the laird's body, the hypnotic quality of his tone. Fiona was losing track of their conversation. "Are we talking about food, or the size of tables?"

"Neither."

"Neither? You are interested in neither?"

She leaned against him, the words suddenly becoming even less important as she became conscious for the first time of his faint masculine smell—so unfamiliar, and yet so oddly pleasing. His legs were hidden beneath her cloak and dress, but Fiona could feel the raw sinews of his thigh muscles pressing against her. Looking down, she realized that her hand was resting on the warlord's rock-hard forearm that lay across her waist. The contrast of her slender arm and his, so massive and strong, was both disconcerting and exciting.

"I am interested in both, but that is not enough." Alec's arm tightened, pulling her snugly against him.

"Not enough?" Fiona tried to focus on what they had been saying, but the pressure of their bodies together was suddenly too much for her. She looked up at him, her eyes dreamily questioning.

"Not enough," he responded, his eyes searching hers for a sign.

Her look never wavered as his mouth came to within a breath of hers.

"Fiona, how does your order look upon kissing?"

"Kissing?" she whispered, her eyes lingering on the sculpted fullness of his lips.

Alec's mouth descended upon Fiona's, and his kiss was gentle, the flesh of his lips pressing lightly against hers, brushing softly across the silky smoothness of the skin.

Fiona's eyes fluttered at the sensation, and Alec knew that, however her order looked upon it, she had never been kissed before.

She remained motionless, not knowing what to do next. Her body was rigid in his arms, as if lightning had struck her. The flash of brilliance that filled her threatened to burst through her skin. She was being scorched from the inside, and she knew not how to express what she was feeling. Deep within her Fiona could feel a molten spot forming, a white-hot seed that startled her with the power of its very presence. With a gasp that barely escaped her, she moved her hand lightly along his arm.

Alec felt the gentle caress of her hand. He tasted her lips, pulling back slightly, but then alighted again. His lips traveled along her cheek, her temple. He could see the way she looked at him, the way her desire and curiosity were carrying her along. When his mouth returned to hers, she was waiting. Her lips moved beneath his, trying to kiss him the way she had been kissed.

This was all the encouragement Alec needed. With raw animal passion, he took possession of her mouth, devouring her lips, tasting, seemingly unable to get enough of her.

And Fiona's response, her eagerness to learn, continued. Willingly she followed where Alec led, unknowingly and unerringly driving him to greater desires.

An inferno was ablaze within him, but Alec was suddenly conscious that it was a fire that needed to be controlled. He forced his lips away from hers. Lifting his hand to her upturned face, he lay her head gently against his chest, caressing her lips and cheek lightly with his thumb and his fingers. Turning his gaze toward the disappearing sun, the young laird filled his lungs with air in an attempt to conquer the passions now raging in his loins.

In her most rebellious acts, in her wildest dreams, Fiona had not thought this possible. She closed her eyes, resting her head against his broad chest. Feeling the possessive grip of his arm around her waist, the sensuous caress of his chin against her hair, she was suddenly in a world she had never known. Her heartbeat was still drumming in her ears. Fiona ran her tongue across her lips, remembering the texture, the fullness of his lips against hers.

She could feel his strong fingers stroking her side.

She opened her eyes, lifting her head and looking up at his profile. She could see him looking straight ahead, at the horizon. She could see the firm set of his jaw. His look was disconcerting.

"Have I done something wrong?" she asked quietly.

"Of course not," he said gently, his gaze drifting to her face. "What makes you say that?"

"It seems as though you are upset about something."

"Fiona, I am not upset." Upset was the wrong term. *In agony* is more appropriate, he thought, feeling her firm body resting so comfortably against his.

"Then, why ... all of the sudden ... You are so serious."

"I am trying to control ... well ..."

"Yourself?"

"Aye, myself. I am trying to control myself."

"From ... kissing me again?" she asked, smiling up at him.

"Fiona, this is a dangerous time to be reading my mind."

"Is it? Why?"

"You had better stop asking these questions or you will soon find out." Alec focused on the shadows that were stretching across the rolling farmlands that led to the Priory.

Fiona looked at him, her eyes widening. If what he

talked about had anything to do with kissing, she definitely did not mind that. Sitting there on his lap, she let her eyes roam over his face, his hair, his perfectly shaped ear. Alec Macpherson was a perfect and an incredibly beautiful gentleman.

"Stop looking at me like that."

Fiona dropped her gaze immediately to her lap. "How do you know I was looking at you?"

Alec smiled. They needed to talk about something else. Anything. He needed to occupy himself with something else, before his good intentions went straight to hell.

"Fiona, tell me about your people."

"The lepers?" she asked, surprised at the shift in the conversation.

"Nay," he responded. "Your family."

"I've already told you all about the Priory."

"Not the Priory; your own family," he said. "Where are you from? Who are your people? Your parents? Or are you really some fairy king's daughter?"

"Oh, don't tell me you believe that story."

"Shouldn't I? How did it go?"

"Really, m'lord . . ."

"Let me see." Alec paused. "Something about a fairy maid who falls in love with and marries a laird. Do I have it right?"

"Nay, that's just a fairy tale. Not real life."

"Then you tell me, Fiona. Tell me the tale of you and your kin."

"There is nothing to tell," she said simply, her voice echoing an emptiness inside. "I . . . I have no one, m'lord."

Alec stared at her, surprised at her response. His words had visibly disturbed her. Who was she? Orphans were not educated to run convents, as far as Alec knew. But this young woman had been.

"All teasing aside, Fiona, how did you come to be there at the Priory?"

"Walter told you. He found me nearly drowned and took me there."

"How old were you then?" Alec thought back over the story Walter had told. Who could have left a child to wander?

"I must have been about five years old. I do not really know for sure."

Alec envisioned Fiona as a bedraggled waif, crying for her mother on a stormy night. His heart went out to her. No wonder she cared so deeply for the old leper.

"Do you remember anything from before?" he asked, pressing. "Do you even know which clan you came from? There are only MacLeods and MacDonalds on Skye."

"I come from neither, that I know of. As for before? Well, sometimes bits and pieces come back to me, but I do not recall anything that makes sense." Fiona gazed with unseeing eyes as they drew near the perimeter of the Priory village. "Water. I remember being in cold, cold water. It felt like days, but I know it wasn't. Before that, I do not . . . I cannot . . ."

Fiona closed her eyes. She did not want to remember. She did not want the nightmares to return.

Alec could see the distress in her expression. He dropped the reins and gathered her to him with both arms. Her hands circled his waist. She buried her face in the crook of his neck. The black charger slowed and stopped.

They held one another for a long time, neither speaking. The evening was descending around them, and Fiona sat, comforted by the support of his nearness. She could hear the night sounds that she knew so well beginning to creep into the air. The bark of the dog, the cry of the owl. Fiona felt the troubles of her unknown past slipping away now. For the moment, at least, here in this man's embrace, Fiona was safe.

"I didn't speak for a long time . . . almost a month, they tell me. The prioress did not know if I could even talk. But I could cry. And David says I did a lot of that."

She smiled faintly as she lifted her head from his shoulder. She was feeling stronger, brighter, more herself.

"But I don't cry very much anymore."

"And you have also overcome your hesitation about talking, Fiona," he teased, adding, "I am happy to say."

"Are you saying, Lord Alec, that I talk too much? Proverbs tells us that a word spoken in due season—"

"Nay, lass, I should say you are just perfect."

Fiona lifted her face, surprised at the quiet strength in his voice. As she did, his mouth once again took hers—gently sucking her lower lip as he pressed her tightly to his chest.

Alec found himself enchanted by this young woman. When he was near Fiona, it was as if another power were taking possession of him. Even as his lips were joined with hers, he knew he had to go slowly, gently, for fear of frightening her off. And then a conscious thought suddenly flashed in his brain: He was wooing her. He was concerned with her feelings, with her response to a simple kiss because he was pursuing her—pursuing this innocent. And he did not deny it.

The world closed in around Fiona as her body molded softly to his. The darkness wrapped itself warmly around them. And there was no one in that world but the two of them. Her arm slipped under his shoulder and she felt the rippling muscles of his back. Fiona felt a jolt of excitement travel through her, and then it was she who was kissing him.

This has to stop, he thought, suddenly aware of the pulsing whir that was growing in his head. It was the beginning of a roar that he knew would soon block out all sounds. Of a desire that would soon be uncontrollable. This has to stop now.

Pulling his face away from hers, he reached behind his back and took her hands in his. Bringing them to his lips, he kissed the tips of her fingers, the palms of her hands. He looked into her face and took a deep breath.

"We need to get you home."

Fiona paused, her mind gradually clearing of the sensuous wisps that were hanging like a mist in her vision.

"Come out to the bluffs with Malcolm and me tomorrow," Alec said quietly.

"To the bluffs? But you're going out there to capture a hawk," she protested mildly.

Alec brushed her lips with his own, and then, tracing a line to her ear, he whispered softly.

"Come tomorrow."

Fiona tilted her head as his lips nibbled her earlobe, kissed the skin of her neck.

"Come."

"Aye, I will come," she answered dreamily. "Someone needs to scare away the birds."

Alec pulled his face back a bit and smiled at her. The young laird then swung his leg over the charger's back and dropped lithely to the ground. Reaching up with both hands, he took Fiona by the waist. Her hands clung to his shoulders, and their bodies touched as he lowered her gently.

They were standing just outside the cluster of village huts, and their eyes were locked in the evening's last embrace.

"We have to get you home," he repeated.

"Aye," she sighed, looking away toward the Priory walls beyond the village.

Hand in hand, they directed their steps up the lane to the Priory gate.

"I think I will be safe from this point," she said. Fiona needed a moment to clear her head before facing the ones she knew would be waiting for her inside.

"Till tomorrow, then," he called as she walked away. "You will tell Malcolm?"

She nodded with a final backward glance before disappearing inside the Priory walls.

Chapter 8

Who can overcome peril, misadventure?
Who can govern a realm, city, or house
Without science?
—ROBERT HENRYSON,
  "The Cock and the Jasp"

She'd escaped once. The warrior vowed to himself that it wouldn't happen again.

"Kill her, and the boy as well."

She was here, exactly where they had intended her to be all along. If he'd only known. He'd have put that knowledge to use. Profitable use. But her time for usefulness had passed, now. Too bad. All these years and they hadn't even known she was here.

But now he knew. When he first saw her, she'd looked so familiar. And then, as if by magic, Andrew's message arrived. Aye, he knew. And he would do what needed to be done. Andrew would pay him well—he had been promised that. And if the brat dies along with her ... well, so much the better!

"But you said the laird has his eye on the bitch," Crossbrand muttered. "What if we can't get at her?"

"I have given you everything you need," the thugs' leader spat at them. "But do not try to start thinking now. Just do as you are told."

"But ... what if we kill the laird? Will there be more in it for us?"

"It is not him I want dead, you dolt. It is she. Killing the boy will add ample dishonor for your ... laird. But do what you have to do."

The pony trailing behind him pulled at his tether, and Alec glanced around at the small brown and white pony. Malcolm is going to love this lively fellow, he thought.

The sun was warm on his face as he threaded his way along the path toward the Priory. He wondered if Fiona had awakened thinking of him, as he had been thinking of her. For the first time in quite a while, Alec had slept well, his sleep undisturbed by visions of kings and crowds.

It had been a late night for Alec questioning the company at Dunvegan. But in spite of all he had done, he was disappointed that he had no information to give Fiona about Walter's attacker.

Based on what he was able to ascertain thus far, any number of men on the Isle of Skye could have been the assailant. Though the common folk loved Father Jack, he had to be a threat to the power structure of both island clans. He was more a counselor to the people than their leaders were, and that had to anger the ruling hierarchy of the clans. Both the MacLeod and the Mac-Donald leaders could easily have grievances with the old hermit, and to pin his death on an outsider made perfect sense. Unfortunately, there were several black horses at Dunvegan besides Ebon, and Alec was certain a Macpherson tartan was obtainable.

But despite all this, the warlord had not given up hope. Walter's grandson, Adrian, still offered the possibility of identifying the man. And having warned the MacLeod men of his intentions of getting to the bottom of the attack, Alec now wondered how they might respond.

"For me? For my very own?" the lad blurted out. "Oh, David, can I really keep him?"

"We will clear it with the prioress, of course. But I don't think she will object to Lord Alec's present."

"Oh, thank you, Alec. He is so handsome." Malcolm ran his hand admiringly over the coat of the little pony. "Can I ride him to the bluffs? What is his name?"

"His name is Rogue," Alec said. "But I think the stable yard is a very good place to get to know one another first. Do you agree, David?"

"Aye, Malcolm's a very able rider, but that is a fine idea."

"A horse and a falcon, all on the same day," Malcolm said excitedly, turning to the older man. "Alec and I are netting a young falcon today. One that I can train."

"I know, Malcolm," David said, smiling at the boy.

"One to keep. Is that not so, Alec?"

"We'll try. No promises, but we'll try to find you one of your own."

Alec's eyes swept over the Priory grounds. There were groups of nuns working in the gardens, and a merchant traveler and his manservant were just mounting their horses by the hostelry. Through the gates a steady stream of village folk were bustling back and forth, but there was no sign of Fiona.

"She is in her workroom," David said, smiling slyly at the laird. "She did not know when to expect you, and the prioress had a few things she wanted done."

"Oh," Alec responded, surprised by the older man's astuteness.

"If you would like, m'lord, I can send one of the boys—"

"Nay," the laird broke in. "I know where it is. But perhaps we shouldn't disturb—"

"Disturb?" David laughed. "She has been out here looking for you every quarter hour since sunrise . . . well, since prime, anyway."

Alec could not help a smile from creeping into his features. "Then I will just go and get her."

"Hurry back," Malcolm's young voice broke in. "We don't want to get to the bluffs too late. Fiona is in a good mood this morning. If we catch my falcon now, she might let me keep it."

Fiona put the stopper in the bottle of ink and blew the last entry dry.

"Done. Done. Done. Done. But where is he?" she muttered to herself. Gathering up three of the farm ledgers and some scrolls, she headed out the door. "Well, I'll just leave these for the prioress, check on the—"

The open door suddenly became a wall—a human wall. Stepping back, she smiled up into the face of Alec Macpherson.

"You're here," she said brightly, conscious of her quickening heartbeat.

"Aye," he said, backing her into the room. His eyes traveled over her, taking in every aspect of her. Her beautifully flushed face greeted him with all the welcome he had hoped to find. The gray dress she was wearing, demure as it was, did nothing to hide the slender curves of her body. She was wearing no veil, and the light of the single window picked up the flaming highlights of her neatly pulled back hair.

He reached over, while holding her gaze, and took the paraphernalia from her arms, depositing it unceremoniously in a pile on the corner of the table. Without pausing, he backed to the door and pushed it closed.

"M'lord," she whispered, her eyes widening. "Is this proper?"

"I don't give a damn if it is or not." Alec stepped toward her. "I've missed you."

"So have I." She took a hesitant step toward him as Alec closed the distance between them.

Their bodies met in a whirlwind of desire.

"You've entranced me, my fairy maid," he whispered, his lips a breath away.

"I'm the one spellbound," she breathed, raising her mouth to his.

Wrapped in each other's arms, the two met in a kiss that ignited sparks in their souls, lighting up the very core of their being.

Alec pressed her to him, suddenly unconscious of anything but the soft mouth and body yielding to his own. His mouth took hers, pressing against the soft full lips, and when his tongue flicked across the inside curve of her lip, he felt her shudder in response.

There was a fierceness in their embrace that had not been present the night before. It was as if the new day had brought with it new feelings, new desires, new thresholds to cross.

Inside Fiona, flames were leaping up, torching all reason, all care. She felt herself being engulfed in an immolation of passion that she scarcely thought possible. She could feel his silent demand. Her hands clutched at his back as her lips parted to accept his darting tongue.

Alec tasted the sweetness of her lips and delved deeply into her mouth, exploring the texture, the soft, warm recesses of her. He angled his mouth to move more deeply into her, and Fiona turned slightly in his arms, rising to his need.

As he felt her turn, a raw desire swept into him, and an urgency began to take hold of him. Her hips were pressed against his hardening manhood, and Alec was suddenly conscious of a growing power that was building with unchecked momentum. He backed her against the table. He wanted her.

Fiona found herself instinctively arching against him. His muscular leg moved between hers and pressed against her intimately. Her hands traced the muscular lines of his back. Her tongue became as wild as his, as undisciplined. Within her, she was suddenly half-conscious of an entirely new woman awakening, one with feelings, with desires. Desires so real . . . so alive. Her senses flooded with a raw hunger that matched his— a hunger that could not be denied.

Emboldened by the feel of his hands on her back, she reached up, taking hold of his shoulder and neck. As his strong fingers caressed her back, sliding ever lower to the curve of her buttocks, she pushed her hips against his powerful frame and felt one hand lift her thigh. Her breath caught in her throat as he nestled his hot arousal tightly to her. She felt his hardened manhood throbbing intimately against her, and suddenly a moment of panic flashed into her consciousness. Instinctively, Fiona tried to move her hips away, but with the table at her back and Alec's coaxing hands and mouth stoking the fire in her, she found the relevance of her fear fading rapidly into oblivion. Fear surrendered to physical desire, and Fiona found her whole body straining for more of him.

As Fiona moved against him, Alec felt his body shake with desire. Her body's movement was feeding the rivers of need building within him. Alec withdrew from the kiss, moving his mouth to the silky skin of her neck.

"What are you doing to me?" she whispered, running her fingers through his hair and tilting her chin to give him better access.

"I'm paying the fairy tithe."

He drew a line with his tongue from her ear to her collar. A gasp escaped her lips, and her hand took hold of a lock of his loose blond hair. His own hands caressed her side, moving gently and steadily to the soft round fullness of her breast. He heard her sharp intake of air as she pressed even more tightly into his grip.

"Fairies . . . are creatures of habit," she panted, feeling his fingers undoing the buttons that held the back of her dress.

"Habit? You could become an obsession." He pulled the collar of her dress away and pressed his full lips to the soft whiteness of her shoulder. The strap of a chemise slipped down onto her arm.

"I could?" she whispered huskily.

"You already have," he answered, pulling her dress down off her shoulder. "You have already taken hold of my heart."

Alec looked into the desire that clouded Fiona's eyes, and pressed his lips to the exposed flesh of the top of her breast. He pulled the gray wool of the dress lower, freeing her rose-colored aureole from the confines of the chemise and taking possession of the nipple with his mouth. She groaned as he suckled, her head tipping backward.

The creak of a door opening in the corridor wrenched them back into the reality of the place. Breathless, Fiona leaped aside, her hands hurriedly pulling her clothes back into some semblance of order. Her fingers flew to her neck, fumbling to close the buttons at the back.

Alec stood where he was, his blue eyes piercing her with intense desire.

What had come over her? Fiona could not explain, even to herself, the rush of feelings she harbored for this man. They seemed to dominate her rational thoughts, her ability to think straight. And this was so different from what they had experienced the night before. Affection had suddenly turned to desire. Tenderness to unbridled passion. As their eyes locked again, she felt her body melting under the heat of his gaze.

"I can't . . ." she stammered. "We shouldn't . . ."

"We've done nothing wrong, Fiona."

"You don't understand. I . . ." She turned and retreated to the small window of the workroom. Standing there, inhaling the fresh air, she tried to calm her senses, to comprehend somehow what had just occurred.

Alec could not tear his eyes away from her. Passion. Ambrose had asked him that question last night. About where a relationship such as theirs could end up. He had listed reason after reason why Alec should let her be. Fiona, with no family, no name, had at least a place and a future that Alec should not tamper with. Ambrose had talked of things Alec had not been ready to answer. About whether this affection for Fiona, this innocent, might simply be a reaction to Kathryn. About using Fiona to recover from his own hurt.

Alec had been angry with his younger brother for asking these things, and he had let him know it. But he had thought hard about what his brother said. Everything Ambrose said rang with the possibility of truth. But now, looking at her, he knew what he had known last night, what he had known for days. That what was driving him was a force very different from what Ambrose envisioned. But it was something he had not been ready to admit. Not to Ambrose. Not to himself.

But it is simple, he thought now, looking at her by the window.

I need her. Just her. As she is.

I love her.

Voices could be heard in the corridor. They passed by the door. Alec watched her face turn slightly as she listened to the sounds recede. He turned and opened the door.

"I promised Malcolm I would bring you right back." Alec smiled. "I had the best of intentions."

She turned and looked steadily at him. He looked so calm, so much in control. So unlike her. She was a mess. Fiona took a deep breath, trying to get some grasp on all that had just happened between them.

"Malcolm is very excited about today, m'lord."

"No more 'm'lord' or 'Lord Macpherson,' Fiona," he replied seriously. "It is just Alec from now on."

Fiona could not answer him.

Standing silently, she looked at the handsome Highland nobleman. Though her workroom was not small, his huge frame dominated the space. An aura surrounded him of confidence, wealth, ability ... power. Everything about him marked the differences between them, from his fine white linen shirt to the jeweled clan broach that held in place the tartan crossing his chest. Looking at him, she knew all too clearly ... she was a commoner without a family, a woman with no name. She lowered her eyes. Yes, she knew all too clearly.

Lord Alec Macpherson was laird.

"I am ready to go," she whispered.

"Before we do, I have something for you."

"For me?" she asked, surprised.

"Aye. A wanderer like you—determined to go off on her own—needs something to defend herself."

From the pouch that hung by his long sword, Alec drew out a small dagger in a leather sheath. Crossing the room he held it out to her. Its handle of brown wood was polished until it shone. On the hilt there was a steel circle, and Fiona could see from where she stood an embossed family crest. *His* family crest.

"M'lord, I could not accept a gift. . . . I—"

"It is not a gift," he said, thinking quickly. Of course she would not accept a gift. What could he have been thinking? "It's for my own peace of mind. For protection. There are other maidens, Fiona, who wear these all the time."

"I do not require protection, m'lord," she said firmly. "Though I am certain those other maidens would cherish such a weapon, especially coming from someone of your stature."

Immediately she regretted the sound of her own words. She herself heard uncalled-for notes of jealousy.

"I am not interested in other maidens," Alec responded, his face stern. He reached out and took her hand, placing the dirk in it. Before letting go of her hand, his voice softened. "It is *your* safety I am concerned with right now. Only yours."

"I still cannot—" she began softly, shaking her head.

"Fiona, wait. Let me explain," he said, pausing, his eyes looking earnestly into hers. "You told me that a man and a woman must learn from one another. I am learning. The thought of you roaming those woods alone angered me at first—now it worries me to no end. But I am learning that I cannot stop you. And I should not try to mold you into something you are not. All I want is to help you and to keep you safe. Or rather, help you keep yourself safe. Now, you take this from me or I'll have you followed wherever you go. So which is it?"

Fiona closed her fingers around the dagger. On the

insignia at the hilt, a cat was sitting above the depiction of a ship on a shield. Its claws were outstretched, threatening. "But you don't understand. I could never use this on another human being. That is simply not my way."

"When the need arises, we all do what is necessary." Alec looked at the young woman contemplating the weapon in her hand. "And besides, you may need it to protect yourself from overly passionate lairds."

Unexpectedly, Fiona smiled up at Alec and tucked the dirk into the cord that encircled her waist.

"You have convinced me."

"I have?" he responded, astonished.

"Aye, m'lord. Overly passionate lairds seem to be a growing threat on this island."

"Well, I suppose I should be glad you've accepted this," Alec replied, his smiling face suddenly showing potential misgivings. "But considering what's persuaded you, I believe I already regret the whole thing."

Malcolm was indeed excited about their outing. Astride his new pony, he was waiting with David in the open area in front of the stable yard. A stable boy held Ebon, and David was holding another saddled mount for Fiona.

"Do you like my new pony, Fiona?" the lad blurted before Fiona and Alec had even reached them. "Alec gave him to me! His name's Rogue, and he likes me."

Fiona's eyes traveled from Malcolm's thrilled expression to the restless pony beneath him. She thought his life had been so complete here at the Priory, before all this. Before Lord Macpherson had stepped into his life. But now, looking at the excited young boy, Fiona knew she had been wrong ... as she may even have been wrong about her own life.

"How could he not like you?" she agreed, glancing up at the laird. "He is a lovely beast, is he not?"

"Since you three have some distance to go, I thought perhaps you would want to ride, as well, today," David suggested, looking at Fiona pointedly. "After all, while slowness is needed for ripening, it also brings rot, you know."

This had been a sore subject between Fiona and David for as long as she could remember. She liked walking.

David hated it. Walking offered her the freedom to use back trails and to come and go unnoticed. David never felt comfortable with that. So he had taught her how to ride. And Fiona excelled at it just as at everything else, but she continued to avoid it. He, in turn, continued to insist that she use a horse going back and forth—for safety's sake. But, of course, Fiona always refused.

"Very well." She sighed without agreeing, noting David's raised eyebrows. Fiona was not going to dampen Malcolm's excitement over the pony. "Though we have perfectly good legs for walking." She mumbled the last words under her breath.

Alec watched as Fiona easily mounted her horse and straightened the skirts of her dress. He could not help but feel disappointed that she was not going to ride with him.

Alec mounted his horse and followed behind the two.

As the trio headed for the Priory gate, the ancient porter, James, unexpectedly scuttled toward them, his long staff held to block their way.

"Nay, lass, ye cannot go today," he cried, clearly worked up over something. "Take the lad back."

Fiona slid off her horse, moving quickly to her distraught friend. Alec looked on, feeling uncomfortably as if he had witnessed this scene before. The porter's blue robe hung open, and his old shirt showed the signs of wear.

"What is it, James?" she asked, putting a hand on the old man's shoulder.

"My mother has sent me to warn ye. Do not do what ye are intending to do, for ye will not fare well, I tell ye!"

"Your mother, James?" Fiona asked. She glanced quickly at Alec. The old porter had to be close to eighty years old and lived alone with his son, the village smith.

"Aye, lassie!" James lowered his voice confidentially. "It is the rain. It will be a deluge. Loch Dunvegan will be flooding o'er the strand."

"But the sun is shining, James," Malcolm piped up. He did not want this excursion put off.

Fiona never took her face off the porter. Her kindly hazel eyes showed her concern as she comforted him, trying to soothe his anxiety.

"Thank you, James. But we are going south—away from Loch Dunvegan—to the bluffs that look out over those little islands—"

"MacLeod's Maidens," Malcolm chirped in cheerfully.

"We will not be far from you if it . . . when it starts to rain."

The porter's troubled look was hardly diminished as he glanced up into Fiona's eyes.

"Very well, lass, if you think . . ." he muttered unhappily, turning and working his way slowly toward his place by the gate. "But my mother, she . . ."

As the old man moved off, Fiona listened until his voice trailed off in the space between them.

"Could we please go, Fiona?" Malcolm pleaded.

With a last look at James, Fiona mounted again, watching the ancient porter, who now sat shaking his head sadly.

"We will watch for the clouds, James," she said reassuringly as they rode past him.

"There is not a cloud in the sky, Fiona," the lad whispered, looking hopefully at Alec.

"We will be fine, Malcolm," she replied quietly. "James is just getting . . . well . . . he is just concerned about us, that's all."

They rode out of the village in silence, Fiona and Alec each watching Malcolm as he sat proudly on his mount. His eyes were taking in everything around him as if this were his first time out and about.

"This porter . . . James, I mean," Alec broke in. Something was gnawing at the laird. Something about that old man.

"He's strange!" Malcolm chirped in.

"That is no way to talk, Malcolm," Fiona corrected sternly. "He is an aging man. And there is nothing strange about him."

"Is he always like this?" Alec asked. "So worried about the weather, I mean."

"Not always," Fiona said, looking up at the clear blue sky. "He says he dreams of things and the crofters believe him. There are some who believe he can see into your soul. That he has the second sight."

"And there are some who believe in the fairy maid. Are these the same folk?"

"Aye, more or less," she whispered quietly.

"Do you believe him? In what he says?" Alec asked, looking at Fiona. "In what he sees?"

"It is difficult to understand dreams and warnings. But we'd be fools not to believe in things just because we do not understand them. So I suppose I believe anything is possible."

"Aye, everything is possible."

Fiona felt Alec's eyes bore into hers, and she felt her resistance to him again begin to crumble.

She pushed her horse ahead of the two. Everything is possible! Aye, for dreamers and fools, she thought. But what was she doing allowing herself these feelings for a laird? When they had left her workroom, she had felt as though everyone's eyes had been on them. As though everyone knew what she and Alec had been doing behind the closed door. She was terribly embarrassed.

But this is no dream, she thought. It is plain and simple. It is flesh and blood. It is passion and desire and disaster. Old James can see it, and I cannot. What a fool!

And the porter's words were echoing in her mind. *You will not fare well.* That is what he'd said, and she knew he was right. For she was the one who was feeling so helpless. She was the one who would suffer in the end. As Malcolm's mother had. But even knowing this, she could not seem to resist the laird's attentions nor rebuff his shows of affection.

She simply couldn't stop thinking of him. She felt his presence everywhere, all the time. She had already let this go too far. Fiona knew that. But now her curiosity, her attraction to him, were pushing her, driving her on. And somehow, she just didn't mind.

Well, whatever is going to become of me, so be it, she thought decisively. She couldn't stop now. She knew she wouldn't.

Behind her the two were chatting away like old chums.

"And just think of it, Alec," Malcolm said excitedly. "If we are lucky today, I will have my own hawk to take home. Then I'll have a mistress just like you!"

Fiona turned on her mount and cocked an eyebrow at the laird.

In the rolling meadow to the right of the path, a flock

of gulls were settling into the pink-blossomed heather and the grass. The boy turned his attention to them.

"Fiona, is it all right if I take Rogue off the trail for a bit?"

She looked at the lad's excited face. "Of course, but don't go too far off."

With a whoop and a slap of the reins, Malcolm urged his new pony into a dash across the field. Shouting and waving his hand, the boy galloped straight into the flock of birds, scattering them into a feathery and squawking cloud.

"A mistress? One of the new comforts at Dunvegan, m'lord?" she teased.

Alec looked at her with amused surprise. "There is nothing but steel and cold stone at Dunvegan, Fiona."

"What, nothing warm? Nothing to help you wile away an hour there?"

"Nothing but some ugly dogs and even uglier warriors," he responded in a confidential tone. "However, if you're offering to visit ..."

Fiona looked away toward where Malcolm was racing across the meadow. Just when she thought he'd gone too far, she saw him rein in abruptly, wheel the pony, and spur him full speed back across the ground they'd just covered.

"I've never seen Dunvegan Castle ... other than at a distance," she said. "Neither the prioress nor David would let me go anywhere near it while I was growing up."

"Well, it surely wasn't the safest of places for a young woman to visit."

Fiona glanced at him slyly. "I'm not sure it's the safest of places for a young woman now, m'lord."

Alec laughed as Malcolm galloped up to them.

"Rogue is fast, Fiona," the lad panted. "Did you see us, Alec? Did you see us charge those filthy English soldiers?"

"Malcolm!" Fiona remonstrated, her voice rising and falling in exaggerated shock. She turned to Alec. "I see what kind of influence *you* are: falcons and mistresses, seagulls and English soldiers."

"A growing Scottish lad needs to know these things." Alec shrugged good-naturedly.

"We will catch a hawk today, won't we, Alec?"

"Not if I have my way," Fiona threatened. "Just when you think you've got the poor thing, I'll—"

"Aye, Malcolm. We may find one," Alec answered, reaching over and playfully putting his hand across Fiona's mouth. "You might not be able to take her home the first day, though. We may need to keep her at Dunvegan for a time."

"But why, Alec?" Malcolm asked.

"Aye, tell us why, m'lord," she prompted wryly, slapping his paw away.

"You have to be patient, lad. You have to woo her. You have to gentle her. And that may take some time."

"I'm not very patient," the young boy admitted.

"What man is?" Fiona remarked sardonically.

"Patience always has its limits, Malcolm," Alec said, eyeing Fiona meaningfully. "But I've been told I'm a patient man."

"The prioress tells me that patience is the virtue of asses," she put in casually.

"Not always," Alec responded, stifling a laugh and turning to the boy. "It's important to remember, Malcolm, that in hawking you are dealing with a free bird. One that has never been touched by a man before."

"By *any* man, Malcolm," Fiona interjected quietly. "It's important to remember."

Alec's eyes bore into the beautiful creature riding beside him. He had to admit it gave him great pleasure knowing he was the first man ever to touch her. He could still envision the glow of her skin, the perfect fullness of her breast. He could still taste the sweetness of her on his lips.

It had never mattered before whether the women that he'd been with had had other men. It didn't matter, not with any of them. Certainly not with Kathryn. But for some reason it mattered here. With Fiona. When he thought of her, a protectiveness raked through his soul. He wanted her to be his. Only his.

"I just want to know when we can roam the fields and hunt together." Malcolm's voice broke into Alec's thoughts. "When I can take my bird into my room with me at night."

Fiona and Alec looked up at each other in unison.

"Well"—Alec smiled—"as soon as she is used to you. But I do not suppose the Priory dormitory is the place for that."

"No, indeed," Fiona agreed tentatively, smiling inwardly at the irony of the exchange.

"But you *will* show me how, Alec? I have never really handled a falcon."

"Aye, lad," he said, looking meaningfully at Fiona. "The first touches of a man and a falcon are a wondrous thing."

Fiona felt her pulse quicken.

"There is a slow and sure breaking down of a barrier."

She watched Alec's eyes travel caressingly down her body.

"And when that barrier is gone," the giant continued, "the pleasure you will bring to one another is ... well ... incredible to the point of being heaven-sent."

Fiona shivered involuntarily in the warm sun.

Alec knew he had better put some space between them before he pulled her off her horse and onto his lap. What an interesting thought. He smiled. Oh, well. Another time. He turned to Malcolm.

"Come on, lad. I'll race you to where the brook passes that big tree."

"You're on!" the boy shouted, taking off like a shot.

The two tore across the field toward the meandering stream on the far side. Fiona watched them happily as Malcolm eased up at the bank while Alec charged splashing across the shallow water. A brightly colored duck flew up and settled back into the brook a stone's throw downstream.

The boy followed the warlord across and sat watching as Alec dismounted on the other side. They were too far away for Fiona to see what the blond giant was doing, but as they cantered back, side by side, she could see Malcolm had something hidden behind his back.

"Daisies!" she exclaimed, taking them from the beaming boy.

"Alec says bringing flowers might take your mind off my hawk."

"Oh, he did?"

"Lad, you're not supposed to tell her that," Alec murmured loud enough for her to hear. "Malcolm, I'll race you to that boulder jutting out up ahead."

The boy was off before Alec finished speaking, and the two watched the lad fly across the ground.

Directing his horse alongside hers, Alec took two of the daisies from the bunch in her hand.

"M'lord, you're about to lose that race."

Alec leaned across and placed one of the flowers in her hair.

"But I have the prize right here."

Fiona looked at him as he offered the remaining daisy. As she took it, his hand came up and took hold of her chin. Leaning toward her again, he pressed his lips to hers. The kiss was hard, unyielding, warm, and it ended all too quickly. Then, releasing her chin slowly, Alec looked affectionately into her beautiful eyes. He realized they were nearly blue, reflecting the azure sky. Smiling, he turned and took off after Malcolm.

The two raced around like madmen. Sometimes they were behind Fiona, sometimes ahead. But watching them, she felt happy, free. She closed her mind to the worries, the nightmares, the wrongs and the rights, and the future.

And then, listening to them cavort, she knew the sound of Malcolm's laugh, his happiness, was just further affirmation that she was doing the right thing. She looked around at the beauty that surrounded her. The rocky outcroppings, the heather-covered hills, the blue sky, the waterfowl and the seabirds.

"Well, that must be one of MacLeod's Maidens."

Fiona started in her saddle, but then, looking ahead, realized Alec was talking about the top of the island just coming into their vision above the slight knoll that signaled the sheer drop of the bluffs. The two had just pulled in behind her.

"The other one does not come up so high out of the sea," Malcolm affirmed.

The rolling meadows that ended at the bluffs were dotted with groves of trees, and a herd of wild cattle could be seen grazing in the distance. To their left a line of woods ran down to the sea at a point where the bluffs were not so high. A stony beach curved away along the shore.

"Well, we certainly do have a beautiful day for finding you a hawk, lad," Alec said, breathing in the salty summer air. He looked over at Fiona. She was sitting high on her mount. Strands of her hair had escaped their braid and were framing her lovely face in ringlets of red-gold.

Fairy or angel, I love that face, he thought. Alec watched her as she took a deep breath of fresh air. His gaze fell on her body, and he felt a stirring in his loins again. She was looking about her, totally unaware of his gaze, of his desires, of what her nearness was doing to him. She was so truly innocent, so magnificently beautiful.

"How should we start, Alec?" Malcolm chirped.

Alec tore his eyes from her and directed his attention to the young boy.

"First we need to look for a nest. It is a good time to find a young fal—"

The sound of a horse approaching rapidly from behind them stopped Alec midsentence. Wheeling his charger, the warlord spurred his horse to the top of the rise. Before he reached the summit, however, he heard Malcolm's pony following and Fiona's voice calling after the boy. Drawing his sword, Alec immediately spotted a lone rider pounding furiously across the meadow. Squinting his eyes against the bright sunshine, he recognized the flying elbows of his beanpole of a squire, Robert. But as he sheathed his sword, Alec's smile of relief was quickly replaced by a frown at the thought of the lad's great haste. Malcolm trotted his pony up beside him.

"Who is it, Alec?" the boy asked excitedly.

"Malcolm!" Fiona exclaimed, coming quickly up beside them. "You should not ride off—"

"Lord Alec!" Robert called breathlessly, reining his froth-covered steed to a halt. "Sir Ambrose . . . he sent me . . . trouble . . ."

"Catch your breath first, Robert," Alec commanded, lines of concentration marking his handsome features. "Now, tell me what's happened."

"Neil MacLeod," Robert said, still panting for air as he eyed Fiona and Malcolm. "He has killed one of his own men."

"Killed! Why, for God's sake?" Alec disliked the MacLeod leader, but killing a man ... a MacLeod man! What could have pushed a man like Neil to kill one of his own clan? "Who was the man?"

"Iain, m'lord," the squire responded. "You know him. The tall blond-haired one with the missing fingers on his hand. He has a Spanish sword from Toledo and a—"

"Aye, I remember him. What else did Ambrose say? Why did Neil kill the man?"

"I don't know, m'lord. But Sir Ambrose said to come quickly. He said to tell you the man was killed down by the falcons' mews. And there might be trouble."

"What kind of trouble? More than what just happened?"

"Aye, the rest of them ... the MacLeods are angry at Neil. He has betrayed one of his own."

It took Alec only a split second for the message to register. If Neil had truly done as he had been asked to do, then Alec owed him. It must have been very difficult to punish one of his own clan, even if the man was truly the one guilty of riding down Walter. There was only one way to find out. He turned to Malcolm and Fiona.

"I must return to Dunvegan Castle," he said grimly.

"Walter's attacker?" Fiona asked quietly.

"Perhaps," Alec replied steadily. "I'll send or bring you word. But right now we must get you back to the Priory."

"Could we stay?" Malcolm pleaded. "Fiona and I."

"I am sorry, lad, but no," Alec said, looking at the disappointed boy. "I must go back to the castle. We'll do this another—"

"We'll be fine, m'lord," Fiona interrupted. "As long as we are here, Malcolm and I will comb the beach. Then when we come back—"

"Nay, Fiona," Alec exploded, glaring fiercely. "I'll not leave you here—"

"On Priory lands, m'lord?" she challenged. "This is our land. We live and work here. This is our home."

"Fiona," he snapped. "The last thing I need right now is to be worrying about you and Malcolm out here alone."

"Before you arrived, m'lord, Malcolm and I spent a great deal of time out alone," she pressed, matching his glare. "The trouble at Dunvegan has nothing to do with us here. There's no reason for us to return to the Priory."

Alec looked at the hotly resolute face of the beauty and at the anxious face of the lad. He had to go now, and he did not have time to physically drag them back to the Priory. He turned and glanced at Robert, whose face reflected the shock he undoubtedly was feeling seeing his master argued with. Discipline be damned, there was no getting around it. Commanding Fiona to go would do no good whatsoever, and Alec knew it.

"Very well, Fiona," the laird conceded. "But Robert will stay with you."

"It will not be necessary." She glowered at Alec, then turned in the direction of the young squire and gave him a gentle smile.

"Fiona, then you are going back with me." Alec's scowl this time was threatening.

"Nay, I won't."

Alec moved forward, taking hold of the bridle of her horse. On second thought, he would force her if that was the way she wanted it.

"Fiona, if you stay, Robert stays."

She slapped his hand with the loose end of the reins. They glared at one another until suddenly her expression softened.

"Really, you worry too much, m'lord. But this time, I'll do as you wish," she responded, her tone as soft as the summer breeze. "I believe David has enough lunch in this saddlebag for five people, at least."

"One of these days, Fiona . . ." Alec growled.

Fiona smiled in response.

Wheeling on Robert, Alec scowled at the squire. "Robert, you make sure Mistress Fiona and Lord Malcolm get back to the Priory . . . or I'll have your hide hanging on the sea gate at Dunvegan."

He turned back to Fiona. "I'll bring word . . . you troublesome kelpie."

With a wave to Malcolm, the warlord spurred Ebon into motion and galloped north along the route they'd just traveled.

She had a way of driving him crazy. And this wasn't the first time, either. Fiona knew exactly how far to push him. How much to test him. And then always, at the last minute, she would back down. But by then Alec, already worked up, knew that he had lost the battle. He did not know how, but it was lost all the same. The more time Alec spent with her, the more he had to admire the prioress' patience. The elder nun was a saint after all.

But he also knew that such a fate was what he wanted for himself, as well. He might never achieve sainthood, but just the challenge sounded heavenly. And Alec knew he would cherish every moment of it.

Alec worked his way through the meadows and along the Priory lanes. Feeling the increasing breeze, he glanced up at the darkening sky. Overhead, dark clouds were rolling in from the west, transforming the rolling hills into gray and forbidding shadows. Slowing his pace, he thought of those he left at the bluffs.

Perhaps the old man was right after all, he thought with concern. How easy it is to disregard the warnings we receive.

His mind wandered back to a rain-soaked day in the borderlands between Scotland and England, to the fields at Flodden where a king had been destroyed on a hill slick with blood and rain. He, too, had received a warning.

The time was 1513. They were being pulled into war, and King James knew it. Negotiations on several fronts had not gone well. And then the news arrived that the English king, Henry Tudor, had invaded France. The Scottish king was not about to turn his back on Scotland's Auld Alliance with France. He was not happy about it, but he would fight. He had said he would invade England if Henry invaded France, and by God, he would.

Then, only weeks before the battle at Flodden, in the church at Linlithgow, the king was sitting with his closest friends at prayer when a stranger suddenly appeared to him.

"King," the stranger rasped. "Do not pass at this time where you are proposing to go, for if you do, you will not fare well in your journey. Do not go. Heed this, King."

The king stood and placed an arm gently on the old man's shoulder, and his words of response were soothing. For months he had been listening to the fears of his people. Fears for his welfare. King James had been nearly overwhelmed by the loving support of his own Scottish people. How could they not fare well? Indeed, he was certain that even God was with them.

After saying his piece, the wraithlike figure simply walked away, disappearing into the darkness of the chapel nave. In a moment, he was gone. Like a blink of the sun. Like a whip of a whirlwind.

But the king had been warned. Warned of the annihilation of ten thousand of Scotland's finest warriors. Warned of his own death.

Only the king, Alec, and two others had seen the harmless-looking stranger. Just a thin, harmless old man . . . in a blue robe.

A blue robe.

The old porter stepped into the lane in front of Alec's horse. Alec reined Ebon in fiercely, and the charger reared up in response. James's tattered blue robe was flapping in the strong wind, and Alec could see that his eyes were peering wildly down the lane past the wheeling animal.

"I warned her!" he croaked hoarsely.

"What is it, James?" Alec shouted. His blood ran cold at the sight of the decrepit seer. James raised his staff, shaking it at the sky.

"The king wouldn't listen," James moaned. "And they all died."

"You were there, weren't you? It was you!" Alec stared in awe.

"The rain's already begun. Can ye feel it? It's started!"

There was no rain falling, but the wind was swirling around them in gusts. Alec stared at the wild-eyed figure moaning in the path before him. Then James straightened his old body and looked directly into the warlord's eyes.

"Can ye feel it, Laird? Do ye remember the rain?"

Alec's eyes swept the sky. The clouds were ominous, gray, and full.

He remembered.

Chapter 9

They call me Death, in truth I declare,
Calling all men and women to their biers
Whenever I please, what time, what place, or where.
None is so strong, so fresh, nor yet so fair,
So young . . .
—ROBERT HENRYSON,
 "The Reasoning Between Death and Man"

The scream cut through the wind like the shriek of a gull.

"Help me!" Robert cried.

"You move and you're finished." Fiona said through clenched teeth. She had done all she could to coax him up the cliff edge. Encouragement had not worked, so maybe threats were what he needed.

"I'm going to die anyway!" Robert moaned.

"You won't be hurt if you don't move." The words were sharp. "But listen to me. You stop your whining or I'll kill you with my own hands."

Beneath Robert the bluffs fell away fifty feet to the crashing surf. The steadily increasing wind had whipped up the waves into a roiling, foaming beast throwing itself against the shore in a turbulent display of violence and fury.

Fiona swept her thick hair back over her shoulder as she looked over the edge of the narrow promontory jutting out from the line of cliffs. Her fiery red locks had torn loose from the braid, but she had more immediate things to worry about than her hair. Malcolm stood beside her, dismay clearly written on his young face.

"What do we do now, Fiona?" he whispered loudly through the roar of the gale.

"We need to save him," she whispered, glancing over at the boy.

"Do you really think we can?" the lad asked.

"Aye, we can," Fiona responded, knowing that Robert could climb up as easily as he climbed down, were he not so frightened. "Do as I told you before, Malcolm. Run for the horse."

The lad leaped up and scurried to Fiona's waiting mount. The rope they had brought for the hawking snaked across the grass to the place where the horses were tethered beyond the narrow neck of the promontory.

"For God's sake, Robert, take hold of the rope," Fiona shouted when she saw Malcolm had the horse's bridle securely in hand. She removed her cloak and dropped it at her feet. Again her command was curt. "If you move either way, you'll fall. And it's a long way to the bottom."

"Don't you think I know that?"

"I don't know how you would. You've kept your mouth open and your eyes shut the whole time you've been stuck out there."

She was getting exasperated with the lanky squire. It figured he'd be afraid of heights. But it also figured he'd be too much the adolescent male to admit it until he was on the narrow ledge so far above the rocky shoreline.

They had seen the goshawk return to a ledge not far from where Robert stood hugging the cliff wall. He had even volunteered to try to get a closer look. And now Fiona glanced out at the mother goshawk, which was continuing to circle threateningly not fifty feet from the paralyzed squire.

"Just move your hand and grab the rope," she commanded again. "It's only a few feet to the top, and my horse can easily pull you up."

"You won't drop me?"

"*Grab* the rope, Robert!" she commanded.

The terrified squire inched his hand toward the dangling loop of the rope. With a last quick movement, he snatched the line and trapped it between his palm and the rock wall of the cliff.

"Slip your hand up through the loop, Robert." She watched as the young man obeyed. "Now hold on!"

Leaping to her feet, Fiona took hold of the rope and turned to Malcolm.

"Lead her directly away from the cliff, Malcolm. *Now,* Malcolm," she shouted over the howling wind. "But slowly!"

A yelp came from the cliff face as Robert was lifted from the ledge. Gradually the squire rose to the top, and in a moment lay sprawled, still shaking, on the grassy peninsular knoll.

Fiona quickly retrieved the satchel and jug of water from her horse. She was back at the young man's side before he even knew it, holding the water to his trembling lips.

"I am so sorry," Robert whispered, working himself into a sitting position. "I am such a coward. Such a disappointment."

"Hush, now, you are none of those things—"

"Aye, I am," he cut in.

"Robert, we all have fears," she comforted. "And some of them we simply can't control. Being afraid of heights is—"

"Lord Alec has no fears," Robert asserted gloomily, his face reflecting his feelings of inadequacy.

"You can be certain he does. Some people just hide their feelings better than others."

Robert looked up at Fiona gratefully. He took a deep breath and looked around.

"All the same, the laird will have my hide for this," he said, smiling hesitantly.

"He'll do no such thing," Fiona countered, crouching beside the recovering squire. "What happened there was purely accidental."

"He won't see it that way. I was left behind to protect you."

"Robert, we don't need protection."

"That doesn't really matter," he responded seriously. "I failed at the task he gave me, and he'll be displeased."

"Are you really so afraid of him?" Fiona asked in surprise. "He doesn't punish you, certainly."

"He does, mistress. He will."

Of all the mean things ... How could Alec Macpherson punish this young man for a fear that he could not control? She would certainly let him have a piece of her mind about this!

"Alec punishes Robert at least once a day. And it doesn't matter if he needs it or not," piped up Malcolm, who had just joined them.

"How do you know of this?" Fiona turned abruptly in his direction.

"Why, I saw him do it," Malcolm said proudly.

"In front of you? He punished Robert in front of you?" she gasped. The madman! How could he do something so outrageous in front of a mere child? Her eye was drawn to a small, leafy branch that blew up over the edge of the narrow point of land, past them, only to disappear again quickly over the other edge. The wind was continuing to pick up, and between gusts Fiona could hear the restless neighing of the horses beyond the neck of the peninsula.

"Aye," Malcolm said uncertainly, noting the anger flashing across Fiona's face. He had seen this look before.

"Mistress Fiona, it's not really as bad as it sounds," Robert broke in hesitantly.

"Robert talks too much," Malcolm said bluntly in Alec's defense.

They were all speaking loudly, trying to be heard over the gusting sea wind.

"Aye, mistress. I talk too much."

"What does that have to do with anything?" Fiona said, still furious about the laird's totally unacceptable behavior. Punishing a squire in front of Malcolm, indeed!

"That's my punishment!"

"What's your punishment?" Fiona asked, momentarily bewildered by the squire's words.

" 'Peace and quiet,' he says. No talking!"

"I don't underst— *What* 'peace and quiet'?" she asked.

"One meal a day, Robert gets punished," Malcolm explained. "That means he has to keep quiet. Alec says he'll go insane if he doesn't punish Robert at least once a day. Fiona, what is insane?"

She couldn't help but smile at the lad's question. But, honestly, even in the short time she'd spent in the company of the garrulous young squire, she had a feeling she could appreciate and commend Alec's disciplinary methods.

"Insane?" she responded. "That's exactly what you two are making me right now!"

Fiona glanced about her. The sky had turned a grayish green that matched the whitecapped waters below, and she thought it looked like the lid of a pot had been clamped down over them. "If you're feeling better, Robert, perhaps we'd better be getting—"

The four riders stormed over the nearby rise and descended upon the bluffs like characters out of the Apocalypse. In the blink of an eye, the horsemen blocked the narrow strip of turf at the end of the precipice, cutting off any chance for escape.

Instinctively, Fiona grabbed Malcolm by the wrist and pulled him behind her as Robert leaped to his feet, drawing his sword in defense.

There was no question these men intended harm. All had their swords fully drawn, all were looking at the group before them with malice in their eyes.

There was not enough room on the projecting point of land for the attackers to continue comfortably on horseback, so three of them slowly dismounted, swords in hand. The fourth sat back smugly, catching the loose reins of the others' mounts and eyeing the two horses and the pony tethered to a shrub nearby.

The three advanced deliberately, and Robert took a half step forward.

"Stop right there and state your business," he demanded in a commanding tone that startled even Fiona.

The attackers stopped short, but only momentarily, and then the leader half turned to his cronies.

"Well, lads," growled Crossbrand. "We've a young warrior to deal with before our ... fun begins."

Fiona shuddered, recognizing the men. They hadn't left Skye after all. She broke into a cold sweat as Malcolm tried to free his hand from her viselike grip.

One of the thugs grinned evilly as his eyes raked over her body. With unconcealed lechery, the brute licked his cracked lips, while the other just stared, menace etched in every feature of his scarred and bloated face.

"Come on, boy," Crossbrand taunted, waving his

sword back and forth in the gusting wind. "Let's see what a sniveling brat from the Macpherson clan can do."

Fiona felt Malcolm pull himself free of her grasp and, as she glanced over, saw him pull his own tiny dagger from the sheath at his waist. Fear rushed through her at the thought of her own precious one falling prey to these outlaws. Frantic, she considered for a moment telling them that Malcolm was the rightful MacLeod heir, but she dismissed the impulse, realizing that these cutthroats cared for nothing but their bellies and their lecherous bloodlust.

Fiona looked around her wildly. They were hemmed in by the sheer drop of the cliffs. There was nowhere for them to go. Malcolm stood beside her, his little knife in his hand. Oh, Blessed Mother, she prayed, panic flooding her senses.

"You drew your sword, now use it," Crossbrand spat, gesturing for those behind him to move forward. "Unless, like the rest of the Macphersons, you just carry it for show."

Like lightning, Robert sprang into action. The squire's lanky limbs took on the grace of a deer as he crossed the short distance separating him from the attackers. The sweeping arc of his sword crashed in a shower of sparks on the leader's upraised weapon, sending Crossbrand sprawling to the ground. Moving back a step, Robert drew his long sword back again as the other two thugs cautiously advanced on him.

First one, and then the other swung their swords at the squire, and the lad's quick reflexes helped him avoid the slashing path of one while deflecting the blow of the other. Without pausing, Robert wheeled where he stood, whipping his sword around, cutting through the leather buckler and into the shoulder of one of the outlaws.

Clutching his arm, the thug fell to one knee, and the other came hard at the squire, his sword slashing at the lad and driving him backward. But Robert fended off the attacks, and soon the two were exchanging blow for blow at the edge of the cliff.

Fiona watched in horror as the fourth outlaw climbed off his horse and moved past Crossbrand to the side of his injured friend, who stood up, grimly wiping blood from his hand.

And then the sky exploded.

A bolt of lightning detonated in a deafening crash not yards from where Fiona stood. Frozen momentarily by the sudden violence of the blast, the figures on the promontory gaped at one another. Robert's opponent took advantage of the distraction to push the squire closer to the ledge.

Then Crossbrand and the other two turned to Fiona and Malcolm, advancing on them and spreading into a half circle like wolves closing on their prey.

Malcolm leaped at the closest attacker, slashing at the man with his knife. With the back of his hand, the thug sent the boy sprawling toward the edge of the precipice, where he shook his head groggily.

"Malcolm!" Fiona screamed, running toward him.

From behind a hand grabbed a fistful of her hair, yanking her to a halt. Another hand took hold of her wrist, and she twisted around, finding herself so close to the scarred face of the attacker that she could feel his foul breath on her face. Behind her Malcolm cried out. With a hard kick that connected with the outlaw's crotch, Fiona turned back to the boy as the man released her hair.

Lurching out of his grip, Fiona caught a glimpse of Malcolm standing terrified at the edge of the cliff. The injured outlaw was moving toward the lad, and Fiona, screaming, leaped toward his back.

Crossbrand caught Fiona's dress at the neck with one hand, and her wrist with the other. Jerking her toward him, he tore violently at the dress, rending it to the waist. Seeing her white skin, the outlaw's eyes gleamed for only an instant before the look was replaced by one of surprise, and then they took on the dull luster of the eyes of a man at the moment of death.

As Crossbrand sank with a moan to the ground at Fiona's feet, the blade of the dirk slid out from between his ribs.

The dagger was clenched in her hand, and Fiona felt the numbness move quickly up her arm and into her body. As the feeling spread, she could see the room, the men, her mother. The past was there before her eyes as real and as focused as the drops of blood rolling with excruciating slowness to the end of the dagger. Fiona felt the present being pushed swiftly from her by the spreading numbness—she felt her spirit melt into the ground at her feet.

The outlaw angrily straightening himself up from Fiona's kick half turned and watched his leader crumple to earth. The red-haired woman stood motionless, beaten and waiting. His eyes riveted on her exposed shoulder and breast, and a sneer crept across his face as he stepped toward her. He would have her first.

Alec paused at the top of the rise, his eyes scanning the shoreline before him. The wind was whipping his blond hair across his face, and he pushed it aside. He should have met them as they returned to the Priory. Where were they?

Fiona's scream pierced the air. Following the sound Alec's eyes focused on a point to his right. Wheeling his horse, he charged down the rise toward the narrow neck leading out to them.

Before the sneering outlaw could reach Fiona, the crashing blow from Alec's sword cleaved his torso from shoulder to rib, and the brute's twitching body was dead before it hit the ground.

The thug looming over Malcolm spun to face the approaching warlord and, with a quick look for help, saw that Robert stood panting over the dead body of the other outlaw. He was alone, and sheer terror caused him to step back from the terrible glare of the advancing giant . . . and off the cliff edge into space.

Alec whirled toward Fiona. She stood as if in a trance, her torn dress hanging from her waist, the blood dripping from the dagger in her hand. Her face was pale, and tears silently streamed from her eyes.

Malcolm ran to her, throwing his arms around her. Absently, her free hand went to his hair, stroking his soft locks.

Alec removed his tartan, and his hand shook with anger as he gently wrapped the plaid around her bruised ivory skin. His throat was parched and his blood was pounding in his veins as he gathered Fiona to him. Holding her, he knew he would never let go of her again. Never. Taking Malcolm's hand, he gestured for Robert to take the boy. His hand reached down and tried to remove the dagger from Fiona's fist, but she clutched it in a death grip.

"It's over, Fiona," he whispered softly. "It's over, my love. You're safe now."

She looked up into his eyes and released the knife.

"My mother," she whispered, tears rolling steadily down her face. "They were hurting my mother. I was there ... but I couldn't stop them."

Alec wrapped his arms more tightly around her as Fiona began to sob. He held her close and felt his eyes well up at the sound of her wrenching anguish. If he could kill these men again, he would. He held her so tight that she felt a part of him.

Standing there as the wind whipped around them, Alec swore to himself that as long as he had breath in his body, no man would ever lift a hand against this woman again ... and live.

Fiona looked up at him as he gently pushed a strand of hair from her face.

"I couldn't stop them," she said, burying her face against his chest once more as her body shook with waves of sorrow.

Chapter 10

Belief does leap, trust does not tarry;
Authority flies, and courts do vary;
Purpose does change as wind or rain:
Which, to consider, is a pain.
—WILLIAM DUNBAR, *"To the King"*

It had been a full week since the incident at the bluffs.
A difficult week during which so many questions had
not found answers. From what Alec could ascertain,
Iain, the slain MacLeod warrior, had been seen with the
outlaws. It appeared he had supplied the attackers with
horses and swords. But with all of them now dead, the
motives behind Iain's actions were baffling. There was
still the matter of the gold found in each man's possession. More gold than Iain could ever have paid them.

And Neil was gone, as well. Fearing reprisal from others of the MacLeod clan, Neil told Ambrose he was
going to the Isle of Lewis in the Outer Hebrides and
left immediately. He had done his job in finding the
traitor—as Alec had earlier directed him to do—but with
his maimed arm, Neil felt that he would be an easy tar-
get for revenge.

Perhaps most puzzling, though, had been Father Jack's
appearance at Dunvegan the same evening that Fiona
was attacked. The priest had been looking for Adrian,
for it appeared that the lad had last been seen heading
for the castle. By morning, Adrian still had not returned.

Fiona had steadily wept in Alec's arms for the entire
ride back to the Priory. As they rode north through the
wild and rainswept countryside, she had talked in inco-
herent snatches about her mother, about an attack. It
seemed to Alec that she was remembering a nightmare.

A terrible nightmare, vicious and painful to recall. And then the tears had stopped.

He had come every day to her side, but it was heart-rending to watch her lying in despair, pale and drawn, vacant, dry-eyed. But Alec knew the attack had made her remember something. And whatever it was, the memory was tormenting Fiona, so Alec remained at her side, desperately hoping for a chance to help her. For a week he had come, holding her hand, willing his strength into her.

Finally, Fiona's tears had come, and Alec had held her long and fierce.

During those hours, after fighting down his guilt since three of these outlaws were the same ones he had turned loose in the forest, Alec had come to grips with his own feelings about Fiona. In his mind he had relived over and over the terror and the rage he had felt seeing the filthy brutes attacking her. How she must have felt, thinking no one was there to protect her from their vicious desires. It tore at him to think he had almost been too late to save her. All he knew now was that he wanted to keep her safe. To remain by her side. To cherish her as she deserved to be cherished.

And, if need be, to help her forget.

But for the past two days she had refused to see him, and that made him crazy. Then, news from the prioress drove a shaft deep into his heart.

Fiona wanted to become a nun.

"I need to talk to her," Alec said. "But she won't see me."

"I know. Right now she is out in the orchard with Sister Beatrice. Go to her, anyway," the prioress suggested.

Alec paused, then nodded gratefully at the nun as he headed for the door.

"Lord Alec," the prioress stopped him, smiling. "Please tell Sister Beatrice I'd like to see her."

"Aye, Prioress. I will."

"Oh, one more thing. Whatever the outcome of your little chat, I want to speak with both of you when you're done." The prioress knew it was time.

The afternoon sun was warm on Fiona's face as she held one side of the iron pot full of the honeycombs they'd been gathering.

"Let's sit a moment, Fiona," Sister Beatrice pleaded. "This is your first day out of that little room of yours. The sun is so lovely, and the fresh air would do you a world of good."

At first she had been against coming out. But Sister Beatrice had insisted. The nun had gently suggested to Fiona that the sooner she was up and around, the sooner her wounds would heal. The younger woman had acquiesced, but inwardly she wondered how that could be true.

Fiona sat silently in the grass, stretching her legs in front of her. She leaned back on her hands and looked up. The rays of the sun shimmered on the leafy branches overhead. The young birds hopped from branch to branch in excitement. She closed her eyes, giving herself up to the lazy murmur of the nearby spring, to the sound of nature all around her. She had made up her mind. It was time to clear away all that had happened to her, to close the doors to her past—to her feelings—and to move on.

But it was difficult to forget him. For the past week she had longed for his presence. Every time she had awakened, Alec had been there. And every time she had seen him beside her, Fiona's heart had ached to hold him, to tell him all that he meant to her. All she had locked inside of her. Of her past and of the present. Of the . . . love.

Fiona wondered if the way she was feeling now was the way her mother had felt about the man who had fathered her. About the man who had never come back. About the man her mother had never married.

I can't, Alec, she thought sadly. I'll not be my mother.

Sister Beatrice was first to spot Alec approaching. She stood quietly and moved toward him. She was hoping he would come back . . . even after Fiona's insistence on not seeing him. Lord Alec cared for Fiona, the nun could see that. And Fiona cared for him, as well. Even if she didn't want to admit it. During those first days after the attack, Fiona had only rested when he had been there with her. Clearly, the young woman needed and depended on him. Clearly, she felt safe with him.

"Fiona."

She heard the sound of the approaching footsteps. But

as she opened her eyes, Fiona thought she had conjured him. His massive frame blocked the sun. My God, he *is* the sun. No, she thought, shaking her head in denial. This was all a dream, a vision, a part of what she was trying to put behind, forever. But then his voice reached her. He was real. He was here. She got quickly to her feet, looking about her in a vain attempt to avoid his eyes.

Alec drank in the sight of her. He had missed her. Two days of emptiness had torn at him. Two restless, dream-tossed nights had filled him with weariness. Fiona's startled eyes opened, and she looked at him before rising to her feet. But then she paused, quickly glancing away, looking like a bird about to take flight. He stood before her, hardly breathing for fear she would run.

"Fiona, why?"

She looked down at her hands and hid them in the folds of her skirt. It would have been so much easier if he'd just stayed away.

Alec moved closer. He had to control the overwhelming urge to draw her into his arms. She looked so somber, so fragile.

Fiona watched his hands move up and caress the skin of her face. Uncontrollably, she leaned into his touch. He lifted her chin and their eyes locked. Her heart pounded, and she silently damned herself for her weakness.

Weakness? she thought. I love this man.

A tear rolled down her cheek. He wiped it away gently.

"Why have you been avoiding me?" His voice was husky with emotion.

How could she tell him of the torment it was for her to be so close to him and to know she could never be his?

"It's better this way for . . . both of us."

"But why?" Alec pressed, holding her shoulders, forcing her to face him, to answer him. "Make me understand."

"I can't see you anymore." Fiona looked into the deep blue of his eyes. "I've talked to the prioress; I will enter the ord—"

"No, Fiona. You won't."

"You cannot stop me," she argued, looking away. "This has nothing to do with you."

"That decision has everything to do with me ... with us." Alec tightened his hold on her shoulders. He wanted to shake some sense into her. "Look at me, Fiona."

Her gaze traveled up to his face again. She wanted him to pull her into his arms. To make everything well. To make the past go away.

"Fiona, something incredible has happened between us. Something that neither you nor I can deny." Alec paused, trying to contain the feelings that were racing through him. "These past few days, I've had time to think. I ... we can't stop. And I can't let you run away ... not to take a vow ... to make a mistake ... for life. Not when I know how you feel—"

"It's wrong, Alec. It's wrong."

He started to respond and then he stopped. This was the first time he'd ever heard his name escape her lips, and his heart slammed in his chest at the sound of it.

"What can be wrong, Fiona?" His hands traveled down her arms, and he took hold of her hands. Her fingers were ice-cold. Pressing them together, he warmed them with his own. "How can it be wrong for me to feel the way I do about you? To want to hold you, to care for you, to be always near you? Fiona, when I first saw you, I felt as though I had always known you. Now I realize my whole life has just been a series of steps that have led me to you. Without knowing it, I have been searching for you all my life. I can't ... I can't put it into words ... because I thought I was in love once before, but this ... this feeling with you is so much more than anything I have felt in the past. Ever."

Alec raised her hands to his lips. Fiona's body came alive at his touch, at his words. She traced his full lips with her fingers, her eyes fixed on the sensual mouth.

She decided.

She had to explain to him. He needed to know what she remembered, the reasons behind her actions, the decision she was making for both of them. But she couldn't do it standing so close to him, touching him. She softly pulled her fingers from his grasp and stepped away from him.

Alec watched as she wrapped her arms about her waist and moved under the branches of an apple tree. She turned and leaned against its trunk, her eyes coming back to his.

"That day at the bluffs." Her voice cracked as the words left her mouth. Alec stiffened and looked quickly away. "The fear ..."

"I know," Alec interrupted, pain evident in his voice. "I left you. But you must forgive me ... for leaving you ... for what those men ..."

"Nay! That's not it!" She silenced him with her words. "Please, Alec. Please listen to what I have to say."

Fiona paused, and Alec looked at her, his gaze steady. She was clearly searching for just the right words. He reached down and picked up a leafy branch that had broken from the tree. He looked at the soft white wood enclosed in the green inner bark. There were three small apples forming at the end of the branch, clusters of green leaves around them. When she began to speak again, he turned his gaze back to her.

"Those men. The way they threatened Malcolm. The way they smelled as they came at me. They forced me to ... remember."

She squeezed her eyes shut, and Alec could feel her pain. He took a step toward her, but stopped when she held up her hand. A helpless feeling swept through him, and he half turned, leaning his broad back against a thick, low-hanging bough.

"The way they moved. His rough hand on my wrist." She shuddered involuntarily. "It all opened a door to my past. A door that I've kept shut a long time. Since I was a little girl. A door to memories that have become nightmares for me. Things I can neither understand ... nor forget."

Alec paled, and then found himself growing angry. He would not allow anything that had happened to Fiona in the past to stop her from living her life the way it should be lived now. He would do everything he could to make sure those ugly nightmares were replaced by what she deserved ... by dreams of hope and happiness. He would make it happen. He tore a cluster of leaves from the branch in his hand.

"Alec," she said softly, drawing his attention back to

her words. "You asked me once about my people. About the time before I arrived here. And I told the truth then when I said that I couldn't remember. I could not recall my childhood. But last week ... the incident on the bluffs ... many things ... many things have come back to me. Things about my past."

She took a deep breath and tried to smooth the tremble in her voice. "I was raised in a castle far away from here. I remember gardens and open spaces. I was young, full of mischief."

"Not much has changed," Alec whispered, seeing a half smile break out on her lips at his words. "Do you remember your people, your family?"

Fiona shook her head in response. "It was always just my mother and I. I don't remember ever seeing my father, and to this day I don't even know who he was. We had a quiet life ... almost hidden. I had a nanny. There were lots of servants, but I was lonely. My mother and I only had each other. And then, all of the sudden, everything seemed to be changing. It was fall ... I was told my father was supposedly on his way to us. I was to meet him at last."

She remembered her room, and old woman waiting with her, the excitement of the anticipated visit. How quickly it all changed. "And then the men came. My mother told me they were bad people, that my father was innocent of this ... I didn't know what she was talking about. And then I was torn right out of my mother's arms. For years, that was all I could remember. Her cries ... her desperate, frantic cries."

Fiona took a deep breath and bit her lip, recalling the dreadful events.

"I'd never seen those men before. They killed my mother's knight. They carried me out into the night air ... it was cold and wet ... and we rode for what seemed forever. We only traveled at night. Then one night we were fording a river. It was during a storm ... the river was wild ... the horses were swept away. The men were swept away with them. A large branch ... it seemed like a tree ... raced by and I grabbed for it. I held on for a long, long time. Even after it became entangled with the other debris floating in the river, I held on. Until Walter found me."

Alec stared at her.

"I don't know why those men took me, but I know that for a long time before they came, my mother was alone. She had people around her, but she ..." Fiona placed both of her hands on the bough Alec was leaning against. "She had no husband. He was supposed to come to us that night. But he never did."

Fiona turned toward Alec, her face set determinedly. "I didn't understand it as a child, but it is clear to me now. I am a love-child, Alec. Illegitimate. A bastard. My mother never married ... I know that. And that castle, where we were, I don't know if it was ours. I think we were hidden away there, because nobody ever came to visit. There was never any family. No one. We were alone, and there was no one to protect us. I won't let that happen again."

Alec could not keep himself from her any longer. Reaching for her, he drew her into his arms, and she came. Holding her close, he cursed himself for letting her see any similarity between himself and some neglectful, philandering nobleman.

"No, Fiona. *I* won't let that happen." Alec pressed her to him. A wave of possessiveness swept through him. He would never let her go. He wanted her by his side forever. He was sure of that. More than ever. And he would earn her love. "Please give me a chance. Trust me. A relationship like the one your parents had will not make me happy. That is not for me. That is not for us, Fiona. I want you forever at my side."

"No, can't you see? I'm no one. I have no name." She pulled back from his embrace, stepping away from him. "What kind of a life would that be? We belong to different classes. You are a nobleman; I am a nun. I was raised for the convent, and that is where I belong. You were born to govern, and that is what you will do."

Alec's protest was stilled by the sound of Sister Beatrice's humming as she came into the orchard after them.

"We are not finished with this discussion, Fiona. We have much more to say."

"Do you remember this, Fiona?"

The young woman eyed the jeweled cross that the

prioress was dangling from an intricately wrought gold chain. It was beautiful in its workmanship, encrusted with the sparkling red and green of rubies and emeralds. Even in the dim light of the prioress' workroom, the brilliance of the gems was dazzling.

Fiona's heart skipped a beat, but not over the worldly value of the cross. In her mind she saw it hanging from the ivory neck of a loving and lonely woman.

"It ... it is my mother's," she stammered, half rising from her chair. "She gave it to me ... my father gave it to her."

"Aye, lass." The prioress nodded. "You were wearing the cross and a leather purse. They were tucked snug inside your clothes the night you came to us."

Alec looked from one woman to the other. He was glad to be included in this meeting, even though he was not certain of the prioress' reason for having him here. The nun had asked him to stay. She had said that what they were going to talk about would concern them both. The prioress had seen him here every day. His attentions, his interest in Fiona were clear, and Alec did not have any intention of letting her think otherwise.

This was a very private moment, and Alec knew it. But he wanted to know all about Fiona, all about her past. If it was a matter of staying at her side for every waking moment, he was prepared to do that. He would stay by her until she could see they belonged together. He would not let her go with the belief that class differences could keep them apart. Damn nobility and every other class difference! he cursed silently. He would be here for his woman.

When they'd been ushered into the workroom by Sister Beatrice, Fiona had headed for a chair on the far side of the room. But Alec's long legs had covered the distance quicker, and before Fiona could sit down, he'd made a gracious show of carrying the chair to where two others sat before the fireplace. She was stubborn, but he was persistent. Wordlessly, Fiona had followed him and seated herself by the prioress.

The older woman gently laid the cross in Fiona's hands, and Fiona felt a knot tighten in her chest. As she looked down at it, a tear traced a path on her cheek, and the knot grew, threatening to choke her. Then she felt Alec's great hand on her arm, and she felt his strength flow into her. She looked at him quickly and felt the warmth of his blue eyes supporting her.

"There was a letter in that purse, Fiona," the prioress said, going back to her worktable. She picked up a tattered and smeared scrap of parchment, and held it up for the two to see. "A letter from your mother."

Fiona stared at the sheet as the prioress came back to her. She looked from the yellowed message to the older woman's face and then back to the parchment. She could see where the folded edges were dark with stains—the purse had not kept all the water out. She wanted to ask, wanted to grab the letter out of the prioress' hand, but she could not. Her arms felt as if a terrible weight lay on them. She felt as if her tongue were swollen and incapable of speech. Her chest heaved with the effort to even breathe.

Inexplicably, her hand rose from her lap. She watched it as if it didn't belong to her. She saw it take the paper, but it was someone else's hand, and the fingers conveyed no sense of touch. The parchment traveled to a place where she could read it, but Fiona could see no words, only a tear that fell, splashing with extraordinary clarity and definition on an empty space at the bottom of the page.

And then she simply held them—her mother's words—in a pale and shaking hand.

And then she read:

To Robert Henryson, Schoolmaster at the Abbey at Dunfermline,
I am sending you my daughter. Her life is in danger. Please, my good friend, keep her hidden and safe. Fiona is the daughter of the King, and His Majesty will come for her. Trust no one. God bless you.
Margaret Drummond

Stunned, Fiona's eyes read over the words again and again, trying to make sense of them. She could hear the prioress' words coming from someplace far away, and she tried to understand them, as well.

". . . a letter . . . Margaret Drummond . . . the daughter of King James . . ."

Alec stared at the prioress, and then at Fiona. He thought he'd always known her. Indeed, he had. She was the very image of her father. How could he have been so blind?

"My mother ..." Fiona blurted out, the letter still clenched in her hands. "M'lady prioress, what happened to my mother?"

The prioress and Alec exchanged glances. They both knew what had happened to Margaret Drummond. All of Scotland knew.

"The night that you were taken away ..." The prioress paused. She didn't know how to soften the blow that Fiona was about to receive. "Word had it ... that Margaret Drummond took her own life. She poisoned herself and died that very same night."

She was dead. Fiona stood up and walked to the window. She looked out into the grounds, but her eyes saw nothing. Dead. Her chest heaved once as she tried to fill her lungs with air. Dead. Somehow she had always known that. Somehow she'd always known that she was alone. Her mother was dead. Dead.

But now ... poisoned? And by her own hand? Suicide?

"No! That's not the truth," Fiona asserted, looking down at the letter. They were going to hurt her mother. She remembered their threats. In fact, there was more coming back to her. A pouch ... the hidden pouch ... the evil man in the castle whom she never saw.

"Fiona," the prioress called. "There are some things you should know."

Fiona turned around and faced the old nun. "They murdered her. She never committed suicide."

The room rang with the conviction in her words. The prioress and Alec were silent for a long moment as Fiona looked from one to the other.

"How do you know that?" Alec asked, standing and moving to the fireplace.

"Because she wouldn't. She was their captive," Fiona retorted. She tried to remember, still searching for details of that faraway night. "And those men ... they said things."

"What things?" Alec pressed. "Try to remember what was said."

Fiona looked at Alec across the room. "I am trying! But I know they were going to hurt her."

"Who do you mean, 'they'?"

"The same men that took me away."

"But you said earlier that your mother was alive then."

"She was. But they did not all leave with us." Fiona gnawed at her lip, racking her brain for more clues to what happened that night. "The leader, he was a giant. His eyes were cruel. He was like some madman. He stayed behind with some of them."

"What else do you remember?" Alec questioned.

"They were Highlanders."

"Highlanders? What else? What clan did they belong to? Could you narrow it down?"

Fiona looked at him wide-eyed. "I was five years old, for God's sake!"

Silence reigned momentarily as Fiona glared at Alec. She noticed his cool exterior. Something was different in his face. His compassionate and concerned look had been replaced by the businesslike demeanor of the warlord in search of answers.

"You were such a wee thing." The prioress' soft words broke into the silence. Fiona and Alec disengaged their gazes and turned to the older nun. Fiona walked to the prioress and sat beside her. The older woman looked into her eyes.

"I have to tell you why I kept you here."

"Aye." Fiona nodded, taking the prioress' hand. "Why didn't you send me to Dunfermline? You must have known you were risking your life keeping me here."

"Hmmph!" The prioress grunted. "At first you were so frail. So quiet and hurting inside. And I didn't have anyone to whom I could entrust you." She took the letter out of Fiona's hand. "She said to trust no one. I considered waiting until I could send a message directly to the king."

The prioress' voice had a vagueness to it, as if her mind were on something else, on some other time. Her attention suddenly riveted again on the present, and her tone recovered its directness. "But I also thought that if I couldn't get word to the king, then perhaps I *should* somehow send you to the schoolmaster at Dunfermline, to the poet Robert Henryson."

She placed a wrinkled hand against Fiona's smooth silky cheek. "You were just a wee innocent bairn, Fiona. But the Lord had other ideas about that, lass. Henryson may have been a man of learning, a poet renowned as a makar, but he was still just a mortal man. Just before the winter set in, we got word that the great poet had died of the flux. So that road was closed to us.

"And then when spring arrived, David went to Stirling and brought back news that the king was going to marry the English King Henry VII's daughter, Margaret Tudor. King James had resisted marrying for the sake of diplomacy, but after your mother died, some of his nobles convinced him that a marital union with England would be in Scotland's best interest. David was not able to get anywhere near the king."

"I can understand that he would not want an illegitimate daughter around when he was marrying a princess," Fiona said, fighting to keep out the note of bitterness that was edging its way into her voice. All these years he had never come for her. He had never searched for her.

"Nay, Fiona. That's not the truth," the nun protested. "You see, they thought you dead. They all did. The nobles, the court, your mother's family, even your father. We heard later that he was like a lost soul. That is, after your mother's death. And he looked everywhere for you. But I suppose he never thought that your fate would bring you all the way to Skye ... to our doorstep. And then, after that great storm, the king simply gave up."

Fiona looked at her hands silently. There was a deepening emptiness in her chest. She never knew her father.

"After that," the prioress continued, "I never had a clear opportunity to get you back to the court. You know that shortly after the king's marriage, the Western Isles rebelled against the king. We couldn't correspond with those who were allied with him. I certainly couldn't go to him directly. But honestly, I wouldn't have if it had been possible."

Fiona looked up questioningly at the older woman.

"There were rumors circulating that substantiate what you've said, Fiona. The word was that Margaret Drummond had been killed to clear the way for the king to marry the English princess. With Margaret Tudor's circle at court, I feared for your life."

The prioress stopped and gazed at the red-haired beauty she'd come to see as a daughter. What comforts she had not dared provide for Fiona, she had made up for in another way. She had given her the best education she could give. It had been an education befitting a princess.

"What made you decide to tell me now, m'lady?" Fiona asked, taking the prioress' hand in hers.

The old nun looked warmly at the young woman and then turned her gaze to the silent warlord who stood attentively by the hearth.

"I received my answer at last."

Standing up, she went to her worktable. From beneath a ledger book, the prioress retrieved another folded missive. Holding it up, she turned to Alec.

"I believe there is a messenger waiting for you at Dunvegan Castle with a message, as well, m'lord."

Alec looked at Fiona sitting expectantly on the chair. He savored this sight, but this was the last of her innocence. No, she was not yet aware of the impact of this news. Of the life that awaited her. An hour ago, he'd felt the love within him, felt his own strength. He had been ready to move mountains to make Fiona his forever.

But now, everything was different.

The nun returned to Fiona.

"You are at an age when your future must be decided. Now that Torquil is gone and Lord Alec is here, the Isle of Skye is once again part of Scotland. So I sent a message to Lord Huntly, and the nobles on the Council of Regents governing with him during the infant king's minority. Lord Huntly is known to be a good man, and he was always loyal to your father, so I told him that you are with us, and of the proofs that identify you. He has written back to say that he has been able to negotiate two things in your interest."

She handed the letter to Fiona. This was so much to burden the young woman with in one day, but Fiona had to know.

"But do I have any family left? Other than the infant

king, I mean," Fiona asked. Truthfully, she was not sure if she cared for this new identity. With her parents both dead, what purpose would all this trouble serve? Unless there was someone else. Family.

"Your last direct relation was your grandfather, John, Lord Drummond, but he died at Flodden. Your mother had two sisters, but they passed away before your grandfather. Since his death, everything has been held by Lord Gray, your great-uncle, with the condition that you would inherit everything if you were to reappear. Your grandfather never gave up hope, Fiona. I believe he must have felt some guilt about your mother's death. I suppose he truly hoped that the Lord would take some pity on him and restore you to him one day. People often want to make amends the most when they feel they've lost their best chance. At any rate, Lord Huntly has now spoken with Lord Gray, who has agreed to accept you 'with open arms' when you arrive, should the proofs be valid in the eyes of the governing nobles. And should that be the case, he will restore Drummond Castle and all its lands to you. In fact, Lord Huntly sends word from Lord Gray that his daughter Kathryn is looking forward to greeting her 'newfound cousin' en route from Skye."

Alec's thoughts wandered disgustedly back to Kathryn. Fiona's cousin. Now he knew why she had suddenly appeared at the Macphersons' Benmore Castle. Why she was stopping at Kildalton. She had heard the bad news. What she had thought to be hers would now belong to her long-lost cousin. Greeting . . . ha!

"Lord Huntly has also communicated with Queen Margaret," the prioress continued. "And she has agreed that should you renounce any claims regarding the 'crown, crown lands, or rights of succession for any of your issue,' she would acknowledge you as the daughter of the late king and formally welcome you in court."

The prioress sat beside Fiona and took the young woman's hand.

"I know it is not much compensation for the loss of a mother and a father, but what Lord Huntly has done is far more than we might have expected."

Fiona sighed, looking down at the letter in her lap. She was not sure she was quite ready for all this. But there was one thing she was certain of—she had no interest in any of those things which were so important to the queen.

"And there is one more thing. Huntly has conveyed the queen's wish that you go immediately to Stirling Castle."

"She wants to be certain that you take a vow of allegiance to her son, King James, immediately," Alec said from across the room. Before you get caught up in the politics of court, he thought to himself. And before you fall into the hands of such grasping courtiers as your uncle, Lord Gray.

Fiona looked up, startled at the news. Go? To the queen? Leave the Priory? Leave Skye? It's impossible, she thought, getting up and crossing to the window. How can I?

"M'lady prioress," she blurted out, whirling to face the woman who had crossed the room after her. "What of my work here? Malcolm and—"

"Fiona," the prioress soothed, taking her hand. "We will survive. Some of the young nuns are quite capable of dividing up your duties, and Sister Beatrice—"

"But m'lady, I want to take my vows! I want—"

"Fiona, my child, that is impossible." Though the prioress' wrinkled face was kindly, the quiet authority in her voice was unmistakable. "You are a lady, Fiona. Half-sister to the king. You have responsibilities that you cannot deny. Duties that take you beyond the walls of this Priory. We love you, child, and this has been your home, but you have another world that awaits you—a world we have, all along, been preparing you for."

Fiona looked into the confident eyes of the prioress. For a moment she could almost feel the old woman's strength and will flowing into her.

A world so different from her world here. A world where her mother had lived.

Fiona considered that world. A place where a young mother's life could be snuffed out like a candle. Where her murderers could go free while the world would think she had committed suicide.

Fiona thought back on that night. Her mind swirled with the images of blood and men, of her mother rushing about the room.

And then suddenly she remembered the leather pouch and the loose stone beside the fireplace.

The prioress had mentioned rumors about her mother's innocence. If she left the Priory at all, it would be for one thing—to prove the truth.

The only chance Fiona had lay hidden at Drummond Castle. She had to get there, and if the route took her first to the court at Stirling, so be it.

"But m'lady prioress, how do I get there?"

"That has been taken care of, my dear." The nun looked over at a thoughtful Alec, who stood quietly, his arms folded across his massive chest. "Lord Huntly has asked Lord Macpherson to convey you to Stirling."

Fiona turned her gaze to Alec, who quickly averted his eyes. He stared straight at the prioress.

She'll need all the protection she can get, Alec thought. It would not be long before the entire country buzzed with news of her discovery. There was every possibility of someone trying to snatch her away for good as they crossed the Highlands. Every power-hungry laird in Scotland would want to have Fiona tucked away in his own castle. Royal blood is royal blood; and power and fortune would belong to the nobleman who could capture her, impregnate her with an heir, and keep her from giving up her claims on the Crown wealth at Stirling.

"Do you have any objection to that, m'lord?" Fiona asked, her eyes searching his steely face questioningly.

"No, m'lady, I know what I must do." He straightened. "Please send word when you are ready to go. I'll prepare my men."

Alec strode toward the door and, without so much as a backward glance, disappeared into the dark corridor beyond the door.

Chapter 11

What has marred thee in thy mood,
Makyne, that to me thou show?
And what rules love, or being loved?
That law I'd like to know.
—ROBERT HENRYSON, *"Robene and Makyne"*

"Why does Alec hate me so much?" Fiona asked Ambrose.

Ambrose stood, momentarily speechless, unsure of how to answer such openness. Seeing Fiona here at Dunvegan had delighted him to no end. Truly, in spite of the fact that he had taken an immediate liking to her, she had more sense and spirit than Ambrose had given her credit for. And the late king's daughter besides . . . imagine that.

But Alec's sulking was becoming difficult to bear, and Ambrose was certain that his brother could go on like this for quite a while. Because of his past mistake with Kathryn Gray, Alec would perhaps never be ready to talk to Fiona and bring his concerns out in the open. In Alec's mind, Fiona had finally discovered family, people whom she never knew she had. He was not going to spoil it all by telling her the truth about the kind of people they were. And besides, he could only speak from his own experience with them.

But aside from all of this, she was entering a life of glamour and attention. A life Alec had run away from. He could just see it. With her beauty and wit, she would be the toast of the court in no time. This was not for him. He would not make the same mistake twice.

"I'm quite certain that Alec doesn't hate you," Ambrose assured Fiona.

"Then why is he behaving like such a boor?" Fiona paced back and forth before the small fire that was burning in the fireplace of Dunvegan Castle's Great Hall. Outside, the gray day was damp and chilly, but Fiona had hardly noticed as she and David rode up from the Priory. She had told David that she wanted to be there to take Malcolm back after his day's hunting with Alec, but her old friend knew better. She was angry, and when she went directly to Ambrose upon arriving at the castle, the prioress' brother had discreetly excused himself with the pretense of wanting to look after their horses.

"Is he, Fiona?" Ambrose smiled. "I hadn't noticed any change."

Fiona stopped and looked directly at him.

"You know that's not true, Ambrose," she said with quiet authority. "Since we received word from Lord Huntly, he hasn't come to see me even once. I sent him messages, told him that I needed to see him. But he hasn't responded. Not a word."

She resumed her pacing.

"At first I just thought he's been busy preparing for our departure and all."

He's been busy, all right, Ambrose thought. Busy tearing Dunvegan Castle and its people apart for the smallest reasons. The men had practically hidden themselves away from him in order to stay clear of his wrath.

"Then I thought, he must be upset with Lord Huntly for making such a request."

That was true, but a definite understatement. Alec's mood had been the foulest that Ambrose could ever remember.

"But all in all, I was blind to the fact," Fiona said bluntly.

"To what fact?"

"It is me. He hates me."

Ambrose held back his laughter. Between her and Alec, the two of them needed help.

"Fiona . . ."

"It's true! You didn't see the look he gave me when he came for Malcolm this morning. I told him I was coming with them, but he just glared at me and said that he wanted to spend time alone with Malcolm before he *had* to leave Skye. You had to see him . . . his look. It was as if I were nonexistent. His cold stare told me to stay away. To leave him alone. He hates me."

Ambrose listened with some surprise as Fiona continued to vent her frustrations. Pacing back and forth, she told him of a wasted day, waiting, fuming over Alec's unfeeling rejection. Whenever she glared up at him, Ambrose nodded gravely and compassionately. As she talked, he had a sense that she had come to him as an ally, though not against a common enemy. She had come seeking his support. Somehow, he was certain he would give it.

The sound of horses in the courtyard outside drew Ambrose's attention.

"Robert!" Ambrose shouted, then turned to Fiona. "You are upset and in few moments this room will be full of men looking for their supper. How about if we continue this discussion in Alec's study?"

She nodded in agreement and followed him toward an open doorway at the side of the hall.

"You called, Sir Ambrose?" Robert asked, approaching the two.

"Aye. Tell Cook to prepare a small meal for *two* and deliver it to the study." Ambrose turned in the squire's direction, adding almost as an afterthought, "And I don't want just anyone coming in and disturbing us."

Ambrose led Fiona into a small room lined with maps and books on one end. One wall was adorned with the Macpherson tartan and two shields, one bearing Alec's clan's coat of arms. Fiona's hand went unconsciously to her waist, to the dirk that was inscribed with the same markings, the one he had given her during the time when he was honest about his feelings. She swore under her breath.

She let her eyes travel to the other shield on the wall. That one bore the MacLeod clan arms.

Ambrose pushed the heavy oak door partially closed and pointed to a chair by the fireplace for Fiona to seat herself in. She shook her head and started pacing the room again. Ambrose went to the hearth and struck a spark into the prepared kindling. The small fire caught immediately, and he moved across the room, pulling a chair as far from the door as he could. He was not going to be too close to the action if he could help it.

"Aye, you were saying, Fiona ..." he prompted, settling back comfortably. This should be good, he thought.

"If I knew he cared—" she began, whirling around as the door of the study crashed open.

In the doorway, Alec stood, his feet spread and his fists clenched at his sides. His eyes traveled from Ambrose to Fiona.

"Welcome home, Alec," Ambrose said innocently. Robert had taken more time reporting to Alec than he had expected.

Alec's glare turned only for a moment to his brother's open expression before returning to Fiona.

"What are you doing at Dunvegan?" the warlord snapped, but he could not stop his eyes from slowly traveling the length of her. Damn it! Why must she look so fine? Why must she torture him this way? She was ... well, breathtaking. Damn it!

"I came here to talk to you," she responded, using the same tone.

"About what?"

"About us."

"There is nothing to talk about," Alec said in the most even, unfeeling tone he could manage. Then he steeled himself against the anguish he saw building in her beautiful eyes. The color that rose in her complexion.

She held her breath and stared at him in disbelief. She knew he was lying. It couldn't be true. Alec's face was distorted with anger, but his eyes were betraying him. And then she felt another emotion pushing at the pain she felt at his words.

Ambrose cleared his throat and stood.

"I'd better leave you two alone to—"

"Sit down, Ambrose!" Alec ordered, his eyes never leaving Fiona's. He hated himself for what he knew he had to do. But a clean break now would be infinitely less painful than waiting until they got to court. It would be only a matter of time before she would be swept away by the seductive lures of the court and her family. He wanted no part of that. And then there was the fact that she was King James's daughter. Fiona deserved the best, the noblest of men. She would have the opportunity to wed to kings. She would have the chance to live as a queen. And what did Alec have to offer? A man who had not even been able to save her father's life. It would be much better this way. He had to break it off now.

Ambrose watched in silence as Alec stepped into the room.

"You may go, Ambrose," Fiona ordered in a low voice that hardly hid her rising anger.

Ambrose watched in silence at the two bulls ready to butt heads.

"Sit down!"

"Go. Now!" Fiona's pitch now carried the full sharp edge of her fury.

Ambrose slowly worked his way toward the door. Alec turned around in surprise when he heard the oak door close behind his brother. When he turned back in her direction, she was still standing there, her eyes piercing him with their intensity.

There was a difference in her that struck Alec full in the face. It was in her eyes. There was an unwavering confidence. But he knew that air of assurance had always been there; he had just been too blind to see it.

It was difficult for Alec to imagine that Fiona could become more beautiful, but it had happened. She was no longer the young nun wearing the modest dark habit of the Priory. Now, she wore a hunter-green dress that she looked stunning in. Alec's eyes fell on the jeweled gold cross that hung below the round neckline and against the tight-fitting bodice of the gown.

But it wasn't the change in clothing that had mesmerized him. Nay, he admitted to himself, the change lay not only in her. The biggest difference was with himself.

From the moment Alec had first laid eyes on Fiona, he now realized, he'd only seen her as an innocent. As someone to protect. He had been too wrapped up in his own world. Like a hero in a legend, the savior of the helpless maiden. All he'd seen had been the difference. All he'd done, had been to compare. Fiona was virtue, Kathryn was decadence. He'd been blind to everything beyond that. He'd failed to truly see her, to recognize her, to value her. And now she stood before him. She was unchanged, the same woman ... but at last he could see her.

Fiona had no need of jewels and finery to show who she really was. He knew.

She was Fiona Drummond Stuart. Unchanged. The same woman she'd been from the first morning on that misty path, clothed like a leper, challenging him like a queen. Wit, courage, beauty, goodness. She was the fairy princess. The Angel of Skye.

They glared at one another across the room, both hiding the chaos that was spreading inside each of them. Alec stood, his arms folded across his chest, eyeing Fiona, who faced him, fists planted firmly on her hips, eyes green and blazing.

"The past two days, you have deliberately kept away from me," Fiona snapped. "And this morning, you openly rejected my request to go with you and Malcolm."

"You have many things to do to prepare for your journey." He shrugged, moving toward his worktable. Turning his back on her, Alec was conscious that he did not want Fiona to see his true feelings, feelings he was sure were clearly etched on his face. Yes, he'd kept away from her, but he had longed for her every minute that they'd been apart.

"Is that all you are concerned with?"

"What else is there?" Alec busied himself among the scrolls of paper piled between two wooden blocks on the tabletop.

She gazed at his broad back. He was suppressing his feelings, hiding them from her, pretending he didn't care. But Fiona knew he did indeed care. She had seen it in his face when he'd thundered into the room. His had not been the look of an indifferent man. No, Ambrose knew his brother too well—Alec's response to their being alone together was immediate and explosive. He cared, and she knew it.

"Something has happened, Alec. You're different. Angry." Fiona was going to get his attention, one way or another. She moved directly behind him. He towered above her.

"Different?" Alec responded without turning around. "I'm exactly the same."

"You are not. You have changed so much these past few days. It seems as though another person has taken over and—"

"You don't know anything about me," he interrupted coldly. "Malcolm and David are waiting. You'd better get on your way."

"That's all?" she steamed. "Get on my way? What has happened to you?"

"Nothing!" Alec said, lifting his eyes from the table and looking straight ahead. He did not want to turn and see the hurt in her. "I am the same. You just never knew me. You'd better go."

"You are not telling me the truth, and you know it. And as for knowing you, I do, indeed, know who you are," she asserted, poking him fiercely in the back. "You're a wretched, miserable, fainthearted laird of a rat-infested mainland dunghill."

Alec turned, dumbfounded in the face of her choice description. Her fiery eyes challenged him, ready to take him on. The rosy glow of an angry blush highlighted her silky skin. The firm curve of her mouth reflected the anger boiling within her.

"Deny it," Fiona pressed defiantly, jabbing her finger into his chest.

He glared. "You want me to fight you, is that it?" All at once he wanted desperately to hold her, to pull her close in his arms and to try and undo some of the pain that he'd given her.

"Aye, but I've no fear on that account, you low-down, cowardly son of a tinker."

Alec looked down at the flaming creature standing with her finger still pointed dangerously at his heart. There was no armor that he could don that would withstand a thrust from a weapon held by her.

"Really. Is there anything else you'd like to add?"

"Aye. You're a bleary-eyed, crusty, stiff-necked dwarf. Devoid of decency, kindness, or passion—"

One moment Fiona was standing and railing at the looming form, the next she found herself lifted into the air, her mouth stopped by a kiss.

She felt his lips crushing hers, and her breath caught with the suddenness of the onslaught. His tongue drove into her unresisting mouth, tasting and claiming all that he held. Fiona turned her face to allow him full access to the velvet richness of her depths. She threaded her fingers into his hair, pulling his mouth even harder against hers. Her own tongue swept against his, and a longing for him flared up from the core of her being. Pressed against him, drawing him ever more tightly, Fiona shuddered at the erotic sensation that suddenly flamed in her veins.

Colors whirled within her, setting her heart pounding and her head spinning. As if in a dream world, Fiona sensed she could not control her body, her life . . . certainly not her future.

Alec gripped her hard against his chest, feeling her arms wrap instinctively around his neck. He wanted her. He had tried to fool himself, pretending that he could just will away the longing that he felt for her. But that was impossible, and now the luxurious softness of her mouth confirmed—at a level deep within him—that there was no rejection, no escape, no denial.

But somewhere even deeper within him, lingering like a patch of spring snow in a dark and shaded glen, lay the certainty of a tortuous challenge, one he was not sure yet how to face.

Alec pulled his mouth away from hers, but Fiona would not allow more than a breath to separate them.

"You're not angry?" she whispered, lowering her hands from his neck and caressing the steel sinews of his chest. She could feel the pounding of his heart through the smooth linen of his shirt. His masculine scent filled her, bringing with it a deep satisfaction at being near him.

"I never was," he replied, brushing his lips downward across her temple, settling finally at the silky triangle beneath her ear. He felt her shudder in response to the movement of his lips against her skin.

She pushed him back against the edge of the oak table, and he sat, never releasing her. He pulled her to him, spreading his kilted legs to bring her even closer. She looked at him straight in the eye.

"You are a poor liar, m'lord," she said, kissing him tenderly on the chin.

"I just need more practice, m'lady." His mouth momentarily took possession of hers. Alec's hands caressed her slender shoulders and her back, feeling the full curve of her lower back, of her buttocks. He pulled her hips against his hardening manhood.

Her gasp of surprise was involuntary, but Fiona had no intention of moving away from him. She loved the feeling of him around her.

Alec kissed her again, thoroughly, deepening the kiss with every thrust of his tongue. As his hand moved along her sides to the curve of her breasts, he felt her melt against his touch. As his fingers gently teased the nipples he felt hardening beneath her soft green dress, he heard her groan from a place far down her throat.

My God, she is beautiful, he thought, overwhelmed by the taste and the scent of her. By her unexpectedly open response. By her wholehearted trust in him.

Alec pulled away from the kiss, confused for an instant by a thought which transcended the present moment. A thought of court and of travel. Of a future that was devoid of life. A future without her. Like a rush of demons, these thoughts came, flooding his brain with images of court, of Drummond Castle, of the obstacles and the people that would try to tear them apart. Into his brain came the cold, loveless face of Kathryn Gray. Alec shut his eyes and fought against the unwelcome image pushing its way into his consciousness. Like a throbbing pain momentarily forgotten, the thought came back to him. Nagging. Unwelcome.

But then Fiona's hands settled on his hips, and he looked into eyes that were seeing only him. And they were eyes filled with warmth, eyes that scarcely hid a deep bank of glowing coals, the embers of desire. She was lit from within.

Lightning flashed in his brain when her tongue traced the line of his lower lip. Her fingers dug into him, reclaiming him.

Alec's hands reached around her again, and he moved his hips firmly against her. He could feel her move with him, her warmth grinding gently against his now throbbing desire. He looked into Fiona's eyes. The look in her eyes told him all he wanted to know. Her look matched his desire. Then her fingers slipped under the cloth of his shirt, and a roaring began in Alec's head that blocked out the world.

When Fiona felt his strong hands on the laces of her dress, an excitement raced through her that she had never before known. She knew what was happening, and she was ready for it. Her breaths became labored as the front of her dress opened to his touch. His hands pulled the silk chemise away from her skin, and his fingers gently slipped across the sensitive aureole of her nipple, and Fiona closed her mind to conscious thoughts, unwanted doubt, and unwarranted fear.

Alec gazed in admiration at the firm roundness of her full breasts, freed of the dress and undergarment that had imprisoned them. As he pushed the soft material down, he felt her pulling her arms out to aid him in his passionate quest. His mouth descended again upon the voluptuous flesh of her upturned mouth. Her parted lips received his in a warm exchange before his tongue traced a line from her chin along the line of her throat and onto the startlingly white skin of her breast.

Fiona leaned back as his tongue seared her flesh. She groaned deep in her throat as he flicked at the skin of her breast, but when his mouth took possession of her nipple, blinding flashes of white exploded in her brain, and a molten liquidity erupted deep within her. Her fingers laced his golden hair, and she held his head tightly to her. Fearing that he might stop, Fiona ceased breathing, but not before a shudder racked her body.

The tremor that went through her was enough to tear through the cloud of Alec's desire. The fires that were raging in his loins were nearly out of control, but he knew that he had allowed his passion to overwhelm his reason. He had to stop. He would not take advantage of his position with her. Their actions right now might be right and good, but they would undoubtedly be suspect to those powers that awaited her. With a herculean effort to control his actions, his desire, Alec paused momentarily, raising his head and crushing her against him. His lips found the soft roundness of her ear, and he felt her short breaths against his neck.

"Fiona," he whispered through clenched teeth. "We must stop."

"Alec," she responded breathlessly, her lips tasting the skin of his neck. "Why? Why must we stop?"

His hands grasped the smooth skin of her arms, and he pushed her gently away from him. Looking at the perfection of her body, he drew a great breath and pulled her chemise and her dress up onto her shoulders.

Her thoughts confused, Fiona looked at Alec intently as he resignedly laced up the front of her dress. Fiona placed her hands on his muscular thighs, and Alec stopped as if an arrow had pierced his body. As they looked into each other's eyes, she began to slide her hands up beneath the plaid of his kilt toward the hardened arousal she had felt throbbing against her.

"Don't!" he nearly shouted, his great palms descending on her hands, trapping them between the kilt and his thighs. He glared at her, a half-smile creasing his face. "Fiona, you are not helping me. If you touch me, I know I won't be able to control myself."

"I don't want to stop, Alec," she replied, looking steadily into his eyes. "I want to be with you."

"Fiona, I want to be with you, too," he responded gently. "These days away from you have been hell for me. I've wanted you beside me every waking moment, and the nights have been long and restless. But this ... what we are doing here ... this is not the time or the place, lass."

"Then why did you stay away?" Fiona let her hands drop to her sides.

Alec paused, thinking of all that he wanted to say but couldn't. He knew that the bitterness he felt for court life was a personal experience, and not a shadow that he wanted to cast over Fiona's future. But he had to explain himself somehow. She deserved an answer.

"Fiona, you are about to enter a life that holds a great many opportunities for you." People, position, places. A life he had just turned his back on. One he had no reason ... no desire ... to be a part of. He had been there. As a young warrior, he had been part of that throng. And he had experienced the lust, the greed that went along with it. He had thought himself happy. All the joys of worldly living had been there for the taking. What else could anyone want in this life?

Alec Macpherson had learned the bitter price of such a life. His own betrothed had given him a taste of what he'd given others. He questioned it now. Whose wife had he himself slept with? Whose heart had he wounded? Which man had lain awake for how many nights wondering whose child his wife was carrying? Aye, he'd never thought of those things then. These comic details of court life. For it had never been him. Not until Kathryn.

Suddenly, fears that had never before existed now haunted him. He'd had to get away. For the first time in his life he'd found himself wallowing in a mire of fraud and deception. He found it engulfing him. Drowning him.

Aye, that was court. People, position, places.

Alec cast around for a way to tell her of the constant barrage she would face by those offering sugared and empty promises while at the same time sucking the blood from her veins. Changing her. And there would be the occasional honest courtier, but how would she ever pick him from the pack?

"What are you afraid of?" Fiona asked gently.

"Afraid?"

"Aye. I can see the argument raging within you. And I can also see you are losing. But that's not all I can see. I can see that you are not fighting back. Your fears are holding you back. You've dashed away your armor. You have no sword. No shield. I'm no warrior, but even I would not step into this battle unarmed."

"I did not think I said so much!" Alec smiled.

She touched his fisted hands. They opened and took hers. "Talk to me, Alec. Give me a chance. Perhaps I can help you win."

"I wish it were so easy."

"You'll never know until you tell me. Perhaps it is. Perhaps you are making more out of this than you should."

"I don't think I am," Alec said, letting his hands gather hers in. "It's your future that worries me."

"Is it that bad?" She smiled, drawing a half smile from him.

"Nay! It doesn't have to be."

"Good. Then help me. Show me."

Alec's face again grew grave. "I might not be the best man for it."

"But I say you are. And, we won't know until you try, will we?" she asked.

"How about your future responsibilities? The people? The ones that will follow and admire you? Life has so much in store for you. You may want to wait and see."

"I've seen where such admiration can lead. I am a product of it. And for that my mother paid a heavy price." Was this the cause of his withdrawal, she wondered. She had to make him understand. "Alec, I want no part of it."

"What happened to your mother is not going to happen to you, Fiona. You are the king's half-sister. Your blood is royal. You will have position, power, and wealth." Alec thought of the great matches that might be made for Fiona. Matches with men who were not running to the ends of the earth to escape the deceit of false lovers. With men who had never failed in their duty to their king. With men worthy of her. Better men than Alec Macpherson. "After you see all that brings, you may wish to choose another ..."

"There will be no other, Alec. And those things mean nothing to me without you. I will not stay there."

Alec fought off a surge of joy at her words. He would like nothing better than to build a life with her away from court. But he caught himself. She had not yet seen that life, and Alec was not certain she would still feel the same way, having experienced it. How could she? And who could blame her. He looked into her innocent face.

He knew then that he loved her as he had never loved before.

But he could not let her know. Not yet. Not while her uncle still had a say in her future. Alec was sure Lord Gray would have his own thoughts on the matter. And those thoughts were certain to exclude Alec Macpherson.

"Just tell me one thing," Fiona said, pulling away and moving toward the hearth. "Do you want me?"

Alec gazed at her slender form as she turned to face him. A knock at the door drew their attention, but neither moved.

"More than life itself, Fiona."

Chapter 12

In vice most vicious he excels
That with the vice of treason mells ...
—WILLIAM DUNBAR, *"Epitaph for Donald Oure"*

Malcolm was pleading with Fiona, to which she replied, "I've told you a hundred times. I would *love* to have you with me, but it is not time for you to leave Skye. And more importantly, it is not safe." She looked at the unhappy lad, feeling in her own heart the same anguish she knew he was feeling.

It definitely would not be safe, Fiona thought. Word had come two days ago that their travel plans had changed. Instead of going by ship to Kildalton Castle, home of Alec's friend Colin Campbell, the Earl of Argyll, and then overland to Stirling, Alec had decided it would be best to go quickly overland to Benmore Castle. But this information had to be kept secret. There were dangers, and Alec felt they were not far off.

He had changed their plans because Walter's grandson had returned with startling news. Adrian had indeed gone to Dunvegan Castle the day of the attack on Fiona. Arriving at the palisade-enclosed main stables outside the castle walls, he had spotted Iain walking toward the stables with Neil. Immediately recognizing Iain as the man who had attacked his grandfather, Adrian had secretly followed them, hiding himself in the loft and listening to their conversation. He had been surprised to hear smatterings of words about hurting Fiona and Malcolm, but from what he could hear, it was clear that Iain had acted on Neil's orders in the attack on Father Jack. Then the boy had watched in horror as Neil cold-bloodedly murdered his accomplice when the warrior had turned his back.

Adrian had remained in hiding while men from the castle had bustled about below. He had listened while Neil lied to Ambrose Macpherson about everything that had occurred, and when Neil rode out shortly after, Adrian had crept out, determined to follow him and stop him from hurting his friends.

Neil had ridden north for a few miles, and then had turned east across the Isle of Skye. Adrian followed him, getting the help of a fisherman to ferry him after the MacLeod leader left Skye for the mainland. For four days Adrian followed Neil on foot into the Highlands. Finally he lost him in the land around Ben Nevis, where the Gregor clan lives. Adrian then worked his way back to the Isle of Skye, hungry and tired, but assured that Neil was nowhere close enough to hurt anyone.

Because of this information, Alec was now anxious to reach Benmore Castle as quickly and as quietly as possible. There were two reasons for his concern. One, word of Fiona's survival had spread, and they would be more vulnerable going by boat on the open water. Two, Neil might be able to muster enough troops among the Gregors to try to take Dunvegan in Alec's absence.

Alec had told Fiona and the prioress that a small force, traveling quickly and without advance notice, would have a better chance of reaching Benmore Castle without incident. And he also felt that, once at Benmore, he could get more Macpherson men to return directly to Skye, thereby reinforcing Ambrose. That accomplished, he would feel much more comfortable taking a larger group of warriors from Benmore to accompany them on the rest of their journey.

Now, with all the uncertainty about this trip, the last thing Fiona wanted was to expose Malcolm to the hazards of what lay ahead.

"You could take me," Malcolm asserted, raising his head from the charcoal drawing he was working on. "I'm not afraid. Alec calls me a gallant young knight and says that I am as brave as any warrior he's had."

Fiona smiled at the angelic little face shining with pride. It was incredible to see the effect of Alec's genu-

ine attentions on the young lad. She felt her heart swell
in her chest at the thought of the man.

Fiona shook her head in an attempt to clear it of all
the daydreaming she knew would follow.

"So, what do you say to that, Fiona? I could come
and take care of you."

"Thank you, Malcolm," she said affectionately. "But
don't forget, you promised Alec that you'd take care of
his falcons for him. And I'll come back as soon as I can.
I promise."

"You promise?"

"Aye."

"But *when*?" Malcolm persisted. "When are you coming back?"

Fiona stared at the boy. Pulling him onto her lap, she
hugged him fiercely. She *would* come back. Alec would
bring her back. She'd make certain of that. Her thoughts
drifted to what lay beyond their journey . . . to the court.
But what would come after that journey haunted her.
Drummond Castle. Yes, she needed to find the truth.
Go she must.

"Tell me, Fiona. When?" The little boy's voice broke
into her thoughts.

"Malcolm, if you think that keeping me from my work
will stop me from going . . ."

"Fiona, I don't want you to go away," the boy sobbed.
All of Malcolm's prior show of courage melted away as
the reality of her departure descended upon him. He
stood up and buried his face in her neck.

She held him tight, her own throat knotting at the
thought of leaving him, of leaving all that she held dear.
Well, nearly all.

Alec had sent Robert with word. He was coming for
her at dawn tomorrow. They had not seen each other
since the day she had gone to Dunvegan. These past few
days had been hectic ones for Fiona. Not because her
own meager possessions were difficult to pack, but because of all the other things she needed to do. Dividing
her duties among the nuns. Visiting the farms around
the Priory. Helping the two young novices who had
jumped at the chance to continue her work with the
lepers.

But her trip to Father Jack's cottage had been particularly difficult. True, Walter's leg no longer caused him any pain and he was improving daily. Indeed, although he was anxious to try putting weight on it, he was obeying the curmudgeonly priest's orders to stay put. So Fiona was confident her old friend would continue to heal properly. Walter would, at least, walk again.

But saying good-bye to these two good men had been truly painful, and now, sitting in her workroom, holding Malcolm to her, Fiona felt the tears, wet upon her face.

Alec stood in the open courtyard of the Priory amid a jostling crowd of subdued men and restless horses. The dawn was breaking clear and fresh, and in spite of their effort otherwise, the excitement of the coming journey pervaded the air. Stableboys ran between the stamping horses with buckets of water and feed, while villagers poured into the yard, mingling among the warriors with a growing cacophony of voices. Nuns and servants from the Priory also circulated among the men, distributing bread and skins of ale.

Malcolm had been standing beside him, taking in the bustling scene, but when Alec looked down, he saw the lad was missing. Scanning the yard, he caught sight of the boy talking with Ambrose, who was crouched before the boy, obviously involved in some deep and serious conversation. Alec smiled, wondering what trouble Ambrose was brewing now.

Ambrose had come to the Priory to see that all went as planned. And his part in the journey was pivotal. At the same time Alec and Fiona were going off across the Highlands, Ambrose would be sending a boat with a number of Macphersons aboard as a decoy along the coast to Kildalton. Alec and he had decided that this could be enough of a distraction to guarantee safe passage to Benmore Castle.

"Alec, are you very old?" a small voice chirped worriedly beside him.

Alec looked down into Malcolm's round eyes. The little boy slipped his hand into Alec's.

"What has Ambrose told you now, Malcolm?"

"He's worried about your health."

"How so, lad?"

"He just said that such a long, hard ride with Fiona

might be too much for your old heart to handle. He says Fiona is young and hearty, but that you're getting old and soft."

"Oh, he does?" Alec glared at his brother, who was innocently watching the two from a safe distance.

"Aye, he says what may lie ahead is not like holding hands in church." Malcolm peered intently at his friend. "Do you and Fiona hold hands in church?"

"Nay, lad," Alec responded, never taking his eyes off his brother. "Ambrose has a strange sense of humor."

"Nay, Alec, he wasn't joking," the boy replied. "He was quite serious when he said he'd be glad to take your place on such a ride."

"Excuse me, Malcolm," Alec said through clenched teeth, taking a few steps after the retreating Ambrose. "I have a few things I need to discuss with my generous brother."

But all thoughts of his brother disappeared when the old porter stepped in front of Alec. The warlord had looked for James when they rode in, but the place beside the gate had been empty.

"There's a bairn in the castle, m'lord," the ancient one cackled. His eyes were glazed, his face stern.

"What? A bairn?" Alec's attention was riveted on the man. "At Dunvegan?"

"Nay. At a place where the angel waits. A bairn. She carries your bairn." The seer gazed vaguely beyond Alec's shoulder. "A mother ... troubled ... so troubled. So far away."

"I don't understand, James." Alec placed a great hand gently on the man's shoulder. It was nothing but bone beneath his fingers. "You must tell me."

The porter turned his gaze to Alec's face. His eyes burned into the warrior. "Beware, m'lord. The angel awaits, but the devil lingers nigh." Turning his nodding head, the seer backed away from the warrior.

"James! Wait ... I—"

"Take care of your bairn, m'lord," the porter said, moving away. "I'll tell ye more when I know."

"Something wrong, Alec?" The warlord glanced quickly at Ambrose, who had joined his brother.

"Nay, I ..." Alec looked back at where the ancient porter was standing, but there was no sign of him. Pushing through the throng, the giant caught no further glimpse of the old man. He was gone.

Fiona pushed open the heavy oak door of the prioress' workroom. Already a small fire flickered on the hearth, and she could see in the half-light the nun standing silhouetted by the light of the window.

The prioress had her back to Fiona, her hands clasped behind her. She appeared to be staring out at the activity in the yard.

"M'lady," Fiona called softly, stepping into the room. "I'm ready to leave."

The prioress turned partially at the sound of her voice, and Fiona saw her hand move quickly to her face, wiping away the tears that were rolling down her lined cheeks.

"Aye, child," she answered, her voice clear. "I can see that they are ready for you."

"Thank you for letting David come with us," Fiona said. David had volunteered to accompany Fiona until she reached Drummond Castle. Fiona believed this last-minute offer had a lot to do with Alec's concerns for the propriety of her traveling with a group of men. Sister Beatrice, her initial traveling companion, simply could not travel due to her worsening cough. So David had stepped forward, the logical choice and one agreeable to everyone.

"He will do whatever needs to be done, child." The prioress continued to look out the window. "He loves you like a daughter, as much as ... I do."

Fiona crossed the room, pausing hesitantly within a step of the older woman. The prioress turned and opened her arms to her, and the two embraced with unabashed affection.

"We will miss you, child," the prioress exclaimed haltingly. "I will miss you."

"Will you have me back if things don't work out as they—"

"This will always be your home, Fiona," the prioress asserted, taking hold of the young woman's arms and looking into her face. "You will always be our beloved angel. Don't you ever forget that."

Fiona hugged the woman tightly to her again as the tears began to course down her face.

The two stood in silence, each thinking of the past they had shared, of the moments of joy, and of what each had learned from the other. The prioress could still remember the wild little kelpie running the countryside, skirts pulled up to her scratched and bruised knees, her hair flying behind, on her shoulder a satchel with goods for the poorer folk. And she remembered the young girl sitting by her falcons' empty mews the day Fiona had let them all loose. The prioress smiled, remembering the lass sitting there, fearful and yet brave in the face of certain punishment, but with a constant belief that she had done the right thing.

Fiona's thoughts, too, dwelled on memories of the past. Of the many times when she had lain awake in her bed, banished from dinner and in disgrace for some disturbance she had caused, pretending to be asleep when the prioress would come to her, as she always did, with a plate of food and a gentle word of forgiveness. She thought of the older woman's constant reminders of the things to be concerned with in the wicked world outside the Priory gates ... all the while encouraging Fiona to experience what she could and to apply all that she was learning.

The prioress patted Fiona's back and took her by the hands. The nun cocked an eyebrow at her.

"But don't think these mainlanders are going to rush you off before I give you one last counseling session."

Fiona smiled at the prioress through misty eyes and obediently followed her across the room, sitting in one of two chairs by the fireplace.

"I want you to know, Fiona," the prioress began, leaning forward and taking her hand again. "I have no fear that you will conduct yourself in a manner befitting the blood that flows in your veins."

"M'lady, I am the same person—" Fiona began. She was uncomfortable about the reference to her parentage.

The prioress silenced her with a look and a squeeze of Fiona's hand for emphasis.

"You can't change who you are, child, but what I fear is this unknown past that you are riding into. You have a great, open, and loving heart. But don't trust anyone, Fiona. There was a reason your mother wanted to send you far away to the poet Henryson. The ones that hurt her, the ones she feared ... they could still be there to hurt you."

"Is there anything else that you know about that time, about my mother? Was there anyone else whom I could look to for help?"

The prioress thought for a moment. She wanted to give Fiona any information that might help her, but everything she had learned over the years was secondhand, gleaned from a procession of travelers and friends.

"Of course, there is always Lord Alec and his family. Alexander Macpherson, his father, is a good and decent man, Fiona. But he'll not be at court to help you." The prioress searched her memory. "I know very little about your uncle, Lord Gray, but there is someone else who could be a good friend."

"Who, m'lady?" Fiona looked at the nun expectantly. She had a feeling she would be needing all the allies she could find to vindicate her mother's reputation.

"Lord Huntly. The man to whom I sent word of your presence here. You should know this, Fiona. Because your half-brother, the king, is only a bairn, all the power in Scotland lies in the hands of a group of nobles ... headed by Lord Huntly. He is the most influential man at court. More powerful than the queen. And though he has already done you great service, I believe he will do more if you ask him."

"Why, Prioress?" Fiona asked. "What is his interest in me?"

"From what I have heard, Lord Huntly was ... well, an ardent suitor of your mother's."

"Do you mean he wanted my mother's hand?"

"Aye, Fiona. I mean he was madly in love with her. He made no secret of it, and he always said he would someday win her back."

"But he never did."

"Nay, lass. He never did."

Chapter 13

There I saw Nature present her a gown
Rich to behold and noble of renown,
Of every hue under heaven ...
—WILLIAM DUNBAR, *"The Goldyn Targe"*

Familiarity breeds contentment, Alec thought.

For the first few days, Fiona had been complaisant enough. In fact, she'd been better than he'd expected—following the lead, staying to herself, occasionally exchanging a word or two with Robert. And Alec had been at peace.

Then, starting a second week in the saddle, she'd become restless and agitated. Around midmorning today, she'd galloped to the front of the line, where she and Alec had argued like tinkers over the fact that she'd wanted to ride in front with him. In too brusque a tone, Alec had adamantly refused, explaining the dangers, the difficulty of protecting her there.

But Fiona hadn't listened. When Alec had demanded that she get back, she'd called him names. Finally, after he'd threatened to gag her and tie her to her horse, she'd called him a bully and had marched back to the middle of the pack. She had ignored him since.

He missed her harassment.

Alec knew his disposition had gone downhill from the moment the group had left the Priory gates. All along the way there had been people waiting for them as they went by; crofters and fishermen, MacLeods and MacDonalds, even lepers had come out to wish her farewell. At every turn there had been an emotional outpouring for her. But his response to this attention had grown progressively sullen. After all, for the safety of all involved, he had wanted to leave the island covertly, without too many knowing which way they planned to travel. But with everyone in Skye seeming to know about their route, Alec was certain that the whole of Scotland also knew.

It certainly appeared that he'd been correct. After crossing to the mainland at Kyle of Lochalsh, they had been surprised by a crowd of well-wishers who had gathered at the dock. But the murmurs of support that went through the throng were directed not at a king's daughter. Alec had heard the voices, and he'd heard the word "angel" over and over, like a chant. Like a prayer.

But he had worried as they'd crowded close around her—reaching out, touching her. He knew that his fellow Highlanders' belief in the supernatural was deeply rooted and strong. And Fiona was a living incarnation of that faith. He now knew that her deeds had long ago become legendary in this part of the country and that it was only natural for news of her real identity to travel ahead of them like a brushfire across a moor.

But he could not risk future scenes like this. She had no fear. No reservation. In every instance, despite Alec's objection, Fiona had dismounted and joined the peasants. It was amazing how the people poured their hearts out to her and how she responded. She was all compassion and kindness. All generosity and tenderness. Alec glowed inwardly with a sense of pride looking on her, but he forced himself to focus on his task—her safety was at stake.

When had her safety not been on his mind? Concerns had been dogging him the entire trip, but not without good reason. The attack on Fiona had not been a matter of her simply being an available victim for the outlaws.

Not long after Neil MacLeod had left Skye, a nagging idea had occurred to Alec. It was at least possible that Neil MacLeod himself had instigated the attack on Fiona. But Neil was not a thinking man—he followed orders—and that bothered Alec even more. And the gold they had discovered on the dead men after the attack had only confirmed Alec's theory.

There were powers out there that wanted her destroyed. The potential enemies and the list of motives were plentiful, and scattered across Scotland. There was

Kathryn, who, by having Fiona alive, would lose Drummond Castle and all that went with it. Then there were the men that had killed Fiona's mother. It was very possible they were still alive. Would Fiona be able to recognize them? While she'd been on Skye, after the attack, Alec had made certain that she was guarded and watched all the time. But here in the open countryside, it was a different story.

So as they continued, he had pushed them to travel at a breakneck pace. They had ridden late into the darkness each night, and started out early, sleeping and stopping for only the hours needed to rest themselves and the horses. Alec had planned it so they would skirt villages when they could, following the mountains and the lochs east into the Highlands and finally crossing Loch Ness where it narrowed beneath the impressive profile of Ben Nevis.

Now they were only two days' ride away from Benmore Castle, and Alec was all too aware of the weary but stalwart face of Fiona all day. The last thing he wanted was to jeopardize her health by pushing too hard.

The warriors and the squires were busy setting up camp on the edge of the shimmering Loch Lochy. Above them, a bluff was reflecting the golden light of the descending sun. Alec had been delighted to see the bluff and the ruined stone tower perched on top of it, for this landmark was familiar ground. For the first time since they'd left the Isle of Skye, Alec was beginning to feel at ease.

Casting his eye around the bustling groups of men and horses, he searched for his sparring partner. This journey was taking forever as far as Alec was concerned. So many nights staring up at the starlit sky, he'd wanted to go to her. Having her so close and yet so unreachable was becoming more intolerable with each passing day. And night.

But he'd forced himself to stay away, refusing to give in to longing on his part that might compromise her future.

Tonight, looking around him, he decided enough was enough. He ached for her company, for her barbed wit, for the pleasure of just being near her. That is, if she'd consent to even talk to him.

David was sitting on a fallen tree by the loch, eating his evening ration of oat cakes and dried meat with Robert. As Alec approached, the two looked up at him with a puzzled look on their faces.

"Well, where is our serene little dove?" Alec asked with a smile. "Out upbraiding the warriors for their mistreatment of the horses?"

They stared at him in silence for a moment, the drinking cup en route to Robert's mouth frozen in his hand.

"She's not with you?" David blurted out, leaping to his feet.

Alec looked hard at the two.

"Why would she be with me?"

"M'lord, she left a half hour ago." Robert blurted out.

"Aye," David broke in. "Robert told her you knew the connection between that tower up there and the late king."

"She was asking . . . she said she was going to find out more . . ." Robert stammered.

"We thought she was going to ask you."

Alec turned quickly, glancing up the bluff at the stone pile at the top.

"I'll go after her," he said. "There's no telling what she might run into out here after the sun goes down. We don't want to put any lions or wolves in any unnecessary danger."

"Do you want me to come along?" David asked. "For safety's sake?"

"Nay," Alec said, patting the sword at his side. "I'm more heavily armed than she."

Striding to where Robert had tethered Ebon, Alec leaped onto the bare back of the steed.

"Lord Alec," David called walking up and tossing the rider a hastily assembled packet of food and drink. "She may be more amenable to coming back with you if you're willing to take the time and show her the tower."

Alec held the packet up quizzically. "And what is this for, bribery?"

They both laughed. Then, wheeling the horse toward the steep and winding trail leading to the summit, Alec disappeared into the lengthening shadows.

*   *   *

Leaving the circuitous route the trail was following, Fiona directed her steps onto the steeper, more rugged path up the cliff face. Warm from the climb, Fiona had draped her cloak over one shoulder. She shook her hair free of its braid as she peered up at her goal. As she drew nearer and nearer to the top, she grew too caught up in her own excitement to pay any attention to the sun descending behind her. The old trail she was following was nearly obliterated by the leaves, briars, and ferns that clung to the rocky face of the bluff. When she felt the hem of her dress catch on an encroaching branch, Fiona hiked her skirt up, tucking the hem into the belt encircling her waist.

The sound of falling water came from somewhere above, and Fiona continued the final leg of her sojourn. The evening was warm, and the air on her legs felt good as she climbed.

Reaching a small gorge just below the summit, Fiona found herself facing a shallow and rocky pool surrounded by clumps of birch and green ferns. She breathed the fresh coolness of the air and dropped to her knees beside the clear, burbling water. Swinging her legs around, she removed her shoes and dipped her dusty feet into the cold, spring-fed pool with a slight shiver.

Fiona glanced up past the small waterfall to the tower, just a few yards above her. She'd made it, and a sense of satisfaction swept through her. There was no one around, and the quiet security of the glen offered the moment of peace Fiona had sought.

Tossing her cloak and shoes onto the bank, the young woman unlaced the top of her dress. Cupping the water with her hands, she began to wash the bare skin of her legs and her arms. Then she stopped and straightened up.

This is ridiculous, she thought, looking about her again. Wading to the bank, Fiona unfastened the belt that held the dagger Alec had given her. Then she quickly stripped off the soft wool dress, pulling her arms free and pushing the garment down over her hips. Standing in the glen in her chemise, she felt a sudden thrill of liberation as the warm breeze caressed her naked shoulders. Walking back into the pool, Fiona made her way into the deeper area beneath the falling water and submerged her shivering body in the cleansing spring-fed currents.

Surfacing, Fiona felt the gooseflesh rise at the cold shock of the water, but she enjoyed the sensation. It was a refreshing pause from the hot and demanding days in the saddle and from the strenuous climb. She swam back and forth in the confined space, wondering whether her absence had been discovered yet by those below.

Standing to squeeze the water from her long mane, Fiona paused ... and found herself wishing him here.

True, she was tired of riding in the grimy wake of Alec and his warriors, but she wanted to ride with him, talk to him. She had missed his attention, his wit, the lingering looks that made her skin come alive while those warm, liquid feelings filled her insides with longings she had never known.

And there were so many questions that she had. So many that she hoped Alec would answer. But he had been surly, ill-tempered, and had not been very receptive to her very civil advances.

Safety, my eye, she thought. What she'd already put up with was more than any reasonable person could possibly be expected to endure. Quietly, that is.

Today, she'd reached the end of her patience. She'd felt tired, filthy, and quite fed up with being treated like a cow on the way to market.

But she felt differently now.

Wading back to the edge of the pool, Fiona quickly pulled the wet chemise over her head and dried herself with her cloak. She was shivering uncontrollably by the time she put her dress back on. She tried to dry her hair as best as she could, then ran her fingers through the wavy mass. She hung her chemise on a nearby branch to dry. Then she sat on the cloak, leaning back on her hands, her head tipped back, her hair a blanket spread around her. She felt good, relaxed.

It was true, she had called him a few names. Good ones. They all seemed to fit. Well, she thought with a smile, not exactly.

She took a deep breath, inhaling the invigorating air.

She certainly had not made life very easy for him today. She sighed, again wishing him here.

"Alec Macpherson," she called out softly, smiling at the sound of the name in the serenity of the glade. The name suited him: strong, colorful, noble, beautiful.

"Aye, m'lady," the voice responded from the rocky ledge above the pool.

She leaped to her feet. "You!" Fiona blurted, watching him perched comfortably on the rocks. "You—you scared me half to death."

Alec stayed where he was, captivated by the sheer beauty of the woman before him. His hard ride up from the loch had been faster than Fiona's climb, and he'd arrived at the base of the tower in time to catch glimpses of Fiona working her way up the face of the bluff. When she hadn't gotten to the tower when he judged she would, Alec had started down, only to find her going into the clear waters of the pool.

When she'd begun to swim, he considered calling out to her, but then had quietly settled on the rocks, content to watch her at her simple pleasures, enraptured by the exquisite charm of the scene.

But then, when she had walked out of the water, her chemise clinging so provocatively to her perfectly sculpted body, Alec had stopped breathing. And when Fiona removed the thin wet undergarment, the young laird had thought his heart would burst through the wall of his chest.

She was a vision. Like some wood nymph, like some unearthly being, some goddess, gracing the waters of the glade with her beauty, with her very presence.

Suddenly, involuntarily, Alec averted his eyes. Etiquette called for him not to watch, to turn away, to offer this solitary Diana in human form the privacy she had obviously sought. But then Alec's gaze swept back, drinking in the scene. For this was Fiona, the woman he loved, cherished, and desired. Privacy be damned.

"I don't think I've ever seen a fairy in her element before," Alec said. "And I'm sure I've never heard one call my name under a greenwood tree."

Fiona stood looking at him, her hands at her sides, unsure of whether she should deny the suggestion or not.

"Have you been . . ." She flushed. "Have you been there long?"

"Ages."

With a nimble movement, the warlord leaped from his ledge to the bank beside the bubbling waterfall and strode to where Fiona stood.

"You weren't watching me," she declared hopefully. "You wouldn't . . . would you?"

Alec took her swiftly in his arms and drew her tightly to him, stopping her questions with a hard and thorough kiss. He drew his lips back from hers.

"You tell me, love."

Fiona gasped for breath, her heart racing at the suddenness of his embrace. Where he held her waist tightly against his own body, she could feel his arousal hard against her.

"You are a scurvy rogue, Alec Macpherson," she whispered. But the sound of her words lacked any sign of conviction, even to Fiona. Something within tingled at the thought of his eyes on her, of his hardened manhood pressing against her so intimately. She knew she was blushing madly. She grasped for something to say. Where is your wit now? she thought to herself. "It's . . . it's lovely here, isn't it?"

"Aye," Alec responded, never taking his eyes off her. "It is lovely, indeed."

Fiona's eyes and his locked in an exchange of longing. Then the reality of the moment sank in, astonishing her. She wanted him. And the want was more than spiritual. It came to her plain and simple. It was physical. She wanted him to hold her, to run his hands over her, to kiss her . . . and more.

She had to step away, to clear her head, to calm the violent pounding of her heart. She gently pushed at his chest, and he released her.

Alec stepped back. Then, with a quick movement, he unfastened his sword from the leather belt at his waist, dropping the sheathed armament to the ground beside Fiona. She glanced up at him hastily, startled by the suddenness of the act.

"What are you doing?" she asked.

"What do you think I'm doing?" Alec grinned mischievously, undoing the clan broach that held his tartan in place. He dropped them both onto the sword. "I'm going for a swim."

"With me here?" Fiona blurted.

"With you here," he repeated seductively.

"You'll do no such thing. You can find your own—"

"Don't they even teach sharing in that convent?"

"What?" She watched as he kicked off his boots, exposing his muscular calves.

"Sharing, Fiona." He stole a quick kiss. Then, straightening, he started pulling the shirt out of his kilt. "Sharing. Of course you could, if you like, go swimming with me."

"Swimming? With you?" Her voice trailed off as Alec removed his shirt, and she was confronted with the golden skin of his muscular chest.

Like a god he stood framed by the glowing light of the sun behind him. Like Phoebus Apollo he loomed. Magnificent. Fiona ached to reach out to him, to run her fingers across the rippling lines of his powerful warrior's body. As if the wind had been knocked from her, she stood. Breathless.

"With me." He slowly started taking off the thick leather belt that held his kilt in place.

"With nothing on?"

"Stark naked." Alec whispered. "Would you like to?"

"What . . . what happens if someone comes by?"

"Nobody will," he responded, finding himself aroused beyond belief at the possibility of Fiona taking him up on his offer. "There is only one way to get up here, and that's blocked by my men below."

Fiona couldn't believe that she was actually contemplating his offer. And she was tempted. His mouth came down on hers again for another fleeting kiss. "Do you want me to help you undress?"

Fiona shook her head, looking at him wide-eyed. Her throat was as dry as an old bone. "Alec Macpherson, you're a . . . you're a rascal."

"Only when it comes to you, love."

She took another step back, gathering her hands behind her. "I can't. I shouldn't. Swimming . . . with no clothing . . ."

"I suppose if you're feeling shy, you could wear this," he whispered, pulling the wet shift off the branch and holding it up. The setting sun shone clearly through the translucent material. "And I promise, I won't watch you put it on."

Wide-eyed, Fiona took in his hopeful expression and snatched unsuccessfully at the chemise. As she did, she saw his other hand, with a flourish, come away with his belt.

Tempted as she was to see if his kilt remained on his hips, she whirled and started quickly for the rock trail leading up from the pool.

"Where are you going?" he asked, grinning.

"I'll see you up at the tower," she called back to him.

Lifting her skirts, she clambered up the rocks, pausing halfway up to glance back at Alec. He was hanging her chemise on the branch again, and his wedge-shaped back was to her. The sight of his naked body jolted her like a bolt of lightning, and Fiona gaped at his flawlessly powerful physique, at the muscular curves of his buttocks and legs. As he started to turn, she whipped around and scampered up over the top of the rock face.

Fiona made her way along an overgrown path the short distance to the ruined tower above. Reaching the landing, she saw Alec's horse, Ebon, grazing the soft grass in what seemed to have once been an enclosed garden. On seeing her, the massive charger moved in her direction and nuzzled at her palms softly.

"Some warhorse you are," Fiona whispered, stroking the soft mane of the animal. "The size of a giant, but the gentleness of a lamb."

Fiona made her way through the overgrown gardens toward the entrance of the keep. From where she stood, her view of the pool was blocked by the giant weeping elms that surrounded the outer parameter of the glen.

Entering the dark tower, she could just make out the flights of stairs that ran up, along the stone walls.

She ran all the way to the top, breathless when she reached it. The views from the top were spectacular.

Alec had been correct in saying that there was only one easy way up to the tower. Perched atop a peak with steep bluffs and rocky cliffs on three sides, the edifice commanded panoramic views of the Great Glen and the lochs that traverse it. The sun was resting in a notch beside the magnificent profile of Ben Nevis, and with every turn, Fiona felt her heart flutter at the beauty of the scene.

Moving to the edge of the tower, Fiona stepped out between the high block of the outer wall. Peering down into the glen below, she felt a pang of disappointment that Alec was nowhere in sight.

I should have gone swimming with him, she thought with a sigh. I should have—

Suddenly Alec's swimming form moved casually into the center of the pool. Fiona grasped the stones beside her, steadying herself against the sudden quiver that threatened to buckle her knees. He was truly beautiful, and she could no more tear her eyes from him than she could lift this tower from its foundation. Perched on the ledge, the breeze lifting her fiery tresses, Fiona watched as he slowly emerged from the pool and disappeared beneath the leaves that overhung the bank.

She took a deep breath and sat back against one of the great blocks, closing her eyes momentarily. All she could see, all she could feel, was him. She wanted him. She needed him.

She was a woman now, and she would have him.

His hair dripping down his back, Alec looked up through the darkness from the ground level of the ruined tower. Sections of the two burned-out floors were dangling precariously above him. Strangely, only the top floor of the structure seemed reasonably intact. The stone stairs that ran upward hugged the outside walls of the keep.

Fiona was nowhere to be seen.

"Fiona!"

At first, only silence answered the resounding echo of his call.

"Here, Alec," she answered from somewhere above.

Holding their cloaks and the packet of food under his arm, Alec started the long climb up the four flights to the roof.

The swim in the cold water below had done a lot more than just cool Alec's burning desire. It also had cleared his thoughts, his mind. One of the things that had nagged at him from the moment he'd discovered Fiona's true identity was the inevitability of having to reveal his past relationship with Kathryn, her cousin.

Lazing in the pool, the sunlight flecking the surface, Alec had come to a decision. She had to know, and he was going to be the one to tell her.

He loved Fiona, and it was important that the trust she put in him not be unjustified. He was certain that, knowing everything, she would understand, before the truth of what had occurred was twisted into another lie.

Climbing through the murky shadows of the last flight of stairs, Alec looked up at the light streaming like a mist through the opening to the tower's roof.

Momentarily blinded by the brilliance of the setting sun, he shielded his eyes as he stepped into the fresh air.

Straight ahead of him, standing on the parapet of the crenelated tower, a vision eclipsed the blinding rays. Her red hair was flying about her in endless waves, framing a face of angelic perfection.

Alec could just make out her eyes, but they were clear and warm. Dazzling. Radiating a warm invite. They drew him to her with a promise of fulfillment. He moved silently toward her, suddenly feeling as if his entire life had been one steady movement toward this moment. Toward this woman.

This angel.

"Alec," she said softly, closing the distance between them. Lifting her arms and encircling his neck, she smiled up at him. "I've never seen a place more beautiful."

"It suits you," he whispered huskily, gathering her in his arms.

She looked around them while still holding him, not letting him go. "I feel as if I am perched on top of the world."

"You are," Alec whispered.

Fiona gazed at him steadily. "Is this the way a falcon feels?"

"Aye, I think it is," he murmured. "Just before she takes flight."

"Then I know why she comes back." She reached up and pushed back a tendril of hair that had fallen across his face. "Why she always will."

"And why is that?"

"Love," she said simply, warmly, her hand delicately tracing the line of Alec's jaw, his chin, his full lips.

Alec shuddered involuntarily at the erotic sensation of her touch. He couldn't wait any longer. He knew something within him would burst if he didn't tell her how he felt. About what her simple touch did to him.

"I love you, Fiona."

At the sound of his words, her heart took flight, soaring above into the golden heavens.

Their lips met, and hers parted as his tongue penetrated the soft recesses of her mouth. Her own tongue swept against his, matching his actions, learning and loving the taste of him. As they clung together, she could feel the breezes lifting her, lifting them, higher and higher into the evening sky. Taking them aloft to a realm, a sphere, no two mortals had ever reached.

Alec broke off the kiss, looking deeply into her shining hazel eyes. His hands reached up, his fingers lacing through her silky hair. "Fiona, I love you. I want to be with you—today, tomorrow, forever. Walking through that door, seeing you here, I knew you already ... you were in my dreams before I ever met you. We are meant to be together. To be one. Marry me, Fiona."

"I love you, Alec," she responded, her heart bursting with joy. Emotions surged up within her as she gazed into the face that had become the whole world to her.

Fiona raised herself as far as she could, pulling him down to where she could kiss the skin of his neck where she could see his quickening pulse. One hand pulled at the collar of his linen shirt, and she caressed his hot skin with her lips. She heard the growl from deep in his throat and understood his unspoken approval.

Alec's hands stroked her back, fitting her slender frame tightly to him. Sliding ever lower and onto the sensuous curve of her backside, his fingers pulled her hips hard against him.

His lips found hers again, grazing against them with a tenderness that jolted Fiona, causing the warmth within her to burst into flames.

"But, Fiona," he whispered. "There are things I need to tell you. About the past—"

She put her finger to his lips. "Not right now," she

murmured raggedly. "Now is all that matters. I have no past. We have only this moment . . ."

"And the future," he finished.

"And the future," she answered, grasping the front of his shirt with both hands and pulling it up. Her fingers slipped under the garment and spread across his hard abdomen and chest. She could feel his pounding heart beneath the taut skin of his body.

"Fiona, you're driving me wild," he rasped. He was truly losing control. "If we don't stop now . . ."

"I don't want to stop, Alec," she whispered, pushing the shirt up and kissing his chest.

"Are you certain, my love?" he asked again, his hands coming up and his thumbs circling the hardening nipples of her breasts.

"Tell me what to do." She shuddered as his fingers stoked the flames within her.

Alec peeled off his shirt and dropped it beside them.

A hunger swept through her. Her hands and her lips were all over him, feeling, touching, exploring the sinewy musculature that covered his shoulders and chest.

He, too, felt the hunger. He stepped back, spreading with a single motion his great cloak on the windswept timbers. Encircling her waist again with one arm, his fingers gently pulled at the laces of her dress while his lips again found hers.

Pulling open the dress front, Alec went down on one knee as his tongue traced an erotic trail from her chin to the valley between her full, round breasts. He heard her gasp as he pushed the material aside and kissed the soft flesh. His mouth found the hardened nipple, and he suckled gently, drawing from her a groan of pleasure.

Fiona felt his hands pushing the dress from her shoulders, and she shook her arms free as he pulled the garment down over her hips.

She stood in the last rays of sunlight, and, still on one knee, Alec gazed lovingly at her, the warm summer breeze licking her ivory skin. His eyes swept over her perfect form, the glowing beauty before him.

"You are an angel," he whispered raggedly.

"I am your angel, my love."

Alec drew her to him, laying his head against her full breasts while his hands caressed her back, the soft curves of her backside, the firm flesh of her legs. His fingers explored the contours of the backs of her knees and thighs and gently entered the moist recesses between her legs.

Fiona gasped in surprise as Alec's hand slid to the junction of her thighs. Her body arched against his hand as his fingers softly stoked the raging fire within her. Fiona's fingertips ran across his wide shoulders, pulling his hair ... at one moment pulling his head away and at the next gathering him in.

Alec's mouth moved over one breast, his tongue circling and then flicking the erect nipple. He felt her hands grip his hair and his back as Fiona unconsciously pulsed her hips against him. His fingers continued to stroke the moist folds of her womanhood while he suckled her breast.

"Alec!" she gasped. His fingers were sending waves of heat upward through her in rivers that threatened to burst out through her.

His breath was warm against her damp skin as he whispered the words. "Let go, my love. Let go."

His ragged words sent her soaring.

She rolled her head back as a pressure began building in her that she had never before experienced. Her breaths were getting shorter, and suddenly Fiona felt her body shuddering uncontrollably and she curled inward over him, one knee rising and her leg encircling the steellike tautness of his thigh. Without thought, she followed her need and clasped him against her, pressing herself against the magic of his fingers until a shower of sparks burst somewhere deep inside her. Deep within, flashes of white heat were exploding with unrelenting pleasure as he continued to stroke the sensitive nub. Small whimpers became panting cries as colors in her head swirled and flared.

Alec felt her body shudder and lock against his as her nails gripped his hair and the skin of his shoulder blades.

She clung to him, clasped him to her breast as the throbbing release slowly ebbed.

Holding Fiona tightly while her mind regained control over her body, Alec crushed her thighs and belly against his abdomen and chest. When he heard her breathing grow more regular, he eased his grip on her and reached up for her hand.

She knelt before him. Her passion-clouded eyes spoke a thousand words. "Alec," she whispered. "I never thought ... I could feel this way."

"There is more, my love ... more." His mouth moved over hers. Teasing, tasting, moving in and out.

"I want to touch you ... to feel you," Fiona whispered as she moved her trembling hands down in front of his hard abdomen, lower. She traced his upraised knee until her fingers reached the end of his kilt and moved under. Then, slowly, ever slowly, she moved them upward.

She heard his swift intake of breath as her fingers encircled his pulsating arousal. A savage desire filled her with new courage. She used her other hand and pulled at his belt, tugging the kilt open.

"Fiona," he groaned as if in pain when her soft hands stroked his hard, velvet-tipped shaft.

He throbbed against her touch. She moved her hands over his buttocks, down between his legs, and back up, caressing the silken skin of his manhood. His skin scorched her hands. He was on fire.

"Fiona, I can't wait any longer. I need you," he whispered hoarsely.

Fiona sat on the cloak and pulled him down with her.

Alec's hands were at her waist. He gently laid her down and lifted himself onto her body. Instinctively, her legs opened to accept him. He wanted to go slow, to be gentle. But she wouldn't let him.

Fiona squirmed beneath him. She wanted him. There was no holding back. She could feel his throbbing manhood teasing her moist opening. Her body shook in anticipation of what was to come.

Fiona was ready.

She reached up and took hold of his neck, drawing him close, so close that she could hear the pounding of his heart.

"Fiona." He had to ask. Even though he knew he could not stop, Alec needed to ask. Looking into her passion-filled eyes, he knew her answer before she even spoke.

"Alec, make me yours. Take me now."

He entered her in one swift motion, penetrating her

maidenhead. Fiona cried out, digging her fingernails into his shoulders, shuddering at the sudden pain. Alec buried himself deep within her and became still. He waited, straining to control his own body, a body on fire.

"I'm sorry, love," he rasped. "I'm sorry about ... the pain."

Fiona clung to him, the shock of the stroke numbing the rending sense that tore through her. Then, gradually, she felt herself begin again to breathe. She grew aware of his quick, restrained breaths on her ear, of the faint tremors running though the muscles of his back, of his throbbing member deep within her.

"Alec," Fiona breathed, smiling and kissing the skin of his neck, his shoulder. She already was centering her concentration on the pleasure as the pain receded.

Deep within her, another being was forming. Her hips moved ever so slightly, pulsing to a beat that Fiona knew from instinct. The pulsing life beat. The love urge pulsing ever louder, ever more powerfully. The pressure within was growing again. She could not believe that this was happening to her again. Surely this was not what should be happening. She arched her back and drew him in more. Her need was urgent now. Overwhelming, pounding. She strained to take him even deeper.

Alec felt his discipline crumbling. It was growing physically impossible to hold back any longer. He withdrew and plunged back into her again. Holding her warm flesh, he kissed her hungrily as their rhythm took over all conscious thought. Again and again he rocked into her, accelerating with each love stroke. Driving her as she drew him in. Powerfully moving her, moving them toward the apex of desire.

When at last their climax erupted, two souls took flight, two bodies whirling in an aerobatic dance, spiraling ever upward. Two falcons soaring heavenward in an eternal love gyre. Curling, bending, bursting forth into a crystalline sphere. Far above. Distant. Illuminated by love.

The purpled blue of the deepening sky was stretching into the golden west. As the darkness settled around them, Fiona lay with her head nestled warmly on Alec's bicep. Alec gazed down into her contented face, his fingers absently stroking the silky red hair that flowed over her shoulder and onto her breast. As his hand moved slowly and lovingly through the soft tresses, his fingers from time to time touched lightly on the warm skin that lay beneath it. The mere contact of his skin with hers began the stirring in his loins once again. He filled his great chest with air, thinking there would be time enough.

He loved this place. Here in this tower, so high above the world, they were safe. Protected from the world. Protected from the past . . . and from a present that Alec would just as soon avoid. If only they could take this place, he thought, the essence of it with them. He smiled down at Fiona. As if a mere tower could hold her from experiencing the world.

Far above, a bird wheeled, one last ray of light reflecting off the ruffle of some plumage, or on a talon or beak. Fiona caught a glimpse of the bird and marveled at its ability to rise above the whole earth. She wondered what it could see as it circled so high above. Snuggling closer to Alec, she looked tenderly into his face, knowing that she would not exchange this view for that of the falcon above them.

"This is a wonderful place, Alec," she whispered, her fingers caressing his hand as it rested lightly on her breast.

"It is Crown land," the warlord answered, softly adding, "It was built by your father."

Fiona shivered slightly as an evening breeze swept coolly across their naked skin. Alec reached down and drew her cloak over their entwined bodies.

"I thought it was old," she said, snuggling closer.

"Nay, it was just left like this after the abbot's alchemy works exploded and burned."

"What?" She smiled, looking at him skeptically. "Are you making this up?"

Alec laughed. "Me? Make things up?" He leaned down and kissed her, pausing to look menacingly into her face. "I don't make things up."

"Very well, I believe you." She laughed. "So tell me about it."

"Well," Alec said, rolling onto his back and grunting with pleasure as she immediately pounced on his chest.

"Your father built this place as an outpost during the Western Revolt. We're just beyond the reaches of the Macpherson lands here, and he needed someplace that could monitor the movements in the Great Glen below and to the west."

"It sounds impressive," Fiona interrupted, resting her chin on his chest. "But I think he just put it here for the view."

"No question you're right." He nodded, reaching up and pushing back a tendril of hair that had fallen in her face.

"Tell me more, Alec."

He tried to force his concentration back to the tale, but it was difficult. All he could think of was how incredible their lovemaking had been and how soon it would take her body to get over the soreness, so they could—

"Alec!"

"I'm sorry, love, but you're a great distraction," he continued, trying to ignore the smooth-skinned body that rested so comfortably on his. "After things quieted down in the Highlands and the Western Isles, James let the Abbot of Tungland live here . . . until he nearly blew the damn thing right off this peak."

"The Abbot of Tungl . . . who's he?"

"A charlatan whom your father found, for some reason, entertaining. He claimed to be an alchemist. Had a great line about being on the verge of turning lead into gold."

"Don't tell me my father believed him!"

"Nay, lass. I told you, he was mildly entertaining. But he also claimed that with a quiet place—and a tidy sum to keep body and soul together—he would not only produce gold, but also perfect a flying apparatus that the king could use to visit every part of Scotland in one day."

"He had a flying apparatus?" she asked excitedly.

Alec looked knowingly at her. "You *are* indeed your father's daughter."

Fiona thumped her fist on his chest. "Did he or didn't he?"

"As a matter of fact, he did. Sort of. James brought a few of us out here after the abbot had been living here about six months. He'd put something together that looked like wings . . . made of a leather harness and wax and birds' feathers. It was about a month before the place burned. He'd been sending messages saying that the alchemy experiments needed a bit more time—and money from the king—but that the flying apparatus was nearly ready. So we came out."

Fiona pushed herself up slightly off his chest, her breasts brushing lightly against his skin. When Alec did not immediately continue, she reached over and took hold of his jaw. "Tell me. What happened?"

Alec's arm tightened around her, crushing her breasts against him. "If you don't stop teasing me, we'll never get through this story."

"Me . . . teasing?" she asked in surprise before realizing what he was referring to. Then with a grin she ran her finger down the side of his abdomen, pleased by the sharp intake of breath that spoke of his pleasure. "Tell me," she whispered coyly.

"Only if you promise me you won't stop."

"I promise. But tell me, did he fly?"

"Aye, he had to when his servants wouldn't do it," Alec answered through gritted teeth. "Straight down . . . from the top of this tower into the brook at the bottom."

"No!"

"Aye." The warrior pushed himself up and rolled her onto her back, pinning her down with his leg.

"Wait!" she cried, as Alec eyed her, his intentions clear. "What happened to him?"

Alec paused.

"When we dragged him out of the water, he looked straight at the king and said he knew what he'd done wrong." Alec leaned down and kissed the hollow of her neck.

"What, Alec?" Fiona answered, lifting her chin to give him better access.

Alec lifted his face and gazed into her lovely face. "He'd used chicken feathers, and what he should have used were falcon feathers . . . and they would be expensive!"

"Did my father drown him?"

"Nay, Fiona. He was too generous a soul for that. But he did tell him that his time here was running out. And it was."

"So he blew the place up."

"And left the ruins for us."

Chapter 14

This fair lady ... passed far out of the town
A mile or two, unto a mansion
Built exceedingly well ...
—ROBERT HENRYSON, *"Testament of Cresseid"*

"Let sleeping dogs lie."

"Never!"

Fiona tossed her head angrily at Alec's comment.

The sun was nearly overhead as, side by side at the head of the group of warriors, they crossed over a heather-covered ridge and started down into the valley that marked the beginning of Macpherson lands. If all went well, Alec said, they would reach Benmore Castle the next evening.

Fiona looked out across the wild green Highland hills, across a patchwork of hawthorn and pine groves, toward the high-peaked Grampian Mountains to the south.

They had been talking about marriage, about whether Benmore Castle was the right place for it. There was nothing Fiona wanted more than an eternity of wedded bliss with Alec Macpherson, but Fiona had something she needed to attend to first.

"Alec, I have to go to Drummond Castle," she repeated. "Before I can get on with the rest of my life, I need to do that."

"What do you hope to accomplish there?" he asked. "Why first? Why can't we go there after we are married?"

"Because I'm afraid of getting distracted by the wonderful things life with you will offer," she said honestly, and from Alec's expression she knew he believed her. "My mother did not commit suicide, Alec. I know that."

"Fiona, have you really spent any time thinking about this?"

"Of course I've thought of it. This has been haunting me all my life, Alec."

"Then tell me. Who could be left there to support what you say, Fiona? Fourteen long years have passed, and no one spoke up when even the king came looking for answers. What makes you think they'll speak now?"

Fiona thought of the people who had served her mother. They were all faceless ... nameless, now. All but Nanna. And what were the chances of her still being alive? She'd seemed so ancient then. And why hadn't she spoken up?

"Fiona, there are other things. Things you should consider." Alec's face was grim as he reached over for her hand. Fiona looked up into his face at the gesture of support.

"Suppose, for a moment," Alec continued, "you *were* able to prove the truth of what happened. What then?"

"Then her name is cleared and justice will be brought to bear on those responsible for her murder."

"But what if those rumors about her murder were true? What if that act was perpetrated in the belief that your mother's death was the key to peace with England? That it was in Scotland's best interest. When your mother died, Fiona, King James had no reason to put off marrying the English princess."

"Are you defending those animals?" she asked fiercely. "Are you saying that she deserved to die because some nobles wanted to do business with England?"

"Nay, lass. I'm defending no one's barbarism. I'm just saying that vengeance will be difficult to bring against people who may have acted believing they were doing the right thing."

"Perhaps for you, but not for me. This is my mother, a woman who simply loved a man."

"A king, Fiona," Alec said, looking steadily into her eyes. Wherever her road led, he was determined to travel that road with her. He loved her, and he would protect her with all the might or influence he could bring to bear ... no matter how high the trail to her mother's killers might lead. "But whatever happens, Fiona, your

fight is my fight. I only bring those things up to warn
you of the difficulties that might lie ahead. And if you
want to go to Drummond Castle before we marry, then
I'll go with you. I'll not let you out of my sight again,
my love."

The breeze rippled through her flowing red locks, and
Fiona looked up into his loving blue eyes.

"I need you, Alec," she said softly. "This may all be
in vain. All my hopes regarding my mother may turn to
dust. But I have to try. I have to know."

He drew her fingers to his lips. "We'll find your
answ—"

"Lord Alec, look!" Robert shouted from his position
an arrowshot ahead.

The squire pointed to the top of the ridge beyond the valley. At least a hundred mounted warriors had emerged
from a grove of oaks and were sweeping down into the
valley. Fiona could see the hard-charging soldiers were
coming directly at them, and looked questioningly at
Alec beside her as the horsemen around her reined in
their animals. On the other side of her, David appeared,
guiding his horse up next to her.

"Those are Macphersons, Fiona," David said to her,
nodding at the approaching troop.

"How can you tell?" she asked of no one in particular.

"David knew we're on Macpherson land," Alec responded. "But I certainly know the way my own brother
sits in a saddle."

The thundering of hooves grew louder as the riders
approached. It seemed that in only an instant they covered the ground between them. The air was suddenly
filled with the sound of shouts of welcome and friendly
banter. The ruddy faces, the plaids, and the flash of
metal crowded the valley with the swarm of Macpherson clansmen.

Fiona sat straight in her saddle, her hair flaming in
the bright sunlight. The newcomers looked with interest
at the beauty and murmurs of approval were heard on
every quarter as they streamed around them.

A black-haired warrior rode directly to Alec at the
center of the milling mass, and Fiona watched as he and
Alec embraced one another from the backs of their
horses. He was a handsome man, nearly as large as Alec,

and when he turned his young and smiling face to her, there could be no doubt who he was. They had the same blue eyes, but as Alec's spoke of confidence and years of experience, his brother's spoke of mischief.

"Well, Alec, they said you were bringing back our princess, but they never said she was such a bonny lass."

Before Alec could respond, John spurred his horse closer to her. Circling her steed, he eyed her appraisingly and reined in beside her.

"Good day to you, m'lady," he said, graciously reaching out for her hand. When she took his hand tentatively, John lifted it to his lips in courteous greeting. As he spoke, he continued to hold her hand, his gaze never leaving her face. "I hope my brother, considering his characteristic stubbornness, has not made your journey overly arduous."

"Why, thank you for asking. It is quite thoughtful of you." She smiled, turning her sparkling hazel eyes to Alec as she withdrew her hand and placed it in the folds of her cloak.

"So then I suppose we have to assume it *has* been a difficult ride!"

"Why should you assume that? I have not said as much."

"M'lady, you don't have to," John responded, throwing a roguish look in Alec's direction. "You must be extremely weary from the hard ride ... and from such tedious company."

"You are quite insightful, for being a Macpherson," she said impishly.

John threw his head back and laughed out loud as Alec spurred his charger in next to Fiona.

"Let me assure you, m'lady, Ambrose and I are not at all like him. In fact, it's well known around here that the Macpherson offspring have improved with every birth."

"Unfortunately for John, he was a foundling," Alec muttered under his breath. "Beware of this ruffian, Fiona. He has a soul that matches that black hair of his. I can tell you that truthfully ... for I love him as a brother."

The men around them laughed at the banter.

"Oh, but foundlings are always the best stock," she

said, casting a playfully disdainful look at Alec. "If you recall, I happen to be one."

"Aye, Fiona. But John is not quite the same as you. He was a foundling twice. We *had* no choice but to keep him."

"That is another one of my numerous qualities. I always find my way back," he said to Fiona confidentially. "On that note, m'lady of incomparable beauty, may I escort you the rest of the way to Benmore Castle?"

"Hold right there, you silver-tongued scoundrel," Alec responded, nudging Ebon's massive body in between Fiona's and John's steeds. "And don't tempt me. Though you're a wee bit large to stuff in a wicker basket, they say the third time is a charm."

"Glad to see you admit the truth for a change, Alec," he said, smiling broadly and pulling his horse to Fiona's free side. "Being the third, I am the charming one."

"But, alas, you're also the scrawniest." Alec scowled, eyeing the lad who was every bit as tall and muscular as he.

"It's not with feats of strength that I plan to entertain this enchantress for the rest of the journey, it's with words of homage that will celebrate her beauty."

"She has me to remind her of that beauty, scamp. So thanks for coming out to meet us ... and be on your way."

Laughter rang out from the men around them, and Alec's young brother joined in.

"Ah, so that's the way it's to be," John concluded affably, steadying his mount and clapping Alec on the arm. "Well, this is going to be a merry homecoming, big brother. Won't Mother be pleased. I'm certain she plans to spend a great deal of time alone with you ... to catch up on things."

John turned back to Fiona. "And while Alec is doing his familial duty, m'lady, I'll be at your service to make your stay as pleasant as possible."

John stood up in his stirrups and respectfully bowed from the waist, and Fiona nodded back to him. "Welcome to the Macphersons' ancestral lands, Your Highness."

"Very well, John," Alec conceded. He turned to Fiona, caught her smile, and nearly smiled himself. "You are the most charming in the land. But if you think we're going to spend the whole day here while you show us how courtly a knight you are, we'll all be as brown as Saracens from this sun. We're leaving, so if you'd like to tag along ... Oh, John, this is David MacLeod, a friend of father's and the brother of the prioress at Newabbey."

"Pleased to—" John began.

As his younger brother turned, Alec swatted the flank of Fiona's mount and the two moved side by side through the clearing mass of Macpherson warriors. Moments later, Fiona looked happily at the grinning Alec as they broke into the open with John in hot pursuit. There was no sign of the cloud that had darkened Alec's moods from time to time. He was happy. He was at home. Fiona wondered if she someday would feel this way on these lands. On any lands.

It wasn't long until John caught up with them, and, three abreast, they led the troop of men at a canter up the far slope of the valley toward the forest ahead.

"Well, John," Alec asked as they followed the ridge, skirting the edge of the thick wood, "what really brought you out here? You haven't ridden out this far to greet me since you were nine years old. And you caught hell for it that time, as I remember."

Alec's memory of the humorous aftermath was cut short as John shot a questioning look in Fiona's direction. The young man's handsome face grew serious in an instant, and he gave Alec a meaningful glance over Fiona's head.

"What's amiss, John?" Alec asked. There was no point in trying to hide anything from Fiona. She was his soulmate, his partner, his love.

"There was an attack."

"On our ship from Skye?"

"Aye," John answered. "Three days ago we received word that the ship you sent as a decoy toward Kildalton Castle was attacked."

"Damn," Alec said grimly. "Though I feared as much."

"Was anyone hurt?" Fiona asked with concern. This was all her fault. They were after her. She never should have allowed others to put their own lives in danger for her. Alec had spoken of dangers, and he'd been right.

"None of our people," John responded soothingly, seeing her distress. "One of Colin Campbell's ships sailed into view just as the brigands fired their cannon at our ship. The filthy pirates broke off immediately—"

"Pirates?" Fiona blurted.

"There are sea dogs who will work for any who pay, Fiona," Alec answered. He turned to John. "Did they catch them?"

"Aye," John answered.

"Good! Where are they now?" Alec asked.

"Some are at the bottom of the Atlantic. The Campbell ship's cannons blasted that ship out of the water."

"Any survivors?"

"A few. But none of them knew anything except the mate. He was more than willing to talk, though." John and Alec exchanged a knowing look. Those who raided the western shores and fell into the hands of their erstwhile victims were quick to look for opportunities to save their skins. "The mate is being held at Kildalton Castle. He says that they were waiting for this ship. And that there was a bounty for the red-haired princess."

"Who would gain by having me?"

"Anyone," Alec said. "Every laird in Scotland would give his right arm for you, Fiona . . . but for the wrong reasons."

Fiona reached over for his hand, and Alec grasped it tightly before looking back at his brother.

"Who put the bounty on her head, John?"

"The mate doesn't know. But he said the captain had received a casket of gold in advance from someone in the Highlands. That's all he knows."

Fiona felt a numbing deadness creep through her. It was an emptiness inside that came with the recollection of old and painful memories. Of events that occurred fourteen years earlier. A fleeting thought linked the incidents that were divided by tremendous distance and by even longer years. Somehow she knew they were all connected.

"So that's why we came to meet you," John concluded. "Whoever paid for that attack would soon learn that you weren't on that ship. We just weren't sure how soon the news would reach him."

Fiona tried to recall the events of their trip. "The ones behind this could not have been from Skye or the Outer Hebrides."

"Isn't it a bit early to rule anyone out?" John asked, turning in her direction.

"She is right, John," Alec said thoughtfully. "With exception of Neil MacLeod, who fled Skye a few days before we left, everyone out there knew we took the land route. They would have known the boat was just a decoy."

"Wouldn't it have been smarter to keep your plan a secret?" John asked critically.

"Believe me, I had no choice." Alec turned, looking at the blushing face of Fiona. "This beauty is not just our princess returning to the land of the living."

"No?"

"Fiona is a lot more. She is the fairy princess who rescues those in danger. She is the wood nymph who guards the lepers. She is the kelpie who swims the lochs. She is the rebel ... the beloved rebel who breaks every rule." Alec paused. "This, John, is the Angel of Skye."

John watched as the gazes of his brother and the bright-eyed beauty locked on one another, shutting out him and the rest of the world. He smiled at the sudden thought that Alec, finally, was home. And John smiled, for it appeared his brother had found someone as rare and as deserving as Alec was himself.

The morning was clear and cold as they rode into the great valley that stretched out between the round-topped gray mountains Alec called Monadhliath and the rising forestland of fragrant, red-limbed pines that stretched out as far as the eye could see to the south. The great River Spey wound like a sparkling jeweled serpent along the wide floor of the valley, and Fiona's breath caught in her chest at the beauty of the scene unfolding before her. The farms and the pasturelands of the valley were green and lush, and the workers in the fields raised their hats and shouted welcome to the passing troop.

Shortly after the sun passed overhead, they rounded a bend in the river and Alec pointed to the great castle sitting atop a mound overlooking the waterway. Groves of tall pines flanked the north side of the edifice, and drawbridges crossed the series of ditches and moats that protectively encircled the high stone walls. To the right, a stone bridge spanned the river on seven arches and led into a friendly-looking village of wood and stone buildings that clung to the south side of the Spey.

A few moments later they rode through the arched entry and into Benmore Castle. Fiona slowed her horse, and she fell slightly behind the others. As she entered the courtyard, which was ringed with buildings hugging the curtain walls, Fiona paused at the sight of the movement and color of men and women scurrying to their tasks. Her gaze traveled upward. On the wall of a great building across the close, a large stone medallion displayed the family crest. Her eyes were drawn to the lion at the top of the shield.

Fiona surveyed the entire perimeter of the courtyard. With its three square towers, Benmore Castle was most impressive. But pleasantly so. True, from the outside, it had the look of a fortress. But from the inside, it had more the look of a comfortable residence.

"My parents have been rebuilding this place for the past two years or so."

Fiona looked to her side and saw John there.

"It's absolutely beautiful," she replied.

"It's all Mother's work. She, at last, convinced the rest of us that it's time we lived in a home rather than in a stone barrack."

Fiona looked ahead, her eyes searching for Alec. She was tired beyond measure, but that did not distress her as much as not having had a single moment alone with him in the last two days. She would ride for two more days, if it meant him taking her back to their ruined tower. She longed for the intimacy, for the feel of his skin against hers. She longed for his kisses, his caresses, his passion.

Her eyes found him and he turned, smiling at her. Her heart tightened in her chest. He was standing head and shoulders above a group of people by a stone stairway leading up to a large doorway.

Breaking away from the group, Alec started in her direction, and Fiona quickly dismounted. She was growing increasingly aware of the watchful eyes and curious glances of the people around her. From the circle where he had been, a tall and beautiful woman took a step toward her.

"I want you to meet my mother, love," he whispered as he reached her side. He took hold of her hand. "They tell me Lord Huntly arrived last night."

"Lord Huntly?" Fiona repeated, surprised.

"Aye. He came to greet you himself. But they didn't expect us quite so soon. He and my father are off hunting this morning."

As the two walked side by side, Fiona felt a weight drag down her every step. She wanted so badly to make a good impression on Alec's mother. But all of her insecurities bubbled to the surface at once. She knew all too well that she lacked a noble lady's sophistication and charm. She was just a plain and simple convent lass who had been plucked by fate from the fields and forests of Skye. She could only be who she was.

By the time they reached the stairway, Fiona's insides were tied in a knot. Alec's mother stood quietly, her dark blond hair loosely braided and gathered behind her. Her blue eyes had the same deep color as her son's, and she looked steadily at Fiona as she approached. Fiona thought to pull her hand from out of Alec's grip, but he held on to her tightly.

"Welcome to Benmore Castle, Lady Fiona," Lady Macpherson offered courteously.

Fiona extracted her arm from Alec's and curtsied to the lady of the manor.

"Thank you for having me here, m'lady," she whispered softly, her head bowed. "I am dreadfully sorry to inconvenience you all this way."

Elizabeth Macpherson stood, momentarily stunned by the behavior of the incandescent beauty before her. This modest young woman—so politely demure—this was not at all what she'd been expecting. She had watched her, sitting so tall on her horse, surveying the castle, and she'd thought, Here we go. This is indeed Kathryn Gray's cousin.

She had never liked Kathryn, from the time she'd first met her at court. But she respected her son's choice and had done a fairly good job of holding her tongue. She had prayed for things to work out for the best, and so they had.

But this lass was clearly different. Elizabeth looked at her bowed head, the nervousness apparent in the flush of her perfect features.

She reached out and took hold of Fiona's chin, lightly raising her face and smiling cordially.

"You need not curtsy to me, Lady Fiona," she said softly. "And you need not apologize, either."

Lady Macpherson was the most striking woman Fiona had ever laid eyes on. And then, looking into her face, she saw the sudden warmth in those deep blue eyes and knew that all would be well between them.

"Why don't you come in with me and let the men bring in your things."

"I cannot burden these men more than I already have on this trip," Fiona said frankly. "Besides, it will take hardly a moment to fetch my satchel and—"

"Here it is, Lady Fiona," Robert chirped from behind, her bag in hand.

"That is all you've brought? You mean this beastly son of mine wouldn't even allow you time to pack your clothes?"

"These are my clothes, m'lady," Fiona replied simply. "One doesn't need a very large wardrobe in a convent."

Alec's mother laughed in earnest. What happened to the trunks full of clothes that Kathryn's servants had carted in—and out—when she'd arrived uninvited not even a month ago?

"I believe, my dear, I can be of some assistance to you with that."

Elizabeth Macpherson took the hand of the young woman and started up the stairway leading to the Great Hall, with Robert trailing behind.

"Where are you taking her, Mother?" Alec called after their retreating backs.

"Why don't you just go about your business," Alec's mother answered over her shoulder before continuing in a more confidential tone, "He's never been one to share, Fiona, I have to warn you about that."

Fiona blushed. She was certain Alec couldn't have had time to relate their plans to his mother. But there was something in the warm way she held Fiona's hand that said Lady Macpherson had just joined their conspiracy.

As the two women made their way through the throng of people into the wide-open doors of the Great Hall, Fiona heard Lady Macpherson ordering Robert to take the satchel up to the Roundtower Room. As Fiona stepped into the great room, she noticed a quiet but firm exchange of words between the lady of the house and the squire.

Fiona let her eyes travel the length of the room. Each of the plastered walls was covered with colorful tapestries and hangings of embroidered felt, velvet, silk, and damask. The floors were covered, as well, with woven rush mats sewn together in strips. From behind the two women, the returning warriors crowded into the hall and began filling the trestle tables. The large assortment of dogs that were settled comfortably beneath the tables lazily stretched and moved out into the spaces between, while servant girls hurried in and out with platters of food, fresh vegetables, and pitchers of ale, their bright chatter filling the room with activity and warmth.

Fiona stared, amazed at the happiness that seemed to permeate the air of Benmore Castle.

"If you'd prefer, my dear, we'll fix you up something nice to eat in your room." Elizabeth put on her most motherly face and cast a sternly disapproving look at an increasingly vocal group who were good-naturedly making room for Fiona among them.

"You must be *quite* weary of these ruffians, I should imagine," she said loudly, evoking laughter from the congenial group. Taking Fiona firmly by the arm, she led her to the left toward an arch and into the quiet of a hallway.

As the two made their way along the corridor, Fiona asked her hostess about the history of the castle and the obvious improvements that had recently been made.

Elizabeth Macpherson beamed, delightedly taking Fiona through the rooms that they passed by, showing her the latest innovations—the leaded windows, the new fireplaces in many of the living quarters. She led her through the new kitchens and the brew house, and up a level into some smaller guest rooms directly above. By the time they had worked their way around to the other end of the castle, Fiona was amazed at the effort that had gone into the castle's renovation.

But more importantly, Fiona realized that in no time at all, the two of them were chatting like old chums, quite comfortable in one another's company and both equally surprised at this budding friendship.

Moments later, her hostess led her up a winding stairwell, and Fiona held her breath as she entered the Roundtower Room she was to inhabit during her stay at Benmore Castle.

It was exquisite.

The room was large and airy, with leaded glass windows that had been opened inward on hinges. The base of each window was corbelled with a bow-shaped oak sill wide enough to sit on. A fireplace had been prepared for an evening fire, and a large canopy bed with richly embroidered curtains sat against an inner wall. The floors were made out of oak as well, and an ornate hand-made rug covered only part of the burnished wood.

"This room is fit for a queen," Fiona whispered, turning in Lady Macpherson's direction. "You certainly don't mean for me to stay here, do you?"

"Of course I do!" Elizabeth took hold of Fiona's hand and drew her to the middle of the room. "I have to tell you one thing, though, you are the first person to be staying in here."

"I am?"

"Aye. We started building this tower about two years ago. That was right after Torquil MacLeod and that Englishman, Danvers, attacked us. It was just recently finished."

"It is beautiful," Fiona complimented. "The mason's work throughout the castle is very fine. But this tower ... the detail of the workmanship ... it is absolutely superior."

Elizabeth smiled happily. It was such a pleasure to have a young woman such as this see and appreciate the things she herself had worked so hard at.

"How do you know so much about these things, Fiona?"

"Well, the prioress made it a part of my education, but I've always been interested in it."

"That doesn't really surprise me," Elizabeth said,

drawing her down beside her onto the bench near a small table. "Your father was a great builder, you know."

"Unfortunately, I never knew him." Fiona paused, absently unfastening her cloak and placing it beside her. "I'm learning new things about him every day."

"Sitting here and talking with you, my beautiful child," she said, squeezing Fiona's arm gently, "I can see his spirit lives in you."

Elizabeth patted Fiona hard on the knee to punctuate her change in tone. "But let's talk of happy things. I'm glad you're here, and I'm glad you're to be the first to sleep in this room!"

"Thank you, m'lady," Fiona responded gratefully. She looked around at the furnishings. "Benmore is so large. Why is this end of the castle so ornate?"

"Actually, we really needed apartments for the lads," she said, trying to sound practical. "But this tower and the adjoining buildings on this western wall were really done with Alec in mind. Alexander and I thought ... well, he is the next laird; he should have something more modern than the old pile we live in. We wanted it to be something special, so we sent to Moray for the best masons we could find. . . ."

Fiona thought of Alec and the love his parents had for him. She thought of the love she had for him. She had fears. Fiona still had difficulty believing that her future life lay with him. Seeing herself here at Benmore—growing old beside him—that was an incredible dream that seemed nearly unobtainable. Her thoughts drifted briefly to another pair of lovers whose destinies had been so sadly star-crossed. She knew all too well that fate was a mystery, and often a merciless one. Her dreams of a future with Alec were wondrously joyful, but would their fate allow it?

A knock on the door roused Fiona from her thoughts. As Lady Elizabeth moved quickly to let in the serving girl with the trencher of food, Fiona realized that she hadn't heard the last few words of her hostess.

The next few hours were busy ones for Fiona. She had not even finished her meal when a troop of the household workers arrived with a tub and buckets of warm water.

Relaxing in the jasmine-scented bath, Fiona nearly fell asleep as the soreness of her days in the saddle melted out of her tired muscles.

But that hadn't been the end. No sooner had she put on the quilted silk dressing gown that Lady Elizabeth had sent up than another knock on the door brought the presence of her hostess's seamstress. Fiona was measured and eyed approvingly by the old woman, who disappeared with scarcely a word spoken.

Now, standing in the middle of the room, brushing the dampness from her long tresses, Fiona gazed longingly at the deep billows of the brightly decorated featherbed. She could not remember ever sleeping in such a luxurious piece of furniture.

Fiona moved to the side of the bed and sat. But then again, she could not remember ever sleeping on anything but the hard ground she'd been enduring for the past week. .

Except, she thought with a sigh, for the few precious hours spent at the top of a ruined tower. She smiled. She would trade a thousand nights alone in this featherbed for that one night in Alec's arms.

And dreams of Alec were all she had as she fell deeply asleep.

Chapter 15

Wealth, worldly glory, and rich array
Are all just thorns laid in thy way,
O'ercovered with flowers ...
—WILLIAM DUNBAR,
    "All Earthly Joy Returns in Pain"

"**A**re you certain you are not rushing Fiona?"
Alec's father asked him.

Alec ran his fingers through his hair and smiled wryly as he leaned back heavily against the top of the open hearth of the fireplace. He certainly had rushed her. From the beginning. From the moment when their paths had first crossed. He could see now that he'd wanted her from that moment, and he admitted to himself he'd used everything he knew about women, every bit of his experience with women, to make Fiona his. And it had happened. He thought of the magical night they'd shared as lovers in the ruins of the tower. She now belonged to him and Alec held that dear.

He'd wanted that, and now he would secure it. What was left was to seal their love, their future, by marrying before anything or anyone could get in their way. And Alec would not let anyone get between them.

He'd thought it would be appropriate to break his and Fiona's engagement news to his parents first. But then, he should have known better. Alexander Macpherson always had at least a hundred questions that he wanted answers to, and for each answer he had another ten questions more.

"Father ..." Alec took a deep breath as he continued, "if it looks to the rest of the world as though I'm rushing her, then the world be damned. I love her. I almost made a great mistake once, but this is no mistake. This is the woman for me. And I know when you meet her, every question you have will be answered."

"But have you thought out all the ramifications of such a union?"

"The hell with ramifications, Father! What good did that kind of thinking do last time? I almost married the devil's own mistress!"

Alexander Macpherson eyed his wife's attempt at a serene expression. Sitting across the room, she was trying to look busy tending to the needlework on her lap. But he'd been watching, and she had not completed a single stitch. She was listening to his questions, and from the blush on her beautiful face, Alexander knew that if he didn't ease up on Alec soon, she would surely pounce on him. My God, how he loved this woman! Thirty-two years of marriage and he still felt like a schoolboy when she turned those cobalt-blue eyes of hers in his direction. And now he realized that his questioning stance was taxing her patience. Alexander knew from experience that the next time she looked up, she would be glaring at him.

"Don't get me wrong, Alec," the laird boomed. "I'm not questioning your judgment. But even if I were, you know how I feel about your mother's judgment, and she thinks this Fiona Drummond Stuart is the finest young woman ever to walk on Scottish soil."

Alexander turned to Elizabeth once more, and this time he noted the curt nod of approval from her.

"She is, Father," Alec agreed wholeheartedly. "But aside from that, she is the most disruptive thing that has ever happened to me, something I'm quite certain Mother would approve of. No woman has ever been able to get under my skin the way she does. She continually bewilders me. She is a rebellious, impish, high-spirited kelpie. Finally, there in Skye, I thought my life was taking on some serious purpose. But then she walked into it and suddenly I realized I was just running away from life."

Alec noted the glimmer of a smile that was tugging at the corners of his mother's mouth. She had always said that her son would be truly happy only with a woman of extraordinary spirit and temper. A woman who could rile him up.

"You *do* love her," Elizabeth put in quietly from where she sat. She nodded with satisfaction. "Well, I probably don't have to tell you that she's in love with you, too. This afternoon—the time we spent together—all she cared about, every question she asked, had some connection with you. We walked through every building, and her conversation kept coming back to you. And the nice part of the whole thing was that she was not even aware she was doing it."

Alec smiled just thinking of her. He wondered if she was still sleeping. He'd peeked into her room before coming to see his parents, and Fiona had been curled up in the massive bed, her hair fanned out like a fiery sea around her. He'd had to use all the self-control he could muster to keep himself from gathering her in his arms.

"Have you told her about Kathryn?"

Alec's face darkened at his father's mention of the name.

"Do you always have to bear such unpleasant thoughts, Alexander Macpherson?" Elizabeth asked her husband sharply. Truthfully, it was a question she'd wanted to ask herself. Fiona had a right to know before any formal betrothal.

"Nay, my love. It is just a simple question!"

"I planned to tell her one time during the journey, but . . . well, I didn't get the opportunity. But I will tell her."

"I'd say in the long run it would be a wise move," the laird put in. "Based on what we know of your former betrothed now, one never knows how the demise of that relationship would be recounted if the Gray girl's the one doing the telling."

"Well, from what I can see, that young woman upstairs will not be believing any word said to her by the likes of Kathryn . . . be she family or no!" Elizabeth looked at her son and husband straight on. "Fiona is an intelligent woman who will not be fooled by the vixen's double-edged words; her warped, one-sided stories; nor by her openly slanderous accusations, either."

"Have you forgotten how conniving Kathryn Gray can be, my love?" Alexander asked. "Have you already forgotten the tears, the heart-wrenching words, the way she pretended to pour her heart out to you after the breakup?"

"Nay, I have not forgotten. But I was able to see past all that. And so will Fiona. I know she will."

Alec moved across the room to the window behind his mother. He desperately hoped so, too. He would tell Fiona about his past, about Kathryn. But he knew that even a full accounting of what had happened would not be enough. Somehow he had to find a way to make sure Fiona would see Kathryn Gray for who she really is. For sometime soon Fiona would be encountering Kathryn, and when that happened, Alec could not be certain of what would happen. In spite of his mother's confidence, he just didn't know what Kathryn would say or do.

Outside, the light had taken on the golden hue of early evening, and Alec thought vaguely about how good the weather had remained. Turning, he seated himself on the wide sill, leaning his broad back against one side of the open window and putting one foot up against the far edge. His thoughts wandered back to Fiona. He had to talk to her before dinner. Alec knew his parents would not stand in his way. His mother clearly liked Fiona already. With some prodding his father would come around.

Alec was determined. He had to get her to agree to announce their engagement tonight to Lord Huntly and the others.

Lord Huntly. How surprising it was that the most powerful man in Scotland had come so far to meet and escort Fiona back to the court. Huntly had always been a friend to Alec's father, but the purpose of his visit this time was clearly not social. Huntly certainly could have waited for Fiona to arrive at Stirling, but he hadn't.

Well, that was reason enough why Alec wanted his and Fiona's engagement announced. Friend or not, if Huntly had come to Benmore Castle to protect Fiona from Alec, there would be trouble. Alec had no intention of letting Huntly separate him from Fiona. He would stay at her side until their marriage. He would remain by her side forever.

He looked past his mother to where Lord Alexander sat at the small trestle table, absently sharpening the blade of the new, lightweight sword he'd received as a gift from Huntly. He was busy at his task, but Alec knew from his father's long pauses that he was deep in thought.

Alec could not help but smile at these two people, so well suited, so obviously committed to each other. He wondered if their feeling for each other, when their relationship began, was anything like what he and Fiona felt. They had always supported Alec and his brothers in everything they'd done or attempted, but he knew his parents could never really understand Alec's difficulty with finding one woman to whom he could truly commit himself. For life. Alec supposed that he'd always been looking for a relationship like the one he'd seen in his parents' marriage. He'd nearly given up. And he'd nearly made a grave mistake.

Then he'd met Fiona. And he knew he'd found the mate he'd always been searching for.

Alec's eyes wandered about the room. It was so very much like them.

The fine stonework, the ornate oak paneling, the heavy carved furniture that graced the room, all spoke of solid Scots tastes. Of his father, so solidly a northerner, so proudly a Highlander. But the other touches were there in the room as well, the feminine touches—the wreaths of woven flowers, the colorful tapestries that covered the walls. That was Alec's mother, so staunch in her gentler, broader view of the world. They had come from different worlds and backgrounds. And they had made a home. A happy home. That's what Alec wanted, as well. For Fiona and for himself.

"Well, I say if you're so much in love with this lass," Alexander Macpherson proclaimed, looking up from where he sat, "then marry her. Forget about a public betrothal and all that nonsense. Just marry her. Marry her now! Immediately!"

Elizabeth turned her gaze to her husband in sheer surprise. Alec stood and moved back to the fireplace.

"Would you care to explain that?" Elizabeth asked, voicing the question Alec was about to ask. She knew her husband, and she knew there was something he was not telling them. "What do you know, Alexander?"

"What makes you ask that, love?" he responded casually. "I agree. That's all."

"Father," Alec interjected. "You've just spent an hour giving me hell about wanting Fiona and rushing Fiona and thinking first and on and on. Don't take me wrong, I'll marry her now if she's ready—"

"While we were hunting today, Huntly and I talked about Fiona," the laird broke in. "He gave me some information that I don't believe you're aware of."

"About Fiona?" Alec asked shortly. "What does Huntly know about Fiona?"

"It's not so much about her as it is about her future. Huntly told me that Fiona's uncle, Lord Gray, is already making noise about appropriate matches for her."

"Nay!" Lady Elizabeth erupted. "He's not even seen the lass yet."

"Nonetheless, he knows an opportunity to boost his family's stature when he sees one, and Huntly believes the queen will grant Lord Gray leave to marry Fiona off as he sees fit, once she's got the assurances she wants from the lass about the Crown and the succession."

Alec stared at his father. If he let Huntly take Fiona, he could lose her. He was going to lose her.

"And don't think Gray will marry her off to just anyone," Alexander continued. "He'll find a highly suitable match, perhaps even a royal one. But it will be one that will serve his own power-hungry desires quite nicely."

The old laird looked at his wife and back at Alec.

"And you can wager every sheep on Macpherson land, Lord Gray will never agree to a marriage between Fiona and you, Alec! After all, you publicly rejected his own daughter, and he's a man who never forgets an injury."

Alec smashed his fist into his open palm and turned toward the open hearth. This had been his fear from the moment he'd learned her true identity. His mind raced, searching for other possibilities. He could not let this happen. He whirled on his father.

"What would happen if she were to marry before Lord Gray formally recognizes her? Before she reaches the queen at Sterling?"

"Aye, lad. That's the spirit." The laird nodded, glancing over at the affirming look on his wife's face. "Huntly is the most powerful man in Scotland today, and you know he'll stand behind you. I said before, and I say now: Marry the lass."

Fiona looked at herself in the silvered glass that stood against the wall.

Never in her life had she worn such a fine gown. The ivory-colored dress laced with threads of gold clung to her slender frame and then flared to a long, full skirt below the curves of her hips. The tight sleeves hugged her arms while the velvet cuffs extended over her fingers. Fiona eyed the neckline. It was way too low for her liking. She took hold of the velvet-collared neckline and tried to pull the burgundy-colored trim higher over the top of her breasts. Oh God, she thought, everyone will be able to see all this skin. She moved to the side of the bed and removed her mother's cross from the side table, hanging the jeweled ornament around her neck. Looking in the mirror again, she gathered her long red hair and pulled it over one shoulder, trying to hide some of her exposed skin. Fiona caught the curious look of the young maid in the mirror. She was getting all worked up over nothing. Nobody will even notice it, she told herself. But would Alec?

She had awakened to the sound of Claire, the young maid, knocking lightly before entering Fiona's room. Fiona had been amazed, upon opening her eyes, at the bountiful array of beautiful dresses, gowns, and accessories that had somehow—in an incredibly short span of time—been so masterfully created and then delivered to her room.

Fiona looked up at Claire as the lass busily reorganized the room, hanging dresses and quickly putting everything in order. Fiona picked up a fine silk nightgown, marveled at the soft suppleness of the material and the finely stitched handiwork. Running it across her hand, she noticed the thinness of the fabric and how it molded to her outstretched fingers beneath. She wondered with a suppressed sigh if Alec would want to see her in that. She wondered if he would come to her here at Benmore—tonight—and share her bed. Suddenly feeling ashamed of herself for harboring such thoughts, Fiona began to refold the nightgown quickly and put it away.

"Did you make these clothes, Claire?" she asked softly, looking over all the finery which lay about.

"Oh, no, m'lady," the young woman responded. "Lady Elizabeth's seamstress and all her helpers have been making up these clothes. I'm not so talented with a needle."

"I never have been, either."

"Lady Elizabeth could teach you, m'lady. She has the patience of Job."

"Job knew needlework?"

The young maid began to giggle. "I don't think so, m'lady. In the guild play last spring, Job was left in rags on the dunghill."

This time Fiona was the one to laugh, but the forceful knock on the door cut the moment short. Claire ran quickly, opening the door. From where Fiona stood, she could not see who was at the door. But Claire's quick curtsy before disappearing told Fiona that the maid had been dismissed.

"May I come in?" At the sound of Alec's voice, Fiona bounded for the door.

Before he could react, Fiona had him by the hand and was closing the door behind him.

"M'lady, consider my reputa—"

Rising to her toes, Fiona took hold of his neck and stopped Alec's words with a searing kiss, before pulling back quickly and sliding out of his grasp. Suddenly conscious of her forwardness, she backed to the table, putting a distance between them.

"Does this mean you've missed me as much as I've missed you?" Alec asked wryly.

She gave him a half smile, feeling the heat rising in her face. All she could do was nod slowly. Looking at Alec, quite dapper in his impeccably fitted clothes and standing so comfortably in the middle of that room, was enough to quicken the breath in her chest. She let her eyes travel the length of him, to quench their thirst. A moment earlier she'd been so excited to see him that she'd cast propriety to the wind. Now Fiona felt embarrassed at her own audacity.

"I had to give my word of honor to my parents that I would ..." Alec's words died in his throat as Fiona unconsciously pushed her fiery mane back over her shoulder. His eyes took in the milk-white swells of flesh that beckoned from the framing neckline of burgundy velvet.

"I . . . I told them I'd behave myself and escort you downstairs."

"They made you give your word about such a simple task?"

"Somehow I think they knew it wouldn't be so simple."

"But why?" she teased, coyly leaning against the table.

In the golden light that was streaming in her window, Fiona was more than alluring—she was bewitching. Alec walked across the room to her and lifted her in his arms. His mouth settled on hers, crushing her lips in a kiss that all but answered her question.

"I've told them about us," he whispered in her ear, his mouth grazing the skin of her earlobe, her neck. As he kissed the hollow of her neck lazily, he could feel her pulse fluttering wildly beneath his lips, and the quiet moan that issued from deep within her stirred in him an already gathering storm of desire. He held her closer, even tighter.

"You mean . . . about the tower," she murmured, pushing her hips lightly against his hardening manhood while pulling her head back, trying to capture his eyes. Her hands moved up his chest. She could feel his heart beating hard and fast.

"Aye, I told them everything." His hand moved to the front of her dress and gently caressed her breast as he leaned down and placed a kiss on the exposed swell of milky white flesh.

"Everything?" she asked, her breath starting to come in quick pants. She watched as he slowly tugged down the neckline of her dress. Slowly, ever so slowly, exposing more of her skin.

"I explained in detail about the time you tried to seduce me in my own study at Dunvegan Castle." He leaned down and tasted her freshly bared skin. His hand moved across the smooth material of the garment, pulling it even lower, until finally one breast was completely revealed. She took a sharp breath and ran her fingers into his hair as he cupped her. She gasped as his mouth took possession of the nipple.

"You're a wild thing, Alec Macpherson," she said hoarsely, the sweet torment taking over her senses. Her fingers traced the lines of his broad shoulders and moved again through his hair. "You're driving me wild . . . Alec . . . Alec . . ."

Fiona bit at her lip as his tongue flicked at her nipple, circling the aureole before beginning to suckle again.

"Alec . . . someone might come," she panted. "It's best to stop. Before I disgrace myself before your family."

" 'Tis true, my love." He pulled back smiling, his eyes delving into the incredible depths of her eyes. "I told them what happened in the tower, about how you were finally successful in taking advantage of my unblemished innocence." Alec's thumb gently continued its circling motion around the aroused nipple, and his mouth rubbed caressingly across her lips again.

Fiona fought to catch her breath, and then, realizing what he'd just said, gently pushed his blond head away from her and punched him in the chest.

He glared playfully at her and gathered her in so tightly that she couldn't move.

"Unblemished innocence!" she growled, pushing at his chest. She tried to pull her dress back up over her breast, but he pulled it down again. This time she playfully slapped his hands away as she accomplished the task. "Beast! I'm certain, in this castle alone, I could find a few that might speak differently of your wayward character."

Alec eased himself into the chair at the side of the table and pulled her onto his lap. "Is it that important?"

"Is what important?" Fiona asked, trying to work herself off his lap. She knew what they were talking about, and she was sure he must have been with many women before her. But she didn't really want to talk about it.

He held on tight. "My innocence."

"You were not a virgin?" She asked with mock dismay.

"Nay," he answered matter-of-factly.

"I'm shocked, Alec." She leaned over, giving him a quick kiss on his lips and jumping off his lap. "But please, love, let's not talk about it. What's past is past. I don't want to know which of the women I might run into have ... shared your bed."

Alec looked at her back. She was avoiding his eyes. It seemed to take forever before she, at last, turned and looked steadily at him.

"We don't need any unnecessary bloodshed, do we?" she asked, picking up the dagger he'd given her and tucking it into the gold-linked chain that encircled her waist. "You never know how one might act when faced with unwanted adversaries."

Alec looked at her. In spite of her playful words, he could see the welling of tears in her eyes before she turned away from him again. She was not ready to listen to the things he was no longer willing to tell. About himself. About his past. About Kathryn.

There would be time enough after they were married.

He moved across the room and stood behind her, enfolding her in his arms.

"Fiona," he began softly. "My love, later on, when you are ready, perhaps after some sunny afternoon of making love, while you sit breast-feeding our sixth or seventh bairn, there are things about me that I would like to tell you."

Fiona laughed and twisted in his arms to look up into his face.

"They must be incredibly terrible things, Alec," she teased.

"Aye. Perhaps after the eighth bairn."

"Do they concern other women? From your dark and distant past?"

"Aye," he said, his hands gently caressing her arms. "Very dark and very distant."

"Then I don't want to know." She rested her head against his chest. "What happened to your 'unblemished innocence'?"

Alec buried his face in Fiona's jasmine-scented tresses and lightly kissed the top of her head. "When I met you, my sweet, life began anew."

"So we both have demons in our past."

"Aye, but that past is gone. The present concerns us now. The present and the future. Fiona, I want you to know that everything that I have ever held dear, every path that I have ever walked, every mistake I've made, every breath I have ever taken has only prepared me for the life I ask you to share in. You, my angel love, are the God-given and undeserved answer to another lifetime that I've lived—a lifetime that at times seems only a dream now. A lifetime that has all too often been no more than a horrible nightmare. But you, my sweet, have brought me back to the world of waking daylight, of sunshine and kindness and goodness and integrity. You have taught me what it is to love and to be loved, Fiona. To care and to be cared for. And now I pledge my life—this new, good, dedicated life—to you, Fiona. I love you."

"Oh, Alec," she breathed, her throat knotted as she raised her lips to his. As their lips met, tears spilled over and rolled down her cheeks. "Oh, I love you so much. You ... your words ... are so beautiful, so ..." She stopped, her tears taking over. There was nothing she could say that could describe the way she felt. But Alec knew. She looked into his deep blue eyes and she could see that Alec just knew.

Softly, tenderly, he kissed the glistening beads away. He could feel on his lips the salty wetness of her emotion. He filled his great chest with air and continued.

"Fiona, marry me," Alec said, gathering her face in his hands. His eyes bored into the depth of hers. "Let's not wait. I don't want to wait. We could be married here at Benmore."

His words tugged at her with their promise. Here was happiness. A future of happiness that would eradicate the nightmares of her past. But she needed to think. She needed to do the right thing. Her duty, her promise to herself to find her mother's killers could not be denied. Fiona stared blankly at Alec's shoulders, trying to avoid his eyes. How could she explain? How could she give up all that he was offering?

"Look at me, Fiona."

Fiona looked up into his eyes and searched for her answer.

"I love you, Alec," she whispered. "But I need to clear my mother's name. My conscience will never let me rest until I have done all I can."

"Marry me, Fiona. Marry me now," he coaxed. "I will

go into the fires of hell itself for you. I'll stand by you; and what we need to do, we'll do together."

She reached up and cradled his handsomely chiseled face in her hand. "Alec, I can't do that to you. That's my battle, not yours. I can't damage your reputation. What I'm after, what I might discover, the truth behind my mother's death, will very likely involve others in your class. Perhaps even people you know well. I've thought about the things you told me, about what might have been the reasons behind my mother's murder. I can see it already. I will become a social outcast in seeking the truth and in asking for justice. But you ... you are Scotland's hope, so important to our future. You cannot have a wife such as I. I'll only disgrace you."

Alec started to speak, but Fiona hushed him with her slender fingers, with her words.

"Alec, what you offer—just staying here and marrying you, trying to forget all the demons of the past—this is not an option. Not when it concerns my mother. My conscience will not allow that. So I suppose marriage ... perhaps is not something meant to happen for us. Not yet, anyway."

Alec gathered her fingers in his hand and kissed them gently before starting to speak. "Fiona, staying apart is not an option. And that's not my conscience speaking. My heart, my mind, my entire being cries out for you. And trust me, there is even more. Before we left Skye, I had to give my word to that little warrior of yours that I'd bring you back."

"Malcolm?"

"Aye, Malcolm. You wouldn't want to have his fearsome wrath come down on my head, would you?"

Fiona smiled, thinking of her little friend. Of his smiling, gentle ways.

"Just accept it, my love. The only question that is left unanswered is not *if* we were going to be married, the question is *when*. And now, after hearing your hesitation, your concerns, I am telling you that decision has been made."

"It has? And what might that decision be?"

"We will be marrying before this week ends."

"Have you lost your mind?" she asked, dumbfounded. "Didn't you hear a word I said?"

"Every one of them!" Alec let go of her hand and went to the chest by her bed, opening the top and pawing through her things.

"And that's all you have to say? You don't care in the least how I feel about this?" Fiona fumbled for some response. "And what happened to a betrothal and long engagements and hand festing? If I'm not mistaken, those are still traditions in the Highlands."

He came back to her with a shawl of silk, woven in the Macpherson plaid. She just stood and watched in awe as he wrapped the piece around her neck and arranged it so as to hide a portion of her exposed bosom.

"Nay, lass. Highland engagements traditionally last as long as it takes to get from the horse to the house," he said, eyeing his handiwork appreciatively. "And sometimes not even that long."

"Alec!" She drawled. "You know that's not true."

"If you say so."

"I do."

"But I might remind you," Alec said, taking her chin gently in his hand, "you spent our engagement walking to the tower."

"We weren't engaged then!" Fiona pushed his hand away with a playful glare.

"We certainly were. And I'm planning to tell everyone at dinner tonight that we were."

"I won't admit to such a thing," she threatened mildly. "You can't lie like that."

"Hmmm," he responded. "You know, there is just no limit to how far I'll go when I make up my mind I want something."

Alec lifted her unresisting body into his arms and crushed her lips with his own. Deeply, passionately, thoroughly, he kissed his beloved with a fervor that left her breathless. Standing her on her feet again, with a smile he began straightening her clothes once more.

"Dinner is ready, my betrothed. The festivities have already begun. They are all expecting us."

"You are thick-headed, stubborn, and deaf, Alec Macpherson," she breathed as he linked her arm in his. "I'll not marry you. You can't force me."

"Aye, I can." He placed his hand over hers, press-it into his muscular forearm as they started for the door. "It nearly slipped my mind."

"What has?" she asked cautiously.

"You've forgotten our journey."

"What about our journey?" she asked, her eyes widening in bewilderment.

"Well, so far I've been able to keep Robert from telling everyone ... well ... how worried he was the night—"

"I'll marry you." She sighed, her face breaking into an ironic smile. "And now I know I'll be marrying the most unscrupulous rogue in all the Highlands."

Chapter 16

Be charitable and humble of estate,
Yea, worldly honor outlasts not the cry.
For your earthly troubles don't be melancholy:
Be rich in patience, if in goods you're but poor;
Who lives merrily, he lives lavishly: for
Without gladness, no treasure avails.
—WILLIAM DUNBAR, *"Without Gladness"*

Fiona was smiling brightly as they slipped into the festive hall.

Around them the sounds of Midsummer's Eve revelry filled the air. Pipers were wandering around the hall, and children from the village danced happily behind them. The woven rushes had been cleared from the very center of the huge room, and ale-drinking revelers were boisterously constructing a bonfire. From every side, laughter and merriment enveloped the latecomers, so that no one noticed their entrance.

Fiona spotted David, sitting with Robert at the long table nearest the door, enjoying the company of some of the warriors they had traveled with, and their ladies. Extricating herself from Alec's arm, she bent over David and whispered their news in his ear. Her old friend's expression was one of pure joy upon hearing the news.

By the time she straightened up, a hush had fallen over the entire hall. The musicians ceased playing, and all eyes were upon her. Alec took her arm as she nervously stepped back a pace. She glanced down at the Macpherson tartan that covered her shoulders and she suddenly wondered if the quiet was caused by an outsider wearing their plaid. She had not even stopped to consider the appropriateness of the tartan. Her mind raced to think of what else could have caused such a reaction.

"Think of them as family, my love," Alec whispered reassuringly. "They've been waiting for you, and none too patiently, from what I hear."

"Why are they so quiet?" she murmured back to him. "I've disappointed them somehow?"

"You've got them spellbound, from the looks of things. But how can you blame them?" Alec said, appraising the incredible beauty of the woman on his arm. It was no wonder that the very breathing of everyone in the hall seemed to come to a full stop. Fiona's voice had wavered, but she stood beside him, her head high and her hazel eyes flashing. The smooth skin of her cheeks glowed in the light of the flaring lamps on the walls. No one but he would ever know the sensuous feel of her full and sculpted lips. Her silken mane cascaded in rolling waves of liquid fire over the tartan at her shoulders and onto the ivory gown that so brilliantly highlighted the perfect lines of her figure. She was a vision. And he proudly stood beside her.

With a booming welcome, a silver-haired giant nimbly crossed the floor, Lady Elizabeth and another smaller man trailing behind.

"At last!" he thundered. "At last the lowly laird gets to meet the fairy princess!"

Fiona's nervousness vanished instantly, a smile spreading across her face as Alec's father approached them.

"At last," she responded with a low curtsy. "At last the humble convent lass is honored with a glimpse of the noblest chieftain in the Highlands."

"Ha!" Alexander laughed, offering his hand to her. "The lass has spirit to go with her beauty. The daughter of good King James owes no curtsy to this old mule."

Fiona graciously accepted his proffered hand as she straightened before him. As they exchanged greetings, those present in the hall seemed to be hanging on every word.

"Before I am completely left out of this newfound friendship of yours, Father, I would like to introduce you to your future daughter," Alec said, putting a possessive hand around her slender waist. "This is Fiona Drummond Stuart."

As Alec concluded, the room suddenly erupted with cheers, and the old man beamed with delight.

The laird opened his arms, and, standing on her toes, Fiona placed a kiss on the chieftain's cheek, only to find herself crushed in a bear hug as his powerful arms wrapped around her.

"It's my turn, Alexander," Lady Elizabeth put in, separating the young woman from her husband and warmly welcoming her with a hearty embrace. Her eyes sparkled as she took both of Fiona's hands and looked into her face. "This is wonderful news, my dear. My son is a very fortunate man to have you. And don't you ever let him forget that."

"Don't scare her off, Elizabeth," the laird said. "Alec does have one or two good qualities."

"Aye, you old warhorse, but only if you call having a silver tongue and extremely handsome features qualities." She smiled up at her husband, and turned back confidentially to Fiona. "Actually, Alec has more qualities than that, but those two definitely came from the Macpherson side."

Fiona did not have to look at the men to agree with what was said. Alec's handsome features had been her undoing from the first moment they'd met.

The pipers began to play again, and Fiona found herself surrounded by crowding faces of well-wishers. There were so many questions that these people had, so much they all seemed to want to know about her. And she answered what she could.

Those who came close were delighted with the young woman's responses. There was no falsehood, no haughtiness, no snobbish arrogance. This prospective bride was not at all like the last Macpherson fiancée. Fiona was just herself. Down to earth and matter-of-fact. And those qualities alone captured the hearts of all around her.

When two little girls presented Fiona with a woven garland of daisies, she immediately knelt down between them, and with great merriment the giggling lasses arranged the crown in her hair, to the appreciative approval of the onlookers.

Alec hovered over her, screening her from overly energetic clan members. John was one of the last Macpherson clan members to push his way through the circle to Fiona's side. After kissing her on both cheeks, and noting Alec's watchful gaze, John decided he could not pass up the opportunity of needling his lovestruck brother.

Pulling Fiona closer to his side, John whispered to her in confidential tones loud enough for all to hear, "You're making a grave error, m'lady. There are stories of lunacy in the family. And if you have a moment, I'd like to explain—"

"Move along, John," Alec growled. "The only lunacy in our family, Fiona, is in the third son."

"Alec!" Fiona scolded laughingly.

"As I was saying—" John continued, holding on to her hand.

"Mother, why *didn't* we drown him at birth?" Alec asked, pulling Fiona closer to him.

"It's never too late," Alec's father put in, stepping into the laughing group.

Alec was firmly tugging at one of her hands, while John held fast to the other teasingly. With one swift movement, Alec pulled Fiona around to his other side, detaching his intended's hand from the young scoundrel.

Fiona looked about her, suddenly conscious of the happy glow that had crept into her body. The warmth she was feeling, the welcome, the cheerful banter, the loving feel of Alec's hand on hers, all mingled within Fiona, producing a sense that she'd never really known before ... a sense of family. Around them the party continued on boisterously, people laughing, shouting, and dancing. She looked up at Alec and their gazes locked. She was a part of this, a part of them. That was what Alec had promised.

She had a family. And most important of all, she had him.

In a few moments Fiona saw groups of revelers starting to work themselves back to their seats. Throughout the hall, serving folk were delivering food to the long trestle tables.

Alec's father started leading Fiona to the head table, and Alec and the rest of the family followed behind, still carrying on their animated conversation. As he reached the dais, Alexander halted abruptly.

"Ah, lass," he explained. "There is someone here that you haven't met, I believe."

Just ahead of them, leaning against one of the tables, a handsome but stern-faced older man stood with his arms crossed against his massive chest, and the laird led Fiona toward the quiet figure.

There was no question in Fiona's mind that the balding man looking intently at her was a man of great power. Over his brilliantly white linen shirt and the tartan of black and white, a huge gold medallion hung from a heavy chain that encircled his neck. On it the rampant lion crest of Scotland, signifying his position as leader of the council of nobles, gleamed in the light of the lamps and torches. His expression never changed as they approached, and Fiona felt a sudden chill as the man's blue eyes studied her face deliberately.

Lord Huntly knew he was staring at the young woman, but he made no attempt to stop. After all these years, he thought. Face-to-face with the daughter that should have been mine. Margaret was there in her features, in the stunning beauty of her eyes, in the set of the mouth, the graceful line of the jaw. He had loved her, but she had chosen another. He had offered her everything, but she had chosen a path that had led to her own death. But he had never stopped loving her. Ever.

As the two stood before him, Huntly straightened and bowed slightly from the waist in response to the young woman's curtsy.

"Fiona Drummond Stuart," Lord Alexander said courteously, "I'd like you to meet one of your greatest benefactors. This is the Earl of Huntly."

"It's a pleasure to meet you, m'lord. Finally, I have the opportunity to thank you for all you've done on my behalf."

Fiona took the cold outstretched hands of the man before her. Alexander towered over them, but she could feel the aura of control that exuded from the earl. He'd not stopped looking at her from the moment they'd started toward him, but she had yet to see a single identifiable expression register on his face. Like a mask, the man's face showed no emotion, no pleasure, no disappointment. It was devoid of feeling. There was nothing but the cold blue eyes that peered searchingly into her own face.

"I've only done what should have been done long ago," he said in an even tone.

"You've done far more than I could ever have expected, m'lord."

His gaze never wavered as his strong fingers gently tightened their grip on Fiona's hands.

"I was a friend of your mother's, lass."

Fiona recalled the prioress' words about unrequited love. She looked at the man who had vowed to someday win back her mother's hand.

"Why don't you call me Andrew?" he added.

Chapter 17

Another kind of ravenous wolf
Is the mighty man, having plenty enough ...
—ROBERT HENRYSON, *"The Wolf and the Lamb"*

*A*ndrew.
 Fiona's blood froze in her veins. *Lord Andrew.*
Unable to move, she stood staring into Huntly's eyes. As she did, memories of an evil night flooded her senses. Words began to pour into her brain, pounding her with the sounds and fears of that distant autumn night. *Should I not be down with Lord Andrew?* Sir Allan's voice was right behind her. As in a dream, Fiona heard the echoes of the good knight's words ... *with Lord Andrew ... Lord Andrew ... Andrew!*

The sights and sounds of the Macphersons' Great Hall began to whirl in a liquid kaleidoscope of colors. Fiona felt herself falling ... floating into a garish nightmare of flashing light and muffled voices. *Andrew!* Faces began to appear before her, weaving in and out between purple clouds that swept past in funnels of windless storm.

Andrew!

Fiona felt her mother's arm around her little body. She could feel her breath on her cheek. *No! Take her far away. From him. From Andrew!* Her room ... full now, men looming over them. A pain in her arms. High in the air, the black eyes of an angry stranger. *Torquil. Are you going to let this wee thing best you?* Another man, his sneering mouth and death grip on her mother.

Mama! Her mother's eyes ... wild with fear ... despair. The flaring torches and then darkness ... a blanket covering her ... suffocating her. The horses. The rough hands. A grip of steel. Riding. Forever riding.

Andrew!

"Why don't you call me Andrew?"

Stepping back, Fiona bumped into Alec as the earl released her hands.

"I see you two have already met." Alec's voice snapped Fiona's head around. Looking into her face, he thought she looked suddenly pale, unsteady on her feet. He put his hands on her shoulders and pulled her to his side. His eyes showed his concern. "What's wrong?"

She felt Alec's strong hands around her waist and took strength from his touch. Looking up at him, she became aware of the numerous eyes that were upon her. Waiting for an answer. "Nothing," she said quietly. "I'm fine."

"You have to do a better job taking care of her, Alec," Alexander scolded. He turned to Huntly. "Alec rushed the poor lass here from Skye in a week's time."

Fiona snuggled closer to Alec as she continued to study the earl. As the nobleman exchanged words with Alec's father, Fiona saw his gaze continually travel back to her and to Alec. She saw him glance down at Alec's encircling arm, at his hand holding her comfortably at the waist. She wondered what could be going through this man's mind.

"I haven't offered you both my congratulations, Alec," Huntly said, his eyes darting from Fiona's face to Alec's. Never a smile. Not a glimmer of emotion in the man's hard face.

"Well, here's your opportunity," Alec responded seriously. He wanted the earl's approval of their marriage, but he'd be damned if he let Huntly's cold ways dampen Fiona's happiness this evening. Alec knew Huntly well enough to shrug off the earl's lack of outward emotion, but he was afraid Fiona might construe it differently.

"You appear to be the luckiest man in Scotland, Alec." Huntly paused, his gaze lingering once again on Fiona's face. "I've only known one woman in my life whose beauty equaled the beauty of this young lady. Congratulations to you both."

An awkward silence fell over the group, and Huntly stood motionless, the only one unaffected by it.

"I sincerely hope, Fiona," he said finally, breaking the spell, "that you and I get an opportunity to get to know one another in the days ahead."

"Well, Andrew, you can get started right now," Lady Elizabeth broke in. "It's time we all sat."

"May I have the pleasure of sitting beside you at dinner, m'lady?" Huntly asked, offering Fiona his arm.

"Nay!" Alexander boomed. "You court-bred fox. You'll not be stealing my new-hatched chick!"

"Alexander!" Elizabeth scolded. "You'll have a lifetime to sit beside our new daughter."

"The hell I will," the laird said as he escorted his wife ahead of the others to the table. "Don't you think I know my own son? We'll be lucky if he'll let her visit us at Easter and Christmas."

"Just because you were so keen in keeping *me* only to yourself, that doesn't mean Alec will be like that," Elizabeth whispered to her husband.

"Why wouldn't he be?" Alexander put his hands around the slender waist of his wife and pulled her affectionately to his side. "Do I have to remind you of what we did during those times that I kept you to myself?"

Elizabeth found herself blushing as she looked around to make sure no one was listening. "Reminding is nice."

The laird whipped around, pulling his wife with him. "Well, that does it. I'm exhausted. I'm afraid this party will have to go on without us."

"Alexander!" she drawled. "We have company."

"The hell with them!"

"Stop it, Alexander," she scolded, trying to pull out of his grip.

"Then have them serve a quick dinner," he growled, allowing himself to be drawn to the table. "Hear me? Quick."

Alec, sitting down beside Fiona and Huntly, exchanged grins with his brother John at their parents' amorous actions. Some things never changed at Benmore Castle.

"There, you see," the laird grumbled loudly with a wink at Fiona. "Now I've lost my place beside my daughter."

Elizabeth patted the bench next to her. "Well, you can sit right here beside me and tell me again about how your hunting went today."

When Alec came to her in the night, the full moon had spread its beams across the chamber floor in a carpet of blue chiffon. The heavy oaken door had swung easily on its well-greased hinges, and the warrior slipped quietly into the room, his eyes quickly finding the great bed in the lunar glow. Placing the heavy bar across the door, Alec moved to the side of the bed. Within the semi-darkness of the damask curtains, pulled back in the comfortable summer weather, Alec looked longingly for Fiona.

The bed was empty.

"Looking for someone?" she called quietly, watching him from the window seat. Fiona hadn't been able to sleep, so, wrapping the Macpherson tartan around her, she sat waiting on the window seat, gazing out at a star-lit sky.

"Not 'someone,' " Alec said, making his way around the bed. "I'm looking for you."

She had hoped that he would come. She needed him; she had so many questions that she hoped he could answer. Questions about her mother. About Andrew, Lord Huntly. During dinner, she'd continued to observe the earl. He was a man of very few words when it came to his own affairs, but he'd asked many questions of Alec, of her. He'd been very interested in her upbringing, in the education she'd received at the Priory. And surprisingly, he'd been very attentive to talk about her relationship with Alec. Though his expression showed nothing, it seemed to Fiona that Lord Andrew was extremely curious about her and Alec. About how they'd met, and particularly about what their marriage plans were.

"Why did the earl ask so many questions at dinner, Alec?" she whispered as he moved her aside and sat beside her.

"You're still thinking about Huntly?" he asked, trying to make himself comfortable in the limited space.

"Aye, I am." She stood, trying to give him enough room to get settled. But he just stretched his legs, taking over all the space she'd vacated. Fiona looked at him wide-eyed. She'd just been muscled out of her snug sanctuary. "Are you happy now?"

"No, not yet," Alec said as he reached and grabbed her hands. With a sharp tug, he yanked Fiona onto his lap. He shifted her weight and snuggled her against his chest. "Ah. This is much better."

Fiona looked up into his mischievous eyes and smiled. He definitely had a way of making her forget things.

"You didn't bar your door." His words were neither a question nor an admonition. They had a note of suggestiveness that made Fiona shiver with anticipation.

She looked at him from under lowered eyelids. "I was afraid you wouldn't be able to get in."

"A mere door will never keep me away from you, my love." Alec's lips sought hers, the tip of his tongue tasting the sweet fullness of her. He pulled back, gazing at her. The glow of the moon glistened in her eyes. "I'd hoped you'd be waiting for me."

The flowing mass of hair billowed over her shoulder, and Alec could smell the scent of jasmine in the soft cascading mane.

"What would have happened if I'd been sleeping?" She drawled the last word as Alec's hand gently began to roam her body. His magic fingers played wide circles on her arms and back, caressing the soft fabric against her skin beneath.

"What do you have under this?" he asked in alluring tones, his mouth playing against her sensitive earlobes.

Fiona shuddered in excitement at the feel of his hot breath against her neck, of his strong hands working themselves under the thick cloth of the tartan and onto the smooth silk of her nightshift. "It's a present ... from your mother."

"Let me see it." Alec pushed her off his lap, standing her in the open angle of his massive thighs. He slowly, ever so slowly, removed the tartan from her shoulder and dropped it to the floor. Pushing her hair away from her shoulder, Alec's hands traveled down Fiona's arms, taking hold of the hands that were hanging quietly at her sides. He gazed longingly in rapt admiration at the creation before him.

"You are a goddess." He whispered, his voice husky with awe. The translucent silk of the nightgown molded itself to the sensuous lines of her perfect body. Alec leaned forward, his hands moving to Fiona's hips. His fingers gently caressed the subtle curves of her belly, and he felt her shiver as his thumbs crossed her ribs and came to rest at the base of her firm, full breasts.

"I have to say, this is the best present my mother has

ever given me." He held his breath as one of the shoulder straps fell off her shoulder, revealing the milky-white flesh of her breast. "I'll be sure to thank her tomorrow."

"Nay!" She scowled softly, pulling the strap back up. "You are not supposed to see this garment until our wedding night."

Alec reached up and pulled both of the straps partially down her arms before drawing her back into his lap. "I think you should know something of our parents, love. My father already had my mother pregnant with a child before they married."

"He did?"

"Aye, he did." He placed a kiss on her exposed shoulders, tasting her soft flesh. "I was born seven months after they'd wed. The families on both sides were quite impressed with my size ... considering my premature status."

"Alec?" she whispered. Finding an opening in the white linen of his shirt, her hand moved caressingly against the sinewy contours of his massive chest.

"Aye, my love?" he answered, his fingers lightly brushing over the fullness of her breast. He felt her stop breathing as the tip of his index finger delicately circled the aroused nipple through the silken material.

"I'm ... I'm glad we are marrying before the week's end." She pulled open the front of his shirt and pressed her lips against the solid warmth of his skin. She lay her head on his shoulder, breathing in the manly scent of him.

"Not as glad as I am." He traced the edge of her gown where the tops of her breasts rose and fell with the slightest of movements.

"But ... I'm afraid, too." Fiona's hands ceased momentarily their voyage of discovery.

Alec drew back, gazing into her anxious eyes. "Not of me, I hope."

"Nay," she answered, averting her eyes. "Of me. Of myself."

Gently he took her chin in his hand, drawing her eyes back to his. "How could you possibly be afraid of yourself?"

"How could I not be afraid," Fiona whispered. "All I know of love and marriage is what I remember of my parents. They might have carried all the love of the world for the other, but they could not be married." She paused and let her fingers caress Alec's face. "Perhaps those two things don't go together. Perhaps, for me——"

"Fiona," Alec scolded gently. "Stop living in the past."

"Aren't you afraid that I might be cursed—as my mother was?" she silenced him, laying her fingers tenderly on his lips. "I was an illegitimate child. Perhaps I am fated to live ... and love as she——"

"I won't let you do this, Fiona." This time Alec took her firmly by the shoulders. "Now, you listen to me. Before I went to the Isle of Skye, before I ever met you, if someone had talked seriously to me of fate being the cause of events, I would have laughed in his face. But, today ... well, today I believe in it. Meeting you, seeing the porter, James ... so many things have happened. The reason I am saying this is that I know ... I understand ... your fears. But I am not going to let those fears hinder our happiness. What happened to your parents might have been their fate, but it was *their* fate, not ours. We have each other. We want each other. We love each other."

"But, Alec, they had all these things too."

"Aye, but they also had the people of two countries objecting to their marriage. They had forces beyond their control pulling them apart. We don't have that, Fiona. We don't."

She leaned her forehead against his lips and tried to accept his words.

"Please tell me you are not afraid."

She looked up with smiling eyes. "Do I hear Alec Macpherson pleading?"

"Pleading. Begging. You can call it whatever you like. I need to know you are content ... that you believe. That's all that matters. So humor me and tell me you will not be afraid."

"But, Alec ... that's not all."

"It isn't?" he cradled her face in his great hands. "Good God, Fiona! What else is there?"

"I still feel like a foolish, inexperienced woman." She paused, and then blurted out her other fear. "Alec, I know nothing about being a wife! Not the first thing! I'm afraid I'll do everything wrong."

A smile creased Alec's face.

Her hand dropped to her side, and her finger played unconsciously on the soft wool of Alec's kilt. "Not one thing I learned at the Priory was aimed at preparing me for this!"

"Fiona, you ran the affairs of that place with tremendous skill. Affairs at Benmore Castle and Dunvegan are no different from what you've been doing at the Priory." Alec looked reassuringly into her face, working hard to ignore the heavenly pleasure of her hand on his taut thigh muscle. These were the kinds of worries it would be a pleasure to deal with.

"Alec, the running of castles is not what has me worried," she said softly. She felt awkward and helpless, but what words would make him understand?

His fingers found the smooth skin of her cheek, and it was hot to his touch. Realizing that she was totally unaware of the effect her touch was having on him, he knew exactly what was worrying her. "Fiona, we already belong to each other. Everything you need to know is already inside of you."

"But I hardly know what to do." Fiona stared down at the thick, muscular forearms that held her so tenderly, at the hands that moved so expertly—exciting her, thrilling her. "I don't know how to please you." Her hand waved in frustration, coming to rest on his arm.

"Please me? I can't believe you've forgotten what we shared in that tower."

"Oh, Alec. I will remember what happened there until the day I die. I know what I felt, but how . . . how can I make *you* feel that way?"

"It's easy," Alec said as his hand caressed the sides of her breasts and traveled up to her face. Encircling her face with his great hands, he whispered the words. "Just be who you are, my love. Don't ever change."

Fiona could see a hint of what she thought was sorrow glistening in his deep blue eyes, and then she knew— more than anything else in this world—she wanted him to be happy. She stood and turned in his arms until she faced him. Their gazes never wavered.

"Alec, that's a promise you have from me." She

leaned down, placing a kiss on his full lips before continuing softly, "But if you think that you can change the topic so easily, you are mistaken, m'lord."

Standing there, looking down at his handsome face, she noted the twinge of smile tugging at his lips as his eyes dropped to her breasts. She laced her hands into his long blond hair and, grabbing a fistful, she pulled it roughly back. "Now tell me what I should do."

Alec's hands reached out, softly gripping her firm thighs. Then, slowly—ever so slowly—he began to gather her nightshift up from below her knees. "Use your imagination, my love. Just use your imagination."

Fiona shivered with excitement as Alec's hands slid under the raised hem, moving his palms across her naked buttocks. Taking his advice to heart, she tugged open his shirt until it opened to his waist. Then, reaching down, she started to pull it out of his kilt and up over his shoulders. Dropping the linen garment beside her, she let her hands travel all over the perfectly defined musculature of his back, his shoulders, his chest, tracing the contours. Then, no longer able to stand away from him, she followed her fingers' trail with her mouth, her tongue. She took great pleasure seeing him visibly react to the effect of her mouth on his skin. Slowly, she lowered herself in front of him, and as the tip of her tongue raced a path down his stomach, she heard him take a deep breath and hold it.

Alec's hands reached into Fiona's tumbling mass of hair and pulled it back. Their eyes locked.

Fiona looked deep into the banked coals of his passion and felt her spirit lift. She placed her two hands on his hardened thighs and slid them slowly upward toward his aroused manhood. She felt his hands latch onto her hair, and as her fingers found his manhood, encircling it, she saw him close his eyes and tilt his head back. Fiona felt an urgency race through her when she pushed back his kilt and exposed the throbbing member to her eyes. Moving closer, she reached down and, hesitantly at first, rubbed the warm crown of the thick shaft against her cheek. Then, running her lips the length of it, she felt him shudder, his thighs tightening against her. Moving around the member, her lips parted, her tongue tasting the smooth, velvety texture of him. Then, hearing his restrained groan, she grew bolder and took him deep in her mouth.

One moment Alec was leashing his desire, the next moment he was out of control. Within him passion surged, filling his chest with a tightness that constricted all breathing. His hands again grabbed her soft mane of hair, and he pulled her head back until her face looked up into his. Their eyes met, and even in the darkened room, he could see her own matching desire. Desire that permeated the space between them. Desire that hung like a glistening jewel in their locked gazes.

His mouth descended upon her still parted lips. His tongue thrust deeply into her warmth. He tasted all she had in her. Alec's hands cradled Fiona's face, then moved across the slender shoulders. Gently drawing the silk shift up, he carefully lifted it over her head. Taking her hands, Alec gazed on the vision looking up at him. His eyes drank in the gleaming ivory skin of her shoulders until she slowly, wordlessly, stood up.

In the soft moonlight, Fiona shone as if lit from within. Like a goddess of some pagan rite, she stood motionless in the luminescent glow, her lover's human heart pounding feverishly, his soul committed, his entire being enthralled by the energy of her radiant perfection. She hid nothing from him as his eyes did homage to her resplendent beauty. His gaze traveled from her face, down along the hair that flowed over one breast, past the curves of her belly to the triangle of soft hair that graced the junction of her long, flawless legs. He looked up into her exquisite face and glistening eyes.

Fiona reached out and touched his cheek, and Alec kissed the palm of her hand. Then, placing her arm on his shoulder, he lifted her effortlessly as he stood, moving easily to the bed and laying her gently across it.

He looked down at her as he unfastened the belt that held his kilt. Unwrapping it, he stood naked beside the bed, and Fiona watched him, a hunger spreading like a wildfire within her. She moved restlessly against the soft sheet, wishing his weight upon her.

Reaching down, Alec took hold of Fiona's legs, dragging her slowly toward him until her knees dangled at the edge of the billowy mattress. She began to raise herself, but he met her halfway, taking her wrists and pushing them back, trapping them with one huge hand above her head. His mouth was rough as he took possession of hers, and Fiona responded with a driving passion that matched his own.

He tore his mouth from hers, and his ardor threatened to overflow as Fiona's leg raised and hooked around his thigh. He kissed the hollow of her throat and felt her body arch against him as his mouth suckled a hardened nipple. Fiona moaned softly as Alec continued to caress with his tongue the sensitive flesh.

When his lips moved down the ivory softness of her belly, Fiona held her breath. He parted her legs and his tongue found the sweet, moist darkness and thrust inside.

As he released her hands, Fiona panted his name, lacing her fingers into his silky mane. Never breaking off the intimacy, he lifted her buttocks, raising her up and thrusting his tongue ever more deeply into her pulsating recesses until she breathlessly cried out his name.

Fiona could not take air into her lungs, but she was beyond caring as the blood roared wildly in her head. She felt his weight upon her as Alec took her into his arms and slid into her. Like two clay forms, their bodies molded together with a completeness that Fiona sensed more than thought. As they lay momentarily still, she felt his arms tightly around her, and she felt cherished, valued, loved. When Alec began to move, Fiona went with him, the pulsing rhythms they each felt rising undeniably within them.

Alec tried to go slowly, but with her tight wet sheath squeezing him, her knee coming up to give him further access, her soft mouth devouring his with fervor equaling his own ... it was nearly too much for him. He called on all the discipline he could muster in the growing haze that was rapidly enveloping him, and contained his overwhelming desire to withdraw and plunge again and again with reckless abandon.

Fiona gasped as he thrust ever so gently into the very core of her, slowly drawing out with long, pulsing strokes that ignited waves of white heat within her. Her eyes half shut each time the crown of his manhood reached the sensitized nub of her desire, and each achingly long penetration sent renewed flames of passion scorching through her body. Looking up through the gauzy haze that clouded her vision, Fiona saw Alec's eyes burning into her with superhuman intensity. Her hands moved over his raised chest to his face, but her poised hands fluttered and then clutched at his long hair as his shaft once again slid molten heat into the very center of her. A moan escaped her lips, and a new urgency swept into her. Fiona's hands moved around him, and she clung to him, grinding her hips into him, wanting all of him.

Fiona's breaths became soft whimpers as Alec unconsciously increased the tempo of his strokes. Within his brain, rational thought was breaking apart, and raw animal instinct was taking over as he felt her moving hungrily beneath him. But as he attempted to concentrate on his one fierce desire—to push her before him to that moment of bliss—he felt his long hard arousal expanding within the warm walls of her passage. Yet even as her legs wrapped around his waist, pulling him deeper within her, he bore down, holding on tightly to his will. But when Fiona raked his back, her whimpers now intense cries of ecstasy, he could no longer hold back.

The room Fiona saw now was lit with the flashing whites and reds of exquisite pleasure. Fiona felt no material beneath her, saw no canopy above. The only things she knew to be real were the man she loved and the wild sensations that were threatening to lift her out of herself and into another dimension. Fiona clung desperately to him, the pounding rhythms of the sybaritic labor obliterating the darkness of the castle chamber. Still more quickly she rose, ever higher and higher, until her spirit tore through the curtain of actuality. With blinding speed, the sky opened above her, and like a bird thrown into flight, Fiona soared upward into a crystalline sphere, stretching and circling, climbing into the blue-white reaches of an ethereal realm.

When Alec felt her graceful body arch up and back, moving harmoniously in their dramatic dance of love, he could wait no longer. Feeling her shuddering body rise hard against him, Alec drove himself deeply into her, again and again. Finally, in a violent eruption of volcanic heat, his massive love shaft exploded within her, filling Fiona with the warm fluid of his being.

Transfixed, it seemed they had spent an age lying together in each other's arms. Astounded by the deep passion that they'd shared, Alec's mind dwelt lingeringly on the experience. This night was one that, even in his wildest imaginings, he'd not have thought possible. He had been the experienced one. But nothing in his past had come even close to this union of bodies and souls that had taken place with Fiona. They were destined to be together. He knew that with a fierce certainty.

Resting on his elbow, he traced her beautiful face with his fingers. She turned and gave him a smile that took his breath away.

"Alec?"

"Aye, my love?"

She edged up against him, resting her head on the pillows as she gazed into the deep blue of his beautiful eyes. "What do you know of Huntly?"

"I think I should be jealous," he teased threateningly. "We've just gone through the most incredible lovemaking since the Garden of Eden, and now the first words out of your mouth have to do with Huntly."

"Don't be," she coaxed, running a finger across his full, pouting lips. "But I'm serious."

"Very well." Alec sighed, gathering Fiona in his arms and pulling her even closer. "What is it you want to know?"

"I ... I need to know about his past. About the kind of man he is. If he ever married. If he has any children."

"These all seem like very personal questions."

"Alexander Robert Macpherson, you'd better start talking or else ..." She tried to growl the last words menacingly, but Alec started to laugh.

"Let's see, where is the best place to start with Andrew, the Earl of Huntly?" he lay on his back musing for a moment as she snuggled comfortably beside him. "Well, from what I know of him, Huntly has been a Stuart man all his life. He sided with your father when he came to the throne, and took the king's fight into the northwestern Highlands when Torquil MacLeod and the other renegade chiefs decided to turn their backs on the rest of Scotland. Lord Huntly remained the king's most trusted adviser until James decided to bring the army into England. He warned the king against going, so

James left him to secure the queen, the prince, and Edinburgh Castle. You know the rest."

Alec turned his face toward the open window. For the first time in three years, the bloody field at Flodden seemed so far in the past, so far removed from the world he was living in, so distant from the future he was envisioning with Fiona. He turned his head back to her and kissed her cool forehead.

Fiona Drummond Stuart, daughter of his long-dead king, had brought him peace. Finally, by coming into his life, his heart, his soul, she had slain the demons that had been haunting his memory. Demons of guilt about a hard-fought battle in which his king had died while he still lived. Finally, fate had brought him the chance to assuage his guilt by protecting Fiona, and he would protect her forever. He would have, anyway . . . he loved her.

"Alec," she whispered, running her hand over his chest. "What about before Flodden? His personal life?"

"Huntly is an extremely smart man. All his life, he has been a soldier and a politician. But most of all, he's been a ruler. Even before Flodden, the king left many matters of government to him. He was the king's most capable adviser, so it was natural for your father to have him involved in all of his affairs."

Then Huntly would have known about the king's delay in arriving at Drummond Castle the night her mother had been murdered. Fiona shuddered involuntarily. Alec mistook her shiver as being caused by the gentle breeze that was beginning to waft into the room, and pulled a blanket over them.

"The way he acted tonight is the way he always acts," Alec continued. "Over the years, he's developed a . . . well, a somewhat harsh side to his personality. He's not what you might call sociable or even friendly."

"I thought he didn't like me."

"On the contrary," Alec said, pushing back a tendril of hair from her face. "He liked you very much."

"How could you tell?"

"He asked you many questions, didn't he? If he didn't like you, all the glories of this world and the next could not make him talk. Andrew's dead silence is legendary." Alec remembered the treatment Huntly had always given Kathryn at court. Her charms had had no effect on the aging earl. He'd been a very good judge of character.

Dead silence, she thought. My mother is dead silent.

"He never married?" she asked quietly.

"Nay. He never—"

"Is it true, what they say?" she interrupted. "Was it because of my mother?"

"That's what many people believe." Alec looked with surprise at Fiona. He hadn't expected her to know about Huntly's thwarted love for Margaret Drummond.

"Tonight he told me he's been to Drummond Castle many times."

"Aye, he's had dealings with your uncle for many years."

"Nay, I mean before. When my mother was alive. He said he'd visited her many times there."

"Fiona, from what I've heard, Huntly adored your mother. But when she chose your father, Huntly stepped away. He always has been a man of honor."

Fiona was quiet for a moment, looking for the right words. What was the price of this honor? she thought bitterly.

"Would he have held a grudge, Alec?"

Alec looked into her face. "Do you mean, would he hurt her? Your mother?"

"The prioress told me he was known to have sworn to win my mother back. Is it impossible to think he might have acted irrationally?" her voice became a murmur. She couldn't accuse the earl without proof. Proof that might lie hidden at Drummond Castle.

"Never, Fiona," Alec answered steadfastly. "I've known him all my life, and he would never do such a thing."

Fiona closed her troubled eyes. Alec was loyal to his friend. And that loyalty would never be shaken by any unfounded accusation she might make. No, she had to do this all alone. If her mother's leather pouch was still hidden there, she alone would have to find it. And in finding the proof, Fiona would show Alec—show them all—the long-concealed truth.

Whatever the cost, she would reveal the truth.

"When are we going to Drummond Castle, Alec?"

"Bored already, my love?" he teased gently.

"Not bored," she answered, punching him playfully in the side. "Spoiled. I've been here not even a full day, and already I have a full wardrobe, I'm sleeping in a finer room than I ever thought existed, and I have a family."

"Oh, is that all?" Alec pulled her on top of him, smiling mischievously. "Haven't you forgotten *one* small thing?"

Fiona smiled back at him and kissed the cleft of his chin. "Oh, did I fail to mention *that*? Though I don't think I'd have called anything we've shared 'small.' " She repositioned herself slightly, and as she slid her body across his, she felt his manhood stir against her thighs.

Alec growled, running his hands down her slender back and over the smooth rise of her buttocks.

"Take me to Drummond Castle?" she entreated. "There is so much there—about my past—that I need to see for myself."

"After our wedding, my love," he responded, his face darkening at the thought. There were two people at Drummond Castle that he didn't want her to see before the ceremony. And he had no desire to see Kathryn or her father, either. But later on, he would help her reclaim what was hers. "We'll stop at Drummond en route to Stirling."

"Is it a long journey?"

"Nay, in good weather like this, we could make it in less than two days."

"Then why can't we go now?" she pressed.

"Because I need to go to Kildalton Castle before the wedding."

Fiona lifted herself up, her elbows squarely planted on his chest. "Why?"

"Because the Campbells are holding the mate from the pirate ship that went looking for you. I need to find out what he knows ... before we go on to court."

Fiona began to calculate in her mind the possibility of getting to Drummond Castle and back in the six days before their wedding. Alec watched her and grinned.

"Don't worry, love. I'll get back in time. No one is going to leave you standing at the altar."

Chapter 18

He shall ascend as a horrible griffin
And meet in the air a she dragon;
These terrible monsters shall together thrust
And in the clouds beget the Antichrist.
—WILLIAM DUNBAR, *"The Antichrist"*

Like some unredeemed spirit, the curling smoke from the altar candle hung restlessly in the air of the small church.

Fiona's eyes traveled upward to where the wispy cloud disappeared into the shaft of sunlight. The light from the window high above streamed overhead, illuminating the church's single adornment, a carved cross that hung dark and heavy on the whitewashed wall above the small altar. Her hand closed unconsciously around the heavy, jeweled cross dangling from her neck. Her mother's cross. Drawing a deep breath, she tucked the cross inside the neck of her dress.

"Perhaps I don't understand, Fiona. But you're certainly not helping me any." David stood looking angrily at the young woman sitting so calmly on the bench at the back of the village church. "Why in God's name do you have to go *now*?"

"Because there are things at Drummond Castle that must come to light."

"But you said Lord Alec is planning to take you there after the wedding," he argued. "Why can't you wait?"

"Because I'm afraid, David."

"Afraid?" he repeated, puzzled. "Afraid of what?"

Fiona took a deep breath. It was all so complicated; how could she explain it? She hardly understood it herself.

"I'm afraid that the person responsible for my mother's murder might be a friend of Alec's." She looked steadily into her old comrade's eyes. "A close friend."

The two turned their heads in unison when the heavy oak door of the church creaked slowly open. The old woman who shuffled in hardly glanced at them, but without another word, Fiona stood up and led David out into the sunny marketcross.

Turning toward the bridge that crossed the Spey under the looming walls of the castle, David followed in silence as Fiona walked briskly to the arched span of stone and wood. There Fiona stopped. David looked out across the sparkling stream at a tinker's wagon that was noisily working its way along the river toward the bridge. Even from where they stood beside the low wall at the edge, he could hear the cursing of the driver over the clanging of pots and pans hanging from the cart's high wood sides.

"Have you told Alec what you suspect?" David asked, turning his attention completely to Fiona. "Have you confided in him?"

"Of course not!" she responded tersely. "I have no proof. He'd laugh at me. They'd all laugh at me."

"Is it so ridiculous?" he suggested. "Fiona, I've known you as long as anyone. What you are talking about here is more serious than just about anything that you faced at Skye. You're talking about accusing one of Scotland's most powerful noblemen with a crime that happened long ago. You are about to marry into the Macpherson clan. . . . You can't just accuse the Earl of Huntly without talking with your intended."

"I haven't accused him by name. You are the one who has brought his name into this. But that is exactly why I have to go now. I can't bring these good people into this. I can't involve Alec until I know for sure."

"First of all, Fiona, I don't know what good going to Drummond Castle would do. Whatever it is that you remember—or think you might remember once you're there—has probably disappeared. Your uncle and your cousin have been using that place as their own for the past three years, and they may not even let you step across their threshold. No one but the queen herself can recognize you as the true heir to those lands." David

pulled her closer to his side as the old cart rumbled
onto the bridge. The fierce-looking old tinker driving
the emaciated old ox glared at them through bushy red
eyebrows that crossed his forehead uninterrupted. David
glared back at him and the drover lashed his beast in a
nominal effort at giving the two a bit of room at the
edge of the bridge.

"I only asked you to help me get my horse, David.
But I'm going to Drummond Castle if I have to walk."

"Lass, at dinner last night, I heard you agree to be
married in six days. Are you just going to leave Lady
Elizabeth now and run off? You've always been impul-
sive, but you're not one to be irresponsible."

"I'll talk to Alec's mother before I go—"

David's hand came down sharply on Fiona's arm as
the cart behind them creaked to a sudden halt. She
turned in time to see the driver's heavy club graze David's skull as her friend ducked nimbly in an attempt to
evade the crushing blow. With a sharp cry, Fiona
reached out in horror as David dropped like a stone
onto the low wall before toppling over the edge into the
rushing waters below.

"Dav—" A coarse hand clamped over her mouth as
she found herself being lifted roughly from behind.
Struggling against the one holding her, Fiona saw come
into her vision another man, who drew back his fist,
smashing her viciously in the midriff. Fiona folded in
pain, sagging in her assailant's arms.

Unable to draw a breath of air into her lungs, Fiona
looked up helplessly as the next blow landed brutally
against the side of her head. Yellow lights flashed momentarily in her head before darkness descended like a
shroud around her.

The two men looked about them nervously as they
dumped the young woman unceremoniously into the
back of the cart. From his perch above, the driver peered
over the edge of the bridge into the waters below, looking for some sign of the old man. Seeing nothing, he
quickly gestured the two into the back of the wagon and
whipped the ancient beast into motion. With a lurch, the
wagon continued on across the bridge into the village as
the men in back pulled down the skin that covered the
rear opening. A few moments later, they were rumbling

toward the grove of woods in the foothills beyond the village.

"That bastard left me standing at the altar, and now you're telling me he wants to marry *this* churchmouse?"

Fiona kept her eyes shut tightly. The woman speaking was leaning directly over her. Inspecting her.

The ground beneath her was hard and damp, but Fiona had forced herself to remain still even after the spinning sensation went away and the muffled voices became clear. Now she continued her pretense of unconsciousness while the woman stood above her. Altar? Alec left this woman at the altar? Fiona thought confusedly. Who is she?

"That's a good-sized lump on the side of her head."

"Aye, but she made out a fair sight better than the old bull who was with her."

It took not a moment until the full import of the man's words sank in, and a rush of sorrow ran like a lance into Fiona's heart. David. Oh, God, David.

"Look at her! Look at her clothes!" the woman railed. "She's a mess. Why can't you follow my orders? I told you to bring her here safe and sound. I told you I just wanted to scare her back to the same dung heap she came from. I don't want to kill her, for God's sake. Look at her! She looks like hell!"

"I have to disagree. The lass looks quite bonny, if you ask me."

Fiona could feel the two pairs of eyes burning into her. "Perhaps you're becoming partial to red-haired country wenches," the woman snapped. The razor edge of jealousy in her voice was unmistakable.

"She is a beautiful woman ... whatever you call her. A nun, a princess, a wench. But frankly, I do like the sound of 'wench' the best."

The man's voice was familiar to Fiona, but she dared not peek at the speaker. She knew he was an islander by his accent, but she couldn't quite place—

"Neil MacLeod, you're a pig," the woman laughed shrilly. "Just like every other man in this godforsaken wasteland. You'd probably take her as she is, if I weren't here to stop you."

"Nay, Kathryn. She is not worth it. Now, taking you

... that's a different story. Ah, my love, her beauty is nothing compared to yours."

The woman's long silence nearly induced Fiona to sneak a quick look at the pair, but then she heard the woman move away.

"Of course, you're right," Kathryn asserted with an arrogant laugh. "But you're still a pig, Neil."

"That's why you like me around, isn't it, my sweet-tongued sow?" Neil responded, moving after the retreating woman.

Fiona partially opened her eyes and peered at the two across the room. By the door, under a smoky torch, Neil was standing with his back to Fiona, holding the other woman in his arms. Fiona looked about the small room desperately. She could hear the sound of water running and the regular clunking sound that she recognized as a mill wheel turning. She appeared to be in the ground floor of some mill. But where the mill was, she had no clue. She had no idea how long she'd been unconscious, or how far they'd taken her.

She had to get out. But how? There was only one small slit of a window near the ceiling, and the path to the door on the far side was blocked by the two. Her hands were tied tightly in front of her with a leather cord. She tried to flex her hands and fingers, but they were numb.

"Ha! Sweet tongue. As I recall, the only reason you still *are* around is because of my 'sweet tongue.' " The woman sneered before stepping away from him. "In fact, I believe you'd be nothing more than a carcass if I hadn't used my charm on Alec Macpherson that godawful night at Drummond Castle. I believe he would have gone right out that window after you ... when he found us together. What was the name he shouted as you scampered across the greensward? 'Cowardly knave,' wasn't it?"

Fiona shut her eyes quickly as the other woman turned in her direction. So this was her loving cousin, Kathryn Gray. Is this what Alec had tried to tell her before? That he'd been destined at one time to marry this woman? Could Alec have truly loved this wench? She strained to hear the man's response, but the silence was long and unbroken until Fiona heard Kathryn continue, her tone gloating and nasty.

"What a sight you were, clutching your clothes in your arms as you ran away! Tell me, did you ever mention to him how well that 'crippled' arm really worked climbing down that wall?" Her laugh was low and humorless. "It must have been quite ... demeaning ... having to take orders from Alec out there on that barren rock of yours, hanging as it is over the edge of the world. And all along knowing that he'd slept with me as you had. That he'd given me pleasures ... pleasures far greater than any you could ever dream of giving me. Did I ever tell you that I always enjoyed comparing you two in bed? Aye. You two were always competing. Always. You knew, but he didn't. Even that last night. The night you ran. Ran for your miserable life."

Fiona cringed at the woman's words. Oh, Alec, she thought. What a fool she must have made you feel.

"You told me that he should never know about us," Neil said angrily. "You begged me to keep silent. And as for that night, I jumped out that window to save *your* precious plans! Have you forgotten? I did that for you."

"You did *nothing* for me. You were just trying to save your own miserable ass."

"Say what you like. You used me as you use everyone to get your own selfish way. You knew that I loved you and that I would never deny anything you asked. But Kathryn, you and I both know I acted as a man of honor. And if you'd kept your own tongue, your reputation could've withstood—"

"Man of honor?" she responded, her laughter high and shrill. "Spare me the 'honor' talk. You know nothing about it. But as far as the rest ... don't make me laugh. Compared to Alec, you hardly deserve to be called a man. You lost, Neil. You ran away. You were too afraid to face him. Accept it: You are just a loser."

"You're a whore, Kathryn Drummond," he growled.

"Aye, Neil MacLeod. A whore ... like you," she answered brazenly, pausing to drive her point viciously home. "But I serve no master—unlike you—who has served many and betrayed them all. Don't forget who you're talking to. I know you didn't bring this wench here to just please me, to win back my affection. Someone is paying you. You are still serving others, Neil. Others and yourself. Look at her. Don't avert your eyes.

Look at her. I know what lies buried in your blackened soul. I know whose screams haunt you in the dark of night."

"Shut your filthy—"

"And I know why you want this wench dead," Kathryn snapped. "After all, lackey, she saw you kill her mother."

"She saw *nothing,* you bitch!" he shouted. "She was long gone when Torquil and—" Neil checked himself midsentence. He turned away from Kathryn. No, he was not going to give away his golden goose. Not after so many years.

Fiona's cry caught and swelled in her throat. *Her mother . . . her mother . . .* This lowlife, this . . . animal! Anger, hatred, beginning as a cold, white spot deep in the base of her brain, spread like freezing fire, hardening the skin of her face, her neck, quickening its pace and then racing through her. Hatred. For this evil man and for the ones with him. Torquil. Torquil MacLeod. After all these years. After living under the fearsome shadow of the man for so many years. Now she knew his identity. And she knew that justice had been served. But what about Neil? And who was the other he'd almost named? Neil knew. This criminal, Neil. And in her mind's eye, she could now see his face, his hand, hard on her mother's wrist, wresting her dagger away.

Fiona's fingers clenched involuntarily into a fist, but she gasped in pain as the bonds cut into her sore wrists. As the two whirled around to face her, Fiona's eyes fluttered open slowly and focused on them. She tried to give the impression of one just becoming conscious. One unaware of the time, the place, or the people.

"Well, it appears the fairy princess has awakened." Neil looked intently into her face from across the room. "Aye, a bright face at last in this drab hut."

"Get out of our faces." Fiona watched as the woman spat the words. "*Now!* Get out, Neil."

Fiona struggled to sit, but an ache in the side of her head started the room spinning again as she pushed herself up. Her fingers were stinging, but she turned a fiery face toward the oncoming pair.

"Well . . ." Kathryn drawled, turning to the Highlander, "didn't you hear me?"

"You want me to cut her hands loose before I go?"

"Nay, not yet." The woman stood a step away, still appraising the vulnerable-looking thing before her. "She has to *earn* her freedom. Now leave us alone."

Fiona pushed herself with difficulty to her feet. Her red hair tumbled over one shoulder as she stood, and she raised her bound hands to her face to clear the loose tendrils away from her eyes. Neil looked hard from Kathryn's face to Fiona's. Neither acknowledged he was still in the room. The two women simply stood, facing each other, scrutinizing each other, lost in an eternal glare. Finally, Kathryn looked away, putting a hand to her hair and lethargically patting golden threads that were woven into her flowing locks.

"You're not letting this wee thing best you, are you, Kathryn?" Neil's amused expression turned sour as Fiona directed a chilling look at him. He started for the door. "I'll be outside when you want me."

As Neil pulled the plank door shut behind him, silence filled the small room like a deadening presence.

Fiona looked searchingly at her captor. Her cousin. She was tall, voluptuous, and blond, with eyes the blue of the sun-faded cornflower. Her charcoal dress was trimmed with silk, and the plaid that crossed her breast covered a deeply rounded neckline. Yes, the woman was beautiful. But her beauty was cold, like the skim of ice on a winter loch. Her movements were slow, indolent, languorous even. But Fiona sensed that Kathryn had resources that she held in reserve, hidden.

Fiona cast about quickly for a way to escape. She wasn't sure exactly what Kathryn and Neil had planned for her, but she didn't trust them. She knew now that these were people capable of any crime. Fiona's eyes quickly appraised Kathryn's strength. She thought she could overpower the taller woman, physically defeat her and try to get out of the millworks. But then Neil—and whoever else was waiting outside—would still create an impassable barrier. She knew she couldn't possibly fight her way out of this ... even if she was a fighter. But she had to try. That was her only chance. Fiona couldn't quite tell whether the dirk Alec had given her was still sheathed deep in the pocket of her skirts, but it wasn't much good to her with her hands tied, anyway. Looking

at her cousin, waiting for her to speak, Fiona knew she
had to use every resource she had. She made up her
mind. If they were going to kill her, she was not about
to submit passively.

Or will I? she thought.

Kathryn moved impatiently toward the younger
woman.

Fiona's erect posture began to slip as she, almost im-
perceptibly, began to transform herself. Her chin
dropped a bit, and she seemed to curl inward, her eyes
darting apprehensively around the room. Gnawing on
her lip, she reached up and began to twist her hair into
a thick rope. Shifting from one foot to the other, she
glanced nervously at her cousin.

She wants a churchmouse ... I'll give her a
churchmouse.

Kathryn reached out and took hold of the golden
chain that encircled Fiona's neck. Drawing out the jewel-
encrusted cross, her eyes lit with desire at the beauty of
the ornament. Fiona stood quietly as her cousin looked
covetously at the exquisite workmanship and the sparkling gems. A gleam came into Kathryn's eye as she
turned a contemptuous gaze on Fiona's face.

"Who did you steal this from?" she sneered.

"It's ... it's mine," Fiona stammered in as timid a
voice as she could affect.

"Yours? Ha!" Kathryn laughed scornfully. "This was
made to adorn a *great* lady."

"That's true, m'lady." Fiona's chin quivered a bit as
she stood with averted eyes.

"Then if it is truly yours, perhaps you'd like to present
it to me as a gift." Kathryn looked appraisingly at the
piece. "It would look stunning on me, don't you agree?"

"Well ... aye. It would, m'lady," the captive responded, panic evident in her voice. "But ... my mother
... well ... Who are you, m'lady?"

The tall woman looked down suspiciously at the timid
creature before her. Had she truly been unconscious
while she and Neil had argued? At the sight of the
woman shivering uncontrollably, Kathryn nearly laughed
at the ridiculously unlikely match Alec and Fiona would
have made. But no more. She would not let that happen.

"I am Kathryn Gray."

"Kathryn Gr . . . Lady Kathryn!" Fiona's whole frame seemed to energize at the name. "Lady Kathryn! My cousin! Lord Macpherson and the prioress, God bless her, they told me you'd be coming to meet me."

Fiona stopped abruptly as if stunned by some revelation. She glanced down at her bound wrists and back up into the haughty expression on Kathryn's face. Her cousin released the cross and turned imperiously on her heel.

"But why . . . where are we, m'lady?" Fiona asked, quickly feeling for the dagger in her skirts as soon as her captor turned her face. Yes, still there! she thought exultantly, instantly falling back into character.

"You said Alec told you that I would come for you?"

"He did, m'lady," Fiona said, nodding repeatedly.

"Has he missed me? Did he ask—" the woman cut herself short. Kathryn wondered momentarily if Fiona had detected that note of vulnerability in her voice.

As Kathryn turned away and walked to the other side of the room, Fiona reached in her pocket again and tried to cut the rope on her wrists with the sharp end of the dagger.

"How is it possible?" Kathryn asked, turning to look distastefully at the jumping Fiona. "How is it possible that you are to marry Alec Macpherson?"

"Why . . . I really don't know, m'lady. He said he would be 'willing to have me.' But I don't . . . m'lady . . . I don't . . ." Fiona put her hands in the pouchlike pocket, lowering her face as she started to cry. Her tears coursed down her cheeks, and her body was racked with sobs.

Kathryn looked on, surprised by the outbreak and disgusted with the pitiful creature. As Fiona continued to weep loudly, Kathryn's expression of aversion swiftly hardened into one of overt loathing for her weakling of a cousin.

"Pull yourself together," she commanded sharply. "I don't want to remain in this rat hole all day. You really are pathetic."

Fiona gulped for air and wiped her tear-stained face on her sleeve. Still sobbing quietly, she looked past the hard-faced woman toward the closed door.

"Do you really think you could be the lady of such a

great place as Benmore Castle? Of course, that's after the old witch, his mother, is put away."

Fiona looked at her, wide-eyed and speechless. She had just undone the ropes. Her hands, resting in the deep front pocket, were free.

"And don't begin that disgusting exhibition again," she added, seeing Fiona's eyes glisten. The wench was ready to break down again, she thought disgustedly.

"Nay, Lady Kathryn," Fiona snuffled. "I'm only suited to be a nun. Just the thought of a man touching me ..." She shuddered visibly.

Her cousin's mouth twisted into a mocking smirk as the tears began to run down Fiona's face again.

"I just want to go back to the Priory at Skye," the captive wailed. "I just want to go home."

Kathryn turned her back on Fiona in frustration. Those were supposed to be her words. This was supposed to be her demand. She wanted Fiona to object. And then she envisioned herself ordering her, forcing her to comply. The little bitch was spoiling all her fun.

"How is it possible we have the same blood in our veins?" she said, turning back to her captive.

"I don't believe you have blood in your veins, Kathryn Gray." Fiona's voice was cool and controlled. The point of the dirk was pressed into the hollow of her cousin's throat.

Chapter 19

Then Anger came in with quarrel and strife:
His hand was ever upon his knife . . .
—WILLIAM DUNBAR, *"Fasternis Evin in Hell"*

It took Fiona only one swift shove to pin Kathryn against the wall. The taller woman didn't make so much as a murmur in protest. Fiona's left hand gripped her cousin's windpipe as the right one held the knife to her flawless face.

"It's God's will, not my courage, that is about to cut your throat," Fiona said in a soft whisper. "Would you like to take back what you just said?"

Kathryn whimpered helplessly in response.

Fiona increased the pressure on the woman's throat, causing her eyes to widen and her complexion to blanch as white as new-fallen snow.

"Now, I want you to listen, and listen very carefully, to all that I have to say." Fiona waved the knife back and forth in front of Kathryn's eyes, then slowly laid it against the blond woman's cheek. "What you did by bringing me here against my will was very wrong. What you did to a good, old man was a mortal sin. For that, more than anything, you will pay. And you will pay with your blood."

Kathryn shook her head desperately, causing the sharp knife to nick her own skin. She cried out sharply as a thin red line coursed down her cheek and dripped off her chin. She was quaking with fear when Fiona raised the dagger and she saw her own blood on the knife.

"You are doomed to hell, Kathryn Gray. But not yet, cousin . . . and you had better do as you are told, or your bloody face will look like a Macpherson plaid. But, you know, perhaps that might be a better fate for you. Perhaps when you are hideously scarred, Alec may take mercy on you and not imprison you at Dunvegan."

Fiona whispered grimly as the woman's horrified gaze never left the dagger. "And hear this: Alec and I love each other. And knowing how much he hates you, and knowing how his blood will boil when he learns what you tried to do here, we both know he'll never rest until he gets to you. And then, if I could possibly talk him out of killing you, you can look forward to a lifelong stay in Dunvegan's dungeons. Do you know what those dungeons are like, Kathryn?"

Fiona paused, waiting for the woman to close her eyes in a silent nod. "They are heavily infested with rats, presently. But I'm sure those rodents would love your company." She hesitated a moment. "You are a loathsome creature, Kathryn, but how could they possibly object to such a delectable companion?"

Fiona put on a grim smile of satisfaction, knowing she had her cousin's full attention. "Now, I have a deal for you. You will answer all my questions. And you will do exactly as you are told. Then, when this ordeal is over, I will let you take off for sweet courts abroad. But listen to me, Kathryn. That's with the condition that you never come back again. Now, what do you say about that?"

Fiona let up on her hold only long enough for Kathryn to gulp down air and nod.

"Very well! Who killed my mother?" she demanded.

Fiona let the knife scrape her cheek when Kathryn was slow in answering. The taller woman shook with terror as she stammered out the response.

"Tor-Torquil MacLeod's men."

"I've found that much on my own. Who else was there?"

"I honestly don't know. Please ... please believe me. Neil had told me. He's the one to ask. He knows what happened. He was there. But he would never say who was behind it all."

"You are lying."

"I'm not! I swear it!" Kathryn began to weep. "Please believe me. He wouldn't tell me. Please! I'm sorry for what happened here. For bringing you here. It wasn't my idea."

Her eyes looked wildly into Fiona's. "It was Neil's. I know he's still paid by someone else. Perhaps the same man. His orders are to kill you. He means to do it. But—"

Fiona clamped her hand on the woman's mouth at the sound of someone moving outside the door. Thinking fast for a way to escape, she gripped the woman's tartan and pulled her closer to the door.

"How far are we from Benmore?"

Fiona let the woman catch her breath again.

"It's only a little more than an hour from here."

"Which way is it? How do I get back there?" Fiona demanded.

"This ... this stream runs into the Spey River down past the next bend. The castle is just upriver. It's very close! You won't kill me, will you? I beg you, Fiona. Please don't cut me again. I'll help you. On St. Andrew's bones, I swear I'll—"

Fiona's cold glare, coupled with the tighter press of the blade against the skin of her neck, made Kathryn cease her frantic pleading. Pushing Kathryn against the wall behind the door, Fiona took the torch from the wall and threw it into the pile of old straw across the room. Instantly, the flames leaped up, and clouds of smoke began to fill the ceiling spaces between the rafters. She took hold of the quaking woman beside her and put her lips close to her ear.

"You will come after me willingly," Fiona threatened in harsh tones. "Or you will pay for your crimes the Druid way."

While Kathryn was still nodding vigorously at her wild-eyed cousin, Fiona commanded, "I want you to call for help, Kathryn. I want you to yell 'Fire!' now."

"*Neil!*" Kathryn screamed without hesitation. "*Help, Neil! Fire!*"

Fiona crouched and pulled her cousin down beside her. The smoke was getting thick under the rafters, and she could see the flames licking the wooden walls above the stone foundation. Taking a deep breath, she braced herself for the oncoming showdown.

It only took Neil a moment to burst through the door. He hesitated for only the briefest of moments at the opening, covering his mouth and nose with the cloth of his tartan. "Where are you?" he cried. "Where the hell are you? *Kathryn!*"

As Neil moved through the smoke to where his captive had been dumped earlier, Fiona pulled Kathryn around the door and out into the yard. A semicircle of men stood close, gaping as Fiona pulled the plank door shut and barred it.

She whirled on them as the men moved closer.

"Tell them to back away, Kathryn," Fiona ordered coolly, prodding her in the back with the dagger.

"You heard her," Kathryn croaked. "Get away from us."

"No! Open this!" came Neil's screams from the burning mill. Fiona listened for a moment to the cold-blooded killer. She hesitated, then steeled herself to his cries. Behind them, Neil began to pound at the door. This was the man who had a hand in killing her mother, and this day, he'd planned to kill her for money. But she was not about to give him the opportunity.

The pounding continued as Fiona pushed Kathryn wordlessly along the wall of the mill, the dirk still pressed into her back. The men moved away from the wall, making room, and the two women angled their way across the small clearing toward the cluster of horses tied at the edge of the woods. Fiona could hear Neil still calling from inside the burning building and throwing himself against the door. She looked about her for a path to the river. She couldn't see the stream, but she knew it had to be to their right and beyond the bristly hem of encroaching pines.

Suddenly Fiona heard the cracking of wood and, turning, saw the door split at the upper hinges as Neil kicked the pieces into the yard.

Halfway across the opening, Fiona watched her enemy crawl coughing through the smoke-filled doorway. None of Kathryn's men, nor any of his own paid henchmen, made a move to help him as he stood hunched over, spewing smoke from his lungs. Fiona tried to move the sobbing Kathryn faster, but her cousin stumbled and fell unceremoniously on the grass, her legs splayed in front of her. Recovering, Neil pushed past the dozen or so men and halted at the sight of the bloodied Kathryn sprawled on the grass with a kneeling Fiona behind her, a knife at her throat.

Fiona cringed inwardly at the look of hate in the renegade warrior's face.

"You tried to kill me," he rasped accusingly, taking a step closer.

"Stop!" she commanded, looking steadily at her foe. "You deserve to die, you butcher . . . woman killer. Tell me, how many times have you tried to kill me? You expect me to wait for you to succeed? Do you propose having me lie down like some sacrificial lamb and have my throat slit by you? Stand, Kathryn."

As the two women rose from the ground, Neil took another step forward. The men standing between the smoking blaze of the fiery mill and the three adversaries watched helplessly, unsure of what to do.

"Stop, you fool!" Kathryn spat at Neil. "Don't you see? We shouldn't have done this. We must let her go. It's my . . . it's our only way out of this!"

"Nay, Kathryn." He slowly shook his head. "You were right the first time. This is your only way out of this. But it certainly is not mine."

"What are you talking about, you idiot? She'll kill me, I tell you."

Neil moved in again as Fiona and Kathryn backed away a step. Fiona could feel the heat of the blazing inferno on her face. Flashing the fiercest expression she could muster at her foe, she lifted Kathryn's chin with her blade.

"One more step and she dies, Neil MacLeod."

"Do it!" he cried.

"Neil!" Kathryn cried. "It is I! Don't let this happen! By all the love we share—"

The warrior stepped in again, drawing his sword.

"Neil!" Kathryn screamed, looking wildly past him at her own entourage. *"Stop him!* I'll reward you! My father . . . Neil, I'll marry you! My father will give you a dowry, Neil . . . land and wealth, Neil. *Stop, Neil!"*

"Go ahead. Kill her." His voice had the edge of cold steel biting into flesh and bone. "If you don't, I will. I am sick of you, Kathryn. You and all your kind. I am sick and tired of the dirty, 'noble' blood that runs in your veins. And you are next, Angel. Our little princess.

Ha! You wench! You're the next one to die. No woman fools me. Do you hear? No one. Go ahead and kill her . . . if you can."

Fiona felt her skin crawl in fear at his words. He was calling her bluff. She was finished.

The discontented protest that erupted among Kathryn's men caused Neil to turn back toward the contentious warriors. With a quick look at his own men, he raised his sword, gesturing for silence.

"You dolts," he began. "She's—"

The explosion blew the roof of the millworks high into the sky in a shower of sparks and splintering wood. The blast knocked everyone in the clearing flat on the ground. But Fiona, the farthest away and the most shielded, was up and running before the echoing hills could return the detonation's booming report.

Dashing across the opening to the right toward the sound of rushing stream, she broke into the line of trees. Working her way around the burning building, she prayed that she had picked the quickest route to the river. She prayed Neil would not be able to catch her. Lifting her skirts, she ran with all the speed she had in her. Finally, she came to the stream behind the building, with the mill wheel tilting precariously out over the water. Reaching the edge, she threw herself into the current without a moment's hesitation. Though the coldness of the water shocked her as she was swept beneath the roiling surface, Fiona quickly pushed herself to the surface. Gasping for air, she tried to steer herself toward the embankment on the far side, but the current carried her back into the white foam and then into the clear, fast-moving water above the short waterfall and just beneath the looming wheel.

As she swept under the falling cinders of the mill, she braced herself for the drop, but then she saw the rough hand waiting for her. Fiona struck out with her dagger, but the water kept her off balance. She went under, searching desperately for a way to evade Neil's reach. But the next thing she felt was his hand grabbing a fistful of her hair.

Neil viciously dragged Fiona's thrashing body from the water. Kicking the dirk from her hand, the warrior threw her ferociously to the stony embankment. Putting his knee hard on Fiona's chest, the brute slapped her savagely.

Fiona's head seemed to burst open as his hand fell across her face. Tasting the blood in her mouth, she looked up into the malevolent eyes of the man looming above her.

Neil couldn't react fast enough to avoid the rock smashing into the side of his grimy jaw. When he saw her reach beside her for another, he drew his sword up in one swift motion and lay it heavily across her throat.

"You move that hand, and you're dead."

"I'm dead anyway, you filthy bastard," she retorted, spitting blood in his face.

Neil wiped the spittle with the back of his hand. "I'll be sure to tell your lover boy that even in the moment of death, I wasn't able to dampen your spirits."

"You are a fiend from hell, but you make sure you tell him that. And you know what, devil? You are cursed in this life and in the life hereafter. Alec is going to hunt you down, you Satan. There won't be a rock large enough for you to crawl under, nor enough gold in the world to see to your protection. He'll come to you when you least expect it. You won't be able to sleep, to close your eyes. Because you'll be terrified that when you open them, his sword will be at *your* throat. He'll skewer you on a spit, Neil MacLeod. He'll kill you in a slow and painful way." Fiona saw the man's face twitch uncontrollably at her words. "He'll make you pay! You have my word on it, he'll make you pay!"

Neil lifted his elbow as he prepared to pierce her throat. Fiona closed her eyes, feeling the sharpness of the weapon. Even at this moment of death, anger—not fear—was the sensation that dominated her body.

"Nay. He'll never know what happened to his fairy. So just say your last prayers."

Fiona thought of how short life is. She thought of Alec, the brief time that they'd shared. She thought of how much she loved him and she felt pain at how hurt he would be. In her mind she heard him calling her name. He would be with her in this life and the next. She would wait for him.

Fiona felt the point of the sword push sharply at her throat, and then she felt Neil's weight on her no longer.

What did I ever do, Lord, to deserve such a painless death? she thought prayerfully.

Chapter 20

Turn to thy friend, believe not thy foe,
Since thou must go, be ready at the gate;
Amend in time, and rue not when it's too late ...
—WILLIAM DUNBAR *"Vanitas Vanitatum"*

A lec galloped into the clearing ahead of John and the others and quickly scanned the scene around the burning mill. Four men, holding five horses a safe distance from the raging conflagration, stood dumbstruck at the sight of the onrushing Macphersons. Alec and his men were on them before they could mount their jittery steeds, and the one foolish enough to draw his weapon on them quickly paid the price for his lack of judgment.

Alec sheathed his sword and, leaping off his black stallion, took the closest one by the throat.

"Where is she?" Alec shouted above the sound of the fiery blaze. The hired outlaws behind him exchanged furtive glances until one of them pointed fearfully toward the mill.

"By the river, m'lord," he whined. "But we've nothing to do with him. He—"

Alec threw the man to the ground and sprinted around the side of the burning building. God, let me not be too late. Let her be alive. Those words kept coming to him over and over. Fate had been on his side when he met Hugh Campbell and the pirate prisoner not even a half day ride from Benmore. He was on his way back when, before reaching Benmore, he ran into David, who, bloodied and shivering, managed to inform them of the attack. And then, tracking the wagon, they had seen the smoke rising over the mill.

"Fiona!" Alec shouted as he made his way through

the smoke and shadow of the flaming mill. Turning the corner, he saw the mill wheel hanging menacingly over a kneeling figure. His heart nearly burst when he saw Neil lifting his long sword over the red-haired woman he held pinned to the ground.

Dashing toward them, Alec snatched Neil from Fiona's motionless body like a falcon plucking a hare from the ground. Heaving him to the stony earth, Alec drew his dirk and dove after him.

Neil's shock was short-lived, and before the blond warrior could leap onto him, he rolled away and came up quickly, his sword cutting a deadly arc in the air between them.

Alec, too, was quick to recover and whipped his sword from its sheath. His fury showed in every line of his face, and as he advanced on Neil, the killer backed away, his expression shifting swiftly from grim belligerence to that of unabashed fear.

"You craven dog. Is that what you saved your crippled arm for? For killing a defenseless woman?"

Suddenly, from behind him Alec heard Fiona's voice. Jerking his head around instinctively, he saw her standing beside the millstream.

That was all the opportunity Neil needed. His sword flashed through the air toward Alec's unguarded head.

Fiona cried out as Neil's weapon descended. But Alec's catlike reflexes responded, and his blade deflected the blow in a shower of sparks. Then, wheeling his own sword high overhead, Alec brought it crashing down on the collar of his cringing foe, cleaving bone and sinew with lethal resolve.

Neil sank to his knees amid his own pooling blood, his eyes glazing over as the horrible knowledge of his fate gave way to the shock of oncoming death. As his brain ceased to function, he heard the fading echo of a young woman's curse, " . . . *in this life and in the life hereafter.*"

Alec drove his bloody sword into the ground as Fiona rushed toward him. As he lifted her into his arms, she was shaking with the tumult of relief and exultation that whirled within her.

He came for me.

Thank you, God, for saving her.

Alec stood, his arms closed around her tightly as the heat of battle slowly ebbed from his consciousness.

Her face tilted up to his, tears of joy streaming down her cheeks. He kissed away her salty tears and held her shivering body until he thought their bodies would melt into one another. Her breaths were coming in short gasps as she lifted her lips, seeking his and the comfort they offered.

Hungry for the feel of her soft, yielding mouth, Alec tenderly kissed away the memory of her horrendous ordeal.

"Fiona," he whispered. "I thought I'd lost you, my love." His hand reached up, caressing her face, assessing her injuries. He gently wiped away the drying clot of blood by her mouth, and then, feeling the large lump on the side of her head, he cursed himself furiously for not protecting her the way he should have. Cursed himself for leaving her alone.

Fiona reached up and gripped his hand as it cradled her face. "My mother didn't commit suicide, Alec. She didn't!"

"What happened here, Fiona? Did he hurt you? Did he—"

She placed her fingers to Alec's lips and silenced his words. "Nay, my love. A mere slap is all. But I have to tell you some things."

The sight of John and a few of the Macpherson warriors hurrying around the corner cut Fiona's words short. She huddled tightly to Alec as the men surveyed Neil's dead body.

John's angry tone conveyed his disgust. "Our men spotted a group of men and a woman going over the ridge to the west. One thought it was Kathryn Gray."

Alec looked at Fiona. "Was she here?"

"Aye, she was with him." She nodded toward the corpse.

"Go after her," Alec commanded sharply. "I want her brought back."

"Nay, Alec," Fiona pleaded. "Please don't. I want you to let her go."

Alec gazed at her uncomprehendingly. "Fiona, she was behind all this. Why let her escape?"

"Alec, let her go. I'll explain everything. She was not planning to have me killed. She just wanted me back in the Priory. There's someone else. Neil was being paid by someone else."

"Who else if not Kathryn?"

"I . . . I have an idea. But I know it wasn't her. Alec, I gave her my word she'd have a chance to leave Scotland. But she had to promise never to come back."

Alec looked steadily into her earnest face.

"Please, Alec."

The young warlord turned toward his brother.

"Have her followed, John. Make sure she sets sail . . . even if we have to pay the passage for her."

As John moved off to convey his brother's orders, Alec turned to the shivering woman in his arms. "We need to talk, Fiona."

"Please get me out of here first. I can't bear the sight of this place any longer."

The men dragged Neil's body around the smoldering building, and Fiona and Alec were about to follow when one of the warriors trotted up from behind.

"Lord Alec, you dropped this."

Fiona reached over and took her dirk from the fighter's hand. She smiled up at Alec as she slipped the weapon into its water-soaked sheath deep in the pocket of her dress. "I'm starting to like carrying this around."

Wrapped in Alec's warm cloak, Fiona sat snugly in his arms as Ebon carried them slowly back toward Benmore Castle. John had ridden ahead to spread the news of Fiona's return. Alec wanted everyone to be prepared for her return, and he wanted to alert the other search parties that had gone out from the castle. When he told her of David's survival at the hands of their attackers, Fiona wept in relief. Now she felt a strong inclination to sleep, and only halfheartedly fought the urge.

They rode in silence for a while with the fast-running Spey to their right. Alec bemoaned the fact that Kathryn had been the one to tell Fiona about their past. He wondered what image she had portrayed. He had been a fool to wait this long. He should have confided in her earlier. There were still a few hours of daylight left, but the orange sun was being blotted out occasionally by the thickening clouds that were rolling in from the northwest.

"Did she tell you?" Alec asked softly, breaking into her contented reverie.

Fiona became alert at his question.

"Did she tell you about our engagement?"

"I heard her speak of it with Neil."

Alec's hand took hold of Fiona's chin and raised her eyes to meet his. "Will you ever be able to forgive me for not telling you about the past? About myself?"

"Alec, I saw her and I heard her. I've had a chance to judge her character myself, firsthand, and I also understand why you haven't wanted to bring up the past."

"She told you the truth?"

"Not me. She was reminding Neil of the truth."

Alec shrugged indifferently. "I never had any idea that they even knew each other. In fact, I still don't know what the connection is between them."

"There was a connection, all right. Neil was the man who was with her, Alec, the night you discovered her infidelity."

Alec paused while her information sunk in. Then, reaching down, he brushed her lips with his. "The real truth, my love, is that I don't care who was with her. Nor do I care what other deceptions she was engaged in while she was betrothed to me. All that matters is that I was able to walk away from the biggest mistake of my life and be blessed with the gift of finding you." Alec hugged her tightly to him. "Fiona, I'm sorry for not telling you about her. But the truth is ... I was afraid. Afraid of losing you."

Fiona fathomed his concern. Her fingers caressed his face. It was a simple gesture. But it was one of acceptance. Understanding.

"For most of your life, you have been without parents and family of any sort. I was afraid that you would not be able to see the true face of your cousin and your uncle. Kathryn's father, Lord Gray, is madder than hell to this day for my breaking off the engagement with her. I knew he would not give his blessing to our marriage. I wanted to marry you before you ever became involved with them, and it was wrong of me. I didn't give you enough credit. I was afraid you would be so taken by their false charm, overjoyed at the thought of having real 'family,' that you would want them over me. That you would allow your uncle to talk you right out of my life."

Fiona gazed tenderly into his eyes. "Alec, those people are strangers to me. I would never accept what they say or even listen to them, for that matter. Alec Macpherson, you are my love. You are the man with whom I will spend the rest of my life. Never forget that."

The world around them disappeared from view as their feelings swelled, obliterating everything else. Like a mountain stream in the warmth of spring, the waters of their emotions rose, rushing to new heights, threatening to overflow the banks that contained them. Lost in the depths of Fiona's eyes, Alec saw a falcon in flight—sailing high and clear. Magnificent. Beautiful. And freely choosing . . . him.

"I will never forget that, my love. I never will." Alec's mouth took hers in a kiss that promised fulfillment, trust, faith, and most of all, eternal love.

Moments later, when they pulled apart, Fiona knew that it was now her turn to trust Alec with what she knew, with what she suspected. Neither could afford to have anything between them. She had to trust him.

So she told him what she'd learned listening to Kathryn and Neil in the mill. She told him Torquil MacLeod's men—with Neil among them—had murdered her mother.

"It doesn't make any sense," Alec said thoughtfully. "I don't understand the connection between Torquil and your mother. He was an evil man, but he had no brain of his own. I have a difficult time believing that he could plan and execute such a crime, one that could go unresolved for so many years."

"I think you're right about that, Alec, but I remember Torquil being there in the room. He was the one who had his men take me away. And all these years, living on the same island, we never came face-to-face. Because of the prioress, I never saw him and I never saw Neil until that day by Father Jack's hut."

"You were very fortunate," Alec said, thinking over the danger that she'd been so close to for so many years. "Your memory may have been gone for the time being, but if Torquil had ever laid eyes on you, he would made certain you would never remember."

"You mean he would have silenced me, the way he silenced my mother."

Alec considered the information Fiona had relayed to him. There was still something not right. An important piece of this puzzle was missing.

"This morning in their talk, was anything said about someone else? You said that Neil was being paid by someone else."

"Aye, but I don't know who ... for certain. Neil didn't name him. And later, Kathryn swore that she didn't know, either."

"And you believe what she said?"

"Considering the size of the gash I put in her face, I'd say she had no choice but to speak the truth."

Alec laughed heartily as he gathered his little warrior in his arms. "Is this the same woman who, on the day that I offered her the dirk, shrank away from me, saying that she would never be able to use it on another human being?"

She looked up into his proud, deep blue eyes. "I'm the same woman, Alec. The emphasis was on 'human being.' I don't believe real human beings are capable of doing what some of the things these ... creatures ... do to others."

He pushed back the loose tendril of hair from her beautiful face and pulled her up higher on his lap. "You're right, my love. Certainly no one you've faced has been worthy of the name."

She had to tell him. She knew she had to tell him about Huntly. She had to have faith and trust in him.

"Alec, there is something that ... that ..."

"What is it, Fiona?" He could sense she felt uncomfortable about whatever she was trying to tell him.

"That night ... the night at Drummond Castle, before I was taken away ..." she took a deep breath. She had to tell the events as they happened. She could not mold the facts to suit her own accusatory feelings about Huntly. She wanted Alec to reach the same conclusion on his own. "My mother's knight, Sir Allan ..."

"Tell me, Fiona. What is it that you remember?"

"He came to my mother while I was with her. He

said that Lord *Andrew* was downstairs. Alec, my mother wanted her knight to take me away from that man. I could tell she was afraid of him."

Fiona could see Alec's face grow dark as he considered this information.

"So this Andrew could still be the one behind all this."

"You see it, too, don't you?" she exclaimed. "It is possible, isn't it, that this same man, who ordered my mother's death so many years ago, now is ordering mine? He must be getting quite nervous that his dark, buried secret is about to be revealed!"

Alec shot a look at Fiona. There had been the attack on her at Skye. Then the mercenary pirates. And now this. There was truth in what she was saying. "Whoever this Andrew is," Alec mused, "he is persistent. But you never saw him, did you? You couldn't identify him?"

"I don't have to see him to know who he is."

"You know his identity?" Alec asked, taken aback by her words. Fiona's tone said she had known for a long time.

Fiona looked Alec straight in the eye as she spoke the earl's name.

"It can't be, Fiona. It absolutely cannot be."

She punched her fist into his chest as she looked up in his expression of denial.

"Why can't it be, Alec? Look at the facts. And be fair. Who else would have objected to my parents' marriage?"

"The whole country, at that time, Fiona," Alec argued. "Huntly loved your mother. He would never have hurt her for any reason—in this world or the next."

"But you are talking about a man about to lose her. He was about to lose her for good."

"He had already lost her, Fiona. He'd lost her five years earlier, when she bore the king's child." Alec held Fiona's face in his great hand. "Fiona, when you were lost—when your mother's body was found—he was more upset than the king himself. Months later, when the king gave up the search, Huntly kept on. Fiona, despite what he presents on the outside, he is a man with feelings. He is a man of honor."

"Then what about the name? Lord Andrew. Sir Allan said there was a man named Andrew downstairs."

"Fiona, you know as well as I, every family in Scotland has a son named Andrew. Probably half of the Lowland nobles in the court at that time were named Andrew. Your own uncle, Lord Gray, is named Andrew."

She went silent in his arms.

"Have you thought, Fiona, that maybe your own uncle is the one behind all this? He's the one who has the most to lose now that you've been found alive. He's the one who has assumed stewardship of your land and wealth after your grandfather's death. Now he has to give everything up."

"Alec, we're talking about fourteen years ago. He had no motive back then to hurt my mother, did he? My grandfather was still alive. My mother had sisters who were still living. He was in no position to gain anything by hurting her."

"True. But by the same token, why should Lord Huntly want to hurt you today? You have no proof of any guilt on his part."

"I think I do, Alec."

"You do?" he asked, holding her by the shoulder, looking into her eyes.

"Aye. A packet. A leather pouch I saw my mother hide away in my room in Drummond Castle. The night she was killed. She said . . . she said to show the contents of that pouch to my father. That he would then punish the evil men who had come that night."

Fiona felt a knot form tightly in her throat. As Alec's arm moved around her, she could feel her mother's arm around her. A tear spilled from her eye and trickled down her cheek. She could see her mother pointing. Five stones from the fireplace. Five. She wondered if the proof still lay there after so many years. The filthy animals.

"The only problem is that I'm not certain that . . ."

"You are afraid that the pouch has already been discovered?" he asked gently.

She nodded in response.

"But there is only one way to find out, isn't there?"

"You'll take me to Drummond Castle?"

Alec reached with his hand and brushed away the single tear glistening on her cheek. "I'll take you there. But first things first. We'll have to be married. Huntly told my father that your uncle is already arranging suitable marriages for you."

"He can't!" she blurted, turning to look into his face. "I'm to marry you. He can do no such thing."

"You'll get to know him soon enough, my love. He is not one to understand matters of the heart. I suppose that's where Kathryn learned her perspective on life."

"Then we'll marry before we go to Drummond."

Coming around a bend in the river, Fiona could see the walls of Benmore Castle rising across the river in the distance.

"The village is just ahead beyond the next grove of trees," Alec told her. Raising his voice, he ordered his men to ride on ahead. "Fiona, do we have to invite him to our wedding?"

As she turned her face to answer him, his mouth captured hers so quickly that she had no chance to escape. He'd only intended to kiss her lightly, to ensure her cooperation, but her response to him took him off guard.

Her hands threaded into his hair, pulling his head lower as her soft mouth opened to the pressure of Alec's searching tongue. They kissed deeply, intimately, reaffirming the passion and hunger they felt for one another.

"You're very persuasive," she cooed as they gently broke off their intimacy.

"Good," he responded, running his hand over her full breast, inside the concealing cloak. "But this is only the beginning."

Chapter 21

For as thou came so shall thou pass.
Like a shadow in a glass ...
—WILLIAM DUNBAR,
"Momento Homo quod cinis es"

When they told her that Celia Muir Campbell, Lady Argyll, was in the castle and looking forward to meeting her, Fiona nearly died. After all, she'd heard from the arriving guests that this was the woman who had spirited the infant King James across Scotland and into the safekeeping of Colin Campbell, Alec's best friend. She was a woman acclaimed by the world, a woman of courage, beauty, and wit.

Fiona looked ruefully at her image in the window. Her wild mane of red hair was once again out of control. She tucked back the tendrils of curls that had escaped their confining braid and ran her hands down her skirts, trying to straighten the folds. "It's time, Fiona," she whispered to her image. "There's no point in keeping the lady waiting."

Fiona closed the heavy oak door of her room and trudged down the stone hallway. Claire had brought the message that Lord Alec and Lord Colin were downstairs with the rest of the guests, but that Lady Celia was still in her chamber and hoping they might meet there.

As Fiona reached the door to Lord and Lady Campbell's chamber, a flush of uncertainty raced through her. She had already found out that Alec was well loved by this family, so more than anything else, she didn't want to be a disappointment. "Get on with it, Fiona," she murmured to herself. "Get on with it!"

At the sound of the gentle knock on the door, Celia pulled the shawl gently over her shoulder and covered the head of her suckling daughter. "Please come in," she called softly, trying not to disturb the nearly sleeping child.

She watched as the door gently moved on its soft hinges and opened to reveal the young woman standing beyond.

"You must be Lady Fiona," she whispered, looking at the angelic figure standing hesitantly in the hall.

Fiona stood feeling awkward and speechless. She had not expected the scene before her. There in the corner of the room by the window, a dark-haired beauty—no older than Fiona herself—sat clad in a simple white dress, a babe nestled comfortably in her lap. Fiona gazed at the peaceful image of the mother and her child and knew, at that very instant, she was going to like Lady Celia Muir Campbell immensely.

Two days later and two hours before the midday ceremony, Fiona and Celia hugged each other fiercely as they prepared for the joyous trek to the little church in the village.

"Ready . . . with plenty of time to spare," Fiona whispered excitedly.

"You look absolutely stunning, my radiant friend," Celia whispered in awe, moving behind her as Fiona took a last look in the mirror. "You will knock Alec right off his feet."

"You mean the same way as you knocked him on his backside the first time you two met?" Fiona asked, recalling Colin's story of Celia and Alec's first encounter.

Exchanging a conspiratorial look, the two began to laugh in unison. Fiona and Celia had been inseparable since the first day they'd met. They'd been spending most of their time in Fiona's chamber, due to the Highland custom that mandated bride and groom be kept apart until the wedding ceremony. But that hadn't stopped the Earl of Argyll from coming and visiting with his wife every hour on the hour.

It was a constant source of wonder for Fiona, watching the love that those two shared with each other. And it had not taken long for her to realize what special people her new friends were.

Sitting together that first day, the two women felt at

ease from the very moment Fiona stepped into Celia's
chamber. Neither knew who took the first step or who
raised a welcoming hand to the other. All that mattered
was that they immediately felt like old acquaintances.
Like long-lost friends who had at last found one another.
And then the hours flew by as they chatted comfortably.

At last they became aware that they'd completely lost
track of the time. Celia went to the crib to check her
sleeping baby when a soft knock sent Fiona to the door
as the heavy oak began to swing open. Stepping in front
of the open door, Fiona confronted a black-haired giant,
his face fierce and warlike, filling the door frame. Moving forward with a hand raised combatively toward his
chest, Fiona asked the man to state his business. A deep
chuckle rumbled from the giant's chest at the sight of
the red-haired beauty holding him off, before he looked
hopefully past her at the approaching Celia.

"It's all right, Fiona," Celia said, taking her blushing
friend by the arm. "He's with me. And you might as
well let him in—he'll just break down the door."

"She doesn't just look like her father, she acts like
him, too," the Earl of Argyll said to his wife with an
amused chuckle and kissed her soundly. "Alec is boring
me to death. I've missed you."

Celia's pull on his arms finally made Colin end the
embrace and turn in the direction of the young woman.
But he still kept an arm protectively about his wife.

"I'm very pleased to meet you, Fiona Drummond Stuart. I'm Colin, the man my wife and daughter keep
around for entertainment. And I'm happy for the work,"
he whispered confidentially, "being a bit big as far as
jesters go."

Sitting back down, the three of them enjoyed a very
cordial afternoon of talking and laughing, and Fiona
learned a great deal—serious and otherwise—about her
beloved. The stories that Celia and Colin shared with
her about Alec were both fascinating and amusing to
hear. Colin and Alec had been best friends for their
entire lives, so, needless to say, Colin Campbell had a
fistful of warning tales about Alec that he was just dying
to relate to Fiona.

But it also took Fiona only that first day to realize
that Celia's stories had a bit more credibility than Colin's

did. "My husband," as Celia put it, placing a hand over the earl's mouth, "is just trying to get even with Alec and *his* bedevilment when he learned *we* were getting married."

The days were full and productive, but Fiona missed Alec. Lady Elizabeth informed Fiona that her son was getting a bit testy at not being allowed near his betrothed.

Celia whispered to her the next afternoon that a near war had broken out that morning. Fiona smiled at the news that Alec was not giving up in his efforts to see her. But Colin, being a good friend, and in keeping with the teasing that Alec had given him, was playing shadow to Alec during the bridegroom's every waking moment. But during the night, Alec—well aware of his friend's inability to stay away from Celia—had thought to sneak from his room and go to Fiona. Finding his door barred from outside, he'd been ready to pack Colin up and send him off to Kildalton in the morning.

During these days, Fiona had been able to meet some of the other Campbells as well. Lord Hugh, Celia's father-in-law, was a lovable bear of a man who was inseparable from his granddaughter. And Fiona also met Agnes, the Campbells' head housekeeper, but who was clearly more of a mother figure to both Colin and Celia. Fiona smiled to herself as she remembered how Agnes had questioned Fiona on every turn to make sure that she was deserving enough for Alec. From what Lady Elizabeth had told Fiona, Agnes loved Alec like a son, as well.

Now, as the bright sun streamed through the window, the morning of the wedding, Fiona looked with pleasure at the gorgeous floor-length dress Lady Elizabeth's seamstresses had created. Her red hair, loosely braided with slender ropes of pearl, tumbled over one shoulder of her ivory-colored silk gown. The round neckline was exquisitely embroidered with a delicate pattern of entwined golden leaves and silver flowers. The great bell-like sleeves were short, revealing the lining and tighter silk undersleeves. The bodice clung tightly to Fiona's slender frame, flaring out in satiny folds beneath the cord of woven gold and silver that encircled her waist. From the white skin of her exposed shoulder, the Macpherson plaid—held in place by an elegant jeweled broach—ran obliquely to her opposite hip, and from the cord at Fiona's waist, Alec's dirk hung in a sheath of gleaming oak and gold.

The elaborate broach, depicting a rampant lion on a shield encircled by ten fleur-de-lis—the royal arms of the Stuarts—was given to her the previous evening by Huntly. The gift symbolized the queen's recognition of Fiona as the true daughter of James IV.

Looking in the mirror, Fiona saw the token of her Stuart nobility, but no material remembrance of the woman who had given her life.

Crossing to the bedside, she picked up her mother's cross and hung it around her neck. Turning, Fiona looked into the eyes gazing back at her in the mirror. Her mother's eyes. *Don't mourn the fearful shadows of the happiness that short-changed my soul. Live your own life, Fiona. Live your own!*

Fiona looked into the mirrored reflection at Celia, playing with her daughter on a chair across the room. The bairn was holding her mother's beautiful, auburn curls in both fists and was stuffing them into Celia's mouth. Listening to the baby's giggles and Celia's laugh brought back memories. Closing her eyes with a sigh, Fiona thought over those times long ago. She supposed they'd played those same games. Shared the same joy that these two were sharing now.

Uncontrollably, a tear welled up in Fiona's eye and escaped its pool, dropping to her cheek. Celia was there in an instant, turning her friend around and giving her a warm hug.

"Now, now. Today is a day for rejoicing. For happiness," Celia murmured, wiping the wetness from Fiona's cheek. "The problems of the world can wait. Think of the man who will be waiting for you at the altar. The one who is going crazy at the pain of not seeing you. Isn't it wonderful to be wanted? To be loved? Have I told you what happened when he tried to come to you last night?"

Brightening through her tears, Fiona began to laugh. "What? What did he do now?"

The gentle knock drew the attention of the two.

"If that's Alec, then I'm now a widow." Celia grinned

at the bride as she crossed the room to pick up her child. "At any rate, I think it's time I went and checked on my husband."

Fiona smiled and reached for the cooing child in Celia's arms. The bairn laughed with delight and dove toward her. "I'll keep little Constance for you."

"Nay, my friend. I know the damage this wee one can do to a fine dress." Celia opened the door and said softly, "I'll come for you when it's time."

Fiona watched as her friend smiled at whoever was in the corridor as she left the room. The door stood open, but no one entered.

Unaccountably, Fiona's heart skipped a beat as she hesitantly made her way toward the open doorway. Peering out into the dimly lit passage, Fiona could make out the shadow of a woman. Stepping back, she smiled encouragingly at the reticent visitor.

"Won't you come in?"

When the old woman tottered in, leaning heavily on her gnarled walking stick, Fiona paused momentarily, uncertainty etched on her face. She thought she'd met all the Macphersons, but this old woman . . .

"Nanna!" she cried, choking on the words as she sprang toward her old friend. Tears streamed down her face as she hugged the small, snowy-haired woman tightly to her.

"Oh, Fiona, lass!" Nanna wept. "Oh, my dear, bonny child!"

For many years, the old woman had thought her little angel dead. Many days she had lit candles in the chapel, praying for the souls of the poor lost mother and child. And then Lord Andrew had brought the news. She scarcely dared to allow herself to hope that his words might be true. No, she would wait and see for herself. She gazed into the face of her little girl grown up. This was her loving Fiona. This was undoubtedly she.

"Nanna . . . how did you . . ." Fiona drew her dear friend to the bed and sat her down. "Where have you been, Nanna? How are you here?"

Nanna wiped the tears from her face and gripped the young woman's hands tightly as she studied every inch of the bride's face.

"You have grown into such a beauty, child. Aye, you have the best of both your parents in you." Nanna threw her arms around Fiona, pulling her close. "Ah, lass, I never thought I'd live to see the day when I could be holding you in my arms again."

For a moment they just sat, wrapped in one another's arms, while years melted away like the morning mist.

"Nanna," Fiona asked, looking at how telling the years had been on Nanna. "Did you just come from Drummond Castle? Tell me what—"

"Nay, lass," Nanna broke in, shaking her head. "I left the place after your grandfather died. I'll not live in it while your cousin's there."

"Oh, Nanna," Fiona asked with alarm, "she didn't throw you out? Where could you go?"

"Nay. She didn't throw me out. I wouldn't give her the satisfaction. I left. I went to the man who offered me shelter years ago. I went to Lord Huntly."

Fiona stared at the woman looking with such openness at her.

"I had no one else, lass," Nanna explained. "But I knew he'd take me in."

"Why, Nanna?" Fiona asked, confused by her old friend's assertion. "How did you know him? Is he kin?"

"Nay. But I'd known him for a long while, long before you were born. He was a suitor of your mother's ... before she met the king. And then, later on, he became a devoted friend. He was always there for her. He is a good man. He truly is. But, you know, Fiona, though he was never one to show his feelings outwardly, he is a man who dispenses justice as he sees fit. And he never forgets. When I came to him at Stirling, he provided for me. You know he sent for me to come here."

"Nay. I didn't know." Fiona looked tenderly into Nanna's eyes. "Could you ... tell me? Please? About ..."

"I know. I know, my dear. I met Lord Alec before coming up here. He told me you'd be wanting to ask about it. You want to hear about that evil night, when I was hurt—"

"They hurt you, too?" Fiona asked in a rush. "What happened? Tell me everything that happened."

"My child. There's plenty of time for this after your wedding. You should be thinking of your—"

"Please, Nanna. I must know now."

The old woman looked anxiously into the young woman's face. So much of her father's impulsiveness, so much of her mother's intensity.

"All right," she agreed. Taking a deep breath, she began. "Though I'm afraid what I have to say might not make sense. Let me see . . . it was a few days before that evil night. I remember being called to Margaret's room, one early afternoon. She had just come back from visiting someone."

"Who it was that she visited?"

"She never told me. But she was quite upset when I saw her. As I entered her chamber, she was just handing Sir Allan a sealed letter."

"A letter? To whom?"

"The Earl of Huntly. I remember Margaret repeatedly stressing the urgency and confidentiality of the correspondence before he departed."

"Did she ever tell you what was in there?"

"Nay, she never did."

Fiona looked out the window as she tried to remember the pouch which was hidden in her room. Could it have contained an answer to her mother's letter? No, it was too small.

"What did the letter have to do with the attack?" Fiona asked.

"Perhaps nothing. Perhaps a great deal. You'll have to decide. At any rate, the night your father was to come, I left you with your dear mother when she sent me to get Sir Allan. I met him just coming from the Great Hall and sent him up the back stairwell to the nursery, just as your mother asked. Your poor mother . . ."

Fiona squeezed Nanna's hands gently as the woman's voice trailed off in the memory of her long-dead loved one. "Please, Nanna," she encouraged tenderly.

"Aye, where was I?" the sad woman paused as she tried to gather her thoughts. "When I went out the rear door into the castle close, some of those wretched barbarians were waiting. One of them dinged your old Nanna on the head, and I remember nothing more until I became conscious a couple of hours later. I was left to die on the dungheap." She wiped away a tear from her reddening eyes.

"I'm sorry," said Fiona consolingly.

The woman patted her young friend's hand. "Nay, lass. You needn't feel sad for me. I survived that terrible night. But something *did* die inside me when they told me of your mother . . . and of you."

"Who told you?" Fiona asked, looking intently at her dear friend. "Oh, nay. First, tell me who was in the Great Hall, Nanna? When you went for Sir Allan."

The aged duenna gazed perplexedly at her beautiful inquisitor. "In the Gr— I don't know, Fiona."

"Well, when you became conscious later, who was there in the castle?"

Nanna thought back through the haze of long years. "Well, when I awoke, Lord Gray was there. He found your dear mother. And Lord Huntly—"

"Lord Huntly was there when you awakened?"

"Aye, lass. They both arrived that night. Lord Huntly came ahead of your father. The king was delayed, and he sent Lord Andrew ahead. Your father didn't arrive until the next day."

Fiona clenched her fists. "Tell me more. Please tell me what was happening when you went back inside."

"The whole place was in a chaos. They had found your mother's body and the note she'd left behind. Lord Gray was getting his men ready to search for you. And Lord Huntly . . . Lord Huntly . . ."

"What about him? Please, tell me."

"The earl went mad that night. As crazed as a loon. He must have been, for he's not one to act the way he did. I never to this day have seen a man more upset than he was. In fact, I heard he was running through the castle like a madman, looking for something. I just can't help wondering if it had something to do with the letter your mother sent him."

The pouch. The proof of his guilt. He was looking for the pouch, Fiona thought.

Twenty-eight Years Earlier, 1488

Separated from his soldiers, King James III lay before the miller's hut in the muddy lane of the village of Ban-

nockburn. The great sword of Robert the Bruce still strapped to his side, the king kneaded his ribs and his leg, gingerly assessing what injuries he'd sustained in the plunge from his horse.

The miller, recognizing the king, moved his thick body quickly toward the fallen nobleman and helped him into his hut.

Outside, two men reined in their horses as the miller reemerged, running for help. Leaping to the ground, one of them took the stocky man roughly by the arm, while the other ran his short sword pitilessly into the miller's back.

With no show of emotion, the leader stepped past the twitching body and ducked inside the hut. On the straw in the corner lay the king, looking weakly at the two men.

"I know you, Andrew," whispered King James, spying the clan broach the young nobleman wore. "You're no help!"

"Nay, m'lord," he answered, his blue eyes, so pale that they were mere reflections of the ice in his soul, glimmering malevolently. "But I am here to help you into the next world."

Behind him, his crony stepped into the king's vision.

"Torquil MacLeod . . . I should have hanged you when I had the opportunity."

With a glance at his companion, the Highlander moved back a step, a shadow of fear crossing his face.

"Don't fret, Torquil," said the blue-eyed warrior over his shoulder. "This old man knows opportunity must be grabbed by the forelock."

Andrew crossed the room to the king and covetously eyed the gleaming ring of Robert the Bruce—symbol of Scottish kingship—that encircled the monarch's finger. "And that, old king, is exactly what we will do," he whispered harshly. "When you are dead, your son James will be king. Aye, we'll make him king. But not for long. Power belongs to the strong and the quick . . . and soon I will rule Scotland."

Then, raising his sword, Andrew thrust the bloody blade again and again into his king's chest.

* * *

Edinburgh trembled with the news that James III had been found slain in the miller's hut, and that the monarch's ancestral ring, the symbol of his power, had been missing from his hand.

But there was no information as to the identity of the assassin.

Chapter 22

Her gown should be of Goodliness,
Well ribboned with Renown,
Adorned with Pleasure in every place,
Trimmed in the finest Style . . .
—ROBERT HENRYSON,
  "The Garment of Good Ladies"

Alec's breath caught as Fiona stepped into the open
doorway.

From behind her, the brilliant sunlight radiated in a
thousand luminous streams, shimmering as it dispersed
in the dim half-light of the church's interior. Alec moved
into the space before the chancel, gazing with pride and
open admiration at the woman of his dreams.

The crowd inside, dressed in their colorful finery, had
been jovial and restless, but now quieted into a hushed
silence as every eye focused on the red-haired beauty
crossing the threshold.

Looking past them, Alec felt all other senses fading
as the enchantment of the vision before him grew
stronger. Even the majestic sound of the lone musician,
piping Fiona's approach to the altar, became a vague
background to the look of love that was being directed
toward him. A look of love from an angel floating se-
renely through the crowd to him.

When Alec had ridden down from the castle an hour
ago, the villagers and crofters who had lined the sun-
drenched route were a festive crowd, cheering and singing along with the roving groups of bagpipers. The children, running back and forth amid the housewives who
were handing out food and sweets, continually raced up
to the groom and his escort of armed warriors. Alec

smiled as the fierce, tartan-clad fighters, their polished armor flashing in the sun, constantly reached down and scooped up the shrieking youngsters for short rides along the way. Even his squire Robert, dressed in his new chain mail, his sword gleaming by his side, looked quite manly as he joked with the other warriors and the flower-throwing maidens that they passed.

Crossing the bridge into the village, Alec shook hands with the gleeful folk as the shouts rang out, announcing his entrance into the hamlet.

The buildings of the town itself were decked out for the celebration, sporting new coats of bright blues and yellows, reds and greens. Banners and the Macpherson plaids waved in every window, and the residents risked toppling from the upper stories onto their neighbors in the streets, in their excitement and revelry.

Everywhere there was laughter and music and exultation, and Alec's heart overflowed to think of how this jubilant greeting would transport his beloved bride when she traced this joyous route to the church.

As the young warlord turned with a wave at the top of the short flight of steps to the church, the crowded marketcross again erupted with tumultuous sounds of gladness and gaiety, and the pipers continued to add their melodious strains to the boisterous gaiety of the event. Suddenly a moment of regret struck Alec that his brother Ambrose couldn't have been here for the celebration, and he thought that probably Fiona was feeling the same way about the prioress' absence. The message had arrived though, from both, that a big event was being prepared to celebrate Fiona's and Alec's marriage once they returned to Skye.

But the extemporaneous parade of bagpipes and dancing folks that began to move around the village square drew a broad smile from the groom, and as he watched, many of the guests and even his brother John joined the happy revelers. Pushing back down the steps to the thunderous ovation of the crowd, Alec, as well, joined the festive marchers with a single lap of the marketcross. Then, with a laugh and a shout to answer their clamor of approval, he vaulted the steps once more and disappeared into the church.

Now, standing spellbound by the vision of loveliness

gliding toward him, Alec felt his heart thundering in his chest as he gazed in rapt admiration at his fairy bride.

Fiona, too, saw nothing but her beloved.

Her eyes traveled over the magnificent warrior before her. And he was magnificent. Alec's long blond hair was tied back in an orderly fashion. Arrayed in his finest kilt and a shirt of gleaming white silk, a tartan of Macpherson plaid crossing his massive chest, the groom cut a bold and dashing figure as he awaited her before the altar. The light of a thousand candles flashed on the hilt of his long sword and on the clan arms inscribed on his golden broach.

But it was the look in his handsome face that captured her. His blue eyes shone with such love that Fiona felt herself melting inside. And her own love—glowing, fluid, molten—threatened to burst through her skin as her eyes locked on his.

Colin Campbell, the Earl of Argyll, sitting on the same bench as the Macpherson family, put a gentle hand around his wife's shoulder and pulled her tightly to his side. Leaning down, he kissed away the joyful tear glistening on Celia's beautiful face.

Alec's father traded a happy glance with his wife as they both recalled the time when they had stood in this same chapel to exchange their vows.

The Earl of Huntly felt the tightness in his throat as once again he mourned the only woman that he'd ever loved. Looking up, he watched Margaret's beautiful child step to the altar and offer her hand to the young laird.

The sound of harps that replaced the piper as the two lovers joined together at the altar, the Latin chants of the priests and the acolytes, and the quiet exchange of vows all gave way to the joyous acclaim of the congregation when Alec and Fiona turned to greet their friends and family as husband and wife.

Fiona, too caught up in her own excitement, didn't wait for Alec's signal. She tumbled down the hill in a rush despite his threatening grumble from behind. She ran, stumbling, past the two barking and excited hounds, down the slope of the steep hill. Leaves, brushes, and crawling ferns brushed against her legs. Lifting her skirt above her bare knees, her hair flying in the breeze of the hillside loch, she ran with the speed of a doe, as if windborne.

This had been their first day away from the castle, all on their own, since they'd wed. The day was hot and the sun high when Alec had lured her out to the stables with the promise of showing her the Macpherson crofters and their efforts. She'd been welcomed and delighted by the folk of the region around Benmore Castle, but as they turned for home, Alec had snatched her from her horse and planted her on his own, leaving the mare and his two hounds loping behind.

And then he had brought her here. Heaven could not be more perfect, she thought, than what she was seeing, standing on the ledge, looking down at the peaceful loch nestled below. High hills, covered with heather in bloom, surrounded the water on three sides, while a white beach of sand and stone beckoned to them at the bottom of the slope. All Alec had to do was suggest a race to the beach. Fiona, not even waiting for him to complete his challenge, kicked her shoes away and bolted for the sparkling blue lake below.

She slowed as she reached the water and, with a look back at Alec, pulled her skirts up above her knees and waded into the cold, spring-fed waters. The chill of the small waves licking at her legs made Fiona shiver slightly. The sun was still high, and its rays were warm and gentle on her face.

"The bottom drops off quickly not far from where you're standing," Alec called from the shore. Fiona turned to see her husband dropping his tartan and a satchel on a smooth spot on the beach. Looking out at her, he quickly stripped his shirt over his head.

"Thanks, but I'm known to be a good swimmer," she responded, flushing slightly at the sight of his muscles, taut and glistening with the heat of the run.

Fiona realized how silly it was to feel even the slightest embarrassment at seeing Alec's body. After all, the time they'd been spending since the wedding had given them both ample opportunities to experience the pleasures of each other's body. Fiona had never known four days and nights could be so sensually full, so physically exhilarating, so sexually satisfying.

But that had all occurred in the privacy of their own chamber—the door barred, the deep down mattress of the huge bed rising up like the Western Sea around them. Fiona shivered again, but this time it wasn't the chill of the loch that was causing it.

Alec smiled, kicking off his boots. "If you don't take that dress off, my lovely wife, you'll be wet for the entire ride back to Benmore."

Fiona waded back toward the shore as Alec unfastened his belt. Unwrapping his kilt, he stood naked in the sunlight, like some visiting Apollo, ready to take flight like a golden eagle into the sun-drenched sky. Her heart was drumming loudly in her chest as she faltered, then neared him.

"Do you think you'll be able to save me?" Alec whispered as Fiona moved within a step.

"Save you from what, my love?" She stared at the sinewy musculature spanning his chest, feeling too self-conscious to let her eyes waver any lower.

"From drowning." Alec reached for the laces in front of her dress and ever so slowly started to undo them. His knuckles gently caressed the soft skin coming into view at his continuing effort. "I'm not the best swimmer."

"Celia told me you used to get seasick," Fiona said as her fingers achingly reached up to touch the golden curls on his chest, "but that you're cured now."

"I still might need help." He pushed the dress off her shoulder and down past the flare of her hips.

"I saw you swim at the pond by the tower." Fiona stepped out of the mount of her skirts. "You didn't look like one lacking any skills."

"I knew it. You were peeking."

"I—I was," she stammered as Alec's fingers undid the top two ties of her thin chemise, partially exposing her chest.

"Good. Because I was watching you, too. While you were swimming." He leaned down and brushed his lips over the full round perfection of one of her breasts. "And since that day, I have been dreaming of doing just this."

Fiona felt her breath shorten, just hearing his words.

"Come!" Alec pushed the strap of the chemise up onto her shoulder and took her hand. The two stepped into the crystal-clear loch until the bottom fell away and the water rose around them.

They swam side by side, splashing and floating, laughing and diving into the darkness and chill. Fiona loved the feel of Alec's hands as he circled about her, caressing her, holding her tightly at one moment and pulling her beneath the surface in the next moment.

Taking a deep breath, Fiona dove deep into the darkness of the tarn, opening her eyes and looking up as her love followed her down. Propelling herself a few yards closer to the shore, she surfaced, bursting into the warm sunlight with her hair hanging like a thick rope behind her.

She turned and stood, her feet just touching the sand where the bottom dropped off, waiting for Alec to surface. The water around her was smooth and silent as the lengthening moments passed. A flash of anxiety raced through her as her eyes quickly scanned the beach and the unbroken surface of the loch.

"Alec!" she shouted, her voice echoing off the heather-covered hills.

Fiona took a deep breath, preparing to dive, when suddenly from beneath her she felt his strong hands gripping her waist and lifting her high out of the water. Holding her in his arms, he pushed smilingly into the waist-high shallows, and Fiona punched him playfully in the chest for his prank.

"Don't you ever scare me like that!"

"I wasn't trying to," he said, eyeing the wet linen clinging provocatively to her breasts. "The view under there was just too incredible to give up."

"What view?" she said shyly, knowing full well his meaning.

"I'll just have to show you."

As Alec's mouth descended on hers, his hands pulled her hard against his chest. Suddenly Fiona wanted to bury herself in him, lose herself, drown in him. Her fingers locked themselves in the strands of his wet hair as she pulled him closer. Just a brief second of loss, of not knowing where he was, had driven her mad beyond measure. And now that madness had turned to a desire, a need for his touch, for the feel of his body against hers. She arched her back as she pressed against him, her breasts aching inside the wet fabric, aching for his touch.

As their mouths caressed searchingly, Alec's hands traveled across her breasts, finding the strap of her chemise and pulling it down over one shoulder.

"Just hold me," he said huskily, drawing back from her as she wrapped her legs around his waist.

As he held her close and she ran her fingers along the muscles of his chest and neck, Alec's eyes wandered lingeringly down over the transparent slip clinging provocatively to his love's perfect form. Pulling her higher, he lightly kissed her chin, and as he ran the tip of his tongue down the hollow of her throat, over the glistening ivory wetness of her chest and into the valley between her breasts, he heard her gasp and felt her body go rigid.

Fiona felt his breath hot and strong on her breasts as his tongue reached the top of her partially untied chemise. Opening her eyes, she tried to concentrate on the sky above, deep and blue with ragged wisps of white streaks that disappeared behind the green of the surrounding hills. She closed her eyes again as one of his hands moved down, drawing up the hem of the garment billowing around her body. The colors of blue Fiona held in her mind's eye flashed into swirls of yellows and reds as his fingers gently reached between their bodies and slid into the cleft at the apex of her thighs. As Alec's fingers expertly found and began to massage the sensitive nub, waves of heat broke through Fiona's body, lifting her until she was no longer aware of the water around them. She was weightless, enraptured, afloat on a golden cloud. With him.

With a soft moan, Fiona arched her body as another surge of heat welled within her, and she unconsciously rocked against him in harmony with his caressing touch. Her body was molten now, the waves of heat cresting again and again, her breaths shortening into gasps until—her entire being exploding in an ecstasy of white heat and light—Fiona let out a cry and rolled back her head as her hands clawed at the flesh of his broad back.

She clung to him, her mouth ravenously seeking his and finding it, their tongues searching out the deepest recesses of their desire. Her hands kneaded the muscles of his back, and as Alec held her, Fiona could feel his erect manhood pressing against her intimately. Lowering herself in the water and standing up, she ran her palms down over the firm flesh of his side, her hand sliding into the water, her fingers closing around the massive arousal.

Alec heard himself groan as she took hold of his throbbing member. He'd intended to pleasure her, to take her to heights of sensual experience she'd never dreamed of. But right now, looking into the fires of desire raging in her blue-green eyes, he simply wanted her. He wanted to be inside of her. Deep inside of her.

"It's my turn," she whispered seductively, smiling coyly into his handsome face, her fingers lightly stroking his manhood.

Alec looked at her. The rosy peaks of her nipples strained to push through the transparent linen of the chemise. He would not be able stand much more of this.

He let her push him backward toward the beach. A few feet from the edge of the water, he drew her down beside him. Fiona lay his head back against the sand just beneath the surface. She gazed at him, his body glistened in the sun as the small waves lapped at his sides.

Pushing her hair back over her shoulder, she knelt down beside him and ran her tongue across his lips, her hand wandering lovingly over the rippling muscles of his belly. Trailing hot kisses onto his chest, she swirled her tongue around his nipples and felt him shudder as she moved her mouth lower. During these past days, she'd learned so many new ways of bringing him pleasure. And in all cases, what pleased her, pleased him. She ran her cheek along the hot skin of his erect member. Then, tasting the clinging droplets of water, she let her lips roam the hardened length.

"Hold there, my love," Alec rasped, raising himself and pulling her up on top of him. "If you keep on like that I may just go mad. Perhaps we might keep that little torment for another time."

Looking up into her smiling face, he lay back again in the water and, raising the hem of her wet chemise, he pulled her knees up till she was straddling his hips.

Fiona lowered her face and kissed him again as he raised her buttocks lightly with his strong hands. Drawing her face back, she gently nestled herself against the great crown of his arousal and gasped as he lowered her onto him. Deep within her he slid, and sheathing him tightly, Fiona felt again the perfect fit of true love.

Stretching her legs alongside his, Fiona moved her hips and felt him move against her in harmony. An aching desire again began to grow within her as Alec's hands pressed her bottom, grinding her hips into his, burying himself even deeper. Responding to him, Fiona raised her shoulders and shifted her hips, hearing his deep-throated growl even as bolts of lightning streaked from her center into the clouded recesses of her consciousness.

Alec raised his head and, with his lips, pinched her hardened nipples through the damp thinness of the undergarment. Unfastening two more of the ties, he pushed the strap of the chemise off one of Fiona's shoulders. Raising his mouth again, he suckled her exposed breast as she began to emit small cries, increasing the tempo of her pulsing body.

Fiona was moving up and down now, grinding her hips against him. As his mouth pulled at the tips of her breasts, she felt a cord of white heat go taut within her, and the sweet torment of his love grew ever wider, enveloping her, enthralling her, propelling her to an overwhelming crescendo of light and heat and oblivion.

As Fiona's cries grew stronger and Alec felt her body go rigid, he knew he could no longer wait. Rolling her onto her back in the shallow water, Alec drove his manhood again and again into her. Fiona raised her knees, wrapping her leg around his buttocks as he thrust himself deeper and deeper within, touching the very core of her. Finally, with a thunderous roar blocking out all other sounds, a sun exploded within him.

As Alec arched his massive body above her, Fiona looked up at the godlike face of her beloved. And as he pumped his life-seed into her, it seemed as though a new universe was created.

Chapter 23

Yesterday fair up sprang the flowers,
This day they are all slain with showers ...
—WILLIAM DUNBAR, *"This World Unstable"*

"I'm with child, Alec!"

He laughed heartily before lifting her into his arms. Smiling into Fiona's tear-filled eyes, Alec held her close. "So does that explain the retching? The light-headedness? The falling asleep at dinner?"

"Aye, my love. Are you ready for eight more months of such delightful companionship? Not to mention my ... ever-expanding presence?"

"Absolutely. I'll cherish every moment of it ... even the retching." Alec looked at her playfully. "In fact, I've been feeling a bit queasy myself. I wonder if I—"

"If you're looking for sympathy from me—"

Alec whirled her around in his arms as his lips devoured her smiling mouth.

"But to tell the truth, I knew it."

"And how might that be?"

"Nanna told me."

"Before she told me?" Fiona took him by the chin. "Is she another woman whom you've charmed into swooning at your feet?"

"No one else matters but you." Alec took her hand from his chin and tenderly kissed her palm. "But when are *you* going to swoon at my feet?"

Fiona stood on her tiptoes and put her arms around his neck. "Considering what I'm carrying, I'd say I already have," she cooed, kissing his chin.

"Willingly?" he asked, brushing his lips across hers.

"Wholeheartedly!"

It had never mattered to him before about having a
bairn, an heir for the Macpherson holdings. In fact, a lot
of things had never mattered before. But now, with
Fiona, life was not the same. She had captured his heart
and his soul. He wanted to have children with her. He
wanted bairns conceived in her womb. Offspring that
would bloom and grow. A part of them both that could
carry their love forward toward eternity.

As Fiona snuggled comfortably against his chest, she
could hear his great heart beating strongly. She thought
of how much her life had changed since she left Skye.
She thought of her friends whom she'd left behind. Of
the prioress, whose advice had been so valuable, so true,
in keeping her from becoming a nun. She knew now that
she belonged beside Alec, wherever he was. But there
was still the matter of Drummond Castle.

Fiona's fingers caressed the muscles of his encircling
arm.

"Alec?" she questioned, pulling her head back and
looking up into his deep blue eyes. "You'll still take me
there, won't you?"

Fiona had thrilled with the realization that she was
carrying a child. Both Nanna and Elizabeth had been so
positive and so affirming that morning in their
agreement and their advice. But as Fiona considered the
prospect of having a bairn, that thrill was tempered by
a tinge of anxiety about what she had yet to face.

After all, their trip to Drummond Castle had been
delayed until the details of the queen's agreement with
Lord Gray could be worked out. In truth, Fiona didn't
care if her uncle kept the place. She certainly didn't want
a feud on her hands. Her interest only lay in going back
to search for the truth. But based on all she was hearing
about court politics, things were becoming quite involved. It had become apparent that Fiona needed to
accept her rightful inheritance formally, for if she didn't,
the question of how much more she wanted would still
be left unanswered. As the king's daughter, now married
to one of the most powerful warriors in all Scotland,
Fiona simply had to put an end to such speculation. The
Crown was not what she was after.

Alec had been busy conferring with his father when
the messenger had arrived from court. After reading the

letter, he'd gone directly to Fiona with the message folded and tucked into his belt.

Now, standing in their chamber with the late summer breeze wafting lazily through the open windows, he was both relieved and excited about their news . . . and about the future. All that was left was to get through the affair at Drummond Castle, so they could get on with their lives.

"Are you certain you'll be fit to travel, love?" he teased.

"I'm as healthy as a horse. Alec, it's important that I—"

"We're leaving for Drummond Castle in two days."

Fiona stopped and looked up into his handsome face. As she did, the apprehension she'd been feeling about whether the pregnancy would interfere with her desire to go there simply melted away. His blues eyes were warm and reassuring.

"This message arrived a few moments ago," Alec said, pulling the folded missive from his belt.

Fiona took the letter that he held out to her, and looked at the wax seal. A two-headed eagle, surrounded by a circle of raised dots. She looked up questioningly at Alec as she unfolded the document.

"Lord Gray," he said, responding to her unanswered question. Fiona scanned the contents as Alec continued to speak. "It appears he is putting on a banquet to celebrate your return. He is going to turn Drummond Castle and its lands over to you officially. And apparently the queen will be present for the event."

"And we're going," she said soberly. Finally, she would have the opportunity she had been waiting for. Perhaps finally justice would be done. Fiona turned her gaze to Alec. "Do you think my uncle hates me? After what happened with Kathryn? And now taking his home away from him?"

"Drummond was never his, Fiona. That place has always belonged to you. Your grandfather made that very clear before his death. And as far as your uncle is concerned, he has wealth of his own. And in my opinion, I think he and his daughter both are getting better than they deserve. Kathryn Gray should be wasting away in some dungeon for what she tried to do."

"Please, Alec, let's forget about her," she pleaded. "She is out of our lives for good." Kathryn was not the one who worried her. There was still that someone else, the person paying Neil to kidnap her. But she didn't want to think of that now. Fiona knew that all those questions would be answered once she had her mother's hidden packet.

"Alec . . ." Fiona paused, looking for the right words. "Can you get along with him? My uncle?"

"Nay, my love. Not in this life."

"Could you try? For my sake? He is the only family connection I have with my past."

Alec cringed at the thought of having to be civil to the man. Their last meeting had almost ended with the drawing of swords. It had been Huntly who'd saved the man's neck, barely stopping certain bloodshed.

"Alec?"

"I'll try. Only for you."

As the light of the dying moon washed over them, Alec stirred from the depths of his slumber only long enough to gather his beloved tightly to him.

Again he felt them around him. Pushing at him. And then they stopped. Standing back, they peered vacantly. Faces. The same, familiar, nameless faces. Alec pushed past, and then the path opened through them.

He was walking with the king. Alec turned to speak to King James, but no words came. He looked behind them. There was nothing left of where he'd been. All had disappeared. The faces. The past. Gone. Thick mist, like the spray of an ocean surge, had washed away every trace.

The king smiled at the warrior and nodded ahead. A door.

Alec heard the voice. It was the old porter's voice.

"Your angel awaits."

Alec turned and looked at the king. The old man stood with him. He followed their gaze to where the door was opening . . . beckoning. The light beyond was spilling through.

"The evil is nigh, Alec Macpherson. Deliver her from the foe. The fiend is lurking."

Alec looked at the two men, unsure of who spoke the words. But he ran. He ran.

Drummond Castle loomed on the first and taller of two ridges, and the Macpherson entourage circled east from the little stone and thatch village, around the high gray walls to the imposing arched entrance. Craning her neck from her study of the warlike edifice, Fiona looked out at broad, rolling valley stretching out to the south, and at the blanket of gray mist that lay so heavily upon it.

Here, on the ridge, the brilliant rays had burned through the fog, and the sky showed pale blue around a warm and hazy sun, but Fiona's hands were clammy and cold. After all that had occurred, after all the waiting, she felt no thrill at returning to her childhood home, only the distress of facing the vague unknown, and a sharp burning sensation just below her heart that would not go away. Fiona gnawed at her lip as the horses labored up the hill toward the castle.

For the past hour, she'd been hoping for some glimmer of recognition of the place of her early childhood, but nothing had struck her until this moment. There was a sense of familiarity in this view that swept through her, but Fiona still could not really say that she remembered any of it. She shifted in her saddle, restless and disconcerted, but she told herself things would be different once they were inside the keep's gates.

Coming up to the large, flat space between the castle and the heavily wooded ridge just beyond it, the travelers were met with the sight of tents and soldiers and the smoke of cooking fires. The area was alive with the activities of warriors at leisure, of men passing the time in friendly sport and competition, and the sounds of bagpipes and laughter mingled with the ringing sound of steel.

Fiona looked at the loud and widespread festivities. All this just for turning over a place that only carried one memory. One very sad memory for a very young child.

Turning away from the amiable shouts of greeting and challenge, the Macpherson retinue climbed the hill toward the gates. Gazing over at Fiona, Alec reached over and squeezed her damp and ice-cold hand. She looked up at him, a tinge of uncertainty flickering across her face.

"Everything will be fine," he said reassuringly, noting her discomfort.

Together they rode across the dry moat over the heavy wooden drawbridge and into the castle close, their horses' hooves clattering loudly as they entered the large open yard paved with cobblestones. The select number of Macpherson warriors who had been chosen to accompany them filled the space around them, and they all dismounted as a small group of men came out into the close to greet them.

Fiona recognized no one but Lord Huntly. And then she spotted a tall well-built man with a shock of white hair who was crossing quickly to them. He smiled broadly and opened his arms to the newcomers. His tartan was clasped with a broach of gold: A double-headed eagle, surrounded by a circle of red rubies.

Her uncle. This was her uncle.

"Well, little Fiona with the fiery hair has returned home at last," Lord Gray called in a warm voice as he came directly to her and clasped her in his arms. "Well done. Watching you make your way up the ridge, I knew I would have recognized my beautiful niece— anywhere, anyplace, anytime. Do you remember me, little one?"

Fiona stepped back and looked into the man's rugged face. His eyes mirrored the light summer sky and sparkled as he looked on her.

"I'm afraid . . . just too many years have passed."

"Don't fear. We'll have plenty of time to catch up on those long-lost years. Welcome again, my dear. Welcome to your new home."

"Thank you . . . uncle," she said, feeling Alec's hands alight on her shoulders.

"Like her mother, a truly beautiful woman," Gray said softly, almost to himself. Looking up at Alec, he nodded, and his voice became cooler. "Well, Macpherson, like it or not, I guess this means you and I are kin after all. Welcome to Drummond Castle."

Alec nodded in response.

From the side, Fiona felt the heat of Lord Huntly's gaze upon her, and she turned to acknowledge him.

"Hello, Fiona," Huntly said, bowing stiffly with one hand on the long sword that hung at his side. "Well, Alec. I see marriage agrees with you. But we need to discuss some business, if Fiona wouldn't mind sparing you for short time."

She looked at her husband reassuringly. She had to be cool and collected. They were here, at last. She could not afford to raise Huntly's suspicions. Not yet. "Please go, Alec. I'll wait for you inside."

"Are you—"

"I'm certain." Fiona spotted Nanna a few steps behind them. "Nanna will look after me until you get back."

"She's among family now, Macpherson," Lord Gray said in a firm tone. "She'll be safe. Rest assured."

Alec restrained himself from growling at the man. But knowing Huntly, Alec was sure he would not request such a meeting now unless it pertained to something of extreme importance, so he leaned down and kissed his wife's cheek softly before following Huntly. But not before signaling his men to stay beside her in his absence.

The remainder of the group moved toward the stone steps leading to the open door of the castle's main building. Fiona gazed up at the building, but still nothing was coming back to her.

Gray's voice broke into her thoughts. "Things must look a bit different to you."

"They do," she admitted as they went up the steps.

"You shouldn't be surprised," he said. "The two buildings on either side of this main building were added about ten years ago. After the fire. But wait until you see the interior."

Fiona looked at him, startled. "Fire?" She glanced around, looking at Nanna.

"Aye, lass," the old woman put in, stepping beside her. "Your grandfather, rest his soul, was in residence here when it happened."

"Aye, and I give him credit," Gray added. "He did a fine job renovating the place. Practically rebuilt the living areas from the ground up. You'll like it. It's quite elegant. Very comfortable."

In a daze, Fiona walked into the Great Hall of a

Drummond Castle unrecognizable to its new mistress. Into a Drummond Castle that she had never known.

And through the fog, Fiona knew that her quest was over. Whatever it was her mother had hidden away, whatever it was she had died for, it was gone.

It was gone forever.

Chapter 24

Thy own fire, friend, though it be but a coal,
It warms the best, and is worth gold to thee.
—ROBERT HENRYSON, *"The Two Mice"*

"Please don't fuss, Nanna."

"It's my job, Fiona. And you're not eating the way you should." The old woman bustled toward the door at the far side of the sitting room. "You should listen more often to your husband, my dear."

"You want me to weigh as much as a boar and never leave the bed?" She grinned at her own words. Hearing about eating was becoming tiresome. But staying in bed . . . well, that was heaven, as long as Alec stayed there with her.

"I know the cook has a fine stew brewing in the kitchen. It'll be just about . . ." Nanna's last words were lost as she disappeared out the open door.

Fiona smiled after her. Laying down the ledger of farm accounts on the table beside the chair she was sitting in, she sat back and looked about her contentedly. After initially learning of the fire at Drummond, she'd not thought it possible wanting to stay at the place. But once again her fate had dictated otherwise.

On their day of arrival, Alec had been summoned by the queen and the ruling nobles. All of them wanted him involved with the future guardianship of the infant king, Fiona's half-brother. Queen Margaret was in a position of marrying again, so it was crucial that plans be cast in iron for the safekeeping of the throne.

So with the king little more than a day's ride south at Stirling, Alec and Fiona had remained at Drummond Castle.

During the past two months, the queen and her entourage had even made a number of excursions back to Drummond, so Fiona had gotten many chances to visit with and hold little Kit, her brother. They called him His Majesty James V, King of Scotland and the Western Isles. She called him the happy little toddler, and he was quite content to be held and loved.

So she did just that. She'd even had Kit in here yesterday, running and playing happily in front of the fire. The queen had been extremely agreeable in allowing Fiona and her half-brother to strengthen the bonds between them. So all week long a constant line of messengers, courtiers, and nobles of the governing Council of Regents had been passing in and out of the castle's gates.

The sitting room was large and spacious, furnished with enough chairs and benches for a clan gathering. Her grandfather's odd idea of installing long rows of shelves for books along the wall on either side of the fireplace was a stroke of real genius, she thought. Books were valuable things, but having them right at hand showed marvelous insight. Letting her eyes wander to the small fire crackling in the open hearth at the end of the long room, Fiona thought of how cozy and cheerful it would be here this winter.

And then, to top everything off, this morning Alec had mentioned that he wanted Malcolm to spend the winter with them. Fiona had been so overjoyed by the news that she'd hardly felt her morning queasiness. Malcolm would be here.

These days, Fiona glowed with feelings of maternal love. First Kit, and now in a few weeks Malcolm. She sighed and ran her hands over her still flat belly. She was more than a third of the way through the pregnancy, but still nothing showed. All the same, she loved this feeling. And she knew Alec did, too. Each night, after making love, the two of them would lay in bed and take turns talking to their bairn. She envisioned him as a boy, with deep blue eyes, and addressed him as such. Alec was sure she was a girl with fiery red hair, and called to her that way.

Alec was due back soon. Her uncle, Lord Gray, and the Earl of Huntly were to arrive tonight for few days of discussions with Alec. Fiona had been pleased at her uncle's attempt to befriend her husband. It seemed as though, in the absence of his daughter, the man had set his mind to capture the affection of his niece. Fiona respected her uncle for trying, but beyond that she still reserved her judgment. It was difficult to get used to family when you had never had any for most of your life.

Dusk was descending, and the room was beginning to get dark. She hoped desperately for Alec to arrive before their guests. For try as she might, Fiona could not get over her discomfort with having the Earl of Huntly as their guest. She could not put the past behind her. Ever.

Fiona stood and moved to the open window. Though the day had turned out dry and fairly warm, the autumn had brought with it cold and wet weather. But it was nothing compared to the harsh autumn weather of Skye. She closed her eyes and breathed in the gentle evening air. The breeze carried with it a hint of dampness as it swept through her unbound locks. She turned away and again sat, closing her eyes and idly thinking of how she could tell Nanna she would wait for Alec to arrive before eating.

The cold arm stole caressingly around her shoulders. Fiona's body became rigid, frozen, and she could not so much as open her eyes when she felt the smooth skin of the icy cheek pressing tenderly against her forehead.

And then she was gone.

Stunned, Fiona sat, too shocked even to call out. But then the sound of horses' hooves thundering across the open drawbridge made her blood run cold as her mother's spirit never could.

Fiona's eyes snapped open, a terrible fear racing through her as her eyes swept the room. Gripping the carved wooden arms of the chair, she vaulted out of her seat and ran to the window. It was no longer the unglazed slit it had been in her childhood, but looking out the opening, she could see the horses stamping as the group of men hurriedly dismounted in the courtyard below. It was the same view.

It happened here, she thought, a strange panic burning in her veins as she whirled and looked about the chamber.

"Mother!" she cried out in the empty room. But she was alone.

It's here, she thought.

Fiona pressed her fingers to her temples to ease the pounding in her head, but as her eyes scanned the room, clearly nothing was the same as she remembered. These rooms had been rebuilt. This sitting room was much larger than it had been so long ago ... when it was her nursery. It was all different now.

And then her glance fell on the fireplace. Surrounded by the long shelves of books, it looked so different. But it wasn't different. Could it be? she thought. In her mind, she could see her mother ... counting over ... pulling the stone ...

Scrambling to the open hearth, she began to pull the books from the shelves to the right of the fireplace. Feeling behind the books, Fiona's fingers grazed the rough stone of the wall. Her haste turned nearly to frenzy, and the volumes fairly flew, dropping to the floor around her.

With one shelf cleared, Fiona hurriedly counted the stones. One. Two. Three. Four. Five. Is this the right height? she wondered. Prying with her fingers, Fiona hurriedly pulled at one corner of the stone.

It moved.

Yanking the stone from the wall, she dropped it with a thud into an empty space among the books on the floor.

Fiona's heart was pounding as she stood, transfixed, before the open gap in the wall. All these years. All that had happened. To her mother. To her. To Scotland. To Drummond Castle itself. Here, buried behind a stone, lay the end of Fiona's quest. Whether the leather pouch was there or not, Fiona knew her search was over.

With a deep breath, she reached into the gloom of the wall.

Andrew stood in the open doorway, watching her reach carefully into the hiding place. He'd known it was here. God knows, he'd looked. But the bitch had hidden it away well. There was no finding it then, no matter how hard he looked. After the fire and the rebuilding, he thought it was gone forever. But no, here she was, and she had known all along where it lay hidden.

I had the right idea, he thought, paying Neil and those

seagoing jackals to kill her. If they weren't so inept . . .
Well, the time had come to take care of this himself.
The time had come to get what was his.

And I will have my final revenge, he thought, his pale
blue eyes glimmering with hate.

Fiona twisted her body to gain better access to the
opening. The space was deep, but she could just barely
feel something with the tip of her fingers. She took a
deep breath and pushed her hand in as far as she could,
and then her fingers closed around it. The pouch.

And then she saw him watching her.

"I didn't hear you come in!" she gasped with surprise.

"I saw the door was open." He took a leisurely step
inside and closed the door behind him. "You could catch
a chill standing in drafts. Your husband should do a
better job taking care of you. Especially considering
your condition."

"There is no need to be critical of Alec," Fiona responded, drawing the packet gently from the wall. She
held it out in front of her and watched his pale blue
eyes focus on it. "I want peace between you two."

"Your husband is a fool to leave you alone like this."
His eyes roamed the room. The open windows drew his
attention. The hard stone of the cobbled courtyard
would provide a suitable landing for her broken body.
"In fact, he reminds me of another fool whom I knew
a long time ago. Your father."

Fiona gazed in shock at the ring and the broach sitting
in her open palm. For a moment the world stopped turning and silence reigned in the universe, but the room
was whirling in Fiona's vision, and the pounding in her
head thundered.

"It was you!" she whispered, holding up the jeweled
broach. The circle of red stones that enclosed the
double-headed eagle still glinted in the light of the room.
And they were identical to those on the broach adorning
Lord Gray's tartan as he stood before her.

"Aye, Fiona. It was I," her uncle sneered, moving
toward where she stood, rather unsteadily, among the
books. Leaning down, he picked up one of the books
that lay strewn at her feet. Glancing at the title with

affected indifference, he turned his cold gaze on the young woman, eyeing her every move.

"But why?"

Andrew threw the book to the floor and laughed, but without amusement. "She asks me why. Don't bother yourself with the ways of men. After all, you're just a fool as well, my dear."

Fiona took a step back toward the window. She would not let him have what she held. This was proof of a crime.

"How?" She needed to buy time. If she moved to the window, perhaps she could call for help. "How could you do that? Your own niece. What evil could possess you that you could kill your own kin? That you could kill my mother?"

The aging warrior pushed back his cloak, uncovering the hilt of his sword. "She had something that belonged to me." Andrew held out his hand where he stood. He could already feel the snap of her neck between his fingers. His cold eyes locked on Fiona's. They were like ice. And he used them as weapons of fear and intimidation. "You have it in your hand. Give it to me."

Fiona looked down at the ring as she stepped backward, away from him. The ring was ornate, even for a sealing ring. On it was a rampant lion over a cross. Above the lion was a crown.

"Aye," he rasped. "It is the ring of Robert the Bruce. The symbol of royal power. Only to be worn by the king of Scotland. Your mother stole it from me."

"My mother knew you were evil. She did the right thing."

"Evil is a necessary part of the universe, my dear. It is the source of power. It is what separates the rulers from the ruled, the great from the lowly, the strong from the weak. The predator from the prey." Andrew dropped his gloves onto the account ledger. He wanted her to feel his strength when his fingers crushed the last vestige of life from her body.

"Evil robs humans of happiness. True power emanates from goodness and decency. You talk about predators? It is the power of God that holds the falcon aloft. The predator does not take pleasure in killing. The falcon does not kill her own."

"You know nothing about these things, woman. Like your mother, who would not listen to anything I had to say. She just wanted to run away. To pour out my secrets ... for love," he sneered. "That ring is mine. These Stuart cowards never deserved to have it. I took it away from your grandfather, James III. Did you know it was I who convinced your father—ah, he was such a gullible child—to ride with my army against his own father? To demand the throne for himself? For the good of Scotland? He made us promise not to lay a hand on his old man. Ha! Fifteen and already he was such a fool."

Fiona shook her head as she felt the edge of the window seat at her back.

"Your grandfather was so weak a king, it made me ill. So I took the ring from him ... while he was running away from the troops of his son. Aye, in a miserable hut, the day I murdered him. Your father never knew how his father died, but he felt responsible. So the boy-king wore a chain under his shirt. He even added a link to that chain every year thereafter."

Fiona remembered the feel of the hard metal. Now she knew his constant reminder of his own guilt.

"And it was I who introduced your mother to him. And as I expected, the morons fell in love. I had him where I wanted him. At my mercy. In the palm of my hand. Under my control. Then the bitch, your mother, spied on me. She found the ring. I offered her a deal. She would have a home and a way to keep her miserable bastard, but she was a stubborn fool. She spoke in dead and empty terms like honor and truth. And then she betrayed me. Margaret stole what was mine, and I made her pay for her crime."

Drummond Castle, October 1502

Spare my child, Margaret prayed. *Holy Mother, don't hold my sins against my innocent child. I know I'm not worthy of your favor. But please grant me this. Protect her from this evil.*

The brute holding the mother's wrists was twisting them viciously, and Torquil MacLeod was crossing the room toward her when the door of the nursery opened. Margaret turned her head and watched as her uncle, tall and cool, glided into the room. Everything in her vision was so clear, every sensation magnified, every detail etched with crystalline precision. In his hand he carried a small blue bottle that he casually placed on the table.

"Margaret," he began, turning abruptly, fixing his ice-blue eyes on her face. "Your household is finished, your child is at our mercy, and your man is a day's ride from here."

The look of alarm that she could not keep from flashing across her face brought a malevolent smile to his. "Aye, in accordance with my own cleverly conceived plan, the king has been gulled into stopping, waiting—as we speak—for an emissary from England who will never appear. A fool is always a fool. He simply trusts me."

An evil laugh rumbled from Torquil MacLeod as the Highlander moved behind his leader. Andrew never even glanced at him, but crossed to Margaret and removed the gag that stopped her mouth. His eyes remained riveted on her.

"Now, niece," he commanded, taking her chin in his hand. "Give me what is mine, and give it to me now."

"Never," she whispered defiantly. "Traitor. Murderer."

Andrew raised his hand to strike her, but caught himself, lowering his fist. "Do not think you can escape my wrath, Margaret. You will give me what is mine."

"You can torture me until—"

"Nay, lass," he broke in, his eyes reflecting the malice in his soul. "It isn't you who will be tortured. It is your bastard child."

"You won't," Margaret cried, terror flashing across her face. "She's just a bairn. Even a monster like you—"

"Ah, yes. A monster like me." Andrew paused and stared grimly at her. "Shall I bring her back up here? We'd intended to keep her. Just another lever to prod the king. But if she must die—and so painfully—simply because her own mother would not give me a trinket that she'd stolen from me . . ."

He let his words trail off in the deadly silence of the room. Margaret closed her eyes to the searing pain. In her heart she knew, no matter what, Fiona's chance of surviving this was practically nil, and the thought of it drove a white hot shaft though her heart.

"Spare your daughter, Margaret. Spare her the—"

At the pounding on the door, Gray whirled toward the sound. The knight that pushed breathlessly into the room halted at the sight before him.

"What do you want?" Lord Andrew snapped.

"M'lord. A troop of riders. Coming up the glen. From the torches, it looks like over a hundred."

"Andrew," Margaret breathed, tears suddenly streaming down her reddened cheeks.

Her uncle whirled on her.

"Aye. Huntly," she shot at him defiantly. "You're finished, you demon! What James is too trusting to see, Andrew will avenge. You'll not be able to get away. Not this time. I sent for him. He'll make you pay."

Andrew Gray stared vaguely at her for the briefest of moments, and then the glimmer returned to his eyes.

"Not quite yet, bitch," he spat. "By the time the meddling fool gets here, Torquil and his men will be gone. And I . . . I will be grief-struck at having just found your dead body."

"Nay . . ."

"Aye," he said with dreadful finality, picking up the blue bottle and removing the stopper. "You are about to meet death at your own hand, niece."

Gripping her chin in his hand, he lifted it roughly and poured the poison down her throat. Stepping back, he watched as Margaret's face turned white, her eyes suddenly brilliant.

"God will forgive me, Andrew Gray. But you . . ." Her legs were beginning to quiver. Her breathing was becoming difficult. "Spare Fiona, uncle."

"Where is the ring?" His face was steeled. His eyes were ice.

Margaret sank to the floor, numbness sweeping through her body. "You will pay for your evil. My friend will avenge me . . ."

"Where is the ring?"

Her tongue felt swollen, and she could hear her words slurring.

"Andrew. My friend will av . . ."

Lord Gray raised his hand. "Give it to me."

As Fiona shook her head in defiance, his hand came

up and took her throat in a vise-like grip, nearly lifting her from the floor.

A movement by the door drew Fiona's eyes, and she felt his grasp slacken as his head turned to see Huntly charging across the floor toward him. Slapping his arm away with all her force, Fiona spun clear of him as Gray drew his sword to meet Huntly's approach.

"You killed her!" Huntly roared, his sword crashing down on the larger man's steel. Gasping for air, Fiona gaped at the earl's pale face, livid with rage, as he swung his sword again at the murderer.

This time Gray ducked out of the way, spinning down the wall away from Fiona. In a shower of sparks, Huntly's blade shattered as it struck the wall, and Gray's return blow knocked the stunned earl to the floor. Moving over him, Andrew Gray placed the point of his sword against his old enemy's throat.

"This will be even better," he snarled. "Attacking my niece. Too bad I couldn't arrive in time to stop you from pushing her over the ledge. I had no chance to stop you, but in killing you, I was at least able to avenge her. It was only justice."

As he raised his arm to strike, Fiona rushed at him, her dirk in her hand. With a sweep of his arm, he deflected her blow, sending her staggering across the room. As she fell, the ring flew noisily across the floor, landing at her uncle's feet.

Andrew, Lord Gray turned his pale, blue eyes covetously downward to where the ring lay. The crown above the lions glinted for him. Again, his plans would move forward. With Huntly gone, another step closer to the absolute power he so richly deserved. To the crown. His crown. An insane and malevolent smile crept across his face as he began to reach for the ring. For his ring.

It was his final mistake.

The room burst open as Alec exploded through the open door. Lord Gray's expression turned from triumph to terror as he saw the young warlord scan the room, his eyes lingering momentarily on his fallen wife.

Rage flashed across Alec's face as he turned his gaze on Andrew. Gray lifted his sword to deflect the oncoming blade, but the force of Alec's blow cut down his weapon and ripped through the bones and sinew of the attacker, driving Gray to the floor in the final throes of death.

Fiona watched as her mother's murderer twitched, his fingers stretching desperately toward the ring that lay just out of his grasp.

And then he was dead, his blue eyes glazing in a cold stare toward eternity.

Chapter 25

"... even though beneath the flowers thorns
do lie, in you, my friend, I have always had a
protector ... a champion to tear out by the roots
those iniquitous barbs. Alas, that I should
deserve such a friend ..."
—MARGARET DRUMMOND, *"Letter to Huntly"*

"I came to her," Huntly told Fiona and Alec. "But I was too late. She was dead ... and you were gone."

The three sat in Alec's workroom, and Huntly leaned forward in his chair, staring at his hands as he spoke. In his hand he held the carefully folded letter he had worn next to his heart for so many years. The letter from Fiona's mother.

Margaret Drummond had written to Lord Huntly, knowing him to be the one man in the world who could bring down justice on her traitorous uncle. She had asked him to come to Drummond Castle, where she would provide proof of the identity of the assassin of King James III. Fearing interception of the letter, Margaret had not dared to mention the name of the killer.

"Looking at her lifeless body twisted on the floor, into her eyes that spoke even in death, I went mad with anger and grief. I was frustrated that I had been too slow to stop what had happened. I tore the old castle apart, looking for some trace of the proof Margaret had spoken of. For the evidence that would prove she hadn't taken her own life. That she'd been murdered. Oh, for a long time I'd had my suspicions of Gray's involvement in the treacherous death of old King Jamie, but I had nothing to bring to your father. He was distraught at the loss of you and your mother, and he could not bring himself to believe any kin of Margaret's could be capable of wrongdoing. In fact, there was probably no one he suspected more than me. After all, how I felt about your mother was no secret to anyone."

Fiona reached over and took one of his hands. "Please forgive me, m'lord. You see, I suspected you, as well."

Huntly smiled at her and squeezed her hand. "I loved your mother, Fiona. And I know she cared for me. Trusted me. She valued me as a friend. I hope you will, too."

Fiona's smile was brilliant when her hazel eyes found his. "I'll treasure your friendship always."

The warm breeze that caressed the earl's face came from nowhere. It was the softest of touches. A gentle sign, bringing a feeling of great peace that went straight to his heart. And then he heard Margaret's voice, drifting toward him through a silvery mist. "Thank you, my friend. Thank you."

He turned toward the sound, but she was gone.

Epilogue

Dunvegan Castle, the Isle of Skye, 1526

The MacLeod heir held up Rory Mor's Horn with two hands.

The silent hush filled the crowded hall. Lord Macpherson poured the claret into the horn. It took a whole pitcher and half to fill the ancestral drinking cup. Malcolm pushed back his long brown hair from his handsome face and brought the ancient vessel to his lips. He knew what he had to do—all at once, no setting it down, no falling down, not a drop missed.

He took a deep breath and drained the ritual cup in one draught.

The clan went wild with cheers and laughter.

Alec raised his hands for silence.

"Your new laird," the warlord shouted.

The hall erupted again with cheers and people rushed to the dais, clapping Malcolm MacLeod hard on the back. But the young leader at that moment had eyes for only two people. He turned and faced the man and the woman whom he cherished more than life itself.

He embraced Alec, who had been a father to him. Who had taught him the values of life, of benevolent rule. Alec, who had kept his promises of bringing prosperity and trade to the people of Skye, while continuing to guide his own clan.

Then Malcolm turned to Fiona, who sat quietly smiling amid the uproar. The young man could see the pride radiating from her beautiful hazel eyes, and she stood as he drew her to him.

Fiona felt his strong arms close around her. He was so tall and broad. So different from the scared little boy who had been brought back to the Priory so many years before. He belonged here. The times were changing, and Malcolm was prepared—physically and mentally—for the challenges that lay ahead for him.

She looked back at Father Jack, who stepped forward and laid the dark box on the table. She pulled back from Malcolm's embrace and glanced at her husband, who was gazing intently into the crowd.

Following his eyes, Fiona caught a glimpse of the old man's blue robe just disappearing behind a throng of tall and boisterous youths. She continued to look, but she knew old James was gone. He'd been gone for a long time, now.

Fiona looked back at Alec and saw him looking at her.

"Malcolm will be fine," Alec said quietly. "Old James is watching over him."

She smiled gently and nodded.

Father Jack raised his hand to the gathered clan and beckoned to Fiona. She moved to the table and opened the box.

The silence in the room was deep and profound, and all eyes were on her as she drew the ancient banner from its resting place.

Gasps could be heard as the clan members recognized the long lost, long hidden Am Bratach Sith—the Fairy Flag.

Wrapping the yellowed cloth around Malcolm's shoulders, Fiona smiled broadly when the hall once again exploded with excitement, and Malcolm was lifted to the shoulders of his people and carried triumphantly around the room.

Over the sound of the bagpipes and the singing crowd, Alec slipped his arm around Fiona and spoke into her ear. "Well, my love. Is it time to go home?"

"Aye, Alec," she responded, squeezing him tightly. "Do you think our little angels have leveled Benmore Castle yet?"

"If you are talking about the same little imps we left there, the chances are fairly good the place is in ruins."

"Our boys are not imps, Alec Macpherson."

"You're right, Fiona. They're just like their mother." Alec smiled into Fiona's loving face. "I just wonder how many of my falcons they've set free . . . this time."

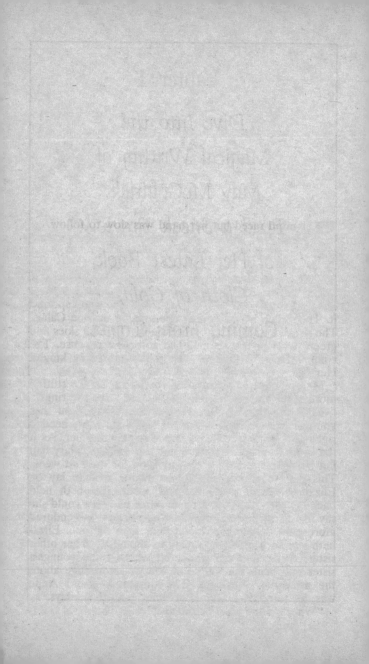

Chapter 1

Her mind raced but her hand was slow to follow.
Elizabeth dipped the brush in the paint mixture
and once again raised it to the canvas.

"What are you calling it?"

"The eighth wonder of the world!" Elizabeth murmured as she took a step back and studied her latest creation. The Field of Cloth of Gold. She had captured it. The sweep of the rolling countryside outside Calais. The majesty of the royal processions. The blue skies and green fields of late spring. The colors of promise. The competitive thrill of the joust. The conquering knight. Her best work so far.

Mary shifted her weight on the couch as she stuffed more pillows behind her head. "Could I see the ring?"

Elizabeth turned in surprise and looked at her younger half-sister. This was the last thing Mary needed right now, with this illness that was plaguing her. As if the sores from the pox were not bad enough, Mary had not been able to hold down any food for the past week. This once beautiful and robust young woman lay on Elizabeth's bed, exhausted and spent. Elizabeth held back her pity—and her tongue. After all, what could she say to this seventeen-year-old who already had endured more pain than others might bear in a lifetime. Elizabeth's mind wandered vaguely to thoughts of her other sister, Anne, and she wondered whether the youngest sister had been the source of Mary's knowledge about the afternoon's incident. The thirteen-year-old Anne was, for most part, Mary's eyes and ears these days.

"Where is the ring, Elizabeth?"

"I don't have it anymore."

"For God's sake, don't pity me." Mary turned her face away, speaking as much to herself as to her sister. "He took my innocence. He slept with me. He used me. So what if you are the one that ends up with his ring."

"You slept with the Scot?"

"Don't be funny, Elizabeth. You know what I'm talking about."

It was no secret that Mary had been the mistress of Henry VIII, King of England, in the recent months. The affair had begun immediately after Mary and Anne were summoned to England and to the court by their father only four months ago. From what Elizabeth had been able to gather from Anne, their father had clearly encouraged Mary to respond in kind to the handsome young king's amorous advances, and Sir Thomas had even gone so far as to arrange private meetings in the hunting lodges away from court . . . and away from the Queen. It was common knowledge that the king had long ago grown tired of the woman who could bear him no son.

Ten years back, after the death of his second wife, Sir Thomas Boleyn had sent Mary and Anne to France to be brought up in the company of Elizabeth, his daughter from an earlier liaison. From early on the bonds were strong between the three young siblings. Elizabeth, then ten years old, was only three years older than Mary. Nonetheless, from the start she had taken on the role of guardian, and had looked after and offered guidance to her newfound half-sisters.

Growing up together in France in the household that their father, Sir Thomas Boleyn, kept in the court of Queen Isabel, the three black-haired beauties had very early on attracted the roving eyes of courtiers and knights from France and from many different countries. Of the three, Mary had always been the one drawn to the glamour of that fashionable life. Indeed, something in Elizabeth's sister had always cried out for the fawning attention of the court rakes, but nothing had ever happened. Not while Mary had been under Elizabeth's care.

Then, when Elizabeth found herself unexpectedly summoned to Calais by Sir Thomas, she found Mary sick and bedridden with pox. Ever since arriving, the older sister had been tending to Mary with loving care. There was no need for scolding the younger woman—if the syphilis didn't kill her now, then she could look forward to a lifetime of suffering.

Though she herself had always shunned the allure of the court and its shallow inhabitants, something within Elizabeth kept her from condemning Mary for becoming the love interest of the most powerful man in England, the man who held their father's future in his hands. After all, Elizabeth had always had her talent—her painting—her secret life and her hopes of becoming a great painter. Those dreams offered all the passion that Elizabeth sought in this life. They made her independent, even as a woman. Lost in her art, she needed no man to look after her, to protect her. But Mary was different. She needed attention. She wanted glamour. As Elizabeth strived to be the observer and to capture the image, Mary had always taken pleasure in being the object, the observed, the center of all attention.

Elizabeth thought now of the price her sister was paying. She picked up the brush and started to paint the puffs of clouds scudding across the clear, blue sky.

"Anne told me everything that happened today at the tournament," Mary whispered, watching the smooth strokes of her sister's brush. "I have to warn you. He is a womanizer."

"You know him?" Elizabeth asked without breaking stride.

"It is hard to not notice him. That Scot is a good-looking man. But don't worry, sister. He is clean. I haven't slept with him."

The crash of the jug against the floor jolted Mary to a sitting position. She looked down sheepishly, trying to avoid the blazing temper of her older sister.

"I warn you!" Elizabeth took a step toward the cowering creature. "If I hear you even one more time belittling yourself as you have been—" She took a deep breath to control her anger before continuing. The walls of these tents were too thin for her liking. "You cannot hold yourself responsible, Mary. If someone should take the blame, it is that king of yours for giving this God-awful disease to a mere child."

"Then you believe me that he is the only one I have ever slept with?"

"Of course I believe you."

The soft tears that left Mary's eyes did not go unnoticed by her older sister. Elizabeth moved quickly to her and gathered the young woman in her arms.

"Henry doesn't. He hates me. He called me ugly. He said he never wants to see my sickly face. The night before you arrived, I went to him. I was delirious with fever. He wouldn't even let his physician tend to me. He called me a . . ." Mary clutched at the neck of her sister and wept.

"Hush, my love. That's all in the past. That's all behind you now. Just think of the future. A beautiful future." She knew her words lacked conviction. Elizabeth bit her lips in frustration as she thought of the cold and selfish king. But they were all like that. Men! Born free to do as they wished. They claimed what they said was theirs by right, but abided by no rules. Where is the logic in that? Where is the compassion?

"Oh, Elizabeth! No man will ever want to look at me. I'll never have any place in society. No one will want me, not even as a friend. I'm already shunned. I just want to die. Death, where are you? Come and take me!"

"Stop your foolish talk, Mary. That will not happen."

"Why not?"

"Because the Angel of Death has to face me first before he gets to you."

"You think you could scare him off the way you scare me?" Mary asked with a weak chuckle.

"Of course!"

Mary closed her eyes and took comfort in the protective embrace. Everything would get better now that Elizabeth was here. She would take care of her, the way she always had. She would never be alone. And she'd get better. Her sister had said so. Elizabeth had already sought the assistance of the French king's physician in examining her illness. The man had been here twice and was coming back this afternoon. He had sounded quite hopeful the last time.

The gentle footstep outside the tent separated the two. Elizabeth moved quickly to her painting and threw a sheet over it.

"Why don't you want me to see it?" The young girl stood in the opening of the tent, watching her eldest sister with a pout on her pretty face.

"Anne, you should not march in on grown-ups as you do. It is not proper." Mary whispered in her weak voice from the couch. "You know very well that Elizabeth doesn't want anyone looking at her pictures."

"I am not anyone. I'm her sister. And what you say is not true. I saw her show her paintings to the Duc de Bourbon."

"She did?" Mary turned to her older sister in surprise. Elizabeth had sworn Mary to secrecy years back. No one was to see her pictures. No one was to be told. Mary knew it was Elizabeth's greatest fear . . . that if people learned of her painting, it would be taken away. After all, it was not proper for a young woman to pursue such hobbies to the extent Elizabeth did. Mary had been shocked in seeing that some of Elizabeth's paintings actually portrayed nude men and women.

"I saw her with my own two eyes," Anne broke in before Elizabeth could respond. "In fact I saw her accept a bag of gold coins from the Duc and leave one of the paintings with him."

Mary jumped out of her place and flung herself at her older sister. "My God! You did it. At last! You sold your work. Which one? How did you convince him to buy one of your paintings? A woman's painting! How did you approach him? How much did you get for it? What made you do it?"

Elizabeth looked up and captured the gaze of her excited sister. She couldn't relate the truth. Not all of it. After all, she had done it for her. To pay the French physician's fee. But she couldn't let her know.

The Duc de Bourbon, for the past couple of years, had been a persistent pursuer of Elizabeth. But that had been a situation the young woman could not accept. She just was not interested in becoming an ornament, tucked away and brought out from time to time for some man's pleasure. As her mother had been . . . so many years ago. And she had let the Duc know her feelings. But the man was not giving up. In their most recent encounters the Duc had been most devious in his efforts to seduce her. She'd been regularly infuriated by his persistent antics and his pathetic tales. So now Elizabeth thought with some satisfaction of how she had earlier today been able to mislead the young nobleman over the painting. She had made up stories that were too unbelievable, but the Duc had for some reason accepted her tale.

"Tell me, Elizabeth," Mary asked again. "How did you convince him to buy your work?"

"I lied. He thinks he's become the patron of a very talented, though as yet unknown artist. An unknown male artist. He thinks I was just playing the part of kind-hearted liaison."

"I would have thought he'd be a jealous monster at the thought of your acting for another man."

"I don't see why," Elizabeth sighed as she cleaned and put away her brushes. "My relationship with the Duc has never been anything more than an innocent friendship ... at least on my part. I've never led him on."

"No? Do I have to remind you how men think?" Mary moved back to the couch and sat down. This topic was one in which she had more expertise than her older sister. "It doesn't matter what you say or do. The fact is, Elizabeth, you don't belong to any man. You are fair game."

"Oui! I know the poems—we women are the 'tender prey' for these overgrown, 'love-struck' boys. Well, I'm not. Though I guess I may have embellished the story to take that into account. I did tell him the artist is a crippled nobleman with leprosy who hides himself away in a priory and never sees visitors." Elizabeth removed her apron and tucked it away. "I suppose after hearing that story there was no reason for the Duc to feel challenged."

For all her words, though, Elizabeth hoped she would not cross paths with the French nobleman for the rest of her stay here. With the heartache of her sister's ailment, she was in no mood to deal with a persistent courtier.

"Father wants you, Elizabeth." Anne's voice had the singsong quality of a child who knows a secret. The other two women both turned to her in unison.

"Father? What does he want?" Elizabeth had seen her

father only from a distance since arriving in the north of France. Their relationship had never been anything more than politely detached. In fact, unless it was due to Mary's illness, Elizabeth had no idea why her father had summoned her, a daughter he'd openly referred to as his "other daughter—the stubborn one."

"I'll tell you for one of those gold coins—" As the words left the girl's mouth, she leaned over and grabbed a couple of Elizabeth's brushes, bolting for the tent's opening.

It took Elizabeth only a moment to realize what Anne had done. She turned and ran after her.

"You spoiled, greedy monster." The older sister chased Anne into the bright afternoon sun. There was no sign of the girl. She was as good at disappearing as she was at appearing.

Elizabeth's eyes roamed the setting before her. There were people everywhere. Squires and stable boys, soldiers and servants, some people dressed in finery and others in rags. Horses and dogs, dull gray carts and brightly painted wagons. The very air was vibrant with action. The gold cloth of the tents reflected the rays of the sun. It looked as though the ropes had captured that celestial orb, holding it down. Elizabeth made a mental note of that. Another touch for her work.

"I have to admit that I feel offended."

The soft, masculine burr of the accent made Elizabeth turn slowly in the direction of the voice. It was he. Uncontrollably, she felt her heartbeat quicken at the sight of the giant warrior dressed in a Scottish tartan now standing only a step away. His deep blue eyes were unwavering as they gazed into hers.

"I'm Ambrose Macpherson. What's your name, lass?"

"Why did you say you were offended?" Elizabeth heard the change in her own voice. Her next painting had to be of this man in his kilt. The sight was definitely too impressive to go uncaptured.

Ambrose smiled.

Elizabeth's heart skipped a beat.

"You were giving this dirt-packed alley more attention than you did to the joust earlier today." Ambrose took a step toward her, allowing a horse cart to make its way past. He noticed that she didn't retreat. But he did see a gentle blush spread across her perfect ivory complexion. As her eyes wandered away from his to the groups of people moving by, the young warrior's eyes roamed the young woman's body. She was hardly the most beautiful woman he had seen in his life, but there was something about her that was quite compelling. Up close, her eyes were the alluring banks of coal that had gotten his attention to start. She had her hair hidden under a severe-looking headpiece, but from a loose tendril that lay against her forehead he could tell she was dark-haired. The dress, discolored in spots, was rolled up to her elbow and untied at the neck. The tease of what lay beyond the next tie was tempting. She had the stance and the boldness of a noblewoman ... but the appearance of a maid. Ambrose let his eyes fall on her lips. They were full, sensuous, inviting.

"You fought a good match." She caught his eyes on her.

"I haven't seen you before. Did you just arrive today?"

"You could have broken your neck at the joust, standing in your stirrups as you did."

"French or English?"

"Did you get that scar pulling a stunt similar to the one you pulled today?"

"You are not married, are you?"

Elizabeth turned her eyes back to the activities in the alley. "There is so much more to see here than at the tournament field."

"Any jealous lovers?"

"Real people, in their element." She hid a smile. "They are so interesting to watch."

"My tent, tonight?" Ambrose reached out and took her hand in his. His thumb gently stroked the soft skin as he lifted her fingers to his lips.

"I have to go." Elizabeth pulled back in haste and, without so much as a backward glance, ran down the alley in the direction of her father's tent.

WE NEED YOUR HELP

To continue to bring you quality romance
that meets your personal expectations,
we at TOPAZ books want to hear from you.
Help us by filling out this questionnaire, and in exchange
we will give you a **free gift** as a token of our gratitude.

- Is this the first TOPAZ book you've purchased? (circle one)

  YES   NO

  The title and author of this book is: _____

- If this was not the first TOPAZ book you've purchased, how many have
  you bought in the past year?

  a: 0 - 5   b 6 - 10   c: more than 10   d: more than 20

- How many romances in total did you buy in the past year?

  a: 0 - 5   b: 6 - 10   c: more than 10   d: more than 20 ____

- How would you rate your overall satisfaction with this book?

  a: Excellent   b: Good   c: Fair   d: Poor

- What was the main reason you bought this book?

  a: It is a TOPAZ novel, and I know that TOPAZ stands
     for quality romance fiction
  b: I liked the cover
  c: The story-line intrigued me
  d: I love this author
  e: I really liked the setting
  f: I love the cover models
  g: Other: _____

- Where did you buy this TOPAZ novel?

  a: Bookstore   b: Airport   c: Warehouse Club
  d: Department Store   e: Supermarket   f: Drugstore
  g: Other: _____

- Did you pay the full cover price for this TOPAZ novel? (circle one)

  YES   NO

  If you did not, what price did you pay? _____

- Who are your favorite TOPAZ authors? (Please list)

- How did you first hear about TOPAZ books?

  a: I saw the books in a bookstore
  b: I saw the TOPAZ Man on TV or at a signing
  c: A friend told me about TOPAZ
  d: I saw an advertisement in_____magazine
  e: Other: _____

- What type of romance do you generally prefer?

  a: Historical   b: Contemporary
  c: Romantic Suspense   d: Paranormal (time travel,
     futuristic, vampires, ghosts, warlocks, etc.)
  d: Regency   e: Other: _____

- What historical settings do you prefer?

  a: England   b: Regency England   c: Scotland
  e: Ireland   f: America   g: Western Americana
  h: American Indian   i: Other: _____

- What type of story do you prefer?

    a: Very sexy
    b: Sweet, less explicit
    c: Light and humorous
    d: More emotionally intense
    e: Dealing with darker issues
    f: Other

- What kind of covers do you prefer?

    a: Illustrating both hero and heroine
    b: Hero alone
    c: No people (art only)
    d: Other_____

- What other genres do you like to read (circle all that apply)

    Mystery   Medical Thrillers   Science Fiction
    Suspense   Fantasy   Self-help
    Classics   General Fiction   Legal Thrillers
    Historical Fiction

- Who is your favorite author, and why?_____
  _____

- What magazines do you like to read? (circle all that apply)

    a: *People*
    b: *Time/Newsweek*
    c: *Entertainment Weekly*
    d: *Romantic Times*
    e: *Star*
    f: *National Enquirer*
    g: *Cosmopolitan*
    h: *Woman's Day*
    i: *Ladies' Home Journal*
    j: *Redbook*
    k: Other:_____

- In which region of the United States do you reside?

    a: Northeast   b: Midatlantic   c: South
    d: Midwest   e: Mountain   f: Southwest
    g: Pacific Coast

- What is your age group/sex?   a: Female   b: Male

    a: under 18   b: 19-25   c: 26-30   d: 31-35   e: 56-60
    f: 41-45   g: 46-50   h: 51-55   i: 56-60   j: Over 60

- What is your marital status?

    a: Married   b: Single   c: No longer married

- What is your current level of education?

    a: High school   b: College Degree
    c: Graduate Degree   d: Other: _____

- Do you receive the TOPAZ *Romantic Liaisons* newsletter, a quarterly newsletter with the latest information on Topaz books and authors?

    YES   NO

    If not, would you like to?   YES   NO

    Fill in the address where you would like your free gift to be sent:

    Name: _____

    Address: _____

    City:_____   Zip Code: _____

    You should receive your free gift in 6 to 8 weeks.
    Please send the completed survey to:

Penguin USA•Mass Market
Dept. TS
375 Hudson St.
New York, NY 10014